PRAISE FOR **WHO IS RICH?**

"Who Is Rich? is a very funny, very frank, and often shocking book about an affair between a man and a woman at an annual writers' conference at a beach town. It is shocking for its intelligent sex scenes and for its Matthew Klam–particular observations and its outrageous humor about the way people behave when they're in crisis. It is a book-long meditation on the nature of a marriage under the stress of children and financial pressures."

—*Vulture*

"By turns fierce, disturbing, and outright hilarious, *Who is Rich?* is much more than a novel of midlife crisis, it's a frank exploration of what it feels like to struggle as an artist and a man. Klam writes like a surgeon, with the sharpest of scalpels, and cuts to the bone."

—Jonathan Tropper

"Crazy brilliant—imagine a satirical, ruthlessly funny Richard Ford or a Philip Roth novel with bite."

—*The National Book Review*

"Who Is Rich? is a tantalizing novel—acute and smart and stark, but mostly it's unrelentingly funny about a large number of very inappropriate things. It's one of those rare books: You open it, then you're up all night. I was."

—Richard Ford

"Sometimes, miraculously, a writer manages to breathe some new life into the subject. . . . Matthew Klam, author of *Who Is Rich?*, turns out to be one of those writers. . . . Maybe it's a love story; maybe it's just a lust story, but either way, it's a fine accomplishment. Here's hoping we won't have to wait another seventeen years for the return of this singularly gifted writer."

—*The New York Times*

"*Who Is Rich?* is a gem within the canon of infidelity literature. [Rich Fischer] is a wonderful narrator, lacerating and gentle."

—*The New Yorker*

"I've arrived late at the brilliant bash that is *Who Is Rich?* and there's simply nothing left for me to say, except that I agree with every word my fellow partygoers have beat me to saying."

—Peter Cameron

"Bitingly funny and surprisingly relatable . . . Think John Irving with a side of Maria Semple."

—*PureWow*

"It's amazing to wait so long for a book, and for it to be everything you wanted. The most singular quality of Matthew Klam's writing is how alive it is. I loved every page of this book. It got into my bloodstream—and kind of destroyed me."

—Curtis Sittenfeld

"Matthew Klam's long-awaited second book, *Who Is Rich?*, is one of those novels with the rare power to mesmerize. . . . Klam is writing in the tradition of Updike, Bellow, and Roth, unspooling an unabashedly masculine account of midlife crisis.

But his female characters are never reduced to caricature. He sees in them a distinct but nuanced struggle for selfhood, [Rich's] wife, Robin, haunted by the death of her brother, while [his paramour] Amy contends with a mate who brutalizes her. . . . Klam has brought to life an indelible character, a man painfully alive on the page, cowardly in actions but utterly fearless in confronting hard truths we spend most of our lives evading."

—*The Boston Globe*

"Rich is a hard man to like, but he makes you laugh."

—Scott Simon, NPR

"Twenty-five years ago (it hardly seems possible) I read a story in *The New Yorker* called 'Sam the Cat' that made me laugh so hard I think I actually peed in my pants. Every so often, in the years that followed, a new Klam story would appear, as eagerly anticipated by his discerning fans as Salinger's in the fifties. Then the stories were collected in a book, the book was rightly acclaimed, and a long silence followed. My point? Matthew Klam is back, with a novel that's just about the last word on marriage, the creative life, and the pathos of middle age. Let us celebrate with tears of mirth and gratitude."

—Blake Bailey

"*Who Is Rich?* is the best dirty book of the summer. [It's] the story of an extramarital tangle between a self-lacerating graphic novelist and a one-percenter Connecticut mom. It's both bleak and joyous, creeping between the isolation of a fuckless marriage and the elusive thrill of the affair."

—*Men's Journal*

"With a perceptive eye and biting humor, [Rich] skewers the participants at the conference, 'an open-air looney bin,' including his own students and fellow faculty members. Rich may be a mildly depressed neurotic in the midst of a lengthy midlife crisis, but Klam ensures that he is also a profound, often-hilarious commentator on marriage, child rearing, and artistic endeavors."

—*Booklist*

"The book is hilarious. *Who Is Rich?* is also an important work of fiction, not only for the mastery of narrative techniques, but for the boldness of imagination. Not since Richard Yates's *Revolutionary Road* have I read a novel that delves so provocatively into the often painful machinations of marriage and the complexities of life with small children. Nothing has been withheld or dissembled. Matthew Klam is an original American storyteller of the first rank."

—Philip Schultz

"Love, lust, humor, jealousy . . . [*Who Is Rich?*] is everything a reader could hope for and more."

—*Travel + Leisure*

"Matthew Klam is a brilliant satirist and keen observer of Unequal America, and his new novel takes a hard look at society's extravagant hypocrisies. His work is thrilling and distinctive—and political in a way that is not always noted because it is also so funny. *Who Is Rich?* is long-awaited and first-rate."

—Lorrie Moore

"A sharp satire about art, sex, and money."

—*PopSugar*

"What a thrill to experience the fusion of Matthew Klam's fierce, kinetic prose with the mysteries of fatherhood and domesticity. *Who Is Rich?* is an electric amalgam of frustration and tenderness, wonder and rebellion: a paean to the obliterating power of parental love."

—Jennifer Egan

"Klam's first novel is an irreverent and at times absurdly inappropriate (which makes it all the more hilarious) story that touches on middle-life crises, parental love, and what it means to be an artist."

—*Domino*

"I just finished *Who Is Rich?* and I seriously, deeply love this book."

—Michael Cunningham

"Matthew Klam's *Who Is Rich?* totally reinvigorates the literary cliché of the male midlife crisis."

—*Slate*

"Like many people, I've been eagerly awaiting another book by Matthew Klam—and here it is, and it's a stunner. This, his first novel, is funny, dark, big, and bold. I read it straight through, with great pleasure and awe at all he knows about art, money, family, sex, kids, mortality, and shame. *Who Is Rich?* is not to be missed."

—Meg Wolitzer

"A tale of middle-aged ennui that gets sharper as it gets funnier."

—*Kirkus Reviews*

BY MATTHEW KLAM

Sam the Cat
Who Is Rich?

WHO IS RICH?

WHO IS RICH?

A Novel

Matthew Klam

Drawings by John Cuneo

RANDOM HOUSE

New York

2018 Random House Trade Paperback Edition

Copyright © 2017 by Matthew Klam
Drawings copyright © 2017 by John S. Cuneo
Q&A between Matthew Klam and Curtis Sittenfeld copyright © 2018 by Penguin Random House LLC

Published in the United States by Random House, an imprint and division of Penguin Random House LLC, New York.

RANDOM HOUSE and the HOUSE colophon are registered trademarks of Penguin Random House LLC.

Originally published in hardcover in the United States by Random House, an imprint and division of Penguin Random House LLC, in 2017.

Grateful acknowledgment is made to Aragi, Inc., for permission to reprint an excerpt from "Sea-Level Elegy" from Stag's Leap by Sharon Olds, copyright © 2012 by Sharon Olds. Reprinted by permission of Alfred A. Knopf, an imprint of Penguin Random House LLC and Aragi, Inc.

Library of Congress Cataloging-in-Publication Data
Names: Klam, Matthew, author.
Title: Who is Rich? : a novel / Matthew Klam.
Description: New York : Random House, 2017.
Identifiers: LCCN 2016051687| ISBN 9780812987539 (paperback) | ISBN 9780812997996 (ebook)
Subjects: | BISAC: FICTION / Literary. | FICTION / Family Life. | FICTION / Satire. | GSAFD: Satire.
Classification: LCC PS3561.L22 W48 2017 | DDC 813/.54—dc23
LC record available at https://lccn.loc.gov/2016051687

Printed in the United States of America on acid-free paper

randomhousebooks.com

9 8 7 6 5 4 3 2 1

Book design by Caroline Cunningham

FOR DANIEL MENAKER

Once, each summer, I howl,

and draw myself back, out of there, where

desire and joy, where ignorance, where

touch and the ideal, where unwilled yet willful

blindness—once a year, I have mercy,

I let myself go down where I have lived, and then,

hand over hand, I pull myself back up.

—FROM "SEA-LEVEL ELEGY" BY SHARON OLDS

WHO IS RICH?

WHO IS RIGHT?

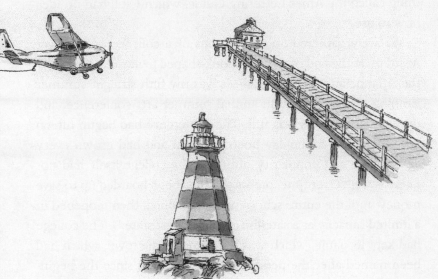

ONE

Fog blew in Saturday morning. I sat under a big white tent and drank some coffee while my chair sank into the lawn. I talked to a kid with a heavy beard in a mangled straw hat who last year for some reason we started calling Swaggamuffin.

A girl wearing a name tag passed out rosters to faculty. A guy walking behind her handed me an info packet. I sat there eating toast, looking at my notes. Other people were out there too, chatting and smoking. I said hello to a dozen familiar faces from over the years and drank several more cups. The fog burned off. A lawnmower buzzed. The sky was a flawless aquamarine blue.

I'd written a three-part lecture, on drawing techniques, brainstorming, and plotting, and also found some handouts with exercises from last year or the year before that. We supplied them with pencils, erasers, pens, nibs, brushes, and paper—100-pound acid-free Bristol board for comic applications—and a little plastic thing called the Ames Lettering Guide, which I still had no idea how to use.

We were gathered on the campus of a college you've never heard of, at the end of a sandy, hook-shaped peninsula, bound by the Atlantic and scenic as hell. It was my fifth straight summer running a workshop at an annual summer arts conference, and once again my class was full. The conference had begun fifteen years before as a one-day poetry festival and had grown every year in size and popularity, although the college itself had not fared as well. Over time, pieces of it had been boarded up to save money until the entire school was abandoned, then reopened in a limited capacity as a satellite of the nearest state U. The college had kept its name, which was the name of the town, which had been named after the people who'd been here since the beginning of time, who'd made peace with the English settlers, teaching them to fish and hunt, helping them slaughter neighboring tribes, before they too were wiped out by disease or dragged off and sold into slavery.

Nada Klein, with her long French braid and dark wolfish eyes, walked through the tent with her shawl dragging on the ground. She beat cancer every year, and showed up late to her own slide talks, and was widely mocked and imitated. Larry Burris was back, too. He skipped his meds one year and wore a jester's cap to class and lit his own notes on fire, and had to spend the night in a hospital. He stood beside me now, beneath the tent flap, patiently signing a copy of his book, and handed it back to a woman who hugged him. On the faculty were many friends I'd come to know over the years as intellects, historians, word-smiths, talented performers, storytellers with big fake teeth, ad-dicts, drunkards, perverts, world-famous womanizers, sufferers of gout, maniacs, liars—embittered, delusional, accomplished, scared of spiders, unable to swim, loveless, and cruel. I noticed

Barney Angerman, who'd won the Pulitzer for drama the year I was born, and Tabitha Portenlee, who'd written an acclaimed incest memoir; she was helping Barney through the breakfast line as he gripped her arm. This past winter the conference director had asked me to name another cartoonist I could vouch for to teach a second comics workshop, but I didn't answer him. I worried, because of the way my career had gone, that I'd be hiring my replacement.

A little before nine I went to the Fine Arts building. Hurrying down a long hall, past students and teachers, I looked for my studio. There were classes in the annex now, landscape photography, felt making, fresco on plaster, whatever that was.

When I got there they were pulling out their stuff, giving each other the once-over. I flipped through my notes. A woman who lived in town was complaining about beach traffic. A skinny kid stared at me, wearing a sundress, mascara, and a pearl choker. A young Asian woman stared at him, clutching her pencil case. A young man in a white polo, a craggy-looking old guy, and a girl with button eyes and tiny feet were talking with affection about their dogs.

I opened the info packet and read the bios of the other teachers and guest speakers printed in the conference pamphlet. There were different levels of us, unknown nobodies and one-hit has-beens, midlist somebodies and legitimate stars. As I read, I could hear my own labored breathing. I tried to slow it down but felt worse, graying as the blood left my brain. I read my course description from who knows when.

MATTICOOK COLLEGE SUMMER ARTS CONFERENCE

CARTOONING STUDIO: SEMIAUTOBIOGRAPHICAL COMICS

with Rich Fischer

July 18–21. Tuition: $1,500. Ages 18+. For-credit option:
$1,900.

Are you ready to take your cartooning to the next level? Start

from scratch, or bring your own comic in progress to our

4-day summer intensive, and we'll help you do just that. . . .

A murmuring of bodies came from the hall. Fans turned slowly over us. An old galvanized ventilation system snaked around the ceiling. A thin woman stepped cautiously into the room, walked out, then came back in. Wild brown hair, sharp elbows, bony wrists, redness around her mouth, raw, wounded-looking lips, a long skirt, moccasins. Was she the kind of person to take time out of her busy life to make a fictionalized comic about herself? Apparently.

I moved across the studio, faking a slight limp in order to give my movements in flip-flops and canvas shorts a more tweedy gravitas, and adjusted the blinds. In this way I became the parent, the benign elder, with knowledge and some intangible quality of goodness that would allow my students to project onto me the power to contain their aspirations. I'd be the vessel, I'd hold their dreams, whatever. When it was quiet, I asked them to go around the room and introduce themselves.

I wasn't a teacher. I didn't belong here. I'd ditched my family and driven nine hours up the East Coast in Friday summer high-way traffic so I could show off in front of strangers, most of whom had no talent, some of whom weren't even nice, while I got paid almost nothing. They'd blown their hard-earned money to come to this beautiful place not to swim or sail but to sit in a room all day writing and drawing their guts out, telling themselves it was a dream come true.

I'd driven up here for the first time the summer after my only book came out. This conference was one of many good things that had come to me in those days. It was maybe the only thing left. Every time I pulled into town and saw the blinking neon lobsters, the bowling alley, the giant plastic 3-D roadside sandwich, it gave me a big feeling, reminding me of a once-limitless future.

Melanie Lenzner taught high school art in New Hampshire and went on too long, acting like it was her class, not mine. Helen Li, a biomolecular engineering student, said she didn't want to start med school in the fall. Nick, the trans kid, said his father had thrown him out of the house and that he—or she—lived in her car. Carol, faded red hair cut short and stalky, looked alarmed, and asked how long he or she'd been homeless. George had gone into the army at eighteen, had fought in Vietnam, lost his wife twenty years ago, and had a daughter named Sonya who lived in Buffalo. Sang-Keun Kim, mustache, ponytail; I thought I'd seen him back in the eighties in porno movies. Frances, a granny in a white cardigan, so happy to be here. Vishnu wanted us to know that he'd taken workshops from cartoonists more famous than me. Rebecca, the skinny one, worked in Hartford as a midwife. Behind the sinks, a teenage girl wearing a wool hat, deerskin slippers, and flannel pajama pants looked up through a face screened in acne. I asked her to move closer. She said no. Her name was Rachel.

I passed around a ream of eleven by seventeen and asked everybody to take some.

I hadn't published anything in six years. I worked as an illustrator now, at an esteemed magazine of politics and culture, a venerated institution of American journalism and the second- or third-oldest magazine in the country. Illustration is to cartooning as prison sodomy is to pansexual orgy. Not the same thing at all. Anyway, you might've seen my magazine work but didn't know it—unless you happened to be scanning for names with a microscope. Some watered-down version, muted to satisfy commercial demands.

I'd been so full of promise, so amazed to have graduated from the backwater of fanzines and college newspapers to mainstream publishing. I had an appointment with destiny, I'd barely started, then I blinked and it was over. Nobody writing to beg for a blurb, no more mysterious checks arriving in the mail, no agent's letterhead clipped to the check, no more calls from my publisher, not even to say go fuck yourself. What I missed most of all, had lost or forgotten, was the making of comics, triangulating the pain of existence through these bouts of belligerence, shame, suspicion, and euphoria, writerly noodlings and decipherable images organized into an all-encompassing environment. No more bragging, no more swagger, no more tasteless personal revelations. Cartoonists still made comics, and I hated them to the core of my filthy soul, and prayed for the return of 1996, when everything that would happen was about to happen, when I'd try to imagine how far I'd go.

If you've experienced precocious success, you know it's rare. At first it seems like there must be some mistake, but you get used to it in a hurry; you're sure it'll always be this way. You travel, and meet famous cartoonists; they praise you, you chat like old friends and get to know them personally, you get sick of their whining and quickly lose respect for anyone on earth who struggles or complains. You come to expect fan mail, strangers popping up to kiss your ass, a certain deference or tone of voice. You start to think that anyone making comics who is without a national reputation, or miserable or obscure and lacking attention from jerkoffs in Hollywood, is a fucking moron.

I wrote on the board, *Plumber, Hitler, moneybags,*

"Let's just take a couple minutes here—"

hayseed, hottie, hobbit,

"—to sketch these—"

lunch lady, Nabokov, beer wench,

"—keep the pencil moving—"

Sasquatch, sous-chef, snowman.

Then I walked around, trying not to look accusingly or even curiously at anyone, offering praise, encouraging spontaneity, saying positive stuff.

"Love it" . . . "Yes!" . . . "Lusty!" . . . "Good!"

The whole idea of this doodling was to lower the anxiety level in the room, to lighten the mood, to give them a feeling of poise and excitement, to discover in any character the autonomous core—

"Maybe another minute to wind up the one you're on—"

—to raise the body temp and get the molecules bubbling. Then I went to the board and drew a snowman with a grin made of coal, and an indent where the nose should be, and this huge honking carrot, slightly bent, sticking out below the equator, you know where. Underneath the snowman I wrote, *"Hungry?"*

They laughed.

"Humor arises from the surprising juxtaposition of text and image."

I drew a rabbit with a worried face, staring at the carrot. Then I erased the rabbit and put the carrot back where it belonged. I drew Satan in an overcoat, with a scarf around his neck, leaning on the snowman, complaining on the phone that the thermostat was broken. Then I got rid of Satan and drew a second snowman saying to the first, *"Why does everything smell like carrots?"*

"When you look at a comic, do you read the words first? Or look at the drawing?" We went around the room and shared our thoughts.

Then I broke them into groups, and for the next twenty minutes they made a racket, shouting, telling tales, arms flapping. They exchanged ideas, offered feedback and helpful insights, discussed, dissected, and ripped each other to shreds. In an email I'd sent out a month earlier, I'd asked them to bring along notes, a script, and some art, exhorting them to bravely mine their personal experiences for therapeutic and artistic gains, in order to come up with the one important story they'd develop this week.

Rebecca had in mind a moment inside an ambulance, her younger self in a paramedic's uniform, leaning heavily over an old man, working to restart his heart, failing to, panic setting in. Sarah wanted to do something light and fun about her job in a bookstore. Brandon, in the white polo, made notes on his first gay pride weekend, bleaching his hair, snorting amyl nitrate, realizing, in the end, *If you've seen one drag queen, you've seen ten thousand.* They had four days to turn their thumbnails into finished pencil drawings, which they'd then ink and letter, scan and reproduce, and present to the world by Tuesday afternoon, in time for open studio.

I asked if anyone needed help. Mel fumbled with her pencil sharpener. I heard crickets chirping in Sarah's empty head. Then I walked to the back of the room and looked at the floor. I heard pencils and paper, the steady breathing of humans at work. I stood behind the printing press, my hands on the wheel, like a sea captain trying to get on course.

TWO

By the time we took a break, other classes had also made their way outside to the picnic tables in the courtyard. A breeze as light as champagne bubbles swept over us from the bay. Sailboats dotted its sparkling waters. I felt relieved. I'd been nervous before class, and almost puked at breakfast. That first lecture always unhinged me, but I'd gotten through it.

But there was something else not right, and it took me a second to figure out what it was: Angel Solito, walking out of Fine Arts, squinting into the sun, coming toward me. He wore a navy blue hooded sweatshirt with long white strings. His arms hung down at his sides, and he wore eyeglasses. I said something, and he reached out a hand. His face was bumpy, as if a rash was trying to come through from underneath, and his hair had been slept on or pushed up into a ridge.

I couldn't tell if he had any clue who I was, but I knew an edi-
tor of a British anthology who knew him. I said her name, like I
didn't care either way, and sternly congratulated him on his book.

"Uh-huh."

He was the cartoonist who Carl, the director, had hired. Solito
was young enough to be my son, if I'd had a son at fourteen, and
on closer inspection the whites of his eyes were laced with red
threads and his head tipped forward as if he had horns. Maybe
he'd been heading to the big black plastic coffee urn on the picnic
table behind me and I'd gotten in his way. Maybe he didn't care,
and just needed to vent, and would've talked this way to anybody.
He shook his head and said, "Man, it's been crazy," and told me
how exhausted he was, how he ran out of money two days ago
and was waiting for a check from his publisher. As soon as the
conference ended, he'd be hitting the road again.

"The book rolls out overseas, in Sweden and Denmark—"

At some point I realized he was confiding, I was being confided
in, and I guess I appreciated that.

"—then the big rollout in Europe, at the end of the summer,
beginning of fall—"

Chewing his lower lip, blinking at me, talking about some
French fellowship, oblivious, harassed, as if French people had
been calling all night and he hated to disappoint them, as a
woman appeared at his side, with flyaway hair and skin so fair she
was glowing, hugging his book to her chest.

"I'm so tired, man, I haven't done any work in, like, months—"

As another young woman walked past us in pigtails, then
stopped short when she realized it was him.

"—new idea for a book but I need to get into a quiet place, and
hopefully kind of erupt—"

"Sure, of course."

"You've been living the life for, like, ten years!" he said, taking a step toward the picnic table and his waiting fans. "You gotta tell me what it's like. That's why we gotta hang out!"

"Absolutely!" Fuck you.

He gave me a tired wave, a polite smile, almost sad, and I gave him a reassuring nod.

Tell you what it's like, Angel. I sold ten thousand books in the last six years. He sold a hundred thousand copies in hardback in three months and foreign rights in thirty-eight countries. That's, like, a million bucks in royalties. The woman in pigtails hesitated, but the blond one had her book ready and jumped.

I'd seen his work somewhere, maybe I saw an excerpt in some anthology, or maybe his publisher sent me a galley, or I might've seen it in a bookstore, in a stack on a table in front, and stood over it for however many hours it took to read the thing from start to finish, before stumbling back out into daylight, shivering and mumbling to myself, groping my way out the door.

Ran out of money. That fucker!

Angel Solito traveled from Guatemala to California, mostly on foot, mostly alone, eleven years old, walked a continent to find his parents, and finally did but never found the American dream. His story was rendered in clear bold lines, with faces delicately hatched, with big heads and a ferocious expressiveness. Reviews of his work had been universally frothy. In the days after I read it I had strange moments, traveling to some breathy place, almost happy, imagining that it was my book, my story, that I'd walked three thousand miles to find my parents, four and a half feet tall, eighty pounds, and alone.

He stood by the picnic table as more bodies surrounded him. He had caramel skin and shiny black hair. I felt the thrill of being him, like they were digging me, thanking me. I'd dreamed of the big time, and here it was, so beautiful, so real! Then I remembered that I didn't get robbed by soldiers and chased by wolves. I didn't crawl across the Sonoran Desert. Where I came from, eleven-year-olds could barely make their own beds.

I grew up in a middle-class suburb with good public schools an hour north of the G.W. Bridge, under a stand of white pine trees in an old house with wavy wooden floors and a loose banister. Walking thousands of miles to find my family would've been unnecessary. My brother lived across the hall. My father sold life insurance and other tax-dodging instruments from a skyscraper in New York City. My mom taught music to fourth, fifth, and sixth graders, in an attempt to make up for her own artistic failures. We lacked for nothing in that house except talent.

Back in the studio, a dozen people sat bowed, bent over their desks—doing what? Trying to pump life into a poorly realized, made-up world. Brandon didn't know where to put his word balloons, and Rebecca needed a beveled edge, and Sang-Keun couldn't figure out how to draw a cowboy hat.

"It's round but curved," I said, leaning over his shoulder. "Like a Pringle potato chip. A disk intersecting an ovoid."

What did he see as my hand flew across the page? Several cowboy hats, spilling out of a pencil. Did he notice how each one was unique and expressive, reflecting the life of its owner? Did he note the skill or understand how hard I worked to make something difficult look effortless?

He touched the collar of his T-shirt, staring at the drawing as I moved to the next desk. He didn't know anything. He didn't care. I showed Sarah how to turn on the light box, and walked to the sinks and looked out the window, and tried my best to stay out of the way as a new generation of artists pounded at the gates of American graphic literature.

THREE

After class I cut across the lawn with a girl who wore cat-eye glasses and had small, pointy teeth, and a man with clay dust all over him, whacking it off his clothes, and Vishnu, who kept bumping into me.

"Professor," he said, "in an interview you said male cartoonists are derivative whereas women are all original. Isn't that kind of sexist?"

"I think I said guys have to shake off Batman comics. Women don't have that as much."

"Did you ever play Five-Card Nancy or stay up all night to do a twenty-four-hour comic?"

"No."

"Why not?" He gave me a canny look, one cartoonist to another.

"There's no point."

"I couldn't agree less." He was a thin, beaky young man with a hollow-boned lightness and no romance in his heart. His hair was thick, blue black, and chopped above the ears. "Do you use a drawing tablet?"

"No."

"Well, what's your favorite inking tool? And what kind of ink, and which nibs, and how do you hold and use the nib? Can I get a demo tomorrow?"

"Sure."

"Have you ever used a toothbrush for texture?"

The problem of walking and talking on a hilly, shifting terrain presented itself.

"Do you like to use a smooth paper or something more grainy?" He thought I knew the secrets and could lay them out for him like coconut macaroons. I told him we'd discuss it in class.

At the beginning of class he'd corrected my pronunciation of his name: "Not Veeshnu. Vishnu." At the end of class he'd asked if I planned to cover self-publishing and self-promotion, and if I had advice on how to get his self-published work into circulation. I said no, but I only said it because I felt that a person who showed up with a stack of sophisticated mini comics to a class advertised for beginners could go fuck himself.

For the rest of class he'd just sat there, though when I asked if he had an idea to work on, he seemed to nod toward his massive accomplishment, his minis, and said he was deciding between a few possibilities, then asked if I had a pub date for my next comic, to draw a comparison I guess, that I wasn't producing anything at the moment, either. When you're the new guy, with a new book out, they treat you one way. When you're the same guy six years later, it's something else.

In the main office, a blond kid had me sign a tax form so I could get paid. He told me without smiling that they needed people after lunch for softball. According to the contract, teachers were expected to play.

FOUR

In order to reach this place I'd crossed several state lines, mounted several bridges, exited highways, and ridden others until they ended. I eventually headed down a coveted stretch of land, surrounded by water on three sides, known by painters for its light, somewhat unto itself most of the year but overrun in July and August, and finally reached my destination.

Everybody knows a spot like this, a fishing village turned tourist trap, with pornographic sunsets and the Sea Breeze Motel. Out of respect for the powerful emotional attachments people form to such places, I'd rather not say exactly where I went, in the event that the detailing of my location causes even more congestion on the streets of that nicely preserved, remote southern New England coastal town.

A Dutch windmill stood at the highest point on campus, a replica or maybe the real thing, brass plates screwed to its siding from an ongoing fundraiser to repair it. On the distant practice fields, yellowing in the heat, the college held a lacrosse camp for high school boys and girls. It sat along some quaint national seashore, amid a high number of colonial-era buildings, among shifting mountains of sand, speckled with dune grass. A frolicsome place, a remote place, a place I'd barely heard of before coming here to teach. We arrived by bus or ferry or train or car, or airplane service direct from Boston. Because of its location, the conference had an easy time attracting artists, oil painters, memoirists, old guys, skitterish teenagers in search of illicit pleasures, driftwood sculptors, printmakers, actors, and playwrights.

They offered a filmmaking workshop. They taught all kinds of crafts. In the afternoon there were shuttles to the beach and a Ping-Pong table in the main building and shows in the gallery and staged readings of plays in the auditorium every night. The writers took classes in red brick buildings with white shutters. Other buildings were crumbling or had been condemned and were barricaded behind tall metal fences with posted signs. The actors camped out in the auditorium. The studios were over the hill, on the far side of the windmill, in what had once been a shipyard. Fine Arts occupied a long, skinny two-story wooden structure that creaked like a sailboat, shingled and faded, and there were cinder-block dorms where they'd put me the first two years, and a wharfy, flaking cottage where they stuck the gang of interns.

This year they'd put me in the Barn; it really was a barn, chopped into apartments for staff during the year, and still partly unfinished. The door to the top-floor apartment wasn't locked, it didn't even close, it thunked against the doorframe, swollen from the seacoast weather. It was one big open room with the angled walls of an attic, rusted skylights and a windowed cupola in the peak, and a narrow swath running down the middle of the room where you could stand up straight. There was a kitchen, frying pans whose handles fell off when you touched them, a coffee table and dresser, a white plastic fan, a filthy plaid couch, and two twin beds crammed in along the eaves.

I'd arrived on Friday at five and hung up my shirts, my head at an angle, hitting it once hard enough on a beam that I expected my skull to crack open and my brain to fall out. I stood on the bed and with some effort cranked open the skylight, stuck my head through, and looked out across campus. I heard a seagull bark like a dog. Over the rooftops of the little town I saw blue water, the harbor jetty, and a dinky lighthouse I'd never noticed before. I felt like I'd shimmied up the mast of a ship.

No humidity, no horrifying summer heat, no buses banging down the avenue, no garbage trucks, no marital rancor, just a clean white mattress on a low metal frame, and nobody to wake me up in the middle of the night by punching me in the head, or barfing down my neck, or giving me a heart attack every two hours with his bloodcurdling screams. Nobody else yelling "Daddy!" through the shower door. When I tell her to stop she begins kissing the door, because that's how much she loves me.

I loved them, too. What would I do without them? All last week, I'd had moments of fear and excitement, waking up with a stomachache, worrying how they'd live without me, while peeling Kaya's carrots, packing Beanie's diaper bag, but also feeling less owned by them and maybe cocky and probably gloating, unintentionally ignoring Robin, and she'd noticed it, shaking her head and muttering how I'd already checked out or was too lazy to marinate the fish, rolling her eyes when I forgot to put ice in her water, not wanting it when I came back with the ice tray. Kaya picked up on it too, woke up in the night and needed to pee, wondering if she could have some potatoes, telling me about Louis, the turtle at camp, as we walked back from the bathroom and I tucked her into bed. Maybe it was all in my mind.

We shared our babysitter with the family of a girl named Molly. Robin had picked them up from Molly's on her way home from work on Friday. I'd called them from the highway in the last hour of my drive. Her mom and stepdad were coming for dinner if they could get it together. I heard Beanie, grunting and sucking, and Kaya going, "Horsey horsey," which meant Beanie was on Robin's boob and Kaya was on Robin's knee.

"Maybe they won't come," she'd said.

Her mom was in the late stages of dementia, and her stepfather was attempting to drink himself to death. Her sister lived three thousand miles away and never called. Her brother had faded into myth.

"It'll be fine," I said. "Make your frittata."

"All right," she said to Kaya. "Knock it off."

"Kaya," I said, knowing she could hear, "get off Mommy so Beanie can eat."

"She used to make jokes: 'When I'm drooling in the corner, smother me with a pillow.'"

"She's not drooling."

"Yet. But maybe this is when I'm supposed to kill her."

"Don't kill her tonight."

"All right."

"Or at least make it look like an accident."

"Don't tell me what to do. Kaya, stop it."

"Sorry."

"What's wrong with you?"

I didn't know who she was talking to.

If Robin needed help she'd call Elizabeth, who lived eighteen feet away. They liked to stand in the alley between our two houses and talk intensely as the girls rode up and down on their tricycles. Robin talked about Beanie's sleep patterns and Kaya's emotional IQ. Elizabeth talked about her fourteen-month-old's language

problems and her seven-year-old caving to the mind games of her
five-year-old. They talked about clients Elizabeth saw for psycho-
therapy and a story editor who tortured Robin. They discussed
clothing, did fashion shows for each other: can I get away with
this, is this consistent with my persona? They talked about cut-
ting off their hair, glass beads, making jewelry, maternity under-
garments, the anti-inflammatory properties of turmeric, hot
yoga, colon cleansing, the perils of a Montessori education, the
naughty spanking trilogy, the sexy vampire movies, postpartum
body issues, hip pain, back spasms, stretched stomachs, cosmetic
surgery where they freeze your fat. If you got her talking long
enough, Robin mentioned her weight, that she was bigger now,
so she thought her head looked too small. They talked about sex
and marriage, aging parents, the transformation of a loved one in
decline, the terrible suffering of their mothers, helplessness and
guilt.

I hung up and drove the last fifty miles to campus. After un-
packing the car I went to dinner and ate barbecued chicken under
the big white tent, at a table with Howard, a bald guy with a
tanned, polished head, and Tina or Dina, who'd come here last
year and made sculptures out of wire. After dinner we crowded
onto the porch, where a poet read a poem. Carl gave his welcom-
ing remarks, urging us not to climb through windows if we lost
our dorm keys. Then we went off to see the theater company do
a mash-up of Chekhov plays, set in the 1930s, with Uncle Vanya
shooting himself in the second act, wandering in and out with a
bandage on his head. In the big hall of the main building I heard
Tabitha give the same talk she gave last year, about her spiritual
journey beyond incest, into alcoholism, then past that, into group
sex and casino gambling, ending in healing and forgiveness. In the
gallery there were photos taken by an American soldier during
some of the hundreds of trips he'd made while bringing fuel to

stranded convoys all over Afghanistan, of the landscape, people, and culture, before he himself was finally blown up and killed. The photos survived. I ate some chocolate-dipped strawberries and talked to a woman with blue streaks in her hair.

Then I went back to the Barn, hung my pants on a nail in the wall by the refrigerator, and thought about Robin, what she was doing, what I'd be doing at that hour if I were home. It was just the usual struggle to stay in love, keep it hot, keep it real, the boredom and revulsion, the afterthought of copulation, the fight for her attention, treating me like a roommate, or maybe like a vision of some shuddering gelatinous organ she'd forgotten still worked inside her.

First a guy sticks something in you. Then a thing grows inside your body. Eventually it tears its way out, leaving a trail of destruction. Then it's outside your body, but still sucking on you. It makes you weird, these different people in you and on you. Robin had had two C-sections and felt that they'd put her back together wrong the second time. A cold electric twinge shot down her back, down her leg, while walking, sitting, standing, or lying down. It defied any cure, painkillers, epidurals. For a while she wore a small black box on her belt that electro-stimmed her buttocks.

In a previous life, she bit my neck and licked my ear when we did it. After Kaya, I worried about courting her in my pajamas, with our little angel breathing down the hall, and lost focus and cringed as Robin's patience ran out if I finished too fast or not fast enough and overstayed my welcome. Bad sex was better than nothing, but Beanie effectively ended the badness. Fuckless weeks, excused by parenting, turned weirdly okay. Like our anniversary, we weren't sure anymore when it was supposed to happen. And, with the exception of my tongue on her clitoris every who knows when, she didn't need to be touched. She had vibrators for that. I think she mostly thought of what I did as a way to save batteries.

Our sex life hadn't been mauled by depression, routine, or conflict as much as it had been mauled by distraction, diffusion, a surfeit of beauty. Was that it? Our children's vitality and strangeness, their softness, shocked me every day. Their lightness and willingness and spirit and stupidity surprised me, their readiness to bravely step into a world they couldn't understand, packed with swimming pools, speeding cars, blazing sun, fanged dogs, stinging bees, heat, silent anger, slammed doors, inexplicable demands, funny hats slammed on their heads, and constantly from every direction these giants with twelve-pound heads, ten times their weight, five times their height, grabbing, pushing, shoving past, talking loud, telling them how to think, what to want, how to treat their own impulses, which ones to kill, which to love. No to crawling inside a dishwasher or smacking your food when you chewed. Yes to climbing trees and sucking your toes. I was sad for the bleakness of a little kid's bumbling existence, envious of the simplicity of their cause. They faced the world because they had no choice. Someone was crying. Someone had pooped his pants. They were explorers in a new land. Robin and I stood by them, in parallel formation, to witness and guide them.

Parallel, as if on the same track, running at the same speed, but not touching and having no way to touch. Parallel like people who went to bed without remembering to say good night, or saying it without meaning it, or meaning it but not saying it. I appreciated how on those rare occasions when my wife would kiss me, she did so with flat lips, popping them the way she did when she smacked at her ice cream. In this way she turned my face into something more palatable.

Was it a good life? Was I more joyful, sensitive, and compassionate in my deeply entangled commitment to them? Was there anything better than seeing the world through the eyes of my nutty kids? Was my obligation to Robin the most sincere form of love? Or was I living despite their obstruction, intrusion, whatever? Had I instead been saved by the transcendent power of my ideas and work connected to the larger world, drawings I'd done for the magazine that illuminated trivial or important events of our time? Was I doing all I could to enrich and enhance and enliven my time on earth, or was I doing all I could to destroy, limit, or block any growth or connection? Or was I doing nothing, imitating real suffering while my time ran out, goofing around, rotting, sexless, ugly, and bitter?

Was this as close to love as I was ever going to get? The closer I got, the more I wanted to destroy the things I loved. Something rose up in me, threatening me. I had to deflect it somehow.

I'd never been able to beat back the loneliness of a solitary life, but as part of a couple I felt invisible and deformed, and even at those times when I meant what I said, my words of affection had to be forced through sarcasm and shame. When I misbehaved, acted out discreetly, impulsively, I felt unbreakable and invincible, although of course the guilt eventually tore me apart. And sometimes I examined those parts, and sometimes I pushed them away, but that was just pushing myself away, the pure, monstrous reality, the real me, and without those parts I was an empty shell. The longer it went on, the worse I felt, until I was out of control and panic seized me and I ran back home.

FIVE

I'd spent the winter engaging in daydreams, fantasies, alternate realities, while flipping through emails in a secret folder, and looking at selfies of this same beautiful woman, barely clad in a towel at a fancy resort in Zurich, or on the swings with her kids at the park, or modeling the necklace I'd sent her at Christmas.

We met here a year ago. She took a class in the studio next to mine and pulled some late nights; we shared a bench in the courtyard, downwind of a cigarette. She was a nice woman with a few complaints, suggestible, not finished, wrapped up in her kids. She was unmoved by her own painting and thought her classmates were hilarious if a little hard to take: the lady who painted in her bra, the hipster who flirted with her in his little fedora. We bumped into each other in the laundry room, and went for a walk on the jetty at sunset, and talked about marriage, and stayed out late, and spilled our guts.

Wasn't that the whole point of this place? To take a break and clear your head? And who really gave a fuck what two people did at an arts conference in some swinging summer paradise? Real life was so lonely anyway, and I figured I'd never see her again, so on the last night we went back to her dorm room and goofed around.

When the conference ended, we started zipping notes back and forth, just a few, then more and more. For a while I thought she'd leave him, and if she left him, maybe I'd leave Robin. But then she didn't, and I didn't, either. I saw her once in the fall, for an hour of furious hand holding and making out in a candlelit booth in New York City. And once in March, at her house in Connecticut. Then things got heavy and she stopped talking to me.

In June I sent her a birthday card and asked if she'd be coming back to the conference. It took her three weeks to say maybe. And now, after signing my contract and promising to play softball, as I headed to the tent for lunch, I thought about what might happen if she did. It didn't help to think about it, but I'd spent a lot of time thinking about it anyway. I got excited. I still had passion. I came over a rise and the whole town lay beneath me, the buildings old and stinking of charm and practically spilling into the bay. I caught a whiff of sea life, a funky low-tide odor. For so long, I'd been deprived of even accidental physical contact. I needed love; short of love, I needed something. I saw myself as adventurous, amorous, and brave. I got stuck in some loop of possibilities and had to stifle a ridiculous little moan. I felt a dog-eared excitement, and rode that familiar surge of energy. By the time I reached the tent, people had worn a muddy track across the lawn between the check-in table and the buffet.

"Ha ya doin'? Everything good at home?"

"Yes!"

"You believe we're back here again?"

I got something to eat and scanned the tent for the face I'd kissed and held, for those long legs of such smooth, glassy skin, striding briskly in the fresh breeze off the bay, for that stranger who'd hovered over me, gasping and weeping.

I didn't see her, but students sometimes walked into town for meals. I went over by the brick wall and sat with some other faculty members, Vicky Capodanno, a painter, Tom McLaughlin, an old guy who'd written a memoir of his childhood, and this idiot biographer named Dennis Fleigel, who was waving his sandwich in the air. He had his foot propped on Vicky's chair as she cut her salad.

"I read your book," he said. I put my bag on the wall and downed my lemonade. I just wanted to eat. "Graphic novel, comic book, whatever you call it. What do you call it?"

"I'm not in that argument."

"Do you check the number on Amazon?"

"It's not in print." I was eating some kind of chef's salad, dry raw beets, chunks of cheddar, and these mysterious white cubes of something. This was a new, wholesome food service. "Hello, Vicky. Hi, Tom."

"Richie," Tom said. "How are you, bud?"

Vicky looked at me with deep intensity. "How *are* you?"

I couldn't remember if I'd ever responded to her last email, from Vermont, where she'd gone to take a break from New York, trying to quit smoking, childless and out of romantic options, wondering how I was, asking for photos of me with my kids, or just my kids, or any cute kid stories—and I grinned at her like a lobotomized dope.

"I was just saying," Dennis said, "that my book was selling, it sold pretty well, Amazon number below ten thousand for two straight years, word of mouth was good, but then that movie came out."

"What movie?"

Ring-a-Ding Ding. It's about Sinatra, and when it came out, my Amazon number went from ten thousand to a hundred and fifty thousand, and it never went lower ever again."

Charlene Wetzel joined us, smiling, and said, "I think I have a stalker." More people sat down. "He wore sunglasses in class," she said. "Last year, it took a few days. This year, first day: stalker."

Heather Hinman, who taught poetry and had a coiled energy that included her hair, said that one of her students asked what font she typed in. Roberta Moser put her plate down and told us that she'd just finished an interview with the local NPR and that the questions were dumb.

I began to feel hopeless and desperate in a familiar way.

Dennis explained that NPR was fine for pushing an art film or a book, but that the machinery that promotes a studio movie is so much bigger. "*Ring-a-Ding Ding* the movie killed *Ring-a-Ding Ding* the book, and it never recovered."

"What are we talking about?" Roberta asked.

"My book *Ring-a-Ding Ding,*" Dennis said, "and how it got killed by *Ring-a-Ding Ding* the movie, which I also wrote."

Roberta smiled at Dennis. "I still don't understand."

Tom McLaughlin brought over a bottle of wine. Frederick Stugatz sat down with Ilana Zimmer, who put some wine to her lips and said, "I just got back from six weeks as artist in residence at the University of Bologna."

Heather took a drink and said, "After this I go to Ole Miss."

Frederick said, "After this I go to Berkeley." He turned and stared at Ilana, who ignored him.

Dennis said, "*Ring-a-Ding Ding* the book is about a sensitive brute who happens to be the twentieth century's greatest entertainer. The movie *Ring-a-Ding Ding* is a piece of shit. But that's not my point. My point is that the kid who's supposed to be eighteen was played by a twenty-six-year-old, and the eighteen-year-olds who saw it thought the guy looked like a senior citizen."

Dennis had red hair and a pink forehead and surprisingly bright blue eyes. If you tried to make eye contact, he couldn't see you. I liked to think of this as the result of some head trauma. It was a kind of blindness that made him unlikable but high-functioning. He'd written four biographies and two screenplays and went on morning talk shows when his books came out. I could imagine back in caveman days someone like him being cut from the tribe, dragged away, and thrown off a cliff.

Heather buttered a roll. She used to be a drunk but now wrote poems about bartending, drinking binges, blackouts, and AA. Roberta was a filmmaker. She'd been making a documentary for the past nine years about corrupt black mayors of major American cities, filming them in jail, running for office again, taking walks with their aged mothers. Frederick taught the musical book, whatever that was, and had been the genius behind last year's musical about Karl Rove. Ilana Zimmer had headlined an indie rock band, with one hit in the eighties, then had a ho-hum solo career, and now dabbled in kids' music. She ran a songwriting workshop every year in Frederick's class. Vicky had paintings in museums around the world that were violent, cartoonish, biting, dark, and funny, that dealt with war, religiosity, porn, rape, but also the cost of art education, women's bodies, and people who lived in garbage dumps. And Tom McLaughlin had been a high school English teacher for forty years, then retired and wrote a rambling memoir of his childhood growing up over a pool hall in Alffia, Texas, population 71, with wrenching scenes about killing cattle and the death of the town; it became an instant classic, then a hit movie. He sat there like the most relaxed guy in the world, his face heavily lined, familiar in a way from posters of him around the conference—they were hard to miss, his head gleaming and speckled with age spots.

The thing to do here was relax and not worry about where I ranked among them. I pushed my plate away and started drawing on the tablecloth. I drew the bay, a single steady line, wispy clouds in the distance, and walking along the shore I drew Batman, the Caped Crusader, looking a little haggard and overweight. Last year's tablecloths had been made of a thick, toothy paper, with a spongy plastic coating underneath, but this was thin one-ply, and the ink bled like I was drawing on toilet paper. It was a waste of time, but I didn't care. Batman was the first superhero I'd ever drawn. I hadn't drawn him in thirty years. Why now? Drawing him middle-aged with a big keister seemed to answer something. He stood in the surf at low tide with a touristy camera around his neck and his tights stained dark from wading.

One line led to another, the feeling of deadness went away, and this arrangement of markings became a scene with a little girl about Kaya's age holding Batman's hand. Was it a memory? Was it cathartic? Did it work? I didn't care. I kept going, surprising my eyes with what my hand could do. In Batman's other arm I drew a little boy in a swim diaper—my knees bouncing under the table—until, shading in the bay around their ankles, I pressed too hard and tore the tablecloth.

Then I thought of home and felt my throat close up. I wondered how I'd protect my kids from hundreds of miles away. I worried that Kaya would ride her tricycle into the renovation pit from the construction next door. I worried that Beanie would suck the propeller out of my old tin clown whistle. Joey, the high school kid down the block, sometimes cut through the alley in his Subaru with his foot on the gas, even though a dozen kids under the age of ten jumped rope and played games there. A spasm of electric jolts shocked my heart, from the heady mixing of blood and guilt that brought on flashes of horror and feelings of dread and excitement, the fear that I would do something sexy and rotten and get away with it.

Stewart Rinaldi pulled up a chair and said, "What did I miss?"

"We're talking about my book," Dennis began, *"Ring-a-Ding Ding."*

No one could stop him from explaining that the movie killed the book. When he finished, no one spoke. Beside me, Charlene folded things into a sandwich.

"Pass the salt."

We had nothing else to say, or didn't want to try for fear of starting Dennis up again. We didn't discuss the news of the day or the presidential campaign or politics in general, power, money, greed, or war. As members of the cultural elite, we didn't believe in any of that. We'd been teaching together for years. We sat in circles, bragging about things that mattered only to us. We were artists. We believed in ourselves.

And yet, things were happening out there. Obama had drawn a red line but Assad refused to back down, while hundreds of thousands fled, in what was looking like a massive refugee crisis. "Call Me Maybe" held steady at No. 1. Ernest Borgnine died. Kim Jong-un had been named Supreme Being of North Korea. The Republican primary had been brutal, awash in dark money, the first since the Supreme Court decided that mountains of secret cash in exchange for favors was totally fine. Romney emerged as the nominee, a hollow, arrogant flip-flopper. He'd spent the summer refusing to release his most recent tax returns, while his legal representatives explained away the Swiss bank account stuffed with tens or hundreds of his own millions. He was in London this week, having FedExed his wife's half-million-dollar dressage horse over to compete in the Olympics.

We didn't care about that stuff. We cared about art. We cared about lunch. Finally Dennis stood, picked up his bag, and walked out of the tent, past the drinks cooler, toward the library.

"Ring-a-ding ding," Roberta said. "Does that ring any bells?"

"Forget it," Tom said.

People liked Dennis as a teacher. Around the faculty, though, he lost control. He engendered pity, which must've bothered him. The interns were clearing off the buffet table behind us, watery bowls of lentil salad no one wanted. Roberta said Dennis's wife had moved out, and Charlene shook her head and said it was a long time coming. Frederick turned to stare at Ilana, who pretended not to notice. Vicky asked why we had to sit here, year after year, talking about Dennis Fleigel, and wondered if anyone wanted to go for a swim in the ocean, and gave me a deep, meaningful look, but I didn't want to linger, to catch up, didn't want to be her beach pal. I couldn't listen to the grievances of childless grown-ups anymore, their boredom with their free time, wondering what they'd missed. Whatever had caught up with them was making them depressed.

SIX

In college I couldn't figure out what to major in. Over in English they were complaining that language itself had become brittle and useless, and over in art, so-called postmodern painting was being taught in a way I didn't understand, as the subject as object ran into ontological difficulties that couldn't be solved with a paintbrush. I started making comics for some relief—leaning heavily on my own journals, since I'd never learned how to make up anything—an episodic, thinly veiled series of stories about a girl and boy who fall in love, stay up late, eat pizza in their undies, make charcoal drawings, create installations of dirt and light-bulbs, hate their fathers, move into an apartment together, build futon frames, flush their contact lenses down the drain, throw parties with grain alcohol punch, get knocked up, have an abor-tion, read Krishnamurti, graduate, break up, fuck other people, and move together to Baltimore, to an abandoned industrial space where sunlight comes through holes in the roof, dappling the walls.

After college I published it myself, on sheets of eight and a half by eleven, folded in half and pressed flat with the back of a spoon, stapled in the middle, and handed it out personally at conventions for a dollar. Making comics kept me from going apeshit. Later, at the ad agency where I worked, I upped the production value, made the leap to offset printing, sending it through on the invoice of a client in St. Louis, who, without knowing, paid for my two-color card-stock cover. I didn't dedicate myself to it, didn't plan on toiling for years. I figured I'd do a few more, get a job as a creative director, drill holes in my head and use it as a bowling ball.

One day I got a call. "We like your comic. We'd like to publish it. Would you be interested in that?" I remember walking around the office, heat boiling my face, wondering who to tell. Soon my work began appearing in a free alternative weekly. A year after that, I cut a deal with a beloved independent publisher for a comic book of my very own. When I finally held it in my hands, twenty-four pages, color cover, I lifted it to my face and inhaled. I caught the attention of agents and editors, and a couple of big-name cartoonists, who championed my work, and the thing took on a life of its own.

All of a sudden I'm cool, phone's ringing, there are lines at my tables at conventions. My cross-hatching improved; my brush-work became fearless. I put out two issues a year. The comic grew to thirty-two pages, then forty-eight.

TV and film people started calling. I quit my job and helped write a pilot. I flew to Brussels to be on a panel of cartoonists. I designed a book cover for a reissue of On the Road, did a CD jacket for a legendary L.A. punk band. I lived on food stamps, even as my ego ballooned. I broke into magazines, and caved to the occasional job for hire, and torched my savings, and somehow got by.

But in my own comics, I handled the hot material of my life. My characters were shacking up, doing PR for the Mafia, suffering premarital anxieties and fertility issues. My publisher suggested collecting these comics into a book. The book held together like a novel. It came out six years ago.

They couldn't sell the TV pilot. The book went out of print. I couldn't tell stories about myself anymore. I'd flip through my sketchbook, dating back to before Kaya was born, life drawings, junked panels, false starts, art ideas, rambling journal entries, then babies in diapers and crawling and wobbling, and all this tearstained agonized writing about how tired I was. Then I'd start to think about What I'm Capable Of, but then I'd think, Who cares. Fuck comics. I couldn't write about these scenes of domestic bliss, maybe because they lacked the reckless, boozy, unzipped struggle of my youth, or maybe because my wife and kids were some creepy experiment I couldn't relate to, or maybe because they were the most precious thing on earth and needed my protection from the diminishing power of my "art," and writing about them was evil.

In my stories I'd been some kind of wild man, some bumbling lothario wielding his incompetence, mistaking his sister-in-law for a prostitute, knocking over the casket at the funeral of his boss, battling suburban angst and sexual constraint in a fictionalized autobio psychodrama. My success at selling that renegade message opened up a sustainable commercial existence, the very existence I'd been trying to avoid. Instead, I embraced conformity, routine, homeownership, marriage, and parenthood, in exchange for neighborly niceties and a sleepy, toothless rebellion in the pages of a crusty political magazine trying to be hip. I worked as an illustrator now, or what might be referred to as an "editorial

cartoonist." I'd also done other types of unclassifiable commer-
cial whore work, promotional posters for a Swedish reggae festi-
val, fabric patterns for a hip-hop clothing company. I had a handful
of regular clients from over the years, a hotel soap manufacturer,
a Canadian HMO, a fried chicken chain in the Philippines whose
in-house art department called when they got totally over-
whelmed, although it had been a while, actually, since I'd done
any of that crap.

Magazine work asked less of me, and paid more, and at times
could almost be fun. I'd done drawings of Anthony Weiner, the
Arab Spring, bedbugs, the uprising in Syria, Walmart slaves,
Obama as a jug-eared mullah, Obama in his Bermuda shorts in
the Rose Garden burying tiny flag-draped coffins, the whole
clown car of Republican kooks who'd been rolling across the
country all year—Michele Bachmann, Herman Cain, Newt, Rick
Perry, and several of Mitt. In one he's waving from his yacht, and
in another he's wiping his ass with an American worker, and in
yet another he's burying his loot in the Caymans. I'd also done
full-page drawings for longer features, assigned by Adam, my art
director: Somali pirates, Gitmo prisoners force-fed on a hunger
strike, and a dozen covers—"The CIA in Damascus," "Stop Eat-
ing So Much Meat," "The Breast Issue," "Our Complicated Rela-
tionship with Drones." I could make a living if I worked fast, on
three things at once, and didn't mind the art department yanking
my chain.

SEVEN

At midnight Beanie got hungry, and at three A.M. he made a sound like a cat being run over by a car, for an hour without stopping. At six he got up for good.

"I hope you have a better night tonight."

"Please don't talk about it."

I regretted having called. They were at the park now, in unrelenting heat and humidity. I sat on a low brick wall by the flagpole, the Place of Good Reception, overlooking the sweep of the harbor, the bridge in the distance, seagulls curling in arcs under high pressure and plenty of sunshine, the temperature a breezy seventy-eight degrees, a skosh below the seasonal average.

First thing this morning they went off to gymnastics camp, where we'd enrolled Kaya for the next four Saturdays, and met a nice blond lady who knelt beside Kaya when Robin tried to leave, and a dark-haired unsympathetic woman collecting the pizza money, and a teenage gymnast, holding a sobbing girl, about Kaya's age, in a pink tutu with a blue lump on her forehead and an ice pack on her wrist.

Kaya had enjoyed the trampoline but not the rope thing. Then some boy shoved her, waiting in line for a cookie. She'd let another boy lie on top of her during circle time, they bumped heads, and now she had a swollen lip. She quit after lunch and said she'd never go back.

Robin's parents had made it to dinner last night after all, but it seemed that Dave hadn't changed Iris's clothes, and her hair was dirty. The last time I'd seen my mother-in-law, she'd used mascara to draw on eyebrows, and wore eye shadow that looked like fireplace ash, and had a bruise from a fall discoloring one side of her face. Every time she walked into a room Robin would walk out, as if an alarm had gone off, explaining loudly that one of the kids needed a cracker, and her mom would sit and tell me how fat people were in Florida, or call Robin's stepfather Dan, or tell me she had a baby in her belly that was painful sometimes.

Robin mentioned the urinary tract infection her mom had, a result of Dave's neglect. He'd done his best to nurse her along, while also resisting and denying the obvious. By the time he'd finally given in and had Iris tested, she'd been tying her blouses in front for a year because she couldn't figure out how to button them. I'd gotten used to the pantomime at dinner, nodding and smiling when she abandoned her fork and pawed through her plate.

Dave and Iris had worked hard all their lives, and this caretaking and dementia were their only retirement. He didn't have religion or children or close family of his own, but he'd confided in me that after Iris died, he planned to take a bicycle tour through the wine regions of Tuscany. He enjoyed the light-tasting Chianti of Florence, as well as the more full-bodied pinot chiefly associated with Pisa. He'd already done the research.

"I need to talk to her nurses," Robin said. "I have to call the house when Dave's not there." I could hear Kaya singing in the background. I could picture the bench where Robin sat at the park by a sweltering playground. "If he's home, they won't say anything."

It was the song Kaya had been singing in the kitchen before I'd left. "Shakira, Shakira!"

"They're not nurses," she said. "They're probably corn farmers. Or soldiers. When did the war end in Sierra Leone?" I said I didn't know. Kaya yelled for Robin to watch her climb. "He's so incapable of dealing with his grief."

Actually, I thought Dave was holding up pretty well, considering. The steroid he took to suppress whatever was choking his lungs had terrible side effects. His face was bloated and his skin had turned red, thin, and fragile. His beard had gone white. He looked like Santa, if Santa started drinking every day at lunch, which Dave did.

"How come this morning at an air-conditioned gymnastics place for seventy-five bucks an hour she wouldn't get off my lap, but we come here in a million degrees and she can't stay off the monkey bars?" I figured it was because she knew the layout, but kept it to myself. "I got so mad at her for quitting. I started screaming, 'You never try. Why *is* that?' I'm sitting outside gymnastics, sweating my ass off, holding Beanie, she can literally see my head from the window, and twice she came out crying, saying she missed me. I just wanted to close my eyes for five seconds. You know how you say I never admit I'm wrong? Well, I was wrong, and I'm not just telling you I abused her to make you feel guilty. I went too far."

"I'm sure you didn't."

"I had to shove him into his stroller so I could deal with her, but he wouldn't let go, and I pressed down so hard I thought I broke his rib cage."

"Jesus."

"At lunch, the nice counselor let her sit on her lap, but the mean one told her she was a big girl and should stop crying. I'm going to find that one and explain to her that it doesn't do any good to tell that to a four-year-old."

"You tell Kaya that all the time."

"That's different."

"Why is it different?"

"Because she woke me up five hundred times last night. Oh, here she is. You woke me up five hundred times last night."

"I'm sorry, Mommy."

"You don't sound sorry." It was true: Kaya didn't sound sorry. I looked out at the bay, the sky, the seagulls, thankful for the distance between us.

"I'm locking her in her room tonight."

"With what?"

"I'll buy a hook."

"Why didn't I think of that?"

"I don't know."

"Because I wouldn't do that to a dog." Two sailboats tacked at the same angle as they cornered around the jetty.

"She's not used to being ignored in the middle of the night. One peep and you're there, hovering over her. Maybe now she'll finally get sleep-trained. Now she'll learn to spend the night in her bedroom alone."

"You're going to sleep-train her in one night?"

It went on like this for a while.

"It's you, you feed and flirt and sing and have conversations at three A.M.—"

The bay, the water, the seagulls.

"When you're here, it's always 'Daddy Daddy,' keeping them out of the basement so you can work, brokering that. When you're not here, it's quiet and I feed them early and put them to bed early, not at nine o'clock—"

"Hey, why don't you take the night shift for the next four years?"

"Because I need drugs to sleep." Beanie let out that piercing cat scream. I heard her whacking him on the back. "And when I take medication, I need more sleep. I'm not doing this for you next summer, so have fun."

"I'm having a blast."

"I don't care what you do up there, but if you give me a disease I will cut it off. Got it?"

"Fine."

"Or shoot you. Or chop off your balls."

"Understood."

Beanie remained quiet, and then we were all quiet.

"I wouldn't mind going to some makeout festival if my body wasn't broken."

"Go ahead."

"As long as you take care of them while I take care of me."

"I should probably get back to it."

"You didn't say how your first class went."

"My class?"

"Yes."

"Fine."

"You say that every year. You worry about that class for weeks, slaving over your notes, 'What do they want from me? I forgot how to teach!' It hardly pays anything, and you're up there having a blast and I'm here killing myself and for what?"

"At least it gets me thinking about comics again. I used to love making comics. I don't know what happened. I have to get a break from the magazine. I have to start something I care about. I have to find a way back in."

"Maybe you're not supposed to write stories about your life anymore. Maybe you outgrew it. Maybe it bubbles up because you're there and you should force it back down where it came from."

"Thanks."

"Or maybe being around those people, you'll have an epiphany."

"Sure."

"Go on, shove it down. Next to your childhood. Next to your parents. Keep shoving."

"You don't know anything about me."

"I know all about you. That's what you're trying to get away from. You think you're worthless, so you make me feel worthless, and when you're gone I don't have that, nobody second-guessing me or giving me nasty looks or turning off my music or criticizing my soul. It's more work, but there's no time to be depressed or think, although I actually can think. Four producers are coming from L.A. on Monday, I'm meeting with the network, it's the busiest time and budgets are insanely tight and Realscreen is right around the corner. I can keep fairly complicated ideas in my head without having any obligation from you to talk and listen. I'm myself. I get love from people at work, and Karen Crickstein wants to meet me for lunch, and Elizabeth comes over and we do the knitting tutorial, and have conversations that matter, and she doesn't wish I would shut up and go away."

EIGHT

The first time I saw her, standing in my foyer, she was holding a giant stick bug in a wooden frame. Robin Lister had moved to Baltimore for a job at the public television station, and knew somebody who knew the sister of this lunatic, Julie, who lived in our group house on Chestnut Ave. Robin took the room of the guy we called Lumpy, who was headed to law school in Denver, which meant we'd be sharing a bathroom.

I helped carry in boxes from her U-Haul. That night I heard her spitting into the bathroom sink, and the next morning I found her in the kitchen, in a thin yellow robe with tiny blue fishes, staring into the garbage, trying to figure out how many cups of coffee she'd already had by the look of the used filter. When I think back to whatever it was that brought us together, it probably happened in the kitchen. She'd been hired to write and edit bilingual scripts for a local children's television program and had tape drives of old episodes to study, but she already had a few things to say about the show's three main characters, a hyperactive skunk, a Hispanic beaver named Anselma, and a wise old chipmunk who protects the young explorers.

I found myself sitting across from her, lingering over breakfast, offering piercing analysis of our roommates' psyches: Nedd, the ladies' man; Rishi, an account exec at the ad agency where I worked; and Julie, the emotionally stunted MBA who talked like a baby. Robin had questions, and I projected a confiding warmth and a loud, Jewish, overcompensating wit.

She was seeing a guy named Jim, who deejayed on the weekends. He was followed by Digger, a cameraman from the Czech Republic who worked in war zones and had always just stepped off an airplane held together with duct tape. He'd been to the Congo, had ridden a horse across Afghanistan. Somehow, a year passed. I'd been dating Eileen Pribble, an elementary school art teacher who stuck refrigerator magnets to the outside of her car.

Robin and I were friends, although she was too good-looking for that. She needed company. I thought I might earn something, through my loyalty, that someday I would collect. At first I didn't know what to make of her, but after a while I noticed how much I looked forward to her coming home at night. After dinner, the two of us would sometimes walk down the street for ice cream. She had hazel eyes, thin, wavy brown hair, and olive skin. The hair resting thinly on a delicate skull held an introspective, self-doubting, reasonable, forceful, somewhat dignified mind. She wanted to get out of kids' programming and work in hard news, wanted to see the world. Digger had friends who could help. In the fall of that year, two Sudanese guys had blown a hole in the USS *Cole* as it refueled in Yemen. The new trend in terrorism, Robin said, was asymmetrical, like a bottle of botulism in a New York City reservoir. She wanted intensity and danger. She was so pretty that guys would stare at us as we walked down the block. Sometimes I worried that one of them would try to kill me.

Eileen and I split, and I thought for sure it would change things. I remember standing in the bathroom when no one else was home, examining Robin's tongue scraper, and found myself pondering the wall that separated our bedrooms, wondering if I could tunnel through it to find her there asleep. There were moments where I'd given up, moments where I got obsessed, moments where I was repelled, moments where I'd grown too emotionally attached. I felt feverish and sick whenever Digger spent the night, trying not to listen while brushing my teeth, long sick sleepless nights until he left for some war zone in East Timor, until he moved back to Prague for good. In the mornings Robin and I had those nattering exchanges old couples have, bickering in front of our housemates or alone, about the missing butter or how long to boil an egg. If her insomnia plagued her, she'd shoot me a look— and I can remember now, the rush of blood in my face. I felt somewhat powerless, and assumed it would pass.

She'd ask my opinion on her clothing before work in the morning, she'd notice my haircut or suggest I stop chewing ice before I cracked a tooth. I wanted her to love me. There was this basis forming beneath us. Sometimes we walked together to the nearby community center for our morning laps. I'd spy on her from underwater, her thin arms balletic and almost lazy in their strokes, a weird, improper technique, her legs kicking furiously, frothing the water around her.

Julie took a job in Atlanta. Nedd moved out. The housemate thing collapsed. Rishi and I found a place in Fells Point. Robin moved into an apartment alone, two rooms with a refrigerator under the counter and the smallest kitchen sink you ever saw. It was fall. One night I brought her flowers and beer and got a home-cooked meal. She was my friend, she took pity on me, I was a pitiful tortured person who could make her laugh. A wall of books greeted me when I walked into the apartment, film theory, life on the Serengeti, prehistoric pottery of the Colorado Plateau, whatever she was interested in.

She didn't want me, maybe didn't trust me, saw something missing, wanted less, a lighter commitment, or was holding out for someone who could take care of things down the line. I couldn't cope with her withholding, couldn't talk to her about us. I played the part of the ironic, submissive romantic, and she played the partially compliant friend of the opposite sex, sexually complicated, rigid, obsessive, a tease. I was protective and patient but losing hope. She was emotionally damaged by the death of her brother and her parents' divorce.

On a weekday morning in December, some lady blew through an intersection and T-boned Robin's Jetta. Thus began the period of her concussion. It lasted through the spring with a sort of merciless momentum. The nausea alone almost killed her. She wore sunglasses at work, had trouble looking at a screen, couldn't tolerate light or music or ambient noise. Went to neurologists, did brain-rehabilitation exercises, memorized colored playing cards. I came and went, brought groceries, made phone calls to her autobody place and health insurance. I still recall the soft shush of a beanbag she tossed from one hand to the other, crossing the midline.

Indoors at night she wore shades under a floppy wide-brimmed hat, looking like a Russian double agent, one I called Farvela Du Harvelfarv. By cooking for her in the stuffy apartment, I earned the right to sit quietly while she talked to her mother, rubbing a certain spot on her temple while she cried, wondering whether she'd ever recover. She became softer, less guarded, quietly resting beside me, resigned to a constant migraine-type vertigo. But because it wouldn't end, it seemed to get worse. She couldn't exercise. Went to bed at eight. Was sad and strange to herself.

Overcome by a wave of anguish, she slept with me. In that way, we began sleeping together. I think it was, even for her, a consolation. And yet, I couldn't help feeling, as I learned to take on her bottomless fears of permanent damage, that the inordinate conditions under which she lived had forced her to surrender. I remember pulling her onto my lap, kissing her head in different places. She was so vulnerable and open. I wished we could always live that way.

NINE

What I knew about Robin at twenty-six has since been overwritten by our twelve years together, by the fuzzing of boundaries that separate us, by events we faced beyond our abilities, by the sound of a four-note wooden xylophone our son liked to beat the shit out of at five A.M., and by the immutable cycles of birth and sleep. It's not an excuse, for anything really, but there were nights Beanie woke up screaming every fifteen minutes. I could count on one hand the times in his life he slept more than two hours straight. It became a secret among us, like domestic beatings, what went on in our house after dark.

Sometimes I blamed our daughter, who fell between the mattress and the wall, or had bears in her dreams, or the rain upset her and drove her out of bed. Sometimes I blamed my wife, who never did figure out how to sleep, who needed protection from the chaos, and wore earplugs and a satin eye mask, and had a bag of prescription drugs she kept hidden in her underwear drawer, and in an emergency had to be shaken awake, and couldn't go back to bed or take naps during the day, and in sleep debt quickly spiraled into anxiety and short-term mania.

But I woke up smoothly and easily when he screamed, and took him from the crib at the foot of our bed and carried him away and fed him or sang him a song, and he went back down for a while. Then I wandered from the bedroom to the couch to the futon in the basement, helpless and itinerant, waiting for his cry, so that the silence became loud, and the quiet throbbed and roared through the stillness like a marching band. If I lay there long enough, I split the worry into so many pieces it started to glitter, and I got dizzy and hopeful and felt grateful for the sounds of cars, birds, dawn.

I did the nights. In the morning I rested on the couch half-dead while Robin got them dressed. Sometimes as I lay there, my daughter came close and made a little ponytail on the top of my head. There were mornings when I wished I could escape or be put out of my misery, but the accumulation of good behavior, the years placed end to end, had also made me strong, although sometimes it occurred to me that it was all too fucking weird, as I struggled to stay the course, all this goodness and responsibility; it seeded an impulse toward endless badness and rebellion.

Sometimes as I lay there Robin bent down to see how I was, touching my hand with a look of eagerness or tenderness in her eyes, almost like hunger or lust, a look I didn't see much in any other context, asking gently for a recap of how bad it had been. Sometimes she brought me toast. I think my pain meant something to her. I think she enjoyed my suffering almost as much as I did. Like lovers using clamps and whips, it somehow brought us closer.

She gave them life, gave them milk from her breasts, nursed

them through sickness and colds, made a throaty sound when she hadn't seen them all day, moaning, kissing them all over. She did the days. I handed over my paychecks, any option money or royalties that hadn't dried up; she pooled it with her money, paying the bills, taking them to kid parties, doctors, setting up playdates, hanging with other mothers, deciding on Kaya's preschool, wondering if I could take a more active role in decisions. Sitting in a little chair by the door of Kaya's classroom last fall for three straight weeks, her back breaking, trying to get Kaya to calm down and hang in there. She was strong, strong-willed, and shouldn't have been surprised that her daughter was, too. She got field producers and actors to do what she wanted, took hours of incoherent B-roll and turned it into tight twelve-minute arcs, understood how the wildlife conservation movement had failed African lions.

For several years, following her time in children's television, Robin worked for an international news agency, and went all over Latin America, and held a camera and got dengue fever and hired soldiers to take her into the mountains. She had friends who were stabbed, kidnapped, or disappeared. Later she worked at the bureau, going out on assignment once a month, and until Kaya was born she ran the desk, Central and South America and the Caribbean, sending out other people to risk their necks the way she once did. Eventually she burned out and quit.

She wound up at the Nature Channel, which was perfect for a mom with a small kid. Her co-workers sometimes arrived still wearing their morning tennis outfits. The newsroom had been exciting and desperate and prone to burnout, but the Nature Channel was ergonomic and well lit and had the congenial atmosphere of a shoe store. She didn't make films anymore; the channel didn't make anything. It bought the finished product, shows about water buffalo, flora and fauna, and also, increasingly, the stuff that filled prime time: a "science" show about people too fat to wear clothes, a "history" show about bombs that fit up someone's body cavity. A show about a man with huge testicles was not yet considered a celebrity vehicle. She still got to travel, but not to the Galápagos. Twice a year her department went to Wheaton, Maryland, for an afternoon of paintball.

Then she had morning sickness, puking her guts out for eight or ten or fifteen straight weeks, it's hard to remember now, wishing she could give me a nonlethal form of salmonella so I could know her pain. After Beanie was born she took time off again, and for the last six months had been edging back in, happy to work part-time at Connie's small production company, whose only client was the Nature Channel, making a sweet little PSA she loved, destined for the wee hours of the night, about girls in poor countries who were victims of early marriage. A former executive producer for the channel, she was now a so-called independent producer, with no benefits, no contract, no real job, at the mercy of bland, plodding, overpaid executives on staff.

Between us we'd had terrifying gaps in employment, clients who'd gone bankrupt, work stoppages, lean times, hospital bills, economic downturns, crises of confidence, bosses who'd lied or disappeared, and projects mercy-killed.

There were moments when I too somehow failed to understand my place in the world or see what lay ahead, when I thought my own good luck would never end, when I mistook the work I did for a skill that builds on itself. I had years where money dropped from the sky, but also disappointments, broken dreams, ill-advised spending on copper saucepans and breathable raingear, troubles with the IRS, and a house we owned whose value had dropped below what we owed the bank. Six years ago, we'd borrowed from Robin's mom to buy it. After the mortgage crisis we were underwater, and nobody would refinance the loan. A year or two later, we went back to Robin's mom. She took out a second mortgage to bail us out. We got money from her dad to buy Robin's car. We got a title loan against the car to pay bills. We set up a payment plan with the IRS guy, asked the worst credit card companies to cut our spending limit, begged them later to maybe raise it back up so we could eat, which, thank God, they refused to do. The magazine paid me on the twenty-eighth, like a monthly salary, although I wasn't an employee, so a third of it needed to be set aside to pay taxes, which was completely out of the question, and would have to be dealt with down the road.

TEN

While I sat there by the flagpole, a pair of gladiator-sandaled feet
appeared on the grass in front of me, and two legs, and above
that, Amy. She held up a finger for me to wait. She was being
polite. She pulled the phone away from her ear and said, "Some-
body wants my money." I feigned outrage. She shook her head.
"I'm on a conference call."

She was tall, with a long neck and good collarbones. She wore
a gray sleeveless T-shirt and close-fitting blue-and-green plaid
shorts. She had the bent posture and crimped mouth of a forty-
one-year-old mom with three small kids. She didn't look like her
photos—ones she'd sent me, from a skating rink, or her bedroom,
or with her oldest kid and a dog—which now seemed like one
more problem to deal with.

She'd tied up her hair for painting class. It looked smooth and glossy. Her cheekbones were high and soft, her arms tanned and freckled. She went back to the phone call, nodding her head as hair spilled from the knot, her wrist bent against her waist, and turned on her toes on the grass, twirling cutely. It bugged me. Her movement said, "I'm busy. I'm needed. I have a life."

In high school she was scouted at the local mall, and got hired to do some modeling, boat shows, department store flyers. Her parents didn't approve. Her father stocked shelves in a grocery store and died young. Her mom was still living, and also tall. Amy had swum competitively, and set a national record in the short-course two-hundred-meter something. Then came a job in finance, to erase the deprivations of her childhood, and marriage to that jackass who made her a fortune. Then she set her sights on becoming some kind of activist, straddling the classes with money and love.

Lately she'd been infusing her artwork with one of her charity concerns. The toxic-sludge painting she'd started here last summer showed aquatic life along the Connecticut shore, deformed by PCBs—which, I guess . . . if you like that sort of thing. Over the winter she'd sent me pictures of another one, more sludge infecting life-giving waters, with these intestinal shapes framing her screwy self-portrait, head too long, one eyebrow raised, a kind of eco-friendly Frida Kahlo thing.

She turned to me and rolled her eyes. I shrugged like, "Oh well." She grabbed her throat and stuck out her tongue. I pretended to gag. She motioned to throw the phone in the direction of the bay. Then she hit Mute and said, "It's beyond partisan politics, but working together to protect our environment I want to thank you all for blah blah—"

She pressed a button on the phone again.

"Ugh. Yes honey, sorry, I'm here."

When the call ended, she groaned. "We're trying to get muckety-mucks to buy a table, and if you really want to know, we can't decide whether to put a seashell in the middle of each table and decorate the seashell with the table number or put the fucking number on a stick."

"Oh."

"Board service."

"You sound bored."

"I like to serve on small boards, with a clear give-get, for a year or less."

"Whatever that means."

"I think it means I have to give them something. Let me tell my assistant the password to my bank account."

For a long time, I didn't think about her money. Then I thought it was ridiculous and disgusting. Although later, I just wanted to get paid. Maybe somewhere in the middle there, for a while anyway, I thought anything was possible, that we were bigger than money, that if we got together, whatever she had would somehow melt away in the heat of our passion. She didn't wear an engagement ring or fancy clothes, and she carried up from birth a grinding Catholic guilt that equated frugality with goodness. She wore diamond earrings, although her generous earlobes made them look smaller.

She ended the call and asked how I'd slept, and I asked how her class had gone, her narrative painting workshop. "You look tired," she said.

She looked thin. She survived for stretches on Twizzlers and Diet Coke. I studied her chipped fingernails, the part in her hair, until I recognized her, the long thin nose with a knob on the end that I'd kissed, and big gray eyes on either side of her head like an extraterrestrial.

I should've asked more questions, wondered how her kids were, the baby who looked like a monkey and ate bananas, the girl Kaya's age who never remembered to wear underwear, or the oldest, who'd had a health scare but was fine now. Or maybe it was better to keep things light, so I did my impression of Beanie eating his first solid food, a Cheerio, chewing it for a minute or two before it flipped right onto his chin, entirely whole. And I told her how Kaya made a schedule of the hairdos of her favorite doll, every day there was a different hairdo, but I didn't go into what they were.

"That's cute."

"Yeah."

"You're a good father."

I hated this fake chitchat. Before she put the phone away, she showed me a photo of her brand-new bald-headed niece in a pink onesie, with a little pushed-up nose, surrounded by her own children and many other neighbors and nephews and other sun-tanned people, beside their swimming pool. It was nice to see her older daughter looking healthy, bright-eyed, and beaming.

"And who's this?" I asked, but I didn't care. I let her talk. There were more photos of kids on horseback in the neighbor's paddock, and girls with juice-stained faces in fancy dresses on the beach at sunset. This one in pigtails was underweight and got gummy vitamins and a chicken leg whenever she came over to play. She lived next door. The mom ignored her but had just bought a $90,000 horse. This boy came to practice piano. He cried if you touched his towel. His dad had moved in with the CrossFit instructor. The lady two doors down had had so much plastic surgery she looked like a marionette. I recognized Amy's garden, now in bloom, her walkways and meandering stone-work. She wanted to move the trampoline so the kids could bounce into the pool, but she worried that if somebody missed the water they'd hit the patio or impale themselves on an umbrella.

"When a big kid bounces a little kid," she said, "we call it popcorn."

In photos the girls danced around in towels or naked; no one cared. "I just let 'em do whatever." She'd grown up in a big family with no money and liked to pretend she still lived on the fly. She wanted me to know that she was the real thing, that all the fancy ladies in the neighborhood had been born rich and ignored their kids. One took the infant and the night nurse with her on business trips. The point was, only Amy with her fun yard could protect the children of utmost privilege from abandonment and cushy neglect. "The nannies like hanging with my nanny, they're all friends, so guess who ends up making lunch for everyone and keeping an eye on the pool?"

"The pool boy?"

"You're getting warmer."

"Looks like fun."

"Honey, I'm always having fun." Her eyes narrowed. Seagulls wheeled over us, screeching like monkeys. A single airplane, high up, left a puffy trail.

"Your pool looks even bigger with the cover off."

Her eyes were pale and slitted. "It's the same."

"And your house looks bigger. Have you been feeding it vitamins?"

"Same pool. Same house."

There were voices coming this way, people walking to the flagpole to make phone calls. She'd spent time thinking about this very thing and wanted it settled.

"It's not my house. It's his. He wanted it. He wanted an even *bigger* place, but I said no."

"That's a beautiful story."

I knew all about her lonely life in the big empty house in the woods. I knew what kind of soap she used on her son's eczema, and the name of her husband's investment fund, and the humiliating details of their sex life, and how many billions in assets, and his unpublished annual haul. I had a hard time imagining that there was anything left to tell me. I knew she'd played trumpet in the marching band in high school, and spit had run down her chin. She'd told me about the ex-boyfriend who stalked her, the summer after high school ended, finally cornered her, tore her clothes, beat her badly, and probably worse—and how she refused to seek justice or retaliate. She missed her father, he'd died a few months after the attack, and in her mind somehow those awful events were connected. One night, when her second kid was an infant and Amy had a bad stretch, her father appeared to her as a ghost at the foot of her bed. She had a high, hard, shining forehead. Some of her hair had fallen out after each of her kids was born.

I noticed her cracked lower lip and remembered my mouth on her salty neck, holding her smooth, bony hip. We locked eyes. I felt it zooming through me again. I heard pretty violin music in my head, the back of my throat went soft, I tried to swallow, and wanted to bury my face in her hair.

A man paced back and forth, talking with one finger in his ear. A white-haired lady stood on the other side of the flagpole in a long denim skirt. "Hello? Hello? Are you there? I'm only hearing parts of what you're saying."

"But you're doing okay?" Amy asked. "And things are good at home?"

"Is that a joke?"

"But how is it for you?"

"I already told you," I said. "I gave her everything I had."

Amy said, "You're a good person."

"No I'm not."

"I'm glad I met you, whoever you are."

"You look beautiful. I'm glad your daughter's healthy."

She nodded. "She's at sleepaway camp, hating every minute of it."

"You got through it. I knew you were scared."

"Yeah, well." She glanced around. "I started to wonder."

"What?"

"You know."

"Huh?"

"If there was a connection."

"To what?"

"To us. All the emails and everything."

"You mean, like, *punishment?*"

She looked up, chin raised. "I'm not blaming you."

"I understand." She didn't want to be mocked.

In March, a week after I saw her at her house in Connecticut, her oldest kid walked off a soccer field and puked and passed out and almost died. Texts and lengthy emails flowed night and day with no punctuation, starting in mid-sentence, referencing jargon and arguments about emergency surgical techniques to relieve swelling in her daughter's brain. Then notes from the hospital at all hours, waiting to speak to the doctors. Her husband was in Milan, working on a deal. Then I heard nothing from her for four months, not a word.

We'd put a lot into our emails. It was a gigantic pain in the ass. If either of us slacked off, the other one got offended. You had to be timely and consistently thoughtful. Although it was nice to know that on nights when I couldn't sleep, at least someone out there was listening. When I started spiraling into my own black hole, or when Beanie went loco at two A.M., or when Kaya cried because her pillow was too hot, or when the magazine sent back my drawing thirty-seven times for revisions and then killed it, or when I received actual death threats for a cartoon I drew mocking military methods of interrogation, or when the dental surgeon sent me a bill for two thousand nine hundred fucking dollars, or the neighbors hated me because my car blew clouds of whitish-blackish smoke, or when Robin said I tasted like something she had for dinner that she didn't feel like tasting again, when I thought that nobody would ever want me again, that I'd never crawl into bed with someone and fall into her arms, grateful, protected, in love—I could say it, through that doohickey in my pocket, and by the power of instantaneous electronic transmission it would find her, rising out of a dead sleep in the middle of the night, and she'd zap back a little something to cheer me up, and that would be enough. Giving voice to every thought in my head, having a place for that, meant a lot to me.

Her kid recovered quickly, and in May Amy took to Facebook to celebrate. In June I wrote to her, wondering whether I'd see her here again, and waited patiently for that iffy response.

"I want to hear more about His holy vengeance, but I have to go play softball. It's in the contract. Part of the fun."

"Oh." She looked miserable.

"You should play. It's the Naked versus the Dead."

"Some people from my class signed up."

"Come on."

"I'd probably hurt myself."

"I hurt myself every year."

"Look," she said brightly. "I took your advice and went to a chiropractor." She turned her head from side to side. She seemed to grow even taller.

"Praise the Lord."

"Although that's as far as it goes."

"Any farther and it means you're possessed by the devil."

Almost sincerely she said, "You are not the devil."

"No, I'm not," I said. "Although it's interesting how you turned that against me, slightly demonic."

"Sorry. It's the possessed part."

"Either way, you're safe from me."

She looked pained. Not too pained, not like she might keel over with blood pouring out her eye sockets, but maybe more like the electric toothbrush she'd been hoping for was permanently out of stock.

"You know what?" Her eyes narrowed again. "I was doing fine until now."

She had been mine. There was that. So it was nice to be close to her, and it was nice to see it causing her pain.

ELEVEN

I went into the dugout and looked through the mitts for one with no cracks in the leather. Tom McLaughlin sat on the bench, reading his phone. Frank Gaspari walked by with his socks pulled up. "Are we ready for this, or what?"

On second thought, I felt scummy and rejected and ashamed. Worse-looking every day, I had a cartoonist's body: shoulders hiked up, head hung forward, face drooping, fuzzy gray hairs coming in on the sides, yellow toenails, my potbelly blousing my T-shirt, forcing me to suck in my gut, to fight the constant hunger of a tired middle-aged man. To be ugly in such a beautiful place was worse, among the shifting sands and rotting kelp and hopeless erosion.

The baseball field was at the far end of campus, inland, breezeless, and hot. You could smell fertilizer baking in the dirt. I watched an airplane fly along the bay towing a Geico banner.

Carl, the director, came across the field, lugging a duffel bag full of bats. He dropped it and jogged around the infield, ass bouncing, change jingling in his pockets, throwing bases on the ground. Then he sat, sweating heavily, on the other side of Tom and told us how much the bag of bats weighed, and where he'd lugged it from, and how an intern named Megan Donahue had locked the keys in the shuttle bus and the cops were on the way, and how the stage in the theater building had been shellacked two weeks ago but according to the theater people was still tacky, so the actors had to act in their socks so they didn't stick to the floor. And the playwrights were all assholes. You had to call them "theater artists" or the "Drama Department" or they got angry. Then he pushed his long gray hair out of his face and went through the faculty, listing who was a piece of crap; anybody demanding a room change or failing to address students' needs qualified, and this year, some of the new teachers seemed to be showing up with dietary restrictions or three names, like Alicia Hernandez Roulet. And the poets pronounced it "poe-eh-tray." If it wasn't for nice guys like Tom and me, he'd quit.

There was a certain headache you got after a day or so, the conference headache, which Carl already had. After three days you got a certain taste in your mouth, conference tongue. He told us how the administrators at the state U had lied and screwed him on funding, they were nickel-and-diming him to death, he had booze in his car that he'd stolen from Marine Bio and Sustainability—then we were quiet there on the dugout bench, and Carl asked Tom how much they paid him at other summer conferences. Tom laughed and said he never left the house for less than five grand but made an exception for this, since we had parties in the windmill.

More people straggled across the field; they seemed fine with the heat, pulling bats out of the duffel bag, dumping the bag to find helmets, testing swings, throwing and catching. Stan, a poet, claimed the mound to calibrate his underhand lob. An old lady with knee braces waited at the plate for batting practice. A security guard stood along the fence, and two women in beach clothes and visors sat in the stands. An able-bodied kid passed in front of the dugout, shirtless, barefoot, wearing jeans that had been shredded below the knee like a castaway's—a fundamentally beautiful young person, covered in downy golden peach fuzz, handing out bottles of water.

A couple of conference-goers in bikinis sat on towels on the third-base line in front of the other dugout, and the able-bodied kid went over and gave them water, then spilled water on them and they screamed. He ran but they chased him and pulled him to the ground and pinned him and poured water on him. Everybody was having fun.

They were perfect and beautiful, whereas I was already a little revolting, although better straight on, but worse from the side. I was forty-two years old, obstructed by the limits of love, grasping at lust, scared to work on a crumbling marriage I'd be sure to hang on to for whatever remaining time we had here on earth.

A young woman dug through the mitts beside me and kept flapping them open and closed until I told her that a righty wears the thing on her left hand. I got a ball and went out onto the grass and showed her how to throw and catch. Her name was Eva Rotmensch. Some people pronounced it "Ava," she said, but they were wrong. She walked with turned-out feet and had a flat pale face with a sharp jawbone and bluntly cut hair. She wore a cropped white blouse and pink shorts so fitted and tiny it would be difficult to imagine any underpants surviving inside them. When she raised her arms, her shirt went with them and I saw her thin torso. She needed me to know that she belonged to the theater company, as opposed to the theater workshop. Never played softball before, no sports, spent the first twenty years of her life in a dance studio. She pranced around on long, strong legs, like she was still onstage, mimicking my exaggerated throwing motion, elbow back, above her ear, and threw it over my head, then threw it into the bushes, then under the stands, waiting each time for me to go get it, like my daughter, who didn't know how to do anything and needed me to show her, as though she were doing me a favor, turning whatever should've been fun into a pain in the ass.

I asked polite questions about her acting career, and mentioned a few out-of-the-way spots where people go to sunbathe, smiling at her, wondering whether she liked the beach, whether she liked swimming in big waves, feeling invisible and ignored, wondering what it would be like if for some reason she put down the mitt and lay on the grass and pulled down her shorts and begged me to fuck her.

Art historian Marilyn Michnick sat behind the fence, smiling and serene, and nearly blind, needing a cane, beside Alicia Hernandez Roulet, whose ugly little walleyed dog yapped around the field. Mohammad Khan, a theater critic, cleaned his eyeglasses with long, delicate-looking fingers, complaining about having to play. "I don't like to get sweaty. I don't like to be wet." Vicky Capodanno came toward us from right field, in the baggy black T-shirt and shorts and combat boots she wore every year for softball, and a few steps behind her, Tabitha wore a baseball cap and a long thing you toss over a bathing suit that looked like a tablecloth. I recognized a couple stragglers, among them a taller lady moving stiffly, hunched and broad-shouldered in her gray sleeveless T-shirt and blue-and-green plaid shorts, who I'd spoken to a few minutes earlier: Amy O'Donnell, who I'd once held as we caressed in the dark, trembling and naked, and later while sleeping in the quiet dawn. I wanted another moment with her, something I could look back on later, to get me through another year, a scene, a place to park my soul through winter months of diapers and screaming.

I looked across the road, beyond the trees, to houses and a cornfield in the distance. Whatever hadn't been watered was dead. A guy in a jungle hat took batting practice, drilling balls into left field, where eight or nine people stood chatting in two clumps, some of them not even facing the batter, and I wondered if one of them would be hit by a ball and killed.

Amy went behind the dugout and started stretching, some kind of hurried knee-bend squat. She was so tall. Her people could be traced back to the northern coast of Ireland, where shipwrecked Vikings raped the villagers, which made them tall and fair. She bent, she hunched, she made horrible faces. Now she squatted side to side.

The guy with the water came through the trees from the parking lot, and one of the girls in a bikini tried to make a run for it, shrieking, and he tackled her and spilled water on her and she screamed. They were young, although not so young, but like a different species.

"What's his problem?" I asked Eva. "Why isn't he playing?"

She watched him, lips parted, not smiling. She said his name was Ryan.

"Is he in the theater company?"

"He's in something in New York, so he's going back and forth, taking the train, so he can't be in anything here."

He rolled around on the grass—he had fine golden skin and a Chinese tattoo on his neck—as she watched him, her poor little blouse straining at every button, her ass floating in the air like a helium balloon. I threw the ball, but she wasn't looking and it flew past her and pegged Stan in the back. He wheeled around, scowling, and kicked it away.

One of these nights, maybe after a rehearsal, under glittering starlight, Ryan might meet Eva walking from the theater to the dorms. And may it not turn into a long-term monogamous relationship, and may it end in a mutual hatefuck. Amen. Behind us, a group of interns stood blocking the dugout, looking sweaty, stealing our water, complaining to Mohammad Khan about having to clean up the tent after lunch.

"The kitchen is a total slime pit!"

"We're totally covered in slime!"

They went on complaining as they tipped up bottles of water: a young woman in a torn miniskirt with torn black stockings and heavy mascara, and her sleepy-looking friend, filling out a T-shirt with the school's name across her chest, and a third one with bouncy, eggy, shiny hair. It was as if the water they poured down their throats went right into their sumptuous breasts to keep them full.

Four more days of this. Then I could go home and choke my wife.

There were enough of us now to split into two teams. People wandered out to take positions so we could start.

I pictured myself heaving over some sullen nineteen-year-old, my baggy old face hanging down, and went along the dugout thinking filthy thoughts, grabbing helmets and lining them up beneath the bench, and asked nicely if anyone had the order, and saw that I was batting seventh. On this broiling Saturday afternoon, where were the cuties of my youth? Women in their forties had replaced them, hunching toward the grave. For so long I'd been young, but that was over, and the thing to do now was teach a little comics and go home, where I could drop my eyeglasses in the toilet, and fall down the stairs in my pajamas, somebody wailing in the background while I stood in my kitchen, in a state of shock, loading the dishwasher.

Vicky came over and put her mitt on her head and said, "Let's get on with it already."

I needed to find someone at this conference, someone who wouldn't harm a married man, or hated being married, or couldn't bear to be alone for three or four days. I didn't have any big strategy here. I liked to flirt. I needed to stay alert every second for a potential alliance in this war against morbidity and death. Were there rules or prohibitions? Some of my colleagues preyed upon the young, their own students, the low-hanging fruit, which struck me as a real character flaw. I wanted a grown-up, maybe with children of her own, someone who was needed somewhere else and wouldn't get hooked. I'd driven the many miles here with purpose and concentration. I had to make the most of my time away from home. Over the last ten years, the stuff I'd done could be counted on one hand: a couple of late-night goodbyes that never got past the talking stage; a wriggling blond woman at a convention in Brooklyn who edited textbooks for a living; Ruth Gogelberg, Gunkelman, whatever, at this very conference three or four years ago. It started when I was sixteen. It started when I was five, the need for a girl to save me, the need to escape, in a panic to get away from my mother and father, out of this empty shell. I always had a girlfriend, always fell in love, and even at my most saintly and sexless, I always liked someone out there, was working at something, moving toward it with intention and forethought, nibbling around the edges until I hated the whole thing, until everything I did became about *not* cheating, *not* doing something, until it was pretty much a foregone conclusion, and all I had to do was pull the trigger and get it over with, so I could slink back to my safe and stable perch and pretend it had never happened and hate myself and think of someone new.

Amy finished stretching and pulled her hair back into a rubber band. Our thing went beyond lusty one-liners and therapeutic confessions. I'd been in love with her for a year. Not love. Whatever it was. And it just so happened that her personal misery, hidden behind a windfall of prosperity, was ironically charged, luridly beguiling, and possibly useful in a practical sense, as fact-based material for the once and future semiautobiographical storyteller. She walked into the dugout. I stood and walked out, pretending not to know her. She found a bat and went behind the backstop and took practice cuts, swinging so hard her helmet fell off.

The game started. A big sandy-haired kid stepped into the batter's box and golfed the first pitch high and gone; it landed in the parking lot, where it bounced as people cheered, as he ran around the bases with his arms hanging down, like a pigeon-toed ape. Mohammad Khan could barely lift the bat, and tapped a base hit. Tabitha got up and somehow outran a dribbler down the first-base line. Then Amy went to the plate, grimacing into the sun, and took a wild cut.

She hit it pretty well. The second baseman knocked it down but couldn't hold on. He picked it up and tagged Tabitha softly on the shoulder, then threw the ball over the first baseman's head, over the dugout, where it beaned the golf cart that had driven Marilyn Michnick here. Mohammad limped home. When the ball is thrown out of play, the runner is awarded the next base. Amy waited at first. I couldn't stop myself and yelled, "Take second!"

She looked at me as though the last thing in the world she needed was a man yelling at her in public; she got enough of that at home. It was a confusing moment. I still had some investment or pride in her, I wanted her to thrive, succeed, whatever, so I stood in front of the dugout waving her on. She ran down the base path, unsure, reached second, and stared right at me as she stomped testily on the base with both feet. Stomped as though to defy me. But no one had bothered to anchor the base, so it skipped out from under her and she fell.

And didn't get up.

The pitcher, Stan, walked to second base. The shortstop knelt. Nobody seemed to be moving. As I got closer, I saw that her whole mood had shifted; she'd come to a sitting position, her arm in her lap. She seemed drunk, the way a drunk is soft, sleepy, in shadows, fighting to stay awake; she was staring down into her lap as if a haze floated in front of her. Looking at her arm, I had to force myself to breathe. It was my fault, I'd done it. I pushed that thought away.

"What's up?" Carl asked, standing so close he was brushing my shoulder. He hadn't seen her fall. Then he looked. I watched his face change. She was sitting with one leg folded under herself, foot turned, knees bent, so that the whiteness of her inner thighs showed.

The girl kneeling beside her talked in a loud voice, holding Amy's forearm. "Tip your head forward, that's good, now deep breath, just relax, you're gonna be fine, don't look, it's okay, I've got your arm," and Amy saying, in a kind of husky, sleepy voice, "I don't want to look," and then a guy in a Red Sox cap came over and draped her arm with a T-shirt.

The security guard called for an ambulance. Vicky walked across the infield dirt, squinted at Amy, then turned to me. Our former and potential closeness made me think she could read my mind. My thoughts were slow and bleating and obstructed, but I noted, finally, that Amy had been a kind of home, a vessel for my discombobulated mind, that my own family treated me like a footstool but this stranger had cared for my soul. At some point, we could hear sirens on the highway. They decided to get Amy out of the sun, and with heavy assistance, she stood and took a few unsteady steps and began lowering herself down to the grass, her legs bending, collapsing, as her handlers bumped into each other, holding her arm, wavering, guiding her down, her legs folded beneath her, all wrong. They raised her up again as though it had been their fault.

"Ready?"

"Sure."

And again she went down, and this time she tucked her chin and went completely out.

"Amy?" the girl said, kneeling. We all waited. "Can you hear me?"

"Uh-huh."

"Do you faint easily?"

She nodded.

"I wish you'd told me that before. I wouldn't have moved you."

Amy's gaze drifted down to the T-shirt covering her arm, as if it were some new friend. "I didn't know until I fainted."

An EMT and three paramedics arrived, asking a series of questions—name, day of the week, name of the U.S. president—and each time Amy answered politely.

"Can you move your fingers?"

"I can but I don't want to, but thank you."

The slapstick fainting, the bone snapped at nearly mid-forearm, crooked and flopping in the sleeve of her skin, not life-threatening but stomach-churning, her broken summer day, her arm lying in her lap, all of us standing over her as Carl used the security guard's walkie-talkie. They strapped her to a red steel chair on wheels. I knelt down and attempted to communicate without making known any extramural bond between us.

"Do you want me to come with you?"

She shook her head. The whole bottom half of her face was trembling. Sweat or some kind of moisture pooled in her eyes.

Carl signed off and handed the radio back to the guard. The hell with it. They wheeled her out.

Vicky stood beside me, sighing loudly, and when I looked at her she gave me a deep, penetrating stare. When I couldn't come up with anything to say, she went behind the dugout and started smoking.

We resumed the game. Other people fell to the ground with injuries. Stan stumbled off the mound, holding his elbow. Luther Voigt pulled a hamstring. During my turn at bat I hit a fizzing pop-up, and felt something go in my back, and couldn't stand up straight, and walking back to the dugout I used the bat as a cane, and watched from the bench as a string of elderly, scarred, limping septuagenarians hit and ran to the satisfying cheers of our team. I had one decent catch in left off a whistling line drive, and another off a deep fly ball. Both times I thought my legs would crumple and I'd fall to the ground, waiting for those balls to bang into my mitt, but I didn't.

TWELVE

In February, I'd spent a week in New Hampshire, freezing to death on the campaign trail, sketching the GOP candidates as they trained their fire on Mitt. The front-runner tried to float above the fray, blaming Obama, smiling with dairy farmers, suggesting that ten million undocumented immigrants self-deport. The same speeches at horrible parties with terrible music and bad food.

Then in March I spent five days at the trial in Boston of the guy who tried to blow up Faneuil Hall, making drawings of the calm, fat-faced, and deliberate attorney general, of the bearded and scowling bomber, and the stolid and weeping families of victims. I wore credentials on a string around my neck, and got there at dawn to stake out a seat, and had nowhere to put my elbows, and learned about forensics, and a training camp in Yemen, and the destructive power of half a ton of nitroglycerin. After three days, my back was so stiff I couldn't turn my head, which other members of the media found amusing.

I finished the assignment and drove south, toward Providence, and a little while later I was following Amy's directions, imagining her on those roads, thinking that this was wrong and delusional, and also sleazy and immoral, which made me dizzy, but who cares. As I got closer, I thought of how racy it was, that the kind of guy who did this kind of thing was usually more chiseled. Turning deeper into rolling hills, darker woods, I figured I could get caught and lose everything and end up alone in a studio apartment with rodent feces and crackers in my beard. People make you do things you don't want to do.

Over the winter, our ten thousand texts and emails had covered a lot of ground—holiday cookie recipes, the tale of the nanny who set the pizza box on fire and almost burned down Amy's house—but also her hopes, regrets, embarrassments, and lots of stories about the man she'd married. She told me stuff she'd never told anybody, suicidal feelings in college, her father's last words, a pitch meeting when Henry Kissinger spoke directly to her tits. By the time the weather changed, the novelty had worn off and our communications had hardened into something else, dogged, rambling, what we had for lunch, but also her fittings for ball gowns and other name-dropping tidbits of the .003 percent, the neighbor who bought a 737, the fund manager who poisoned a local river to get rid of some mosquitoes.

Amy had married a banker who made $120 million a year. He funded tea party candidates and didn't believe in climate change. She'd left a good career to stay home and raise their kids in style. Sometimes, when he walked into a room, she felt goose bumps rising on her skin, a seething animal hatred, although it hadn't always been that way. A world-class salesman, he'd sold her a bill of goods. He had a charitable heart, and a hospital in Latvia named after him that always needed cash. He was a soft touch on early childhood education, the third world, the urban poor. Although when I pressed her, she admitted that there were other things they agreed on. The federal government sometimes got in the way. The answer to our stalled economy would come through less regulation, with certain safeguards, which the president didn't understand because he'd never run a business.

It was easier to ignore things in an email, elliptical phrases, insinuations. Her friends were generous, too, engaged in civic improvement in the Bronx, in farming projects in Togo. It had a certain logic, billionaires to the rescue, that kind of thing.

The emailing of our minutiae had a way of leveling the disparity in our fortunes. I told her how much it hurt to step barefoot on a piece of Lego, so she told me how much it hurt to trip over her son's Exersaucer. We liked to pretend we lived parallel lives. My daughter and Amy's younger girl, Emily, began worrying around the same time that if their baby teeth fell out, their tongues would fall out, too. How many times did we trade photos of adorable kids in pajamas or the bathtub, or end the night with a few pithy words, "dying for you" or something, that kept me buzzing for hours? How many nights did I lie in bed like a twelve-year-old boy from the pain of a thing so stubborn, imagining her over me, pressing myself flat, the cat draped across my dick, getting a contact high from the waves of desire coming off me—either that or its purring gave me a boner—but it was so real, I found myself whispering, almost touching her, knocking myself out in the dark.

She grew up in Leominster, Mass., the second oldest of six, or seven. A grandmother with a brogue lived down the hall. The family car had holes in the floor. She made sure I knew where she came from, that she'd had it rougher than me, which wasn't saying much. Her dad stepped off the boat from Ireland, got drafted into the U.S. Army and shipped to Vietnam, and came home a patriot. Her mom missed Ireland, she thought Americans were crass, but loved nothing more than to sit down on a Saturday night to watch Lawrence Welk. Amy's favorite sister, Katy, two years younger, married a cop. Her older brother sold fighter jets and missile parts to Taiwan. Lots of sidebars about her other sisters' knee surgeries and blockages of breast-milk flow, their kids and husbands, their crummy office jobs. High school swimmer, track hurdler, vice president of her senior class. She was attacked the summer after high school ended, in a field beside the town pool. She told me how she thought he meant to kill her, and recalled the boy who found her, and wrapped her in his towel, and brought her home, and cleaned her up.

She put off college for a year. Worked in a photo lab, took up painting, dated a guy a few years older, but wouldn't let him touch her. Went to a state school on a swimming scholarship, worked nights on campus security, wearing the orange windbreaker. Majored in econ, spent three years analyzing reports at an institutional bank, swore she'd never considered banking until she took the job. But hers was a small unit within a bigger bank, growing rapidly, and soon they moved her into sales, making presentations in high-yield. The women in her department were tall and good-looking, the men were retired professional hockey players, and they all did vicious things to try to steal one another's clients. In place of any sort of imagination for a career path, she'd taken the formulaic route to some abstract idea of success, maybe hoping that one day she'd have security. Or a red Lamborghini. Earnest young people were drawn into an abusive, sexist, money-crazed environment, worked to death to prove themselves, to separate out the weak so that the only ones left were greedy, scrappy, stubborn maniacs.

On the rebound from some long-haired Australian deadbeat,

she met whatshisface, Mike. He was tall and dark and strong as an ox. He could work a hundred hours in a row without setting foot outside the building. Even in the short time she knew him, she could see him changing for the worse. She didn't consider him a friend or a mentor, and he didn't know how to talk to women. Was he shy? Was he tired? That first Thanksgiving with her family, when he wouldn't make small talk, she knew it was wrong but went ahead with it anyway. Planned the wedding, got cold feet, refused to back out. Or maybe the Australian guy had mistreated her and Mike was nice at first. I forget. She filled out reams of forms for an annulment, met regularly with her priest that whole first year, trying to figure out how to get out of it, then got knocked up, and was either pregnant or nursing for the next seven.

Last summer, lying on the beach with her classmates, she wore Italian movie star sunglasses and a white wifebeater, tight against her freckled copper skin, over a screaming blue-and-white flowered bikini, the string loops tied behind her neck as if she'd been dressed that way by some larger being who'd stood over her and tied that bow and then pushed her out into the world. After the beach, a few of us went to play putt-putt golf, where she towered over me by half an inch, and I couldn't stop looking at her legs.

On the final night of the conference we skipped the festivities, went to a fancy restaurant, then drove out to the point. She didn't hesitate, just stripped and ran right into the big booming ocean in the dark. Her bra and undies were white. When we got out of the water I forced myself not to look, forced my eyes up, above her chin. But then I looked. She was breathing strangely, said she hadn't kissed anyone else in nine years. I noticed her breathing, and looked at her hands, and then it hit me: Duh, she's shaking, she's telling the truth.

This stuff happens in movies all the time, but what's interest-

ing about real life is that the longer you live, the cornier life be-
comes, although that corniness, what once seemed corny, now
comes from a deeper place. Desperation doesn't mind corny.
Desperation trumps style. We owned the beach, foam breaking
around our ankles, delirious and alone in the moonlight.

Her bunkmates had already gone home, and Amy had the
room to herself. There were problems with the lighting, curtains,
noises in the hall. Over the next several hours she became awk-
ward, worried, antsy, horny, offended, confused, athletically en-
gaged, panting and moaning, weepy and angry, relieved and
exhausted, until we passed out like two crazy drunks. Then, last
fall in a bar in the West Village, while trying to wrap her legs
around me in the booth, she tipped over a candle and set the table
on fire.

If I took more than three hours to write back she got mad,
then quiet, then started leaking sarcastic and manipulative
desperation—"Who needs you when I've got the weather re-
port?" If I complained about Robin, she flew to my defense. If I
wrote something too sexy, she wrote "Lord!" She had an unironic
religious side that I had the urge to violate. She ran the Christmas
pageant at her church. They used real animals, she put a diaper
on the goat, and sometimes bizarre things came out of her, about
meeting me "in the afterlife," or how she sometimes "worried
about my soul," or that she admired Laura Bush "as a mom," or
that she took classes in Broadway tap.

She wondered if having kids had changed her, made her less
tolerant. Maybe she was the problem, not him. She didn't have
patience for someone who wasn't as small or crazy or helpless,
wasn't as madly in love, who didn't crawl on the rug and play
games or fall apart when she walked out of the room. But then
she'd divulge the peculiar terms of her relationship with the guy
she referred to in emails as M—who spent half his nights in the

city and the rest in the firm's offices in Frankfurt or Shanghai, or at home behind a locked door at the other end of the house, and made contact with her mostly through his secretary, treating her like an employee, barking orders, or worse, since employees never woke up in the middle of the night with the boss in his underwear standing over their bed—and I couldn't help thinking that they were both nuts, that money caused it, that rich people had one goal in life, and were creepy and obsessed and not better than anyone.

She organized events at a school for poor kids and sent me the T-shirt to prove it. She sat beside Mayor Bloomberg at a dinner for twelve, attended birthday parties for the wives of bankers who'd been burned in effigy in recent demonstrations of civil unrest. She did one day in the city every week, on a trading desk, and mentioned in passing that she'd had a short on the euro for so long she could retire to Bali on that money alone. She sent me a hundred dollars last fall, to get a massage when I hurt my neck, and we sent each other a few things around Christmas, sweaters, slippers, gloves, a blouse, though in February she threatened to send me a plane ticket, so that we could meet up at a conference he'd brought her to only to ignore her—in a little town in the French Alps where if you skied down the wrong slope you ended up in Italy, and you had to take a taxi to get back to your hotel. I hadn't skied in twenty years. She might not have meant it. It's easier to say stuff when you're loaded, or when divorce doesn't land you in a tiny peeling apartment counting change for the laundromat—or maybe she just wasn't as scared as I was, like that's how you are when someone really turns your crank, when every single gesture between you is not a marriage transaction or a judgment of who did what or who did wrong.

South of Providence I headed toward Plainfield, then Norwich, then drove down the coast for an hour. Off the highway it was wooded. As I got closer, the road wound scenically along endless stone walls and dense hedges impossible to see through. The pavement turned to dirt and sometimes went beside a field with a lone horse in the middle, wrapped in a blanket or unclothed, with some big house in the distance that said to all who passed, "Get a load of this, you fucking dirtbags." I found the mailbox and pressed the button and drove through the gate, and was surprised at how loud the gravel was, and slamming my door I looked up at the house, holy fuck, fieldstone chimneys, big columns on a massive porch.

In my cursory investigations, Michael Rapazzo's name had turned up on a list of speakers at some economic summit, and on the board of a dozen companies, and as the founder of a free health clinic in Hoboken, and as the backer of a charter school, or a string of them, mostly for profit, in tax-free public spaces. Three-quarters of the $20 billion he managed came from large pension plans of state employees in Rhode Island, New York, Massachusetts, and Connecticut. Cops, firemen, teachers. In 2011 he'd had his best year, and he was up 24 percent in the first quarter of this year.

He'd also appeared on TV financial news shows once or twice, fending off attacks on private equity, citing a study by some think tank or university, he couldn't remember, that proved he'd created eight thousand jobs. But I was drawn to his posture of authority; he was conventionally handsome, and I could imagine him mistreating his family in all the ways Amy had mentioned, growling at breakfast, forgetting birthdays, spending Christmas alone in a hotel in Lisbon, falling asleep at dinner. I couldn't fully assess the debate on carried interest, or whether the companies he'd succeeded in turning around justified the ones he'd accidentally leveraged into bankruptcy, or, more generally, whether bankers should have their intestines wrapped around their throats for wrecking the earth's economy, but I'd heard from Amy how hard he worked to unlock potential value in undercapitalized industries. I worked just as hard to unlock the business in her pants.

I knocked, and was relieved to see how ashamed she was. She looked tall and grim and expensive, and as I entered the house it smelled like citrus cleaner and new carpeting. What could she do for me except destroy my little world? The magazine had coughed up a plane ticket but I'd canceled it, adding twenty hours of driving to my already aching back, hoping my car didn't shit the bed, telling Robin I had to stop in New York for meetings, meetings I didn't actually have—to do the graphics on a can of dog food—all so I could make this sordid little detour. Although I hadn't texted Amy until the night before, since I hadn't been sure how long my work would take, how many days I'd need at the trial in Boston. There had also been the distinct possibility that I would chicken out, which left me feeling less ashamed and disgusted.

Her hair was darker, her front teeth were big and white and slightly crossed on the ends. She wore a gray turtleneck. She'd written back that she had a lunch date, housepainters were there, and her younger daughter had to be picked up at one. We'd have an hour or less, but yes, she'd said, please come. Anyway, I had my own kids to get home to. Beanie had his first cold, and Robin was covered in hives from exhaustion. I wanted to get off the highway and sniff their heads.

Amy led the way, not saying much. The kitchen was long and white, with a couch in a bay window and a dog on the floor sweeping its tail. Annabelle was a rescue mutt and Amy's best friend. The ceilings were eighteen feet high. In the space above our heads you could hang hammocks, rope swings. The marble island was the size of my kitchen and covered with stacks of home design magazines, cookbooks, baskets of fruit, onions, pads of stationery, phone chargers, mail, a box of essential oils, a basket of ribbons, scissors, a stack of delicate-looking white bowls that, when I touched them, turned out to be made of rubber. The island was entrenched with things that could've gone in a drawer, Scotch tape, stapler, pie weights, cutting boards, a pewter mug of unsharpened pencils. It looked like the staging area for a yuppie war.

The doorknobs, drawer pulls, light fixtures, and color schemes were bright and coherent. Somebody had baked a crust in a casserole dish that sat on the counter, although I didn't know if that someone was her; I wasn't sure what she did all day, between the philanthropic commitments and the mommy stuff she claimed to live for, rocking her son in the middle of the night, building a tree house, standing in a pool all afternoon teaching the girls how to dive. What she did in the way of housework and how it resembled what went on in my house I never figured out. On this very day she had a list of things that needed her immediate attention: a local art museum pre-gala speech had to be written to rally the host committee, the lunch in town she couldn't cancel with the sub-Saharan head of Oxfam, and then she was taking her kids to the park. On slow days, she tutored in math at the after-school program they funded in town. She'd been to the hospital they'd built in Macedonia and wanted to go back. She also managed some pile of money. She worried about the Fed's monetary policy watering down the dollar. At Christmas they'd gone somewhere in the Caribbean I'd never heard of. In February she'd skied Chamonix.

Who was this woman? I stood there in my coat, so nervous and guilty I almost choked, and asked for some water. She ran the tap and handed me a glass. A photo on the fridge showed a younger Amy with lighter hair, evenly cut on the bottom, before her son was born, holding Emily as a baby, standing behind the older girl, the beautiful blue-eyed Lily, and the husband, who looked decent, older, balding—beside an even older, smiling, bald-headed guy who I guessed was his father. I noted a pink receipt from a landscaper for "decorative stonework," for $68,342. It was detailed and handwritten in plain language. There was a twenty-dollar bill under a magnet and a phone number scribbled on a business card that named Amy O'Donnell as principal partner in something called Cardinal Growth Fund. In the photo on the fridge she looked happy and serene. They were standing at the folded-out staircase of some kind of aircraft. The husband was tall and thick, with a big head and bags under his eyes. The older man, upon further inspection, was international war criminal and goon for the state Dick Cheney.

"You *know* him?"

He had a hand on Mike's shoulder, smiling with no upper lip. She glanced at the photo. "Mike did a deal. We were friends. He used to take us places."

On the drive here I'd imagined an awkward meeting, which might've led to fumbling intimacy, nymphomania, the hostess lighting candles in a hot tub. But now I felt stupid and drank my water. Her face looked longer, with a pointy chin, and in a low voice she said, "How's Boston?"

"Fine. I'm done."

She leaned against the counter, looking at the floor.

"I've been in a courtroom for the past five days, sketching cops and suicide bombers."

"You're heading home."

"What's wrong?"

"Nothing."

"What do I owe you for the water?"

I saw her hands shaking. Over her shoulder, Cheney held his pose. "I do this thing where I can't stop checking my phone. Do you do that?" I said yes. "Are we supposed to keep this up forever? Is there something else?"

"Like what?"

"Telepathy? Bigger keyboards? Smaller thumbs? I can't keep up this flirting. I'm not cut out for this shit." She put her palms against her eyes. "I lose my phone and until I find it I'm a crazy person."

"It can be a little distracting."

"I yell, and I never yell."

"Don't yell."

"It's bad. We're bad." I couldn't understand the point of that kind of talk. "This whole thing. We're sick."

"*They're* sick. We're the good ones." The stupidity of my response exhausted us.

She stepped through the pantry into a hallway to check on her son, snoozing in his stroller, sucking his thumb. She silently slipped off his corduroy jacket, sighing softly, showing distress, glancing at me for direction. I figured I should leave. Unfortunately, I'd lost my sense of how to retrace my steps. There was a wall of framed photos—the husband made up for his bald head with some hairy forearms. I couldn't help noticing a small black-and-white one of a moonfaced girl with barrettes and a dimpled smile. Amy came closer, breathing next to me, and said, "I think that was the last time I brushed my hair."

She put her hand on my shoulder as some kind of steadying gesture. I knew I was sick. It was a game that made everything else go away. It was as corny as the piña colada song, and as irrational as a noxious fear in the night, a fear of maiming and death by some rich guy's hired thugs while my children watched in horror. The sneaking around demanded exhausting and myopic concentration, and made me schizo and paranoid. There was nothing I could do about the guilt.

Anyway, I couldn't stop myself. My own ethical dilemmas seemed small in comparison. She believed in prayer and public service, a certain godliness, and, even so, couldn't stop herself from texting me photos of her naked butt. She wanted to create a stimulating after-school environment for poor kids in Detroit, and worked at it day and night, using all that moolah she'd ripped from the bones of humanity. She went down the hall. Half in a fog, I followed.

There were some serious crown moldings, beautiful bookshelves filled with new hardbacks, a bio of Rudy Giuliani, some T. S. Eliot. Weirdly, some part of me grew to fill the size of the space. Another part of me felt like the victim of a war or famine, contemplating the high-walled fortress of a conquering army. Envy felt unsafe. The power of her money made almost any interaction disorienting, manifesting in feverish insecurity. Stuff on lower shelves confirmed the unthinkable, an engraved chunk of marble, thanking him, and also plaques and paperweights in wood, metal, plastic, and glass, acknowledging his service on the governing bodies of clubs, hospitals, colleges, and museums. Engraved pen holders, letter openers, staplers, and an actual chair with his name burned into the back beneath the crest of a Midwestern university. A piano sat on a raised area of polished hardwood floor, under a domed ceiling with tall windows on all sides, a sort of dance floor where an orchestra might set up. She'd hosted something the night before, and in fact an orchestra had set up, on that raised area by the windows. There were stacks of rental chairs, tabletops, and glassware in racks.

The inner-city school thing sometimes meant baking three hundred cupcakes and driving sixty miles to sit in class all day letting kids from the barrio braid her hair. The school endeavor was a bigger time suck and sometimes meant flying to Chicago or Miami to negotiate the lease on a building on loan from the Catholic Church. Call it philanthropy, or a kind of grassroots activism, or white billionaires dismantling public education. Although at least she was doing something. She could've just as easily spent every afternoon humping her tennis pro. She had powerful friends, parties, pet projects with which to work out her ten-cent philosophies. The party the night before had been to help clean up Long Island Sound. They'd handed out plastic pails with plans for the next beach cleanup and encouraging data. She offered me a pail.

Last year she'd had two yards of sand carted into the house so the kids could have a scavenger hunt, but the weight of the sand had made the floor joists creak, and when people started dancing she thought the house would fall down. This year Brooke Shields co-chaired the event.

"I have so much leftover food."

I had no zany fundraising stories to share. I felt shaky and middle-class. I had brains and an education and was not lazy but maybe worse than lazy, barely scraping by, donating twenty dollars here and there to the charity of my choice, while the superpowered people saved the world.

We walked on. We passed a big red room, a round ottoman, a Chinese triptych, giant vases. A white room, chrome, glass, glaring bright white sofa as long as a Greyhound bus. Dining room, earthy wooden table, fireplace, wrought iron chandelier like in a Frankenstein movie. We passed an actual painting by Thomas Eakins of a woman looking bored shitless in a pink dress, and a framed photo of an astronaut floating in space, inscribed by the astronaut with a Sharpie, thanking Mike and his investment fund. Then a room that looked like where they actually lived, with beat-up couches, toys, a TV, corduroy pillows with the stuffing falling out, and a kid's piano.

We passed a big guy in a dark T-shirt and sweatpants, splattered with paint, holding a paint roller, talking in Spanish on a cellphone. No flicker of recognition passed between them. She seemed involved in deeper calculations.

We traversed the mud room, gleaming Moroccan tile, blue walls, stone sink, deep shelves, sneakers, shoes, boots, flip-flops, baseball caps, straw hats, rain ponchos, scarves, mittens, earmuffs, gloves, shawls, and capes. Past the mud room we descended into a part of the house where people folded laundry, including a woman watching a hip-hop video on low volume. She sat on the couch in a collared white shirt and a cardigan.

"This is Perlita," Amy said. "Perlita runs our world."

Perlita stared at us. The lower level was bright and airy and entirely aboveground. I'd heard all about her, going to night school, man troubles, car problems, two kids back in the Philippines being raised by their aunt. Amy said, "Wanna yell if he wakes up?" Perlita nodded. Amy smiled, the tendons pulling at her neck.

We went back a different way, and turned and climbed a dark, narrow staircase, and as we climbed I looked out a small window onto her covered swimming pool, with walkways of elaborate stonework. I recognized the barn in the distance, a clean beautiful post-and-beam structure she'd sent me photos of, no animals inside it, nothing at all but her sunlit painting studio, where she made her goofy artwork.

Upstairs we passed a four-year-old's bedroom the size of a bowling alley, with its own veranda. We passed additional seating zones, a paneled library, a gym with chromed machinery and a padded floor, an office—and finally entered a sunny room with high windows. A bed hid behind a rice-paper folding screen. She closed the door and bolted it and put her face in my face and breathed. I went a little cuckoo, recalling the Spanish-speaking housepainter, processing and abandoning scenarios, outcomes, inspecting the place for signs of him, whoever he was, a massive black armoire, a tall, blackened fireplace, some Asian-looking chests. I felt sick and wanted to leave. I had a sandwich and some cookies waiting for me in the car. The bed sat low on a wooden platform with a pea-green silk comforter and gold tassels. It didn't look all that virginal. There were books on the nightstands. It was creepy, although maybe I didn't give a shit. They had a crib by the bed, like us. An invisible kid watched me run my hands up and down his mother's flanks as the surveillance cameras of my imagination whirred away, gazing at us with a thousand hidden eyes. I felt the obligation of it, another insincere gesture to another unhappy mother. "You have a long drive home," she said, letting me go, "and I have stuff to do."

But beyond this room was a smaller room with a ficus tree and a couch and a wall of glass facing the woods. There was a makeup mirror on a desk scattered with jewelry and a walk-in closet heaving with her clothes. On the couch were sneakers and a laptop, where, I imagined, she'd written all those emails. The adjoining bathroom had a floor made of smooth stones and an egg-shaped tub. Moisture lingered in the air, her smell. I believed all of it then: that she had nobody else to talk to, her husband was gay or autistic, a bill of goods she'd sold to me that I was the man and could do what I wanted.

"I have twenty-one minutes," she said, blushing, with sad eyes, all business. "Then I have a lunch that'll probably cost me a million bucks."

Something fell off the makeup table and crashed. I felt myself soaring, brightly, falling over. The couch was too short. I had one hand up her sweater and one down her pants. Her head tipped back as she grabbed my wrist and said, "I feel ugly."

I felt ugly, too. I'd spent five days in an airless courthouse under bright fluorescent lights, eating fried-egg sandwiches. The night before, we'd texted to arrange this rendezvous. After it was arranged, I didn't sleep a wink. I drove three hours with reckless abandon to get here in time.

"I'm not taking off my clothes."

It all came back from last summer—the change in breathing, the hand on my hand, resisting, instructing, guided masturbation.

"We don't have to do anything," I said.

"Yes we do." She tightened her grip. "Every day, all day, you're the only thing I think about, the only person I want to talk to."

It was true that I'd never had that with Robin.

"I married someone who ignores me," she said.

"But you got sick of it."

"But it creeps me out to use some rationalization."

"Like we've been mistreated," I said, "so we deserve this."

"Or we'll all be dead soon and no one will give a shit."

"Don't get mad at me. I'm not the one jerking you around."

"You're so liberated." We hovered in that vulnerable state. I felt her wanting my help getting past it. "Why did you wait until last night to tell me you were coming?" Her breathing changed and became more labored, her eyes on me but not seeing, her anger distracting her guilt. She exhaled, trying to reel it back in.

"I wish this whole thing would blow up in my face so he'd find out and I could stop pretending." She grabbed my hand and shoved it down farther, directing the operation. She made a lovely noise. Her other hand went to my elbow. I found some spot on her that made her go out for a minute and leaned down and sucked her nipple. She came like sneezing, then rested, yawned, ran her hand through my hair and said, "How many other houses are you planning to visit on your way home?"

"I don't even have time to brush my teeth, I'm so busy answering your emails."

We had eleven minutes. I lay there, considering ways to get her pants off. I could ask politely. I could say, *We're old and sad and this is our only consolation,* or, from the other angle, *Let's celebrate our youth, we're not done yet, let's romp.* There was the legalistic approach, citing spousal shortcomings and violations, and redundancies among the various approaches. I tried to think, but as I did she started to fight with my belt, then got onto her knees. "Here," I said. "Let me." She looked at me with pity and clawed at my pants and yanked them open. I guess I just exploded. It might've been the best blow job in my life, except maybe it didn't go on long enough to count, like in professional bull riding, where the judges need at least eight seconds for a qualified ride.

"Do you feel better?"

"No, I feel violated."

"Sorry, I'm out of practice. I don't do that for my husband."

We gave up on the couch and rolled onto the carpet. Her bra hung loose, unhooked, under her chin, and her sweater was bunched up around it. Five minutes. It was important that we not dwell on him. "I missed your face," I said.

"I forget you sometimes," she said, "but when it's quiet you come back to me."

"I always wonder where you're going, what you're doing."

"Even though you were busy in Boston, I knew you were close by. You were more mine. Now you're heading home."

"I'm yours," I said. "I've felt that way for months." Robin was younger and lighter and had finer bones.

"If anyone downstairs asks, I'll say you're my cousin." Amy

was bigger and taller, but laid out against me she fit perfectly into my arms.

"Do you have a lot of cousins?"

"Tons."

"Do you have sex with them on the floor in your closet?"

"This is known as my dressing room."

"I bet you're fun at holidays."

"I bet you're fun, too."

"Not anymore, not even on Christmas. Now all I do is work. That's why Robin hates my guts."

"Mike thinks I sit on my ass all day popping bonbons."

"I don't want to work anymore. I've got other things to do before I die."

"It would be different with us."

"We'd stick our hands in each other's pants."

"I'd take care of everything," she said. "I really would."

"Come home with me," I said. "We'll tell Robin you're my cousin." I felt her go slushy in my arms, losing hope. I tried to let my weight crush her, but she wasn't fragile and didn't mind. What was I supposed to do now, spirit her away in my barf-stained Toyota wagon?

"I have nothing against your wife, but every time you mention her it makes me want to puke."

"I drove all this fucking way to see you."

"I'll be sad when you go."

"I'm sad now."

"I hate this," she said. "Although it's nice to be with someone who doesn't act like he wants to kill me every time I open my mouth."

What could I say to that? "We'll have fun this summer."

"I guess."

"What does that mean?"

"I hate cheating," she said. "I hate lying and planning and scheming."

We lay there, trying not to do that.

"Hey," I said. "What if we meet somewhere else?"

"How is that better?"

"Somewhere less public."

She gave it some thought. "I have a meeting in Anguilla next month."

I'd had in mind somewhere near the Amtrak station in Wilmington. The longer we lay there, the worse I felt. Even if I could afford the plane ride, I'd have to get someone to cover. Our babysitter worked part-time. Who would do drop-off in the morning and pickup at Molly's at night? I'd need an excuse. And I'd have to tip the Caribbean bellhop for incidentals.

"I know it's harder for you," she said. "Mike doesn't give a shit. I've exchanged six words with him in the last thirteen days." I didn't want to hear about that bald-headed fuck. "He's in Holland."

"Good for him."

"I think he had to go buy some clogs."

"You're funny."

"I wish I could help you."

"Help me what?" I asked.

"I'd like to make it easier for you."

"So I can meet you in Anguilla?" We were still having fun.

"I don't mean that. I didn't think you even cared about money."

I didn't want her pity, or her dough, if that's what we were talking about, but as I lay there I thought about hers, and mine, and had the sense that we'd begun blindly feeling our way into a conversation that was not entirely contradictory to my interests.

I said, "I live on sunshine and candy." She told me to shush. You'd think there'd be some formal presentation or specialized language, or explicit demands on those targets she largessed, since it was one of her many jobs now to give money to losers.

"You're successful at what you do," she said, "but it isn't as steady."

I saw us entering into a new type of contract, an arrangement based on lust that offered a dividend, a secret layer of protection. I imagined it then as some monthly number, conceived on the basis of my responsiveness to her needs, money I'd immediately get hooked on, which would open up new priorities and all sorts of sickening conflicts, and eight kinds of pressure to spit out gratitude to justify her investment. I'd learn to beg when I came up short, one more worldly necessity negating my search for solidarity, artistic purity, and spiritual insight. I'd just attach myself to that multiheaded hydra, that billion-dollar death machine, each suction cup lined with serrated teeth, swiveling, perforating my system, jamming its slimy probe inside me. Things would sour between us and I'd wait for the ax to fall, emailing her lackey functionary, some asshole I'd be on a first-name basis with, happy holidays, all that.

"Hey, why don't you take your money and shove it?"

"Hey," she said. "We use our inside voice."

"Oh wow, here's eight cents on the floor. Can I keep it?"

She looked bored, or harried, or a little alarmed. She looked as if she'd stumbled into one of those unnerving conversations with a stranger in a public place where it takes a moment to figure out that they're crazy. Also, it was time to leave.

"How were you planning on funding me?"

She leaned back and touched the corner of one eye, rubbing it. "What are you talking about?"

"I'm pretty sure I can make a living on my own."

"I'm sorry you have to work so hard."

"Say that one more time."

"Sorry."

"You want me to know how it feels to get paid for it, because that's how it is for you." She pulled her arm off me and sat up and fixed her clothes. "I don't mean you," I said, my face burning. The need to clarify took hold. "This whole place is fucked." I offered a poignant description of my earlier disorientation, how I'd lost my sense of direction as we wandered the downstairs, which I'd intended as an illustration of the excess of her house though unfortunately made it sound like I'd wanted to leave from the start but got lost. One last time I gave in to the idiotic impulse to explain. "But that's the idea, isn't it? To crush people so they can't even think. What does it cost to heat that ballroom?" She leaned forward, avoiding eye contact, hunching to get her bra back on. She had long, fine, soft, beautiful hair, nice collarbones. "I feel like a total skank right now, and it's not even my house."

"Will you shut up."

I think she just wanted someone normal, not some broke freelance artist, but not him, either. He didn't put their kids to bed, didn't say good night to her. Her sisters hated him. He enjoyed strip clubs, dining alone in expensive restaurants, borrowing money against companies with hard assets, numbers and video games, but not people. No doubt the burdens of his philanthropy weighed upon him, the politicians who came begging, senators and governors, who he referred to as "a buncha ding-a-lings." His tutoring centers served ten thousand kids a year and needed more space. His hospital in Eastern Europe bled cash.

Hey, I had my own fucking problems. I'd been gone all week, I had a deadline and a long drive home, where I worked beside a washing machine in an unheated basement with a damp floor and a midcentury oil burner that reeked of diesel. In a rainstorm I stopped counting how many wet-vac buckets I carried into the yard.

From where I lay I could see a broken ceramic dish, makeup brushes, loose change on the floor.

"I didn't mean to call you a skank."

"You never called me a skank."

"Well, you're not one."

"And you're not a liar and a cheater."

"If I were rich, you wouldn't have anything to do with me."

"Is that right?"

"I'm not real to you."

"You can stop telling me what I think."

"You think it's cute that I make sixty thousand dollars a year."

"That's the stupidest thing you ever said."

We were both so miserable, waiting for me to shut up. I wasn't about to leave Robin for this woman, although I liked her, she was entertaining, but the financial imbalance made it a nonstarter. What was I supposed to do, follow her around, begging, for the rest of my life?

"When I met you, I didn't know you were loaded. And when I found out, it made it harder to like you, not easier."

She was glad to hear this. But then she was sad, because it was true.

THIRTEEN

A week after that awkward scene in Connecticut, Amy's seven-year-old daughter had a brain hemorrhage while walking off a soccer field. Somehow in Amy's mind there was this linkage of events, which on one level I understood. Overwhelmed with guilt, she took it as a sign. I gave her whatever space she needed.

I spent the spring and summer forgetting her. Although at times when I couldn't forget her, I pictured her at Lily's bedside, or in the woods behind her house, walking the dog, missing me, maybe weeping in the pickup line in her beautiful-smelling German car or on an airport runway on Anguilla, killing whatever thoughts came up.

But cutting off daily contact with her had another effect. Like the quiet that rushes in after a car alarm, it let me breathe, gave me peace, made me strong. In the intervening silence I began to notice you-know-who. I'd been living in my head for so long,

Robin had become strange to me again. You recognize the strangeness as the person you first met.

She put mustard on her hamburgers. She licked her yogurt bowl at breakfast. She stuck her sweaters in the freezer to kill the moths. As winter edged into spring, she had her moles burned off, and over time I saw those burn marks slowly heal. I watched from my side of the bed as she drugged herself into a coma every night, spying on her from under the blankets, noting the fine white hairs on her neck, and little moons that hung outside her undies. In the warming days of spring, her easy-browning, pollen-dusted skin faintly shimmered. I listened to her voice, wafting across the hall as she woke Kaya for preschool, heard it in my sleep, reminding me of my mother. I watched the fingertip she traced along Beanie's ear while he lolled on her nipple.

Her own mother, once the means of her survival, was all but gone. Her sister out west never called. Her brother was long gone, but sometimes haunted her dreams.

Her father was a tall, broad, large-lipped man who, in a lab at a chemical company in the seventies, had accidentally invented a nylon fiber five times stronger than steel. He'd won every important award in chemistry but the Nobel and was loved the world over by people whose lives he'd saved, his invention having protected them from bullets or bombs, lauded by builders of sports equipment, suspension bridges, musical instruments, and medical devices. And yet he was the one who'd left the family all those years ago, for his sexy lab assistant, and could not be forgiven. After the tragic death of his son, he still didn't return, and he eventually married that Turkish hussy half his age. It was complicated stuff. He was sporadically, effusively generous. I wished he'd give us more. He claimed he didn't have a lot of money—his discoveries belonged to DuPont—but he had a lot more money than we did.

We visited them in May, shocked by the cloudless Midwestern beauty of Chicago in late spring. We wandered through the unused rooms of their big brick townhouse, hunted for a wooden spoon in the kitchen they never cooked in, and tried to work the remote of their home theater while they went to the lab or wined and dined their favorite molecular engineers and polymer scientists. They'd always just returned from meetings all over the world and told fun stories of parties in restaurants, famous acquaintances, and the latest in composite materials. After a couple of days of that, I found Robin alone in some unused room, behind a cloud of agitated motion, knees shaking, breasts pumping, starry-eyed, hunched, vengeful, cursing the wife, eating meat off a chicken leg. The wife insisted that our kids call her Jenny, rather than Grandma or her real name, Mujgan. Mujgan sent us home with toys, and Dopp kits she'd collected from Lufthansa's first-class cabin, and beautifully wrapped clothing she'd already worn with no tags and no receipt, which Robin draped against herself and thanked her for, then brought home and tried on, full of sarcasm, then gave to Goodwill.

They also owned a vacation house we'd been to once or twice, off the coast of Florida, on an island made of garbage.

It was hard to believe they had ever been a family. But there they were, in framed photos in her dad's study, with Mom too, squinting under sun hats when the kids were small. And there they were a few years later, during a trip to France, on a research fellowship, after her brother was killed, in an image mostly devoid of grief, with Mom out of the picture, showing instead the snazzy purse her dad wore in Europe, and Mujgan in a macramé bikini, and Robin's familiar scowl, and her sister's nearly fatal eating disorder.

In old photos, her brother, Eddie, had been the smiling one. If people tried talking to her about him, even now, it made her angry. Picture something so terrible that for the rest of your life it never changes and you never figure out how to deal with it. I was sad for her at Christmas and at times when without warning his absence became vivid, sad for the past she'd put on ice, for their family's truncated future, sad for who I'd hoped to be to make up for it, the brotherly husband I should've become, for how I'd fallen short. The person she'd married was part of a future I couldn't live up to.

It's hard to approximate the sweep and fullness of a twelve-year relationship while diminishing and giving evidence against my wife and children in order to validate my adulterous behavior, but on that trip to visit her dad in Chicago this past spring, I felt especially tired of my marital shortcomings and stints of poverty and artistic despair, the failure to meet my own low expectations. I was suddenly aware of the time I'd wasted all winter, trying to lie and sext myself past manic domestic entanglement.

It was just the usual stuff, sooty socks, closet shelves falling apart, the increasing awkwardness of disrobing in front of my wife, the sounds of rodents carrying stray cornflakes behind the stove and up into our walls, along with any lingering nerve damage she'd suffered from pregnancy that radiated from her hip, up into her lower back, down the meridian of her leg, rode her wiring and made her sour and frail. I gave up on screwing, didn't wonder what my chances were, didn't look for an opening, didn't engineer it, didn't beat myself up over an opportunity I might've missed. Lying there as another chilly night passed between us, I was relieved to feel trapped and defeated, to feed it and point it inward and hoard it for myself.

But in the spring, her pain began to fade. She went back to the gym, snapped back into shape, and bought yoga pants that hid nothing. Our lovemaking began again, sporadic and incidental, modest in its meaning, ambition, and duration.

The weather had been warm and beautiful, and then it really was summer. Sun dappled the leaves of our walnut tree. Lawn-mowers hummed in the evening. Somehow, the bill for Kaya's summer camp had finally been paid, three thousand bucks, and the bill for fall pre-K was already late. One night after dinner we walked through the woods at the end of our neighborhood and into the park, Kaya ran ahead, I carried Beanie, Robin and I held hands, and I remember it well because later that night I almost killed her.

There were abandoned tricycles and a basketball left lying on the playground, and I threw an errant skyhook that went over the backboard and into a hedge. At some point, after the kids had been bathed and put to bed, we sat on the rug folding laundry, discussing them, how Beanie liked to sip his bathwater while I read him a story, how Kaya had fallen in love with the ugliest white patent leather shoes in the world, two sizes too big, and pleaded for them, and tripped on the sidewalk and skinned her nose, but still refused to take them off. How, at four, she was less unified, more complicated and skeptical, already bored with having her picture taken, offering a fake smile, and how Beanie would get angry if he couldn't spit cottage cheese into the holes in my harmonica. We wanted them with the madness of a teen-age crush, we belonged to them now, we were nothing on our own anymore, and we placed their clothes in neat piles, amazed at what we'd done. To have a conversation lasting longer than thirty seconds about something other than that day's logistics or strategies she'd learned from parenting books on how to destroy our kids' will left me thrilled and grateful and brimming with hope.

Then I cleaned the kitchen while Robin sat at the table, watching rough edits, making notes for the Nature Channel on a show not about nature, but about a hoarder who lived with fifty-two chickens clucking inside his house. Then she dragged the Internet for the perfect pair of boots and recipes for people who eat flax, while getting whacked on pinot grigio, explaining to me that manganese is good for my prostate. Then she lay on the carpet, raising and lowering her pelvis in a kind of yoga-pants mating ritual, making soft breathy sounds, her nursing boobs rising, moving up her body's absolute geography as her hips lifted, then falling as her butt met the floor. Afterward she did our house bills, pausing for a moment to insult my income and future prospects, to recall my back taxes and lingering debts, until Beanie started screaming. He woke up Kaya, who made one too many demands, and then Robin started yelling too, telling her to stop crying, threatening her with consequences, referring to the chart. The Chart of Good Behavior rewarded Kaya with gifts and gum or punished her with the loss of dessert and weekend television. It went on like that. It hurt to hear. I tried not to. She took it out on Kaya as a way to yell at me, because I didn't like the chart, or because parenting is hard, and she actually didn't know what the fuck she was doing, and neither did I, and that made her mad. My agony at hearing my daughter suffer had to be contained. Because she was a child in this marriage, Kaya's suffering could not be avoided.

After putting them back to bed, we tidied up the first floor, gathering, sweeping, shoving, folding. Robin followed me around, blaming me for sabotaging Beanie's nap schedule, blowing wine breath in my face, punctuating descriptions of a four-year-old with words like "obstinate," "transitional," and "oppositional," educating me along the way, insulting me with her sarcasm.

Perhaps I made it sound worse than it actually was. What I know is, we were mostly kind to each other. It was good at least half the time. All she had to do was walk into a room in her bathrobe, smelling like a baby herself, asking me to check a mole on her back, suddenly small and vulnerable, and I'd give in, my heart blown open like a parachute, a kiss on her neck when I was done.

After the insults, she sat at the table, blouse raised and tucked into her armpits, breast-pump suction cups strapped across her chest, squinting at the milk collecting in the bottle, talking about Beanie's burps.

"Why do you think he has colic?" I asked.

"He's too old for colic."

"That's probably true."

"You're not listening. I said it was something I'm eating. I said my breast milk is pink. I said it seems like colic." She'd pushed aside our place mats from dinner and laid out her knitting project.

"I'm not listening."

"From your tomato sauce last night."

"I know what the problem is."

She didn't look up but cocked her head to the side, suction cups against her chest.

"You think our family's going to fall apart because your family fell apart," I said. "And if you keep it up, it will."

"Keep what up?"

"Your militaristic expectations."

holy crap - so acidic

She squinted at the bottle of tomato-colored milk, slowly filling. "You had your perfect mom. She never yelled, never said no. She protected you from your father because you needed that. But now you're the parent. You don't get to be the baby anymore."

"And you don't get to be my father."

"Why don't you go fuck your mother."

"I don't need to be educated by you."

"If you do to your kids what your mother did to you, they'll end up like you, an emotional cripple, unable to work with others, waiting around for some paradise that never existed, that will never exist because life isn't perfect."

"I know it isn't perfect because you get into a screaming fight with a four-year-old every night so she cries until you bribe her with a cookie and packs of gum."

"You're the one who treats people badly, you cut me off at dinner," she said, "and if you do it again I'm going to take my fork and stab you. Do you want me to stab you?"

"Every night you talk about how broke we are, while I'm trying to eat."

"This from a guy who sleeps till noon while the babysitter my father pays for takes care of his kid."

"That's bullshit, but how would I even know? I never see a dime of that money."

"And you never will, because you'd blow it."

Kaya stood at the other end of the kitchen, holding the cat, listening.

"She plopped on my head." She said to the cat, "I want you to apologize for biting my chin. I give you an apologize, and you give me an apologize and send it to my brain."

Robin unhooked herself and pulled down her shirt and knelt and hugged Kaya. Kaya spoke to the cat: "You're a cutie wootie. You're a furball. Dat's not responsible, sweetie." Robin put the cat on the floor and carried Kaya upstairs and lay down next to her and fell asleep.

Later I emerged from the basement, having wrecked myself with the illusion of work, and got into our bed, sad and alone, and listened to Beanie snore. I was hoping for a cry, maybe praying for a way to give myself over to anything, anyone who would need me, who I could soothe and hold, as a way to put our family back together.

On our block, you could see which families got along, which ones couldn't be apart, clutching, clinging, which ones couldn't be in the same room together. Across the street lived a heavily pregnant litigator named Shao, married to a jittery math professor named Phil, expecting their second child. Next to them were an old, bent, scowling, poodle-walking hermit—a retired electrician—and his wife, in the final stages and bedridden. Next to them was a house with three boys, hockey sticks, soccer balls, skateboards all over the lawn. They were lawyers in the telecom industry who wrote regulations and then crammed them down the government's throat. Lisa served disgusting slabs of bloody meat for dinner that everybody over there loved. We had a block party every Labor Day with a bouncy castle and an egg toss.

We lived in a Maryland suburb known for its aging hippies, free mulch, and hundred-year-old Victorians, just inside the Beltway, a five-minute walk to the subway, a twenty-minute ride to downtown D.C. We'd been here for six years. Before that, we lived in Baltimore.

You could see how other people's marriages worked, and you could take a wild guess, just by looking at them, who still did it. The ones who didn't do it didn't like you, but they knew they'd get you soon enough. The ones who did, who still seemed to hunger for each other, with their arthritis and their floppy appendages, made you wince at the thought of them naked.

Next to Lisa and Brett lived Amanda and Robert. He was special assistant to the deputy something at the State Department; she wrote talking points for some evil intelligence agency. She had small boobs and lacy bras and it really worked. Some nights before dinner she'd come up the sidewalk with her two little kids and we'd joke around and stand in our yard and she'd keep checking her blouse to make sure the top button didn't come open, and I couldn't help feeling noticed for noticing her.

On the other side of us lived a guy named Steve who cleaned carpets for a living. His wife looked too young, like he'd married his daughter. His daughter looked exactly like the wife, and could sometimes be seen from my upstairs bathroom late at night taking breaks from the glare of her monitor to kneel and rummage through her clothes half-naked. Elements of aging and ugliness now played a role in the corners of our privacy and the marriages around me. More people fatter and in worse shape, but still on some sort of eternal honeymoon. Other people who couldn't get along, and caved and got divorced, destroying everything. Their kids fell apart. People who stayed single were children themselves and their genes were weeded out by natural selection.

Everyone not getting fucked enough, men not fucking anyone, women no one was fucking. What was the point of having a body? Intellectual life was not so satisfying that we could afford to relinquish the physical. The simple act of, or, I should say, when two people who, for whatever reason . . . or maybe it was more about the ability to give pleasure, if that's what married people are up to, or maybe it's just the raw power of sex, to cleanse and heal the body and mind, to simplify, soften, maybe clarify a complicated, heavy relationship, to make strong what is often rough or broken, while putting a fine and graceful point on the coarse and bumbling flesh, while gently nourishing the other, while somehow loosening oneself from the hunger—hey, around here we didn't get enough of that. But just to hold the other and be held in return until the boundaries melt and our bodies hover, float, become weightless in that zero time of unclocked moments—we didn't do a lot of that, either.

So when Beanie finally woke up with a shriek, I figured it was from the waves of unhappiness pouring off me, wafting across the floor. And maybe he wasn't hungry so much as receptive to my distress; maybe I fed his hunger not for some nutritional reason but in order to fill my own emptiness. Maybe Robin was right and I shouldn't have been giving him bottles in the middle of the night at ten months, rewarding him, training him to wake up. I couldn't stop this vicious cycle. She pleaded with me, but I couldn't. I couldn't sleep, didn't want him to sleep either, didn't want to be alone. It was one thing in our lives that I could control.

When he finished his bottle he made a good burp, and what more could you ask for? Then he made a different sort of burp, his eyes rolled up into his brain, I could hear it coming up the pipe, it hit me in the chin first, then in the chest, like a garden hose had been attached to the back of his head. It was warm and smelled, at least at first, like apples. I staggered to my feet and carried him to the tub, to rinse the puke off him, rinse it from my hair, the plumbing whistling right through the wall, to wake whoever slept on the other side, and after I put him back down Robin and I met in the upstairs hall.

Quietly at first, we exchanged strongly held parental philosophies. She sighed, softly breathing sly accusations. I handled her inauthentic parroting of facile ideas, barf on the lapels of my pajamas, hoping to enlighten her. She deftly batted away my objections, invading my space, so I held her back, so she kicked me and tried to scratch my face off. I begged her to stop, or maybe I urged her on, like, "That the best you got?" I used my hand to keep her away, but not a flat hand, more a sort of curved grip, noting the sensation of the thin, soft, frail neck of my wife in my hand, like, "How did that get there?" A voice in my head, a tiny stage director, said, "Careful, careful," until I let go.

That was followed by the abandoning of her post, the dragging of blankets past me, the knocking of stuff off low tables, the destruction of personal property as Robin went downstairs to sleep. I followed her to the living room, where she made up the couch, draping windows with towels for curtains as I stood, arms folded, sadder than I'd ever been, admitting everything, asking forgiveness, wishing her a good night's sleep. After our fights I felt tender and protective.

"Go on, keep talking," she said. "I'm calling the police."

When I met Robin, she was a cute kid who could do impressions of the wackos who worked in televised puppetry: Lois, head puppet wrangler, who built each of the characters by hand; Brenda, who talked to them as though they were alive; and Kyle, who played Anselma. Sometimes her impressions overtook her: grabbing an oven mitt, pretending to be Skunk, saying, "I love you, Chippy, DIS MUCH," her cheeks flushed as she got tongue-tied and disoriented, wiping away tears.

But a year after we met, the world changed. Our nation came under attack, and Robin started calling everyone she knew in TV news, friends of Digger's in Istanbul and Karachi. She wanted to go somewhere with a "-stan" at the end, where troops and air support assembled for the war.

And while she never did manage to get to the Middle East, over the next six years she worked for a couple different newswires and later Japanese, Kuwaiti, and British agencies, sometimes shooting a story for a few days, other times gone for a week or two, on the road 180 or 200 days a year. This was back when no one gave a shit about Latin America, when coverage down there was still a rinky-dink operation, and even a phone call was sometimes difficult, and satellite hookups were sketchy and slow. Her assignments took on a familiar pattern: gang murder, prison riot, kidnapping, coup. She covered dire poverty, guerrillas, narco-trafficking and cartels in Colombia, Venezuela, Mexico, and Honduras. The ups and downs of Haiti, Aristide, Duvalier, mudslides, fires, FARC, Chávez, some horrible plane crash in Paraguay, body parts hanging in a tree. After a childhood marred by divorce, illness, sibling tragedy and death, she'd gained some resistance to human suffering, or maybe had a greater appetite for it.

And then she went corporate and learned to handle the blow-dried West Coast bosses of a vast public media company, while fending off the flattering advances of one Danny Katavolos, grandson of television pioneer Johnny Katavolos, and for a while she ran the Nature Channel's moneymaker on sharks—she came up with the idea to stick a guy in the ocean off the coast of Somalia wearing underpants made of chum. She faced the irregular participation of her dad, and her mother's steep decline, and didn't ask for my advice on how to raise our kids. I wasn't prepared for her to blossom into womanhood.

It was easier to be around her during the hours of the day when our kids were awake; it was safer and more fun, as we cleaned the kitchen while Kaya dragged her little brother around, saying, "Hey, look! Baby Beanie can walk!" Then I'd go to the basement while Robin did her yoga tape in the living room, her lady yogi's Southern drawl burbling through the ceiling above me, her feet pounding the rug as if to flatten, to pulverize me. I'd come to bed hours after her, turning the doorknob like a safecracker, crawling past the crib on my hands and knees so the floorboards didn't creak.

I liked to hear Beanie snore, and the quieter sounds of Robin sighing in her sleep, soft high sweet sounds like a secret baby was hiding inside her. Tiptoeing beside the bed to find my pajamas,

I'd study the mess of our blankets, tracing beneath them the contours of her body, staring down into the husk of her discarded jeans at my feet, the soft-looking, brightly colored underpants still inside them, so that I stood naked where she'd been naked, as though an echo of our once-naked selves intermingled on some alternate plane. Then I'd climb in beside her, calling up the ghosts still resonating in the air between us, and remember something better.

What was better was this: a receptive, neglected accomplice in the well-groomed horse country of Connecticut, suffering a similar fate, transporting herself over e-waves of desire through the magic of her cellphone, down the East Coast, to find me hiding under the blankets, texting with one hand. Someone who needed bodily updates, and remained curious and enmeshed, and kept the bloom on our flirtation, and cut it off for reasons I hadn't yet understood—matters of life, death, and the supernatural.

It was too late, I was too far gone, I'd spent too much time thinking up filthy stuff I planned to do when I finally got the chance, knowing I'd be sprung for a week in July, at my annual summer arts conference. There had to be someone else out there. I couldn't let it go. Despite the lack of communication since mid-March, despite the long silence, my feelings for Amy had grown even more intense, because I didn't need to filter or censor them, didn't need to shove them in an email and wait for the response to know they were real. In my loneliness I had to resist going back to study every word she'd ever sent, although I did, about four times a day, but it was more the knowledge that someone out there waited, trapped in her life, thinking of me.

FOURTEEN

I went into town and rented a bicycle. Pedaling through the village, I fell in with other cyclists as we dodged tourists bumbling off sidewalks in floppy hats, crowding Main Street, trampling the town green, which overlooked the harbor. A sinewy man, shiny with oil, stood beside an old cannon, eating a caramel apple, in nothing but a shimmering green Speedo. A lady with a gray mullet played guitar on a bench, singing "Your Body Is a Wonderland." The town had a history as a noisy, unconventional haven. A window displayed T-shirts with slogans: I MASTURBATE AND I VOTE; MY PARENTS ARE GAY. Art galleries, a side street paved in cobblestones, rainbow pinwheels strapped to lampposts. Not a cloud in the sky, bright blue hydrangeas, white boats sailing by.

Even though my phone didn't get a signal, I kept checking. I had a feeling she might call. And in the bay a single motorboat, a line of white foam behind it, an airplane above it in a mirrored dome of continuous blue. Old stone church, bait and tackle, a kids' playground in the sand. Riding out of town there was nothing, no coverage at all. The weight of the phone in my pocket was a nameless erotic impulse. It had always been the only way in.

I passed tiny clapboard houses, sharp green lawns, blooming rosebushes. Across the bay to the south I saw the tall bridge you took to reach the interstate, to leave this place forever, a bridge I'd be crossing soon enough. I thought of Amy, bleary-eyed and trembling, facing backward in that chair they used to roll her off the field, staring ahead at nothing. I figured her conference was over.

Past the massive stone breakwater that crossed the bay to the lighthouse, I joined other cyclists heading to the beach, and left them at the entrance to the state park, and rode by the Coast Guard station, its bell softly clanging, seagulls swirling out over the dunes. I followed the shoreline for a while, along a golf course and a grassy, lonely unnamed bay, and saw houses up in the hills. I found a quiet road with no markings that eventually turned to dirt, with smooth humps and soft potholes; I rode on to a parking lot with a boat ramp where the road dead-ended in a berm of sand. Two kids stood ankle-deep in tea-colored water, collecting something with a net, as a guy in surf trunks baited hooks beside his truck. A woman on the tailgate with long black hair stared at me as I leaned my bike against a guardrail and sat, my back against the sand, sipping water. I pulled off my backpack, took out my sketchbook, and attended to feelings of worthlessness.

The general shape of the truck emerged. Squinting, I delineated sand dunes to the east. Then I struggled to grasp the human figure. Do you think of the skull first or the contours of the head? When we move, all manner of compensatory things happen. The woman opened a cooler and fed the kids. I couldn't get the trees right, then began addressing areas of light, shade, and texture. The windshield didn't look like glass. The bay didn't look like water. With a white-out pen I plastered over my mistakes, waiting for them to dry, blowing on them, staring out at the flat-bottomed clouds on the horizon. Before I could finish, the family packed up. The tailgate slammed. The guy walked over. He stood behind me for a minute.

"That's why I take pictures," he said. "It's faster."

"Thanks. I never thought of that."

They drove off. I sat alone in the silence.

On Friday, during the long drive up, sitting in traffic, I'd phoned Adam, my boss, the magazine's art director. I'd already sent him a dozen sketches, and he'd sent back two thousand emails, tweezering over every detail, nitpicking me to death until he finally approved one. I had those rough illustrations in my sketchbook, and sifted through them for the one he liked best. I had to finish that drawing, maybe later today, and get started on a full watercolor painting of Chinese factory workers.

The drawing would accompany an article about our failed wars with the Muslim world, our trillion-dollar experiment in nation building, the nightmarish lessons of history, and some other stuff. It was written by a famous crank who'd been at the magazine for decades.

The magazine had been around for 160 years, and as with other august, oldfangled publications, it required the protection of a benefactor. It had recently been bought in a fire sale by Jerry, a twenty-six-year-old who'd made a billion dollars starting a social-networking site. Jerry wanted a fresh look, a fresh feel, and had worked closely with Laura, the editor in chief, shuffling the staff, designing a new logo. They still ran pieces of straight investigative journalism, still published essays and criticism on society and the arts, but they also made room for lighter fare, satire, photo spreads of naked dudes and women in lingerie, kooky stuff, snackable content, diagrams and charts taking potshots at businessmen, movie stars, and politicians. I guess my work was part of that zany new look.

The article more generally assailed our disastrous record of regime change and our role in unleashing extremism. Adam wanted my illustration to connect a possible GOP White House with the neocon wackos hoping to get back into power to pave the Middle East. Big oil, American exceptionalism, party of war. In the sketch Adam picked to go to final, Romney rode a bomb toward Iran, Dr. Strangelove–style, dressed like a Mormon door knocker.

I could be happy working as a magazine illustrator. Cartooning, on the other hand, was lonely and difficult, and it savaged my personal life. Mainstream critics loved to talk about a new golden age of comics, and there was more money around and plenty of good work jumping the barriers, but a semiautobiographical story told in arty-farty black-and-white panels of a heterosexual white guy, contemporary daddy under stress, needed a reason for being, a plot, a hook. Whereas a magazine illustration already had a reason for being, and it failed if the number of viable interpretations rose above one. I liked that precision. I liked nailing the assignment. As an illustrator, I got paid to worry about what Adam worried about, his canned lefty politics, his prepackaged cultural commentary, his conventional ideas of what looked good. And while my salary wasn't enough to undo the lie we were living in a house we couldn't afford, it definitely helped. The anticipation of that monthly paycheck arriving in my bank account had become a more complacent and regulated panic, the money a modest return on a sane and expected amount of work. Anyway, making your own comics is the road to hell.

A magazine illustration is a rational, defensible complaint. Prescribed, safe, part of the conversation. It served some function in society. Exploring my failings in a comic book was something entirely different, a selfish, sadistic experiment, a cry for help. It was also an awkward and imperfect method to attach thought to action, to think through my worst impulses and hopefully cleanse my soul. I guess that was what interested me. That was what I'd given up.

I finished the drawing of the truck, overdoing it, fixing it until it was ruined. I drew my hand, with veins and tendons flexing. I drew middle-aged Batman, at low tide, with a clam rake, staring like an idiot at some women undressing, stripping down to their bikinis. I drew fat Batman on the beach as he cavorted on a blanket with those chicks. I drew a little girl and her brother, waving to Daddy and blowing kisses. And I drew Robin, in her sports bra and yoga pants, saying, "I'm gonna buy a gun and shoochoo, muthafucka!"

I looked at my phone. It had one bar. Then it had none. It said, SEARCHING FOR NETWORK, then said, NO SERVICE. You had better luck on the other side of campus, by the flagpole, toward the highway.

I met Amy one night outside Fine Arts, downwind of a cigarette, sitting in the courtyard. We talked in a soft, sideways lukewarm rain. She leaned in close and bumped my knee. Then it spread across hundreds of miles and emails and photos that blotted out reality and ruined my life.

I drew a woman, easily and quickly, arms flung to either side, on the grass, unconscious, in the middle of the infield. Beside her I drew a shorter, bearded man with glasses and checkered shorts, and who is this man but my cartoon self, my hapless and poorly imagined alter ego. I drew the baseball field, bordered on one side by the campus, the clot of buildings in the old shipyard, and on the other side by a golf course and railroad tracks and a two-lane highway.

The pleasure of seeing my experience represented here came at me in a rush and my pen moved fast, zip, zip, no guessing, no stopping, everything where it should be, extraneous details excised, coastline neatened and simplified. A little wooden biplane flew in the vast expanse over the ball field, towing a banner: FLOOPSTEIN COLLEGE SUMMER ARTS CONFERENCE.

I started a comic strip, thumbnailing panels, this woman, this man, they meet, have a fling, fall in love. A year later they're back. Ideas came pouring out and I worked sure and fast, the way I had when I'd first started drawing comics, before I knew what I was doing, when everything came easily, in one draft, and there were no consequences, or there were but I didn't know it yet. I wanted to tell the story of my affair and, in the process, explain how I'd lost my way, what I'd done for love, for fatherhood, for the sake of good material. This comic would retroactively validate my years of making nothing. I could work on it in my free time, and surprise my publisher, and in four or five months I'd push thirty-two pages out into the world, and Robin would read it and throw me out of the house. In a year, I'd be halfway done. In three years, I'd have a book. I'd cough it up—the ugly, urgent truth—and deal with the fallout later.

I sketched the cover and titled it "What I Did at Summer Camp," in a woodsy font made of logs, and along the margin I drew a quick approximation of my own disembodied head, inside a sunburst, a corona with lines radiating, and beneath that I drew Marilyn Michnick's face, smiling, cockeyed with crooked glasses, and Mohammad Khan, sweaty and pleading for relief, and Tabitha Portenlee, and Vicky Capodanno, and Alicia Hernandez Roulet's ugly little dog, and gave each character a new name and a brief bio: "Vivian Friedman, expert on Florentine sculpture," "Ali El-Amir, prone to heat rashes," "Magdalene Ton-silman, interested in gambling and incest," "Emily Carbona, can't quit smoking," and "Sméagol, the walleyed goblin."

I made some notes about my doppelgänger—a cranky art director—his constraints and encumbrances, his seascape painting hobby, his family back home, with a vague similitude to Robin and my kids, changed their names, flipped their sexes, older boy, younger girl. In a box beneath the notes I scribbled, "The Adventures of Clark Kornblatt, Advertising Executive, Artist, Lover, Sportsman, Husband, Father, Adulterer," and "Costarring Natasha Monaghan-Rinaldi, Rich Lady from Connecticut, Hasn't Had Sex Since the Mesozoic Period."

Then I sat there and rested, and looked it over. An encounter at an arts conference. A woman of means and her dingbat boyfriend. Underlying theme: monogamy blows. Jeezum, how bold. I lay back against the sand and thought about cheating, until it became unbearable.

sense of place in this chapter is

FIFTEEN

Back in town I walked my bike along the pier, past tugboats, by the ferry landing, and took in the stench of the commercial fleet, game-fishing boats, rusty trawlers. I fiddled with my phone, hoping for a text from Amy, and dropped it in the street. I hadn't gotten a signal in two days. I wished they'd put up some cell towers in this stinking fishy hellhole.

Sometimes out here it seemed that the wind would blow a signal into your phone, and suddenly you had messages from hours or days ago. I squinted down into my hand, holding it at a delicate angle. Had she been carrying her phone? Please text me already, goddammit! Fuck. I walked my bike down Main Street because it was too crowded to ride, gawking and depressed, staring too hard at everything.

The town in summer was many things. It had beautiful light. The sky always changing. The breeze softly luffing. The sun like a hand resting gently on your shoulder. The buildings old and practically falling into the ocean, the streets narrow and crooked, walled in by Victorian B&Bs with fancy paint jobs and front yards heaving with wildflowers. Rainbow flags on every corner celebrated tolerance and diversity, the freedom to love. This place had been known at one time or another for whale hunting, Portuguese immigrants, sand dunes, herring shoals, shipwrecks off the point, but also for a certain kind of seeker or desperate kook, Puritans, dropouts, communists, frazzled intellectuals, painters from New York, experimental-theater types, alcoholic fishermen, sailors stationed here between the wars, stubborn or demented individuals hoping to escape persecution. It was seen as a haven for artists, a place of open-mindedness, and throughout the world for the last hundred years as a center of unconventional living, as a gay summer resort.

Two men ate ice cream cones in booty shorts under a sign advertising a drag show, beside a store selling taffy, a store selling kitchen gadgets. A guy in tight teal jeans drank coffee with a woman with jingly gypsy sandals outside a bar smelling of fried oysters. An elderly woman with gray dreadlocks buzzed by in an electric wheelchair led by dogs in rainbow collars. In this town even dogs could be gay. A massive shirtless guy with gold nipple rings in a Viking helmet wove through pedestrians on a booming Harley with a ferret in a crate wearing little goggles. Where did they come from? Would they ever go home? If I stood here forever, and the human traffic never ended, I could let it pass through me and live as a ghost and never have to think about myself again.

I locked my bike next to a cluster of bikes and followed the flow of traffic through a covered arcade, past a children's boutique, and entered a jewelry shop behind two men with matching sunglasses, matching sideburns, matching pectorals. I put my hands all over everything. I thought Robin would like one of these bracelets, and with the help of an easygoing and solicitous clerk, I found the exact one on black leather twine with a waxy finish, strung through a half dozen large, metallic, shimmering black pearls.

The men walked out and the older woman who'd been helping them joined the clerk beside me. From this distance, Robin couldn't do anything to stop me. I'd worked hard to earn these precious funds to buy a gift she didn't want or need, to signify my love.

We tried several bracelets on the young woman's lovely wrist but kept coming back to the nicest one. Robin's ingratitude and insults, her slights about my earnings, her sexual inattention, were beside the point. Or maybe they weren't. I'd show her. It happened quickly. I thought it said $300; $300 would've been a stupid waste of money, but then I noticed the third zero. I'm still not sure why, but when my credit card was declined, I pulled out our debit card in a state of almost total disbelief, and wiped out our checking account.

Back out on the street, I passed two women with matching silvery-blond crew cuts, rollerblading by with clomping strides. I read the receipt. No returns allowed except for store credit. I took in long, damp sheets of breath, to keep from blacking out. That made it worse. It erased my salary for the conference and then some. After our house and car and first child's emergency cesarean birth, this was more money than I'd blown on anything in my life. I passed an immensely tall, fabulous-looking drag queen, and a little skinny gum-chewing drag queen, flyering the crowd in the hours before their shows. I attempted to interpret my irrational action. Had I ever done this kind of thing before? No. A life in the arts requires vigilance and restraint. Was my behavior out of character? Yes, technically, and also terrifyingly, although it was possible that this was merely the culmination of a period of interior deadness and anger, that something had been building for months, or years, that the recent and ongoing stresses had pushed me over the edge. I tried to figure it out. Robin would be stunned into something beyond hatred, more like fear. She'd think I lost my mind. This was the kind of thing borderlines did before they burned down the house.

Pedicabs and kids on bikes fought for space on Main Street with muscle boys in packs and day-trippers and families with small children hauling beach stuff, imported Bulgarian teenagers rushing to work for an hourly wage, women who looked like librarians, wrapped in each other's embrace. They were happy, proud, and in love. I'd just spent the amount we'd saved to send our daughter to pre-K in the fall on a piece of waxed leather strung with stuff made by a mollusk. Whatever other cash we had coming was already set aside for regular expenses, to be disbursed during a weekly, unpleasant, nauseating triage of deciding what got paid first. A small blue velvet bag had been placed inside a white paper bag, and I held it tightly in my grip and continued my stroll down Main. I needed to gather myself and return the bracelet. If I had to murder everyone in that store, they would refund my money.

Health-food store, bait and tackle, taffy store, war monuments along the town green, motels, bars, benches full of gawkers, sipping espresso in little paper cups, big rusty anchor mounted on cement. Across the street, beside a sandwich board advertising tonight's cabaret, a big, blond frightening drag queen in a full-length white sheath joked with tourists, hawking her wares. A massive white clapboard building with black shutters and a witchy-looking clock tower, the town hall, cast a cool shadow across the green. There were police cars lined up along the wide front steps, a familiar-looking ambulance parked there, too—like an ice cream truck, clean and white with red and yellow—and beside it, a small brown building with partly tattered shingles, with a brown wooden sign that read, OUTER BEACHES MEDICAL CLINIC.

I crossed the street. I'd gone in there once for a band-aid and they had shellacked swordfish hanging on the walls. The real hospital was an hour away. She'd think I was harassing her. But wasn't I also her friend? Who would turn their back on a friend at a time like this? I went up the wooden stairs.

Inside, the waiting room was windowless but bright, fluorescent lights pulsing overhead. I passed a woman in a bathing suit jiggling a baby, and an old man with his arms folded across his chest. At the nurses' station, three people in scrubs were quietly typing and filing papers. I walked down the hall, past examination rooms with the doors ajar, some ogre coughing to death in the first one, a kid screaming in the next one, and at the end of the hall found a curtain; it was white and looked disposable, with a foot of mesh at the top. I stood on my toes and peered through the mesh.

Amy lay on a gurney, wide-eyed, head to the side, jaw hanging open like a drunk's. I felt sad and achy and sorry this thing had happened to her, and at the same time a little fascinated and unmoved and almost unable to believe it was real. A man in scrubs stood over her, medium build, angry complexion, receding curls.

"Every break is different," he told her. "Some people come in sobbing and begging for morphine. Others, like you, hold it together."

She licked her lips and said, "I gave birth to three kids without drugs."

"Well," he said, and sat on a stool and turned his back to her and began very nerdily measuring strips of white stuff, cutting and laying the strips on the table. I thought he was talking to himself, then realized he was telling the nurse how he planned to manipulate the break back into place.

"Because what you usually get in some Podunk town on a Saturday," he said, turning back to Amy, "is a medical assistant who's never done one of these before, so you have to wait for the surgeon to get off his boat and get in here." Then he gave a nod to the nurse. He mentioned a Something splint to deal with the swelling, then ice and elevation, and a new compression splint ten days from now, depending.

Another nurse pushed past me and threw back the curtain. I followed her in. Burt Feeney, the provost of the college, sat in the corner. He got the call if anything happened on campus—public urination, fire alarm, underage conference participant naked in the lacrosse dorm at three A.M. Behind him hung a poster of Diseases of the Digestive System. The doctor moved past Burt to check the X-rays on a light box on the wall. Burt called the doctor Henry. Amy turned to me as though she knew I'd come, and I thought, Don't do anything, don't scare her. I looked at her as though I'd known her all my life. Her T-shirt had ridden up against her armpits, against her boobs, and her plaid shorts were twisted and her face hung to the side. Her T-shirt looked soft. When I looked at her, it softened me. I stood there, staring like a creep. She was mine. She had been all along. There was dirt on her socks from the base path, and an IV in her good arm, but the puffy orange thing they'd put around her other arm on the field was gone, the arm lay there on a silver tray, bare and still, deformed.

"Does it hurt?" I loved her and wanted to tell her.

She shook her head and seemed to go away. She seemed a bit

high on goofballs. Her eyes closed and her eyebrows went up like some bored waitress's. When she came back she said, "I have a distal radial fracture with displacement."

The nurse unwrapped some rolls of gauze. "Folks," she said, to try to clear the room. I had to back up to let Feeney pass. He knew me from dealings at school, and gave me a friendly nod, like, "Look who's here, one of our depraved faculty members."

He taught marine bio and gave tours of the lab he helped run, out on the shoals—I went my first year here, forty-five minutes by boat, in the rain. His students warned us about the dangers of overfishing the Hamanausett Bay, then Burt got up on a milk crate and talked for two hours about the seals he tagged, a steady stream of water running off his hat, and I wanted to shoot him with a tranquilizer gun and implant a radio in his head. He'd actually been born in this town, and was tall and stooped with a gray beard and the accent of some Nova Scotian cod farmer. His wife, Edna, gave lectures every summer on heightened feeling in paintings of the late rococo period, and had a gonzo Afro like Phil Spector's, which was probably fine if you lived here year-round.

The nurse yanked back the curtain again, and another nurse, a tech, brought in a machine. The doctor spoke in a voice so gentle he seemed to be pretending. "What I'll do now," he said, "is administer the local." Then he gave Amy an injection right at the point of the break, the needle hunting inside, the doctor angling the syringe athletically, and I almost puked. I stood beside Burt, just beyond the curtain. Amy sighed, and moved her tongue around as her eyes bopped across the ceiling. He loaded up the syringe and did it again, a little higher.

Then he left, and the tech set up her machine while the nurse complained to the tech about how far away she lived, on a military base an hour inland. The tech was slower, quieter, with purple-powdered eyelids. They were waiting for the lidocaine, five more minutes. Then they walked out and stood down the hall.

"She slipped on second base," I told Burt, "because nobody nailed it down." Behind my words was the threat of litigation, but he didn't care. He wore a faded T-shirt with a turtle on it, with the name of his environmental alliance, and the biggest green shorts you ever saw, army surplus, with the fly not completely zipped.

"You don't have to stay," I said. "I can do it." I'd come to rescue her. He took out a red bandanna and blew his nose so it honked.

"Okay." He put away the hankie and went down the hall, tilting to one side like an old seaman. At the end of the hall he met the doctor, who put an arm around Burt's shoulders. I felt dizzy and alert.

Despite the local color—smelly artists who lived in unelectrified dune shacks, transvestite parades, stores selling cock rings—the town itself had the narrowness of an isolated colonial fishing village. The locals hated you, the annual scourge, the six-day summer renter in search of local flavor. You could see it in the backs of their eyes when you asked them what time high tide was, or between their teeth when you walked across the dunes through the plover habitat. Somewhere around Memorial Day the streets became too crowded for a car to pass, and every week after that the town's population doubled, and by the time I got here the locals were in retreat and droves of idiots were going around in those funny lobster hats with claws and jiggly eyeballs or trying to kill you in their avocado-colored Mercedes-Benzes on some crooked side street laid out in 1690 and not much wider than a bridle path; they strode in and out of restaurants and stores selling overpriced crap nobody on earth could actually afford. I bet Burt was sick of the whole thing. I didn't blame him. I'm saying I understood.

Then he came back down the hall and asked how I planned to get her back to campus. I said I didn't know. He smiled like he didn't care either way, and leaned through the curtain and called out, "Feel better, Amy," and said he'd see me at the fundraiser that night, one of those cocktail parties that all faculty were required to attend.

SIXTEEN

Up close, she looked a little loopy. I took the stool the doctor had been sitting on and brought it to her bedside.

"How is it?"

"Eh." Her voice had that nasal breaky tone of a drugged person not exactly keeping it together.

"I was worried," I said, as though I'd walked through a blizzard, calling every hospital within a hundred miles. Her cheeks were red, like those of a kid who'd woken up from a deep sleep under heavy blankets. "You'll be relieved to know that I'm a doctor, although unfortunately I did my training in cartooning. Now, what seems to be the problem?" I touched her knee. "Does this hurt?"

"Will you cut it out."

"You're not left-handed by any chance?"

"No."

"Hey, how many more bones were you planning on breaking this week? Because if this keeps up, I'll have to find someone else to play the accordion."

Her face twitched. "I'm going home." She wiped her eyes. "The nurse had to zip me up when I went to the toilet." Tears ran down and hung on her nostrils. "I can already see my kids going pooey if I can't string beads for Pretty Pretty Princess."

The bracelet sat in a blue velvet pouch, inside a white paper bag, on my lap.

"Stay. You can still go to class."

"And do what?"

"Listen. Soak it in."

"I'm not really a painter. I just pretend. You're the artist."

"Well, your kids will survive without you. Your nanny can handle it."

"Yeah, except it's hard to get good help from eight thousand miles away." Her sister had the kids until Tuesday. Amy had sent Perlita back to the Philippines to see her own kids. Then she sniffed her tears in, and I started to feel responsible, entangled, whatever. I held out the box of Kleenex, took the wet tissue when she finished, and threw it away.

"It's a clean break?" She nodded. "And you don't need surgery?" She said no. "Did you want to call anybody?"

"No."

"Did you leave a message at home?"

She shook her head. "The only one who'd get it would be me."

"But what do you do in an emergency?"

She looked at me as if that had never occurred to her. "I call his assistant, and she contacts him, then relays a message back to me if there is one."

"So did you call his assistant?"

"No."

"Why not?"

She had to think. "He's in Frankfurt."

From the second I'd met her I was assigned to hate him, so no surprise there, but still, I wondered, why did she marry him unless she wanted to be ditched?

"It's okay. I have people helping me. It's all pretty seamless."

"Cool."

"What you don't understand is, I work for him. And they work for me."

"Sounds good."

"Oh, fuck you."

"I'm just glad to hear your marriage still stinks. It's not any better?"

"No."

The nurse came in and tapped her arm once, twice. I tried not to look. She did a few things behind us. On the wall beneath the light box, a computer monitor and keyboard were bolted to swinging metal arms. The nurse left.

Out in the hall I could hear the nurse and the tech waiting for the doctor, complaining that five minutes was up. Amy's rib cage raised and lowered softly. I could feel it, in waves, coming over her. Every once in a while she tipped her head back and yawned. I yawned, too. I didn't want to leave. Everything out there was a mess.

A cop went down the hall, past the crash cart, in sunglasses, telling the nurse at full volume about an arrest he'd made the night before, unpaid bar tab, the drunk daring the cop to cuff him.

"Hey, guess what," she said. "I talked to someone."

"About what?"

"I thought I was going nuts."

"Oh."

"She seemed to think it was fascinating, but I got bored hearing myself complain."

"You mean you went once?" She shrugged. "What did you think would happen after one visit to a shrink?"

"I was trying to figure out what to do with you."

"Yeah, I know what you mean."

She said my name, nicely. It seemed to emanate from her, without shame.

"You remember my name."

"I say it all the time. You're the only person I talk to."

"Like in your head?"

She didn't look at all embarrassed.

"What do we talk about?"

She shrugged as though I wouldn't understand. I thought she was a fucking lunatic.

"Aren't you afraid God will hear?"

"No." She looked stoned and windblown, with fuzzy, staring eyes. The nurse strode back in. With this injury came a new honesty—a layer of defense had been breached—and, beneath it, a new vulnerability. Beneath that, though, was another unreadable layer of defense. The tech tapped at the keyboard of her machine. The bright light of this place exposed blue veins in Amy's temples, they were raised and greenish, but it also lit her eyes, blue gray with gold flecks. I touched her knee. She had soft, smooth legs. "I'm sorry about everything, and I'm sorry you broke your arm." I opened the velvet bag and took out the bracelet. Giving it to Robin would've been worse than throwing it in the gutter.

"I bought this for you." I put it on her uninjured wrist and tore off the price tag. There was a way of fitting it to her, pulling the ends through the knot. She looked at it, then back at me.

"You didn't have to do that."

"It's nothing."

"It's not your fault."

"I'm aware of that."

She didn't care about the bracelet at all. "They're after us, no matter where we go."

"We'll move to New Zealand."

"They'll get us."

"We'll raise sheep and have blond babies."

"Can I get a bike with black fenders?"

"Yes," I said, "and we'll make sheep yogurt."

"Can I put a bell on the handlebars?"

I said yes. It was better to pretend. She looked at the bracelet again and thanked me.

SEVENTEEN

He wore a loud apron, neon blue, to protect him from the X-rays. The nurse went behind Amy, taking hold of her upper arm with both hands, telling her to buy cast bags at Lowell Drug. Umbrella bags worked too, they were cheaper, you could get them at Costco. In this way Amy could keep her arm dry, as she looked ahead to showering, as if the business at hand was almost done. The doctor's hat and gloves were blue, and he took the stool I'd been using and held her wrist in his lap. I stood behind them, at the edge of the curtain. The doctor pressed with his thumbs, facing the nurse, walking them calmly down her arm toward the deformed place as the nurse held her upper arm steady. He bent her broken arm. The nurse seemed to brace herself as Amy's eyes opened wide; he bent it farther, as if flexing an ankle, and all the air went out of her. He yanked it toward himself with a sudden snap, and she groaned.

He pulled it across the drum beside him, a portable X-ray machine with a dark glass surface. The tech kept her white-sneakered foot on the base of the machine, as if pressing down on a gas pedal, watching the monitor on the wall, not lifting her eyes from it. The bones overlapped by half an inch. She told him, "medial," "proximal," and cues down to the millimeter. The doctor seemed lost, mushing Amy's arm, kneading it like bread dough, the blind thumbs looking for the broken ends to mesh. Amy sucked in air, hissing through bared teeth. The lidocaine obviously did work, since her body remained flat and motionless, but something must've leaked through, some synapses must've blown.

The nurse braced Amy's elbow as the doctor stood, lifting from the balls of his feet, grimacing, throwing his weight up to the ceiling, the way you would if you were trying to yank a fence post out of a hole, gloves streaked white against his knuckles, the black hair on his knuckles showing through the latex, blue hat going crooked. Amy made a growling noise that shocked me, then suddenly flung herself against the gurney, ripping off the paper sheet. I thought she'd knocked herself unconscious. She said she was light-headed and thought she might pass out. The nurse said, "BREATHE," and she did, eyes peeled. I saw her silver fillings, black in bright light, her tongue pressed against the gloss inside her mouth.

Sweat ran down my armpits. The doctor checked the screen again. Still not right. My arm started to throb. I felt it twisting and tearing as an imaginary ice-cold hypodermic needle went into my forearm and scraped the bones.

We'd bonded over the shock at how our lives had turned out. One of us had peaked too early and failed to live up to his potential, and the other one was trapped and enslaved and felt prickly hatred upon her skin whenever her husband walked into the room. We filled our emails with every complaint, trying to make our lives sound more tragic, and idealized and taunted and swore to the other, and promised an escape, sometimes hourly, and went ahead causing more pain.

The doctor stood again. My eyes moved from the eyebrows of the nurse, to the purple eyelids of the tech, to the tip of the doctor's tongue, to the floor. He'd never get it right. I wanted to rip his filthy hands off her. I didn't really love her, I wasn't even sure I liked her, although maybe I liked her. But did I like her because I was lonely and she was hot and rich? Or was it because I didn't get any sleep and had brain damage from speaking baby language? Or because Robin's booty had snapped back into shape but touching it was still a no-no?

I spaced out and saw myself watching the scene. I thought about the events of this afternoon, and with some satisfaction I began to note sensations and the placement of people and things, for later use: the equipment, the doctor's canted hat, Amy's hideous moans, stuff I could play with in the narrative of my forthcoming work. I'd have to massage the dialogue to show vulnerability, humanity, the intensity of the lovers' bond.

Then I felt bad because I really loved Robin and my two little zipadees. I could still make it right. If I had to break Amy's other arm, I'd get the bracelet back. My kids were the whole show. Without them I was lost. Without Robin my life was garbage. In the mornings I dropped Kaya off at preschool and she ran, skipping, waving, jumping in the air, blowing kisses. Beanie bounced up and down in my arms, yelling nonsense. I wanted to squeeze them both and chew on their little craniums. I couldn't sit here another second. After all this hocus-pocus, I just wanted to go home.

Then he stopped, and in the strobing grayscale on the screen you could see the ends met. The bones lined up.

EIGHTEEN

I'd fallen asleep in the waiting room, under a plastic fish, a bluefin tuna, waiting for her paperwork, and woke up with stinging eyes, my head pounding, in a terrible mood. The thing in my pocket buzzed and jangled. It was Robin, asking if I had a moment to speak to my daughter. She sounded oddly at ease. In some bizarre anomaly across the waves of electromagnetic particles, the phone call came through in a clear connection. I could hear Kaya whimpering in the background, and Beanie too, though he sounded more indignant, like a weary traveler upset with his hotel bill.

Some issue required my immediate intervention. The endlessness of it, the detail work, the centrality of children, the sudden refusals, inexplicable urges, stunning meltdowns, the marital pieces spinning around that core, flung with force in every direction—in one day I'd forgotten it all, and I'd probably forget it again as soon as this problem resolved itself or the connection died, but I remembered it now. The late-night interludes of drunken oneness, the smooth articulations of the umbrella stroller, the tiny bite marks in their hand-cooked leftovers, the fantastic expense of our babysitter, regardless of my father-in-law's help. So exhausted at dawn that the sight of the neighbor's softly mown grass brought tears to my eyes for the beauty of this world.

"Is everything okay?"

"Kaya rode her tricycle into the pit behind Elizabeth's house."

I held the phone sweatily, feeling the floor of the waiting room sway beneath me.

Our kitchen windows looked out on that scene. Blue tarpaulins hung off the back of their three-story renovation, flapping day and night like a sailboat. Curtis and Elizabeth's yard had been excavated and was now occupied by their new foundation, but the permit for the dumpster was late, so the rest of the hole had been filled with demolished house, scraps of lumber, metal framing, shredded aluminum siding, and broken glass. In the alley between our two houses, Kaya and a girl named Julia liked to ride down the slight incline with their feet off the pedals, a straight shot into what used to be a patch of grass. During the week, the workmen with their funny nicknames parked their trucks there to block it off. When the girls were in the alley, someone was supposed to stand at the bottom.

"And while Kaya was bleeding all over the bathroom floor, Beanie sucked the propeller out of that clown whistle and almost choked to death." Robin sounded more than calm—loose, almost thrilled. "I had to hold him by his feet and smack him to get him to cough it up." It sounded like she'd been drinking. "He didn't cry, but I cried, and Kaya cried, although she was already crying."

"Please start at the beginning."

"Okay."

"Where were you?"

"Inside getting Beanie."

"You had the monitor outside and you heard him wake up?"

"Yes, idiot, I had the monitor outside."

On one level I understood that somehow Robin had orchestrated these events, possibly in their entirety, out of frustration or temporary insanity from lack of sleep, spun them into something shocking and only loosely based on fact, to punish me, that maybe none of it had happened and my real son and daughter were lying on the carpet having Elmo juice, watching *Fairytopia*, but on another level I wasn't so sure.

"Brett said she screamed the whole way down. She was still holding the handlebars when he got there." I pictured Kaya hanging on to her tricycle like some X Games hot dog. Robin calmly listed the injuries: "A skinned shoulder blade, a deep cut on her hip, a cut on the back of her head, a worse cut on her hand, and two skinned elbows."

The nurse emerged from the hallway and beckoned me. I waved her away. Brett had been in his own yard, ten feet over. I imagined him stepping down that narrow plank the workmen used to enter the pit, an old two-by-twelve that never broke but bent and flexed when they rolled wheelbarrows up and down it. Maybe she'd asked him to watch when she went inside. He was probably the last person you'd want out there looking after your kid. He had a sure-handed nonchalance, a passive negligence, a malicious inattention. He made no move to intervene when a kid fell from a tree or left half her face on the sidewalk; he seemed merely curious, vaguely affirmed, as though their injuries verified or satisfied something. He had three boys. The force of so many sons vying for their mother, wishing him dead, had taken its toll.

"She's shivering now and won't stop crying and says she's hungry but won't eat."

Kaya took the phone, and I heard that familiar modulation of my own voice as it rose and softened, telling her how sorry I was that a bad thing had happened. It was strange to hear myself, that part of me, in the clinic waiting room.

"Dat's okay," she said, showing a maturity and compassion that sometimes shocked me, and then she said something about a boo-boo, I couldn't understand what, and then the call died. I called back. Again the nurse waved at me to follow her down the hall. I called several times, and pictured myself standing over Brett, bringing down the baseball bat, over and over. I tried Robin's cell and got her voicemail. Amy walked toward me, unsteadily, with her splinted arm in front of her, the other hand supporting it. The nurse came up from behind her and handed me a plastic bag with some forms and Amy's wallet and sunglasses and said, "The local wears off in an hour."

"What does that mean?"

"Then it'll hurt."

NINETEEN

The pedicab took a right off Main Street and turned in at the campus gate. I paid him fifteen bucks to drive half a mile and caught her when she stumbled down from the cab, then led her slowly up the stairs of her dorm and found the room key in her pocket. Threw her clothes on the floor to clear the bed, then barred the door when she tried to pack up and drive home. After she promised not to leave, I made her lie down and helped her with the pillows, and hid her car keys, and went back into town to get her prescription filled. When I got to the room, she was resting. I went out a second time, to buy ice.

The little store with rainbow flags had run out of ice. I saw the time on the clock tower above town hall. What had the nurse meant by an hour? An hour from when? I ran to the gas station by the highway, and ran back through the crowds on Main Street with the bags of ice swinging. I'd hoped I could get away for a few days and everything would be okay. I'd thought that at the very least, they'd be safe. I pictured Kaya screaming, falling into the pit, holding on tight.

When I got back, the lidocaine had worn off. I saw Amy arch, her head crowning against the pillow, her mouth open, teeth bared, no sound coming out. She hadn't been able to open the bottle of pills one-handed. She made a noise, a jagged, improvised yowl. I ripped open the bottle, and pills went all over the floor. I accidentally stepped on one and smashed it, picked up another and handed it to her.

They'd put me on OxyContin when I had my wisdom teeth out. I gave it my full endorsement, hoping to calm her, or me: "You're going to be okay." I thought the pain would level off, but after a while she got into something only a great martyr could access. I held a tissue while she blew her nose.

"Hang in there, kid." We really were being punished. Her agony was somehow a relief. One or two of the bedrooms in her suite looked empty and unused, and the others were vacant but had clothing on the floor. Her forehead was smooth and hard and I touched it and felt that numbness again, witnessing her pain. I couldn't help her, couldn't control myself, couldn't catch Kaya when she fell, couldn't protect them. When the painkiller didn't seem to be working, I dug out another from the amber vial and handed it to her. She threw it down with the water I'd brought from the bathroom in a paper cup. There'd been six pills, counting the one I'd crushed into the floor. Now there were three.

I had to get out of there and call home. I wanted photos of Kaya's injuries and eyewitness accounts. After I finished off Brett, I'd use the baseball bat on Curtis for renovating his house. They'd talked about tearing it down but had decided instead to blow out the rear, then beat the height restriction by raising their yard. I had to get back down Main Street to terrorize a certain jewelry store clerk, then hurry to the Barn to look through my notes to get ready for class in the morning. I had to manage my students' egos and frustrations. I had to care. I had to get paid before Robin saw our bank balance, had to get home before she killed my kids. I needed to start on that painting of Chinese factory workers, and call Adam, and then make the Romney drawing in ink and scan it and send it in. Long days waited for me back home, parenting, bandages, differences of opinion, scrambled meals and bedtime sorrows, my sleep carved up by sobs and howling shrieks, and long nights hammering my work into an art director's half-baked, mystifying demands, micromanaged by an erratic twenty-six-year-old publisher who'd never worked at a magazine before he'd bought one. I felt myself fighting against all that rope as the noose cinched itself down. I had to shower and change and get to that fundraiser. Carl, our boss, didn't like those things any more than the rest of us, but the least we could do was go and kiss some donor's ass. If you blew off parties or came late or acted less than thrilled to be there, he made note of it and didn't hire you back. It was part of the job of the conference, the conference as one of the last remaining perks from the good old days, and I couldn't bear to lose it.

She rolled her head from side to side, grimacing. She asked me to take out her earrings. "Deep breaths," I said, leaning across her face, touching the sun-damaged creases on her neck. I fixed the pillow. Her eyes went wild.

"Why did you come to the hospital?"

"I was worried about you."

"Bullshit. You walked by accidentally."

"What the fuck. I thought you wanted me to leave you alone. You stopped talking to me for four months."

"What the fuck do you think I'm doing here?" She started sobbing again. "I came back for you. I wore my cigarette pants to dinner last night for you, I didn't see you anywhere, I had to sit with some old lady and talk about the barbecue sauce!" But I'd looked for her too, and looked for her again at breakfast. "I can't stand it!" She said something about Mike in Frankfurt, gasping in a shaky voice. "I can't live this way anymore. I can't be alone all the time and then treated like shit."

I had the creeping awareness that since March I'd secretly wished her ill, imagined some degrading payback for how she'd boxed me out, for everything, the incidental bragging, about her luncheon with Sting's wife, Trudie, how she got trapped inside a ball gown alone at home and had to cut herself out with a bread knife, but this display of misery had already exceeded my fantasies of revenge. Her eyes had sunk into her head, her skin was greenish and sliding off the plates of her skull.

"'Mommy, are you sad you married Daddy? Does he wish he had no children? Does he hate us?' Emily asks me that now. It's so horrible." He hadn't made one piano recital this year, no soccer games, swim meets, parents night, nothing. He missed the birth of their youngest kid, plain forgot and went golfing. Didn't have a single question for Lily's surgeons. "They're going in there to save our kid's life with an experimental procedure and he couldn't take his head out of the bag"—"the bag" being a derogatory term for the soft briefcase he carried with him, even on canoeing trips, filled with balance sheets for upcoming deals. "I asked the questions! I made the call!" The memory of it seemed more painful than the arm. I took out a third pill in case it got worse, and held it in my sweaty fingers as the coating came off and the thing turned gummy in my hand. "Every night of my life I have to read until I'm unconscious, or else I lie there and worry that I'll die, and all they'll have left is him."

"You're not dying."

"He'll hire some pole dancer to raise them. Maybe she'll let him stick it up her ass."

"It's okay."

"One day you'll hear I'm dead, and you'll be sad but you'll be happy, too!"

"No I won't."

"You never knew how much you mattered to me."

"You mattered to me, too."

Between gasps, her breathing quieted. I touched her forehead with the palm of my hand and promised she'd be home soon, and rubbed the decomposing pill in my other hand. She calmed down and rolled onto her side, and made a soft, hoarse, muffled whimper, like an infant fighting a nap. There was no way to get the bracelet off her now.

My pain was like hers, from wanting her all this time, from wanting out, from being trapped, from wanting life. We made the motions of living but we were dying in a hurry. Soon I'd be gone and my kids would grow old and they'd croak, too. It was a knot, a loop, twisting and choking me off from what I needed, from life. You don't even know, but you're dying right now. She was quiet. I ate the pill.

Below the open window I heard people in the parking lot. Out in the bay, a lone sailboat crawled along the razor line of the horizon. I heard "Call Me Maybe" ringing in the courtyard. A moment later I felt my sinuses release. I took in huge gulps of seaborne air. I tasted life on my tongue. My lips cracked. My mouth was as dry as a chalkboard. The stitch in my back from softball, or from that crappy mattress in the Barn, or from yesterday's nine-hour drive, which had crippled me, was gone. I'd been gritting my teeth, trying to outrun it, but hadn't realized it. The drug came over me in surges of undulating serenity. She closed her eyes, so I took another pill and choked it down.

TWENTY

Light came in waves, sound came in waves. Cicadas out the window sounded like distant machinery.

"It's numb," she said, touching her splint. I had a similar thing going on with my face. I drifted in and out, alert but adrift, in love with mankind. The lower parts of us rhythmically dry-humped. I'd crawled into bed with her at some point. My heart beat time with nature's green machine. I understood the language of insects. I thought this was the most beautiful little room on earth, and humped her harder, the two of us crammed in together on her twin bed. I felt a cool sensation around my mouth. It was drool. I was drooling. She broke her thumb once playing field hockey, something else happened skiing, I wasn't listening.

It wasn't just the ache in my back. My whole helmet was gone, the whole case of mistaken identity that had chained me to the furnace in my basement for the last five years, the whole doomed, provisional future, the sodden memories of rancorous domesticity: poof. I'd drawn a new circle where the head had been.

Out the window an Evian banner chased an airplane across the bay. "Gangnam Style" rang out in the courtyard. I felt sluggish, a little queasy, like a sick kid in heavy pajamas. I slipped my hand in, stroking and cupping her everywhere. Amy leaned back and opened her mouth and reached up with her good hand to feel my face.

"Nobody touches me except my kids. No hands on me, no skin against mine."

"Same deal at my house," I said.

Thoughts of Robin back home raced in and I forced them out, and told her how happy I'd been all those months, to have someone lighting up my phone night and day, thinking I mattered, like sugar in my veins. A good day meant steady updates and flirty pics or news of my appearance in her dreams and fantasies, and a bad day meant no word at all, and when we cut off communication my world went dark, so I talked to her in my head, like a lunatic, the same way she did with me. I listed my favorite photos of her, the one at a fancy lawn party in a short dress, pretending to shoot herself in the head out of boredom, the one of her on a sled with kids on her lap, and the one in pink undies. I recounted her nighttime phantom visitations, and how I could feel her actual body, hear my bed creak, feel her warm weight upon me, her knowing hands and pliant parts, her voice hissing in my ear. Either you've been there and know or you haven't and think I'm nuts, but I swear, it happened. I told her how the thought of Lily's surgery made me cry, how I'd worried about her kid until my head hurt and prayed in my own unaffiliated way for her to pull through. I felt ashamed in confessing, and Amy reached up and whacked me so hard with her splint, it folded and crunched my ear like a bag of Cheetos. But it was an accident, and only meant to be a loving caress. It didn't hurt at all. Every gland in my body felt fine. Her teeth banged into mine as she worked my mouth with hers.

"You know," she said, pulling back, "it's hard to take a picture of your own butt."

"I wondered about that."

"You wave it over your shoulder and hope for the best."

"You had good results."

Her hand lay between us, the fingers turning blue. She slurped at the saliva gathering at the corners of her mouth.

"Oh God." She'd been smiling. "Do other people do this kind of thing?"

"Yes," I said. "That's what I keep telling myself."

The air grazed my skin like velvet. The drug made me feel like a long-eared gnome. I decided to remove my shorts. Underage shoplifting and vandalism, passing out drunk at the wheel and totaling my father's car, knocking up my high school girlfriend, knocking up another girlfriend in college, abortions, miscarriages, loose finances, unrealistic or laughable ambitions, wild statements in art and in life, flushing away all of our money for the thing gently rotating on a rich lady's wrist—these were impulsive acts or the unintended consequences, nothing earth-shattering, but here was another one. I felt stupider in my underwear, and lifted the hem of her T-shirt, and yanked it over her head.

She was bigger and longer than ever. Her bra was padded, cinnamon-colored, with a wire in it. I knew she was ashamed, that she never took it off for him. I knew everything, and followed her nipples around the room until I nearly fainted. The soft arc at the bottom of her breasts described what they'd been, full, on a broad frame that matched her collarbones. Her nipples were small and cute and tasted metallic. Her skin was softer than Robin's, although Robin's was pretty soft. Her underwear was nude with scratchy lace, and she lifted her hips and I threw them on the floor.

"That's it," she breathed wildly. She wanted to be naked, wanted to be stripped. "Let's make a bet," she said. "And if I win, you have to come with me and my kids to Disney World." She touched me with a silky, absentminded caress.

"And if I win, you have to dance around the room naked."

"We'll get Mickey ears and binge on Twizzlers." Her index finger and thumb lazily circled my business, as if she'd read in a Vatican-approved periodical how to apply the minimum of wifely contact to satisfy the required manipulation, though it seemed that between her hand and her brain there was that characteristic disconnect I'd grown used to during intervals of our intimate engagement. Like the hand was into it, even though the head instructed the hand to chill and maintain a demure proportion of modesty.

"Or go someplace out west, with little cabins."

"I missed you."

"Can we talk about what happened?"

"I never should've gone to your house in March. That was a bad idea."

The mention of it seemed to derail her. "When you left that day, I couldn't stand it. I wanted to tell someone, 'That was my boyfriend. We just broke up.'" She must've meant her housekeepers. She never mentioned anyone else. They shared a bedroom in her basement: Perlita, who wiped the baby's ass, and the Salvadoran woman who'd lost her restaurant in the economic crash and now did laundry for a living, and the nanny with scars on her face who babysat on weekends and cleaned the rest of the time.

"For the last two weeks I kept thinking about coming back

here, jumping out of my gourd. Not just excited but also sort of crazy and sad and mean to everyone."

And Tammy, who rolled into the driveway every morning at five o'clock to give Mike his private yoga lesson before his driver showed up to take him to the helipad so he could fly into the city, or to Teterboro, to his waiting jet.

"Abusive and whiny and selfish, didn't want to do after-school pickup or read to them at night or cook anything or walk the dog. I didn't want to come here, and I didn't want to stay home."

"I've been a nervous wreck, too."

"I wanted to tell him."

"Great idea."

"I think he figured it out."

"How?"

"He only digs me when I've got something to look forward to." She wiped the corners of her mouth with a sleepy gesture. "Not just him. Strangers try to talk to me. Babies think they know me. The guy at the meat counter kept carrying my bags to the parking lot, directing traffic so I could pull out." I pictured her, bouncing around the supermarket with an expectant, wide-eyed look, a broad-shouldered, pigeon-toed, six-foot-tall lady.

"Anybody else?"

"Then I get home with the groceries and this guy I barely know is trying to rip my clothes off."

"I thought he was in Germany."

"He left on Sunday."

"I thought he was always too tired to want sex."

"Not always."

"Or distracted by work."

"I was thinking of you the whole time, although you're nothing like him."

"I don't want to know."

"Rips my clothes off, no kissing, bend over, no talking." Even on drugs it hurt to listen. "I forget where he'd been, Wisconsin maybe. He got home early. I guess he was excited to show me how healthy his prostate was or something. It was awful."

"Oh my God."

"Finally, when I couldn't get him off me, I told him about you."

"I can't tell if you're being serious."

"Not your name but I told him I was going away, which of course he didn't remember, and that I was going to see you, which he didn't believe, and it turned him on even more."

"I guess that explains how he knew."

"And when he finished he gave me a present."

"How thoughtful."

"He gives me stuff, trinkets or wads of cash."

"But this actually happened, or are you kidding? I'm still confused."

"Like jewelry, nice stuff." She reached up and touched an earlobe. "Where'd they go?"

I had no idea what I'd done with her earrings. The bracelet had two dangly pieces with pearls knotted at the ends that clacked together.

"Did he hurt you?"

"Nah."

"Well then, how much money would he give you, typically?"

"Like I robbed a bank." I tried to imagine it. "Although fifteen percent of his business is in my name, so it's my money, too."

"But, like, give me a ballpark figure."

"I don't care." She turned serious, although her eyes went in different directions. "I've tried everything. I've tried getting blitzed. It doesn't work. I even thought about hypnosis."

"It's all right."

"One day I'll have something better, maybe not with you, but I will. You don't have to come to Disney World with me if you don't want to."

"I do. I said I'll go to Disney World!" I felt this wild state of believing, familiar and illusory but stronger than ever. She hugged and kissed me. I didn't know whose drool was whose. She tried swallowing my face. I fought back as best I could. The first time in these dorms it had been innocent and authentic, an unpremeditated falling in love. But this time it was more ominous and bewildering. We smooched until our faces melted. I opened and pressed back her knees, kissing her ribs, the cool sveltish bones of her. She flung her head back and I smooched her belly, waggling two fingers slowly into her. I slid down, breathing underwater, and squished my tongue around and around. Her legs jolted and she heaved and wriggled. I had trouble breathing but it was good to shut her up with my tongue, to gag myself with her, to steer her long legs as they banged against my head. My tongue got tired and the muscles in my head ached, and cramped up, and turned to stone. I might've passed out but my tongue kept going. I felt her pulse beating against my lips, her body vibrating from her moans, her hips rising and me going up, dropping down, holding on, wrapping my arms around her.

"It keeps going!"

Then I lay there with my cheek on her stomach, catching my breath, listening to her breathe.

"Holy moly." And a minute later: "Nobody's gone down on me since college!"

She didn't want to stop. "Hey, can you keep doing that while I do this?" She used her fingers on herself while I used my tongue. Her hips bounced, her knees cupped and clattered against my head, my arms wrapped around her, hanging on. "Oh, I need this in my life!" Then more noises, then gasping for air, then she cried while coming, just like last year, and pulled me up and wrapped herself around me.

"Oh, thank you, bunny."

"Sure." What the fuck? I wanted her to respect me, not call me "bunny." Then I thought of Mike, a hundred pounds heavier than her, throwing cash or jewelry on the bed after he finished. Then I remembered the high school ex-boyfriend. In relationships, I read somewhere, men feared being humiliated, while women feared being murdered. Although it didn't seem to be part of her, and really, I admired how she refused to let a bad thing define her, didn't seem to be trying to heal some wound or deal with it in any overt or subconscious way. I admired that strength, the fighter in her, how she'd survived and moved on. Although maybe by refusing to deal with it, she got stuck reenacting it in some endless looping karmic nightmare.

A moment later I felt her good hand tugging on my ass, her foot curled around the back of my thigh, the tendon pulling and drawing me to her, her clublike appendage banging and scratching the back of my head. A trail of saliva ran down the side of her face. I wasn't about to cut diamonds with this thing, but with some angling and shoving I found a way to squish it inside her.

"Is that okay?"

"Mmm."

I got it moving. It worked. I'd been hoping for this, although not exactly this, but I felt held, I felt home. I went into her arms and peeled off my hairy defenses. Robin and I had been screwing for twelve years. We had no idea what we were doing anymore or why. Amy and I had been at it for two minutes on controlled substances and were already spiritually entwined. We were smiling and looking at each other like, Holy shit. I had trouble imagining the awful things she'd been through. Everything but this was in the past.

This was how you did it. You fell in love. You thought about her hourly. You waited for a year. You waited until she asked. I'd been screwing since high school but had had no idea what it was until that moment. Once she asks, you pass it to her. Then she passes it back to you. It's an agreement. You have to ask for it and she has to ask for it. When the vote is unanimous, she passes it back for all women, for the business of the human race, fully aware that time started with this action, an engine lying in the cave of our furry relatives before man arrived. She was smiling. I was like, Thank you, God. The worst sex is a crime that shouldn't define you. The best sex in life is tough to predict and hard to explain.

How weird was it that the closer I got, the lighter I felt, the drunker I felt, the weaker I felt, the more unfiltered or unmasked or honest or in love, the smaller I felt, the less I felt I had to bring, to defend myself, the more easily she could take me, devour me, allow me to disappear inside her. I started to shake, my arms were tired, and she shuddered and I shook back and we held on like two crazy poodles, shaking and trembling. I pushed only half the time, and the other half she pulled, she drew me in, and I was taken up, the cord stretched taut between us, one breath, one body, one of us. Then no one breathing, then looking at each other and madly kissing. Then the pattern again. One. One. One. If I could feel the pattern, I could stay with it indefinitely.

"Oh."

I've got her now, she's mine now.

"Ohh." I'm holding her, I'm in her arms, I'm banging Amy, I'm coming inside a beautiful mother.

That kind of orgasm is inexplicable and impossible to duplicate. It leaves you grateful and mystified, altered and plural, self-less and boundless, winded and imprinted with her soul. She curled into my arms, resting her head on my chest, eyes closed. "Oh, bunny," she said, and drew her knees into her chest. We stayed that way for a while. Eventually, I asked if she was okay. She'd curled into a ball like a pill bug.

"What am I doing?"

I struggled to process it analytically. Although heavily suppressed and encased in narcotic batting, even I could see where this was headed.

"I'm never reckless. I tried to leave."

I stood and was able to put on my clothes. Other responses occurred to me: loss of control of my arms and legs, sudden convulsions, and outbursts of crying.

"I'm bad."

"You said that last summer."

"We're crazy." I found one sneaker under the bed. "I didn't come for this. I came to see your face. I wanted company." I had to toss her clothes around to find the other shoe. "We're out of control."

She fell back and cradled her arm. It wasn't entirely the same as last year: she didn't directly blame me or say she was going to hell, and her tears might've been residual and were certainly in line with recent events. It was certainly not unexpected, and a percentage of her response remained in flux, as she opened her eyes and looked searchingly and even reached out her good hand toward me, maybe moving at an asymmetrical rate to the level of normative discomfort, adjusted for the incongruence of overlapping historical, psychosocial, and physiological—

There was an explosion that rattled the windows.

Maybe it had nothing to do with me. Then another explosion. When I left she was looking at her splint.

TWENTY-ONE

On my way across campus from Amy's dorm there were several more explosions. Every day at five o'clock some nutjob out in the harbor fired a cannon off a sailboat to signal the beginning of happy hour. I walked to the flagpole and called home, twice, then gave up and headed to the Barn. The broken arm. The bracelet disaster. Then my wife tried to kill my kids, and I fucked a plutocrat. Things were definitely out of whack. In the parking lot, two guys were painting stage sets. Past the windmill I fell in behind some people with beach towels around their necks, barefoot, singing, "I Could Have Danced All Night." A woman had some kind of flower in her hair. She'd been the lead in last night's Chekhov mash-up.

As the conference wore on and gathered intensity, attendees who'd been waiting and planning for weeks or even months now burst into creative expression. The frenzy didn't usually start until Sunday night or Monday, but here it was late Saturday afternoon and the terminal cases were hard at work. The barefoot singers harmonized. They turned left at the bottom of the hill, and it was quiet again.

Robin was alone and sleep-deprived and doing the best she could. I forgave her. My children would eventually heal and grow older, have children of their own. Their suffering was distant and unreal to me. Amy was also suffering, tolerating abuse in her marriage. Some kind of emotional blindness kept her strong, helped her negate the severity of these attacks. Around me, though, she felt safe, could feel her feelings, her fear and guilt. I wanted to run back to her dorm room to see if she was okay.

For eight months I'd maintained slavish contact, assembled a long-distance romance for the ages, returned here with low expectations, then saw her through a bone fracture and near-death country-doctoring to complete the most arduous seduction in history. But what she'd needed was a benign and practical kind of help, not another stalker from the meat department. I'd gained a new understanding of the workings of her marriage, one that concerned me. Given her history, her husband's brutality was not surprising. Victims of certain crimes were more likely to be victimized again, were less able to enforce boundaries, disrupt patterns, read signs. I didn't blame the victim, but I saw her as a locus of sexual aggression, a weird convergence of uncontrollable forces.

Sex deprivation had made me desperate, half-blind, and irrationally prone to fantasy, impulse, isolation, and cruelty. The parenting and homeownership, the borrowing, the debt, the load-bearing walls, packed inside that steady, anxious flow of days, nurturing, soldiering, corralling, building a monument to a lifestyle, to be preserved, resold, passed down, passed on. I lived in a sticky web of communal adaptations, minimizations, moderations. It made me cuckoo.

She prayed the rosary and sent money to Rome. I hated that smug superficial authority. I couldn't stand it, how sure she was. Never reckless. Tried to leave. What better time to be reckless than now? She had all the wrong instincts, took her cues from all the wrong people, from a clergy of predators and an old Nazi pope in a crown. Nothing weird about that, nothing wrong with liberation theology in a banking context in a late-capitalist nightmare in the midst of an environmental meltdown. Arcane legislation written in secret by industry cronies on obscure financial practices and windfalls for carried interest had made her rich. She'd been formed by her parents' immigrant struggle, a smoldering blue-collar rage, and the last two bull markets. Socially progressive, fiscally conservative, except the second part canceled out the first. She backed the NRDC, PETA, NOW, and Planned Parenthood, but also believed in trickle-down and thought lazy people who sat in drum circles on private property complaining about corporate greed weren't helping.

Amy had a sense that she'd willed herself up from nothing, the inevitable result of grit, market trends, and globalization. She wanted that for everyone—some version of the American dream. She'd sold bonds—for some companies I'd heard of, multinationals, big pharma, a marauding Russian lumber operation hacking down the rain forest, a Chinese oil corporation building private armies in the Niger delta. Then she moved to private equity, to leverage solvent companies into ruin, strip the assets of the businesses she'd targeted, rationalize their labor forces, and shove them off a cliff. It had all worked out beautifully. Sometimes she mentioned stuff in passing, a lavish thing at Lincoln Center or a birthday celebration for Mike's pal, with Coldplay helicoptering in for a fifty-minute set at fifty grand a song plus gas for the copter. The pal was some chemical manufacturer who I could google and hate, whose pet issues were ending corporate taxes and private space exploration. Then I'd stop speaking to her for a few hours, to let her feel my wrath.

She didn't care what I thought, never saw herself as a leech, said she'd only worked in finance as a means to an end, told me about everything she had to put up with, the locker room atmosphere on a trading floor of mostly men who talked as though she weren't there about who they'd like to screw, bosses who summoned her to dinner at strange hours and pinned her against the wall and slobbered on her face, younger guys who worked under her and stopped by her desk to complain about their sweaty balls, commenting on her blouse, height, legs, while she did her darnedest to get along, laugh it off. Got married so they'd stop harassing her at work. Got pregnant so he'd stop harassing her at home.

She thought of herself as a mom now, pious and demure, lonely as a nun, shooing away her staff so she could interact with her children, drive them to school, stopping by the gym for an hour to see Leon, her hot heterosexual trainer, then conference calls and meetings—sending new equipment to a hospital in Senegal, a check to a women's shelter in Croatia—parent-teacher conferences, bedtime stories, nightly parties. She had a former athlete's can-do spirit, a hankering for immediate and tangible results.

There were twenty-four nieces and nephews and more on the way, and tons more over in Ireland. She paid their dental and hospital bills, and had already sent half of them to college. Picked up the tab for her sister's two knee jobs, owned four or five houses of her siblings and cousins, acting as the bank, had the best rate, zero interest, and forgave them any payments they missed. The list of people benefitting from her went on and on.

I couldn't toss Robin for some libertarian wing nut. My wife, whose negligence had nearly wiped out the next generation, whose panty shields always ended up stuck inside the dryer, who'd stayed by my side not three days earlier as we'd listened together when, for whatever reason, the dishwasher made a noise like a goat eating a tin can. Then it suddenly resumed normal operations. At that very moment we'd been sitting at the kitchen table, waiting to register Kaya for fall pre-K at the Unitarian church, staring intently at the screen like we were about to drone somebody's ass in Kabul. A box started blinking, and at the appointed hour, online registration began. Robin clicked the button once and shrieked in agony. With many more applicants than spots, we were given a number in the low three digits. There were tense moments until we got Kaya's slot. After registration was done, we calmly strode around the downstairs of our domicile, secure in our place in the world, her $3,000 preschool being the cheapest around by two grand, most of that money having been painstakingly set aside in our checking account—until I'd blown it earlier today, and then accidentally gave away the bracelet I couldn't afford to someone who already had all the junk in the world.

I didn't think these things in exactly this formulation, although I should have, but I was too wobbly, hot and smeary from too much kissing, a muscular ache in my head from using my tongue in too many directions, my crotch all sticky and stuck to my clothes. What I'd done was horrible and disgusting. Heaven would take note.

I went to the Barn and showered, and tried to forget the whole thing. I shaved in the mirror, my head wedged against the ceiling, then spent an hour on my painting of Chinese factory workers.

The OxyContin left me calm and contemplative and barely able to draw. After retrieving my clothes from the dresser, I crawled backward on my hands and knees, standing slowly, dodging low-hanging beams. I figured I'd seen the last of Amy O'Donnell, that in the morning she'd head back to her dream house, close the gate, and live out her days as a stooge for a right-wing nutcase.

At seven I went back to the flagpole and tried the house. Then I tried Robin's cell. After a dozen attempts I gave up and left a desperate message, begging her to call. I was stunned by the most excruciatingly beautiful sunset, towering, visionary, in pink-and-orange sherbet, and commiserated with other conference-goers over the inconsistency of the signal, rumors of cellular hot spots, outdated local equipment, and different networks not functioning properly because of incoming weather.

TWENTY-TWO

The streetlights had come on. The town looked soft in purple shadows. I rode my bike past the bay at high tide, bonfires along the beach. Bright paintings hung on the walls of a gallery, the noise from a crowd wafting out the door, the balcony above it crammed with guys. I smelled ketchup in the air, burgers on a grill, spilled beer, mussels in garlic, the clean, funky seaweed of the bay. Showered, tanned people smoked along the railing of an outdoor bar. I sensed the collective rhythm and mayhem, the double macchiatos, broken diets, and reckless spending, Mastercard bills one swipe away from disaster, romantic failures and STDs that would trail them for months or years.

The road split at the end of town. I rolled down a quiet street and looked back across the harbor at the old church steeple against a faded blue with flame-tipped clouds, strawberry streaks in Creamsicle light. The air itself was purple.

Over a little bridge, the land narrowed to a reef of dunes and scrub. On the right, the bay was shallow and weedy and flowed out to the sea. On the ocean side, high up on the dunes, were fancy houses with panoramic views. Every year I passed by here and wondered why I didn't make $4 billion flipping media companies.

A vast modern thing, mostly glass, lit up at night like a shopping mall. A Nantucket-style house on steroids, under construction and still growing. A red brick house with tall columns that made it look like a plantation. Were they that much smarter than me? Was their flesh worth that much more? Actually, yes. A slutty-looking Spanish deal with squirting mermaid sculptures, a sprawling colonial with twelve chimneys, a hulking gray stone thing that looked like it could've withstood a bombardment . . .

Behind them, the sun kept falling through a glorious heaven.

The effect of the narcotics had faded into softly lifting waves, as thoughts flitted painlessly by. I had been held by a one-armed bandit who'd stolen my heart. By a lovely Christian housewife, a stranger really, reeking of midlife boredom and an overpowering daily sorrow mediated only by superstition, lower urges, parental terror, and religious mania. In some other world it could've worked.

I wondered if Beanie was asleep and whether Kaya had eaten dinner. If I'd been there, my daughter would now be glued to my lap, tired and sweaty, and I'd carry her around like a sack of flour while I brushed my teeth. Other than her traumatic premature birth, this was maybe the worst thing that had ever happened to her. I pictured her noodle arms and silken shoulder blades, which fluttered under my hands, and imagined the torn-up skin that covered them now. The cut on her hip was the worst of it. A hellish night of reactive co-sleeping lay ahead. If I'd brought them with me, none of this would've happened. We worry our heads off. The dread is universal. Let nothing happen to my kid. Let her be the one to not suffer. It starts off so simply, and you assume you'll be spared.

I came upon a family of deer, silently cropping manicured grass along the edge of the road in front of a fieldstone manor, a mother and two white-speckled fawns, until a silver Range Rover barreled toward us; as they shot into the scrub, the car almost blew me off the road. Between the nutso mansions were some regular houses from a bygone era when middle-class people could still buy land on this beach. Far ahead, where the road dead-ended, surrounded by water on three sides, was a national park where anybody could rent space for trailers or put up tents, and on the other side of the road, the town's tiny airport, a paved runway that cut through the dunes. I rode by places hidden behind a massive hedge or a gate with a glowing security panel, and turned at a big white one that looked like the Getty Museum.

Three valets stood at the end of the driveway with flashlights. I walked my bike because the gravel was too deep to ride on. Sea grasses blew delicately in the breeze. People dressed in white headed back down the driveway, already leaving. I wore a clean plaid shirt and the canvas shorts I'd had on since this morning. I was hoping to make it to Wednesday without doing laundry.

I heard clattering dishes and music and the low rumble of a crowd, and wound through a maze of parked cars, and heard the roar of the ocean a few dunes away. I'd been to this party three years in a row, and last year, at the end of the conference, there was a smaller party for just a few faculty and the director and his wife, up in the pool house, real swanky, and I got invited. A couple of us stayed late and borrowed swimsuits from our hosts, and after they went to bed we made margaritas, and accidentally broke this glass pitcher shaped like a pineapple, and flung ourselves naked from the hot tub into the pool, and someone barfed on the delicate meandering sidewalk that wound through the dunes. I ended up sleeping in one of the maids' empty rooms, and in the morning got blasted in the face by the unobstructed sunrise, and walked out into the day to discover bagels and hot coffee, and cigarette butts floating in the pool.

In the garage at the top of the driveway a caterer had set up his operation, with steel prep tables and waiters in white coats. I said hello to some of the staff I'd met last year or the year before, standing by a golf cart: a young guy with Elvis sideburns and tattooed arms; a big black guy named Clyde, with a walkie-talkie, who'd given me a lift back into town last summer after I'd spent the night; and an old lady named Peggy, with reading glasses hanging down on her bazooms and a worried look on her face, who somehow remembered my name.

"The ice machine broke," she said.

Clyde said, "You bring any ice?" I said no, but he laughed and said, "Oh, we got another machine at the pool." Then he and the lady hopped into the golf cart and sped across the driveway, into a brightly lit hole in the dunes, a tunnel so wide you could drive through it, into a garage full of gardening tools, golf carts, inflatable pool toys, umbrellas, and kayaks. Above that were guest cottages, offices, and a disco. It was their weekend place.

Marty Azamanian had made his money in parking garages but then started buying movie theaters in the eighties, then got into cable TV and radio stations, rolling them up, thanks to deregulation—until he crushed the regional networks and locked down half of North America. And was credited with helping polarize news, and finally succeeded in killing FM radio—he perfected the formula, whittling down the playlist of every Top 40 station to the same five pop tunes, cutting what was left of local coverage, turning a handful of right-wing talk-radio assholes into national icons. Then he went west to conglomerate Hollywood with a pure business plan designed to hedge against failures and helped birth hideous blockbuster sequels like *Karate Kid III* and the *Robo-Cop* franchise.

Over the years I'd met his tennis buddies and monied pals, who liked to pretend the house was no big deal. Marty's ex-wife was an actress, and there were two kids from his first marriage. He also had a younger boy and girl with Bruce, his partner, through a surrogate, after he came out of the closet. Books had been written about him. He was small and ruthless and had grown up in a housing project in the Bronx, exactly where my dad grew up, on Fordham Road. I figured that out the first time we met.

Then he got into the music business, bought a football team and a two-million-acre game park in Africa, synergizing with his media monolith, diluting the brand, triggering a shareholder revolt, sucking out a billion dollars in dividends before bankrupting or flipping whatever was left. A lawyer of Marty's was found in a parking garage with a shotgun between his knees and his teeth blown out the back of his head, and there were years spent fighting the FBI and the SEC, and he was also sometimes mentioned by name as the reason you can't find any rhinos alive in Zimbabwe.

Anyway, it was Marty's partner, Bruce, who really cared about the arts, a patron of the arts who, along with the wife of the local congressman, had thought up the conference fifteen years ago. Bruce was a short, thin, painfully shy man, a lawyer and aspiring memoirist who, thanks to Carl, was given a slot every year to read from his work in progress. I attended those readings whenever possible. His descriptions of fruit and nature and sailing the Aegean were dry and stiff—they put me in a coma—but the stories of his childhood in Kentucky, the scenes of his grandma's edema and the guy who beat his mother with a fan belt, the child abuse, alcoholism, and violence of the rest of his wacky family really grabbed me.

At the edge of the gravel I waited in line at a card table. A kid checked me off on his clipboard and handed me a name tag. Behind the table, neatly shorn, in a slim gray suit, Bruce greeted each guest by name. Propped on a chair next to the kid was a metal-framed poster that I recognized, because the drawing on it was mine, of a girl under an umbrella, typing on her laptop on the sand; I'd donated it some years ago, said they could use it, then just forgot. The poster advertised a fundraiser for the conference—this fundraiser—the girl bent over the keyboard, adorably lost in thought, water bottle, beach umbrella, bag of chips, different shady-looking men's faces rising in thought bubbles from her screen.

I thought the drawing was not so bad after all. The line work was cold and clean. The skin on the girl's face was immaculate, but beneath a superficial beauty bubbled a percolation of lust. It seemed now not so much that somebody in the office had run out of ideas and found my doodle that had been lying in a drawer for three years and stuck it on a poster but that I still had talent, it wasn't over yet for me, things would turn around. If I put my mind to it, I could do anything. I could write my way out of this mess. I'll wake up every day at four A.M., I told myself, and do the new comic while I'm fresh and full of energy, do my magazine assignments at night, although God knows I'd tried that before and it never worked. I was too tired. Anyway, somehow I'd pull it off. The new piece would demonstrate a maturity and depth and reservoirs of fury. I'd make something so heinous and explosive that my wife would cut my nuts off, my children would pretend I was dead, society would shun me, and I'd move to Croatia and live in a kind of fantastic isolation, burning with remorse and indignation.

When it was my turn, I stepped forward and bent at the waist to receive Bruce's hug. He thanked me for coming, so sincerely, "and for this," the poster, practically weeping with gratitude, and remembered my kids, with a smile that was his usual sad, suffering face, a mix of real pain and boredom. I asked about his kids, the younger boy and girl, who sometimes played in the pool during the party, and the two older ones from Marty's first marriage, the teenage daughter who sometimes passed through the crowd, fresh from some orgy on Nantucket, looking drunk and windburned, sometimes arguing loudly with Bruce over lost privileges or demanding the whereabouts of her father. And the son, who transferred to a new college every year, and wrecked his car last winter and spent a month in a body cast.

Seeing Bruce again, knowing him as I did, as the sane one, hearing the gossip about his struggle to protect the kids from Marty and the mother, gave me a sense of unstoppable organic parental hell. Over the winter I'd heard from Carl that the older son was doing better, taking a break from school. When I asked Bruce how he was—the kid's name was Max—he smiled so that a tooth hooked on his lower lip, and hung his head and thanked me, and I thought that now he really would cry. He said Max was spending the summer at the house but had gone out to meet friends. Bruce was nice. That made it worse.

Despite their billions, he was a small, stooped, fragile-looking person, and for that reason easier to relate to, and according to his memoir had been molested as a child by the old lady who lived upstairs, although when his mom died he moved back home to protect his younger siblings. See? He was a good person. He was the one looking out for those kids, and tried his best, although he was failing miserably, publicly, the outcome somehow inevitable. He went to all the plays and slide talks and openings over at the conference, and was genuinely admiring of everyone on the faculty, envious of any artistic gift, and supposedly bank-rolled most of our salaries, and greased the more famous people to come teach. I got twenty-five hundred bucks a year plus travel expenses. I needed a raise.

On the dimly lit path to the pool I passed a waiter and took a drink from his tray. It tasted like cough drops and lighter fluid. When you came here you had to be careful not to guzzle. You had to fight the urge. You felt drawn to the scene, to the need to blend in, to become what it asked of you. The patio was lit with flickering hurricane lamps, and I stood in front of the bar over-looking the pool, next to Dennis Fleigel, beside a table of cheeses and prosciutto, and a real wooden rowboat filled with ice, with oysters spread on the ice, and a man behind the boat, in a yellow fisherman's bib, shucking the oysters with a knife.

I recalled the events of the past few hours. Making love to Amy had cost me three thousand bucks, fifty dollars a minute. I could say I'd lost my wallet, call my bank and dispute the charge, which would temporarily restore our balance but leave me open to credit card fraud. Although the clerk had never asked for my ID, which meant that if the bank decided to investigate, I might win. It was safer to lie to Robin. On Tuesday, Carl would pay me. On the twenty-eighth, my salary would come through from the magazine.

In the pool house they had stacks of clean towels and a popcorn machine like at a movie theater. Dennis pointed out upgrades they'd made since last summer, the patio wider and longer on this side, stone benches with padded seats around a new stainless-steel outdoor kitchen, some guy in a chef's hat stepping around it like a busy idiot. Warren Schultz, who ran the local theater troupe, banged out show tunes on a piano. Above him, moths bumped into the glass globe of a kerosene lantern. People joined in, but Warren's voice was louder. Below the patio were gardens, a tennis court, and then the ocean. The breeze passed through me like a spirit. When the waiter passed by, I took another drink.

The house sat out on its own promontory, a little farther out than the houses downwind of us, which were huge and lit up like the *Titanic,* but not as nice. The sight of these digs always made my jaw fall open, although really I was fine until I walked up the driveway and started feeling bad about my own house, a small red bungalow with no shutters that our real estate agent had described as "charmless." A ball of shame got lodged in my throat anytime I came here, I had trouble swallowing and kept picking at the thought, like if somebody gave me a bomb right now I'd drop it on that shitbox with my family inside: that kind of shame. This display of overkill sparked a rage of envy and extra shame for my awe, which I couldn't control and was maybe why when I came here I drank like I did, or maybe because it was so beautiful—I drank to kill off whatever neurons grew from that brain activity, but I could feel it in the energy of people around us, the size and power of the place strengthening us as we grew to fill the scale of it, the rush of that mistaken idea, excitement and futility battling it out, making me dizzy.

"It's a nice breeze."

"Every time you inhale," Dennis said, "you owe Azamanian sixty bucks." He had what appeared to be a terrible sunburn.

"And what is this one again?" I asked.

"Negroni, sir."

"And what's this?"

"Boulevardier," the bartender answered.

"What's the difference?" I heard my own loud voice barking in my ear. The bartender poured me one of each. Tabitha clinked my two glasses with hers and said it was making her cross-eyed.

Dennis turned to her, horrified and amazed. "You sold a TV show?" He had a redhead's freakish freckled sunburn.

"Yeah, we got a pickup, or whatever it's called." The show would be based on some parts of her first book, about her crazy mother and her impoverished childhood in a Reno trailer park, and her second book, about the incest and her wild teens and twenties.

"I've got two hundred and fifty pages done on my book," Dennis said, "and two hundred pages to go and two more years. I'm on track." If he kept talking, he could keep his insecurities at bay, so he started lecturing us on his current subject, Coco Chanel, and the failings of lesser biographies, which his book would hopefully trounce.

Heather Hinman joined us. She taught in the English Department at a big university, and liked to complain that her former life as a bartender had paid twice as much and the drinks were free. She'd gone swimming in the bay and said it was beautiful, but warned us about sharp stuff you could cut your foot on where they anchored the boats.

Ilana Zimmer had gone in the ocean and said it was rough. "Lifeguards were running out in pairs—one had the buoy around his neck and the other had the bucket of rope." As if to back up her story, her hair was still wet. Frederick Stugatz stood there, dry as a bone, staring at the side of Ilana's head. Her voice was deep and smoky and reminded me of her one hit song from twenty-five years ago. I heard it on the radio about once a year, and every time, I imagined her cashing a royalty check for fifty-eight cents. She and Frederick made an effort to circulate so people wouldn't think they were having an affair, but then she told us how her son had flunked tenth-grade biology, so he'd enrolled in summer school, but when she'd called home earlier tonight she'd heard the Xbox in the background, her husband didn't care, and Frederick looked at her like he was about to have a stroke.

"That's what happens," he said, "when you drop everything to move to Bologna for six weeks." Ilana stiffened and stared ahead.

All the jealousy and heartache and secret negotiations, all for a hidden spooge in the dark. I'd done it, I'd popped a stranger, it was time to get to work, to use my debasing experiences for the purposes of artistic advancement, in a half-true story imbued with the mysterious behavior of actual humans, their bad decisions and perverse yearnings that somehow delight us. I'd remember this night, bathed in kerosene lamplight, in the silky air.

And I'd return again to the vision of Amy, lying with her back to me, spooning, then moving my arm so her head rested on my chest, then facing her, our lips pressing, in what would become our best and favorite way, with her pale eyes that drew me in but told me nothing, her sorrow shifting gradually to something soulful, as she set aside those baffling values for this yielding, as I pushed until the softness resisted, as she craned her head up, eyes closed. I missed her. We hadn't said goodbye.

I ate salted barbecued shrimp, peeling their jackets, and rinsed my hands in the swimming pool. The narcotics had been vaguely therapeutic, but now I was totally bombed. My confidence raged. I would immerse myself in comics, get interested in cross-hatching again, bang out half a page a day, and sell foreign rights in twenty-nine countries. I'd make millions.

I met a real estate agent named Happy Longworthy, who told me what the taxes were on a beachfront estate on sixteen acres. She introduced me to a little toad who owned the largest private collection of Greco-Roman statuary on earth, which he kept inside his house in eastern Tennessee. He invited me to come see it. Roberta explained that while finishing her film on corrupt black mayors of major American cities, she'd started her new project—

a documentary about teenage hooker gangs of inner-city Phila-
delphia. The toad from Tennessee looked enthralled. Happy
clutched her necklace. I tried to consider myself above all that,
groveling before our donors, with their threat of mind-blowing
patronage, them having a lot of it, me not having any. I tried not
to care while slobbering all over everything. Waiters kept pushing
through with trays. In the dim light, it was hard to see what they
were passing around.

"I don't know what I'm eating."

"It's sashimi," Heather said. Unless you forcibly stopped them,
the waiters handed you another drink. Some idiot fell or jumped
into the pool in his clothes. It was time for dinner.

In the bathroom I had to hold on to a wooden post to keep
from falling down. The pool house had been built to resemble a
rustic Malaysian jungle hut, made from exotic hardwoods, with
an overgrown sod roof you could supposedly eat. I washed my
hands in front of the bathroom mirror and noticed a drunk,
middle-aged fraud whose moment of notoriety and one pub-
lished book had faded years ago. Anyway, who was I kidding? I
couldn't use any of this stuff. Screwing a married lady, ridiculing
her, dumping all over my wife and kids? I'd cause irreparable pain
and harm. The fiction would collapse under the weight of the
facts. And when was I supposed to get it done? Between diapers,
boo-boos, and screaming fights? And scraping melted cheese off
the wall? And waking up in the night when I felt like dying? As it
was, I barely made it through my days. Back when I'd had no one
to worry about and only bare-bones freelance gigs, a thirty-two-
page comic had taken six months, eighteen hours a day, working
like a galley slave. The last issue, seven years ago, had nearly killed
me. I'd be in a nursing home by the time this thing was done.
Someone sat in the stall behind me, grunting loudly on the toilet
like my father.

The sinks were giant wooden tree knots carved into beautiful bowls. There were stacks of crisp white hand towels. I tucked in my shirt and found, in the pocket of my shorts, a Mercedes-Benz key, which I'd grabbed to stop Amy from driving home earlier and had forgotten to give back, and started cursing. Although if I had the key, she couldn't exactly leave. Marty Azamanian flushed and came out of the stall behind me and went to the other sink. He wore a straw cowboy hat and jeans and a Hawaiian shirt.

"What's the matter with you?" he asked.

From the other pocket of my shorts I pulled out two small, sharp, pointy objects, which I held up close and examined. A pair of diamond studs, Amy's earrings.

"Shit. Fuck."

"You got a problem?"

"Me?" I might've stolen them on purpose. "No."

He placed his cowboy hat on the counter between us. "Doing okay?" He checked himself out in the mirror.

"Yeah, thanks for having me. Doing well. Keeping busy."

"Well, I'm sixty-five years old and I look like hell and I'm growing a pair of titties."

I couldn't do it, couldn't shoot the shit with a billionaire. And anyway, he was impossible to talk to, and it felt like punishment to have to thank him for something I didn't want and hadn't asked for and couldn't repay.

He touched the bags under his eyes. "I'm starting to look like my ma."

On that stretch of Fordham Road, black and Italian and Chinese gangs roamed, and if you wandered onto the wrong block you'd better be ready to run for your life. The first time we met I took a wild guess, then told him my dad had lived across from the big playground. Maybe that was why he liked talking to me, and why I never fell for his ghetto dialect and streetwise baloney. I couldn't stand it, the horrible everythingness of his wealth, the crushing blackness and blindness of it, sucking me in, the museum-quality house and cowering domestic partner and fucked-up kids, the thinness of his party costume as one more way to combat the nothingness. I thanked him again, and hoped I wouldn't see him for the rest of the night.

My father also got himself out of the Bronx, and worked to make a better life for his kids, killing himself to get where he was going, blaming us, my mother, brother, and me, not ashamed, as if the whole human race walked around that way. He'd commuted to the city, and every other week to the insurance company's home office in Hartford, and on the weekends he'd used sports and yard work to numb himself, and in that state was often warm and loving, sometimes silly, comic, athletic, and enthusiastic. A health nut, highly intuitive, hypersensitive, and emotionally unresolved. Unconscious, sarcastic, demanding, at times physically intimidating, threatening, destructive, and terrifying, and unable to communicate on an intimate level. He worried he'd end up broke again and back in his miserable childhood. He saw himself as a sellout and eventually decided, when he couldn't stand it anymore, to retire at sixty-two, then ran out of money.

It would be an exaggeration to say they were broke. Their house was paid for. They were fine as long as they didn't buy anything else. They had groceries. They had vitamins. They couldn't afford new clothes or dinner in a restaurant. They didn't buy gifts for each other or anyone else. Their bills were sometimes a problem. A fender-bender deductible last year had sent shock waves through their balance sheet. No vacations, no trips. If you needed him, my father could be found talking to himself in his asparagus patch, in his filthy gardening clothes and a hernia belt, or on the lookout for expenses they could trim. He was in some ways better suited to it because he'd been poor as a kid, although in other ways it was worse for him because his modest success had been his identity. He claimed he wasn't angry, just sick of it all—not depressed, but in his retirement he didn't need human contact, except for my mom, and had become very deep, into nature, and spent fantastic amounts of energy building his woodpile, sweating over it, sawing and chopping and crying into it because half their savings had vanished in the financial crisis and he worried about paying their heating bills. Since the meltdown, he kept their savings in cash and municipal bonds, missing the stock market rebound, and every time he opened his bank statement he thought about killing someone.

People were already taking their seats. On the lower patio there were three long, narrow tables, maybe thirty places at each, and torches at intervals on bamboo poles. Seating not assigned, food on the table, large white steaming ceramic tureens every few seats with boiled lobsters, and small dishes between us of corn pudding and balsamic-vinegar-drenched diced tomatoes. Hunks of Brie, cakes of veiny blue cheese, crusty bread, and purple orchid petals strewn around. I started eating everything but the flowers.

Dennis sat beside me, sweating from his sunburn. He really was cooked, couldn't bend his arms without gasping, kept patting his forehead with a cocktail napkin. The napkins had been printed up for this event; on each of them was the year and the name of the conference, with a tiny reproduction of my drawing of the girl, like a logo, typing on her laptop under an umbrella. A has-been, a never-was, but my drawing had some iconic power.

Roberta sat by Dennis, and Happy and the Tennessee toad sat across from us. The toad wore a ring that might've been from some plundered civilization. Vicky Capodanno appeared, scraping her chair on the patio, and sat on the other side of me, spilling her drink on both of us. She raised her lighter, with the cigarette backward, staring into the wrong end. She liked to follow me around when she got drunk, with the understanding that she was helpless and alone, couldn't take care of anyone else, too fucked up to have her own kids, although a little obsessed with mine, sending them origami swans and disturbing tween novels they wouldn't be able to read for ten years. When I looked again, the filter was on fire and she was trying to take a drag. Still, I was subordinate to her fame and biennials and whatnot, works in major permanent collections like MoMA and the Tate.

"Hey, pal," I said, hitting her on the shoulder. "I love you."

"Hey, pal," she said, and tipped her chin up and winked, sucking hard, blowing smoke. "I know who you love."

I ignored her. People around me futzed and chattered as

though they'd never seen these things before, as though these lobsters had just hopped off a spaceship from Mars. I ripped out the tail with my hands and ate it with butter running down my arms. A guy named Conrad gallantly wielded his nutcracker, shattering the claws for the women around him, telling us about a recent trip to Finland, including a special someone he'd met named Kaspar: "Poet, musician, diplomat, doctor, and I said to myself, 'If this guy's queer, I'll cream my mushrooms.'"

Everybody laughed. I cracked a claw. It shot a stream of warm lobster juice right into my face. A waiter went around, pouring white and rosé. I got both. I took a second lobster and went at it like a badger. At the center table, Carl stood and gave the fundraising speech. I'd already heard it eighty-five times. All around me, they went through stacks of napkins, wiping their faces, sopping up puddles on the table, ruining my drawing, leaving shredded piles of what looked like oatmeal.

Reports funneled down from the other end of the table that Burt had tripped on the sandstone path. There was a head wound and blood. Edna was with him. The party kept going. Paramedics arrived from the wrong side of the pool and had to pass by us to reach him. I flagged the sommelier, who poured me a Riesling.

Vicky put her cigarette out in the middle of her lobster and yawned and winked at me. Trudy Miller warned us not to eat the green goop because of the sewage in the bay. Winston Doyoyo, an old man from South Africa who happened to be a Nobel Prize–winning playwright, emptied the contents of his mouth into a napkin. Everywhere I looked, people were doing disgusting things to my drawing. Trudy said that at her daughter's high school prom, girls were allowed to bend over no more than ninety degrees on the dance floor while pressing their asses against the crotch of a boy's pants. More than ninety degrees was forbidden. Tabitha said her daughter's orthodontia cost six grand.

The wind came up and flung tablecloths and silverware, coffee cups and a tray of cookies onto the ground. They discussed their kids' soccer injuries, calculus, piano lessons, and abortions. I'd have to raise Kaya and Beanie and launch them out into the world. It hadn't even started yet, and then they'd leave and I'd miss them forever and they'd hate me like kids do.

Whatsherface, Bonnie Raitt, got up and played a song, kissing Marty's ass when she finished, telling us how he'd revolutionized the music industry. Marty took the microphone and told her to sit down, and made us clap for his boyfriend for founding the conference. Bruce stood and in his trembling voice thanked the faculty: "For the blessing you give our strident struggle to voice the silence clotting our throats."

"I wish I were back in the dorm," Tabitha said, "reading my students' garbage."

"Do you know how much a billion is?" Dennis said. "It's a thousand million." He'd gotten to the party early, so Bruce had taken him for a spin around the main house. "'I designed this kitchen myself. I designed this ocean myself.' Give me a break, you fucking phony."

The house tour had wounded him. I knew how he felt. The place was so gorgeous you wanted to start ripping planks out of the floor with your teeth. Maybe you'd dreamed of royalty as a child, or you'd fantasized about living in a castle or flying in a private plane, but either way it triggered what you never got or gave up on long ago, something sad and personal, and it was subconsciously exhausting. The house was designed to make you feel awful.

Summer will end, fall will come, then winter, when everything dies. Back home, I'll be doodling in my basement, recalling this lobster feast in the silken air in kerosene lamplight, and the beautiful glimpses of Amy from earlier, our endless afternoon, spliced, assembled, and preserved. I'd been fine until now, but the hours had passed. The further I drifted from her, from our moments, the harder it was to live. But unless she'd hired a tow truck, her car was still here, and so was she.

"Cartoonists must enjoy doing illustration," Heather said, holding a now decomposing napkin that featured my work.

"Sure," I said. "If they want to eat." It was one of those polite, slightly forced, heartfelt exchanges we had when we were stuck together at a fancy thing. Heather said good illustration had certain intangibles. I more or less agreed. The piece I'd started that afternoon would accompany an investigation of suicides at a cellphone factory in China, with 430,000 employees crammed into a dozen giant buildings over a square mile, on three shifts, twenty-five cafeterias running twenty-four hours a day. One guy killed himself after a thirty-two-hour shift, and another one jumped off the roof after working 112 straight days. Average age of suicide: nineteen. Labor cost to build a cellphone: eighty cents. Try drawing that.

Vicky slumped in her chair, eyes narrowed, head back. I winked at her. We were communicating nonverbally about artistic integrity. Then I realized she'd passed out.

Frederick and Ilana slipped behind our table, ducking torches, passing through the crowd as though they were invisible, or we were brain-dead, taking the path out to the beach. Waiters started clearing the other end of the table. The swimming pool was lit but empty. Conrad and some Scottish guy were naked in the hot tub, trying to work the Jacuzzi buttons. A fine rain had begun. Two women from the Theater Department climbed out, bodies steaming, and flicked their hair. Towels sat stacked in the rain. When I looked back again, Frederick and Ilana were gone.

Strong winds came up, spitting rain, then sand, blowing sparks and smoke from the outdoor fireplace, which led to last call and a crowd at the bar. Roberta waved her drink, talking about a kid named Skittles, who lived in his grandmother's crack house and had sex in a McDonald's men's room. Happy Longworthy rubbed her necklace. I followed the footlights off the patio, toward my bicycle.

"Let me ask you a question," Tom McLaughlin said, stumbling. "Will you have a drink with me?" The later it got, the more he drawled like a Texan. I kept walking, so he turned to the sleepy, tulip-shaped intern, one of the interns who'd stolen water from our dugout, and asked her.

"No thanks," she said. "I've had enough."

"These are both my drinks," he said, banging into her. "But this one's younger, so I'm treating it more gently."

Winston Doyoyo sometimes snuck out at night without his wife or assistant and had to be dragged off women who'd agreed to dance with him, even though he was almost eighty. Carl liked to walk through the tent at mealtimes and pull on women's ponytails. Toward the end of the conference, he sometimes threw his tongue down somebody's throat without asking. Ilana and Frederick used the conference as some kind of bidet for them to wash their private parts in, before heading back to their loved ones. The staff was cleaning up.

"Hey, Clyde," I said. Empty bottles, cigarette butts, an abandoned dress, and high-heeled shoes looked like the remnants of a Roman orgy. "How's that ice machine?"

He grabbed the pool house doors and slid them closed. "Time to go home!"

TWENTY-THREE

Weaving in the dark in the rain through the west end of town, I saw the neon sign for the taffy store and passed bars blaring house music and a tea dance raging around the swimming pool of a one-story motel. A garbage bag of ice swung and bounced against my leg as I pedaled. I dodged pedestrians, the street jammed with sweaty dancers three deep in front of the pizza place. I reached campus and drank rainwater off my lips as grass came up under the tires and I fell over and lay there, gasping.

Amy's dorm was locked. I banged on the door. I'd brought this ice for her. Someone opened a window and told me what to go do to myself. I responded with vicious threats and disgusting obscenities. This scene was playing out as yet another storied episode in an epic affair, big, with obstacles we fought through to be together. Someone came around the corner with a walkie-talkie and said he was calling the police, but it was just the kid who played ukulele at open mike. He asked if I knew where I lived.

Up the hill past the windmill I dumped the ice onto the grass. The old Barn sagged along its roofline, under the cupola and weather vane. I hefted my bike to the third-story landing, dropping it and tripping over it on my way in the door. Toilet and shower stall to the left, kitchen straight ahead, grease stains on the wall, dishes in the sink, dented pots, and a flimsy, unpainted partition wall that blocked off a place to hang clothes. It looked like the inside of the Unabomber's shed. A metal table with my teaching notes and papers and four chairs that crouched like spiders beneath the windowed cupola, which even now shed grayish light. And in the light, some half-finished sketches of Chinese factory workers. When they couldn't escape the system or work any harder inside it, they simply took themselves to the roof of the factory and threw themselves off.

I emptied my pockets, banging into furniture, hitting my head on the ceiling, and tried to take off my shoes without falling over. I'd given up everything for cartooning, and for that alone I deserved to die. Then I gave up on cartooning. I suffered psychic grief, low output, self-mockery, obscurity, isolation, depression, all of the deprivations of artistic sacrifice—without making any art. Marriage and parenthood provided a kind of second life, a new beginning, for some failed artists. Certain men thrived in it. If these past years had been any indication, I never would.

In the eaves of the apartment, the roof met the floor. Deep in the pinched area, behind the sofa, a wooden folding ladder had been pitched longways, tall enough to allow someone to change a lightbulb up in the peak. I squinted at the shape of it in the dark. I thought I could use it to reach the antique rafters in order to hang myself.

Did I want to hang myself because I was a lonely, drunken whore? Or because I couldn't figure out how to make a comic about it, to find meaning in it? I didn't know.

I went to my luggage for a belt, crying a little, sick of it all, of cowering, groveling, slaving away for pennies on scut work while dysfunctional tycoons complained about their man titties, or hoarded priceless antiquities, or told my art director what to do with me. Billionaires decided for me, told me where to go, what to think and draw, they underwrote the conference that brought me here to this hotbed of debauchery that fired my imagination and damaged my soul.

I was tired. Or it was the booze and narcotics, and the billion-dollar pay cut Amy would have to accept to be with me. I wanted to sleep. How would it feel to be gone? Had the world been missing me before I was born? Hasn't everyone at one time or another imagined himself gone? How sad would my kids be? This body held and protected them, these arms lifted them in the night, this voice came to them even in the womb. A healthy man who played with them on the floor, he went away and never came home. The children weren't told how he died, and his passing left an empty place, a smaller, meaner, sadder life. I wanted to believe I was worth more dead than alive, but it was about the same, which was nothing.

TWENTY-FOUR

Robin's brother died in a rainstorm coming back from a Police concert his senior year in high school. Five other people, including the driver, who'd fallen asleep, walked away from the wreck. He'd played the violin better than Robin did, had long, elegant hands, aced AP physics, was the editor of his high school yearbook. He was nice. He'd been admitted to an Ivy League school for the fall, and had already written back to say he was coming. When their parents had split, a year or two earlier, he'd accepted the sudden promotion to man of the house and stopped bullying his little sisters, seemingly overnight. It was a Saturday in early spring, and later that night, their family doctor went down to the morgue to identify the body. In the morning, a neighborhood boy knocked on the door, and brought them flowers, and swept their steps, and raked their yard.

And who can say what happens to a family when events occur

beyond their control? If this could happen, what was to stop anything else from happening? If this could happen, why did it happen only to them? And how would it be for you, the younger sibling, next in line behind the boy with nice hands, if you didn't have his smile or easygoing charm? For the rest of your life, whatever you accomplished, you'd have to wonder—or you didn't wonder, but everyone else did—what if he'd lived? It would drive you insane.

We met twelve years later. She didn't talk about it. The driver was still a friend of the family's. He sent them cards at Christmas: "All best wishes." What did he want? What did any of it mean? She dealt with Eddie's death by forgetting him and putting it out of her mind.

After her dad moved out, after her brother was killed, after her trip to France with her sister and the dad's new Turkish floozy, she came home to find a student of massage therapy in Eddie's bedroom. Thanks to her dad's lawyer, her mom had to take in boarders for extra cash. She went to her dad's house on weekends, and sometimes snuck out at night, unchaperoned, fourteen years old, in a green suede miniskirt and purple cowboy boots. And while her sister went to live in a psych unit for eating disorders and their mom accompanied her there, Robin camped out at her father's, and got arrested for shoplifting, and borrowed his keys, and totaled his Jeep. She had rock 'n' roll predilections, and more than once she had to be picked up by bouncers and carried out and deposited on the sidewalk. She was tough, or the family traumas did it, inoculated her against fear, hesitation, whatever. She figured she'd be dead by age thirty.

In high school she loved a lot of skinny boys with curly brown hair who were roughly Eddie's height. She did it on staircases and in tree houses and hammocks and swimming pools and on the hoods of cars. She went to a big university, then switched to an all-girls college, then dropped out. At her father's urging, she attended some kind of archaeological summer camp, in Colorado, set among beautiful Native American ruins, and worked on a film there, or assisted some visiting TV crew, and thought this might be an interesting way to make a living.

Five years later she moved into our group house in Hampden. I was cocky and terrified and twenty-nine, working as an art director at an ad agency with forty employees and a monthly nut of a half million dollars. I ran focus groups of homeless men as they discussed their favorite fast food sandwiches. I designed billboards to trick poor people into getting on a bus to throw away their money at a casino in Atlantic City. Eric had founded the agency but now spent most days in his office screaming at Republicans on TV. In lean times he'd call in whoever it was and hand them the benefits folder, then fire them and let them out the side door. We lived under the constant threat of annihilation.

Robin and I started dating, although I hadn't loved anyone with a straight face for any sustained period except for family dogs, and wasn't too sure what I thought. I thought many things—I thought she was pretty nice, and that I was pretty smart. During our first winter together, the symptoms of her concussion gradually faded. I was so relieved to have found someone. And yet, even an idiot could see this was mostly lust. For a long time I'd just wanted to kiss her, and thought that would be enough, and then I wanted to screw her three hundred times and be done with it.

There was nothing weird or nasty about it. It wasn't new, although it wasn't old, either. It worked every way we tried it; it was amazingly filthy yet absolutely clean. I thought she was powerless to see this kind of doubleness and subterfuge; I thought she was weirdly innocent or blindly trusting, and vulnerable to this kind of deceit. Maybe she didn't have the skill to identify a swindler like me. Her trust left me feeling mortified, and somehow responsible for her, and then miserably stuck. I loved her, in defiance of the sniggering little joker I pretended to be.

Complicating the problem of our personal life was another small detail. I was having my moment. What had begun in a free local alternative paper now ran in syndication in several other college-town papers. My ego ballooned. Within a year of our getting engaged, I'd signed on to do my own freestanding comic. The writing overwhelmed me. For a single twenty-four-page issue, the artwork alone was equivalent to a year's worth of strips. I ditched my job and drained my savings, which left me shaky and nocturnal and chained to my drawing table, which, as you can imagine, made me a real joy to live with.

By then Robin had spent almost two years writing puppet dialogue in Spanish and English and was slowly going nuts. We were still living in Baltimore, in a small beige house in Lauraville that cost almost nothing, with solid oak six-panel doors, louvered transom windows, a claw-foot tub, blah blah, overlooking a massive cemetery that had been featured in *Homicide* and *The Wire*. Seventeen minutes from the Inner Harbor, ten minutes from the interstate, with a new Giant supermarket, a car wash, a Korean barbecue, an AutoZone, and an all-black elementary school under heavy renovation. And sometimes guys standing on the corner with their pants sagging down, selling drugs into car windows and yelling, "You look at me? Keep driving, faggot!" In our own small yard, under big old shade trees, maples and oaks, there were flower beds of irises that smelled like root beer, and a long row of peonies, big white ones flecked with pink.

Robin had a beautiful soul and was sensitive and guarded and jaded and tough, and like any young soulful sensitive person who'd suffered unimaginable pain at the loss of her brother, who'd withstood the family breakup and her own temporary brain trauma, she wanted someone who understood her pain. But she was so fucking pretty, and had a lovely healthy body, and I was so pleased with the fact that she gave herself to me that it pained me. So instead of the soul mate she'd been promised, she got some clod scheming for ways to shove it in her.

The tension dissipated at breakfast, and crept back in at night. She put so much energy toward holding me off, trying to keep herself together, keep to her side of the bed, to keep me from climbing her like a tree frog. I had a beautiful fiancée and I should've been happy, I should've been skipping through rain puddles, celebrating our uncommon love. But love like that doesn't exist on this planet, which somebody forgot to tell me, and then she poked me in the eye in her sleep, and in her nightmares sometimes yelped or moaned, and gouged me with her toenails, and stole all the blankets, and scratched around for pills every morning, and lied to me about finishing the milk, which I thought was nuts, so I wrote it down, and used it in the comic that I happened to be drawing, which only made things worse. To get even with me, she shut me out. And so, to get back at her, I kept writing her into my stories, twisting things she'd said and done, diminishing her, taking our private moments out of context, to frame and punish her.

I'd been conducting these kinds of experiments for years, leaning on details of my personal life, trying to represent the truth, to give form to this confusion, wondering how close I could cut it, worrying how the people involved might react. I didn't enjoy hurting their feelings. If I could've figured out another way to do it, I would've. Certain friends spooked easily and felt threatened by my borrowed or poorly disguised representations, or harbored some innate persecution complex, and became chiding, distant, or hostile, although the ones I'd intentionally set out to unnerve or unmask either failed to get the hint, or tolerated it well, or felt proud to have inspired me. Such are the pitfalls of autobio cartooning.

My roommate Nedd eventually stopped speaking to me, because of injurious depictions of him in cartoon form. My friend Annie unwittingly contributed to the making of the character Anna Boringstein, a bulimic communications flack who just happened to work for the mayor. My good friend Rishi was a tolerant and forgiving guy, but I made too many jokes at his expense, and although our friendship might've fallen apart anyway, it ended forever when he took a job in New York. We'd lived together for years, and worked at the same agency. I resented him for leaving. I miss him even now. In the end, I couldn't face these people out of shame.

During our first year together, I didn't write about Robin at all. But in order to meet the demands of the longer, more burdensome periodical, I put the weekly strip on terminal hiatus, and turned away from themes of twentysomething agitation and incipient adult ennui and toward a world I could reach out and touch, that of a young couple on the marriage track. From sheer fatigue I quit massaging the truth and began dumping in wholesale identifiable scenes and verbatim conversations, which is partly how my comic evolved into something less fractured and more novelistic, but maybe also why I eventually ran out of material. Is it any wonder that after a short while of living with me, she hopped a flight to Managua?

Robin would be gone for weeks at a time, covering a massive piece of the planet, natural disasters and geopolitical events. At first, anyway, she was trying to figure out the rules of journalism. She wanted to get up close, to get ratings, to push advertisers until they flinched. If some butcher went around Lima decapitating children, putting their heads on pikes, she had to shoot it, she had to give her work that feeling of proximity to danger. As a kid, she'd liked it loud, liked to rock, went right up to the band on-stage, stood beside the speaker and got blown around.

She met Danny Katavolos at Telemundo, and together they traveled across most of the Western Hemisphere, before they both quit news and happened to end up at the Nature Channel, first Danny, then Robin, a year later.

She'd come home in the middle of the night, her hair smelling like cigarettes, banging her suitcase through the door, waking me, complaining that her pants were too tight, pacing around the bedroom, stripping, yanking her suitcase open, talking loud and ignoring me, turning on lights, trying on clothes for work the next day.

They were driving from Medellín to Cartagena, a terrible idea even by crazy standards, and approached a roadblock manned by paramilitary troops. Danny was in the backseat, and their pot-head cameraman panicked at the wheel, and the three of them started fighting about their equipment, which pieces to offer up first, which ones they might later exchange for ransom, and then they ran out of gas. Or got a flat tire, I forget. I liked her stories of drug lords, Sinaloa death squads, kidnapping, extortion. I was a good listener. She came home spooked but so intensely alive. There were close calls and bad things that weakened her resolve, until she started saying no to Haiti, not worth it, not going to that part of Mexico again, either. "I can't be killed," she'd say, "for a five-minute story about bird migration."

She'd crawl into bed, too tired to eat the dinner I'd left out, had to get up early to cut bulk footage off the satellite feed and edit the package for seven A.M. Or she undressed at the foot of the bed, ignoring me as she pulled the blouse up over her head, sliding her skirt down her legs as I lay there; it was night, I'd been asleep. Absentmindedly she flipped through her closet, snipped a long string from the armpit of her blouse, elbows out, telling me about some cartel body count, how the killers went into a school and dragged students out and shot them, she got the footage, the bureau was pleased. Robin was brave, and I admired that. I assumed that, at the very least, she'd be killed. I think she hoped she would be.

An old friend of hers, a Venezuelan journalist, got shot in the face in Quito. Other friends had heart attacks, gained a hundred pounds, or took a job writing speeches for a hospital in Cincinnati and never went back to Latin America.

It was a riot inside a women's prison in Brazil that finally finished her off: murdered guards, the building in flames. Or maybe it was the town that was buried under a mudslide, or the time she rented a single-engine airplane to take her crew three hours across the dark ocean, to do a piece about an oil rig burning off the coast of Guayaquil. And stared out the window before take-off as the man on the runway waved his arms at the pilot, pointed at the landing gear on their aircraft, and yelled, "You're over-loaded!" The pilot ignored him, waved goodbye, and gunned it. The man on the ground crew stepped back and made the sign of the cross, and then the pilot made the sign of the cross too as Robin sat there, silent, and the plane barely cleared the tops of trees and headed out to sea and couldn't get any higher, buzzing a hundred feet over the ocean for the next three hours.

I think she felt guilty that she lived and Eddie died. I suppose her work had something to do with it. I think she went looking for death and found enough to cure her, although it took years, and in the meantime there was guilt, like for the little boy who cried on camera in his mudslide tableau. She wondered, Who owns the story? Who gets to decide? Was it right to shoot this scene, to take this piece for herself? Would we know anything at all if we didn't traffic in the lives of strangers? Are we interconnected, or is it hit-and-run? Are your stories also my stories, or are we intact and alone? She came home and dumped out her guilt to me like dirty laundry, and those stories piled up on our floor and what was I supposed to do with them?

She took a Xanax and flipped off the lights and climbed into bed. Her body slim and hot and neatly packed, her ass so small and round you needed a magnifying glass to find it, so sweet and tight that gospel music should've been pouring out of it. We lay there and talked about Honduras, where she was headed next, or maybe the Kuwaitis wanted this refugee camp in the D.R., or the office in Bogotá that rented out equipment insisted on a police escort, and she had to call her guy down there in the morning to figure it out.

Was it her story or was it mine? Did I live only in support of her enrichment? Did my experiences matter? If she had only let me bop her, would I have passed out and forgotten the whole thing?

"When do you get back?"

"I have to check." She got up and put another Xanax in the pill chopper and cursed when pieces bounced onto the floor, and got back in bed and placed the ice-cold bottoms of her feet against my shin.

"Oh my God, your feet!"

"Well, you're like a stove." A little more foot, almost ankle, rubbed against mine. The curves of her feet were stark and dramatic. I petted her hair gently. Her breathing changed. "I'm finally calming down." She had problematically high arches that caused complicated injuries, exacerbated by running. "Thank you for loving me." I would miss her and then forget her, and have to remember her all over again.

"There, there." Sometimes, from stress, she'd get the hiccups.

"I can't do it with you tonight."

I made a soothing humming sound you might use on a baby.

I'm sure I stroked her arm or touched her face. "Hey, what's a few Xanax," she'd say, sounding drunk, "compared to a heart attack?" I had to agree. I had to get used to having her around. Welcoming Robin back into my life was like rejoining a cult: special rules, rituals, foods, a certain way of speaking, figuring out what was permitted, how to avoid those actions now deemed wrong.

"Stop."

I did. "Go to sleep."

She turned and cranked the blankets around her and rolled away. "I call you from wherever I go, desperate to connect, and you have nothing to say, then I come home exhausted and you expect me to fuck you."

"It's okay."

"I don't get you. You avoid me when I'm here, you sigh and stew, you're nicer to the mailman than you are to me, and then when I have to leave you act sad."

I liked the mailman and he liked me. Nice guy, dependable.

"Or, you get on the phone and start to cry, and say what's the point, and try to dump me."

"I thought you said you needed to sleep."

"I'm working hard, I'm doing everything. I don't know why we're still together. Why are we trying to have a baby?" After a few minutes, in a clear, detached voice she'd say, "I've been holding on to the hope that if we have a child, this will have been worth it." And then, interrupting the silence: "I have to let go of the hope that things will improve."

She flung an arm over her head. I lay there, staring at her armpit, realizing that you could miss a thing but never want to see it again. You could hate something but still want to eat it.

She started making teeth-gnashing, sighing, snorting sounds of sleep. And while she slept, I began seeing the panels of an already finished comic, my own work, that didn't actually exist yet. And over here a box with narration. And down below, in a wordless three-panel sequence, the guy on the tarmac making the sign of the cross, and then the pilot making the cross, and finally, the airplane's cross-shaped shadow hovering just over the water, in a long rectangular panel, to indicate an extended period of time.

I could lie there pretending to sleep or go into the bathroom and jerk off into the sink. I stepped over her suitcase and went downstairs and took some notes about the story I'd just heard, making up any details I couldn't remember, feeling like a scheming two-faced calculating fraud. I suppose now that it was some reaction to envy and disappointment, since her return didn't include me in the bodily sense and her storytelling made me feel like her toilet. But it wasn't just something to flush away, wasn't just someone banging a suitcase around and then lights out. She saw a mudslide, a prison fire. I saw her watching, being moved by what she saw. Then I took those pieces and laid them out under a bright light and messed around with them, for weeks, months, and when I was done, I'd done it without anyone asking for it, ever vigilant, in my note taking, of the things that went on around me, a kind of misfit with delusions of grandeur and an overactive fantasy life, although in that case my vigilance led to a story about a young couple in the early years of marriage trying to have a baby, told from two points of view, one off the coast of Ecuador, one closer to home, with an unborn child, and God in the middle. I felt like some kind of predator.

That comic appeared in *Suspicious Package,* Issue No. 5, and sold for $3.95, and went through several printings, and won a nice award at a convention, and later became a key chapter in my book. Marital failings, artistic desolation, the inability to meet expectations, grown-up male alienation. She saw me churn through the material of my friendships and housemates and saw how it tore me up to use that stuff and also how excited and relieved I was to be making headway in the cartooning world. She saw how the irresistible substance of our relationship presented itself and became central to my work and how much richer and more complex my comics became as I struggled under the weight of the material. She wanted me to succeed. I wanted to tell my story, wanted to peel back the onion, uncover the mess, surprise my eyes with what my hand could do, alone at my desk at strange hours, heart pounding, pits sweating, cackling silently to myself and hoping I could shock the world. I connected to a second self, a deeper sense, a subaudible language of colors, shapes, of gnawing contradictions.

You trade security and comfort built up over months or years for a moment of self-expression, followed by more years of confusion, resentment, guilt, all the trust undone, finally earning it back. She felt ridiculed. I had hurt her. It took years for her to forget and move on. Why did I do it? Because I'd been dying for a story and it walked through the door.

Kill your thoughts. Kill your mind. I gave up on dramatic and artful self-destruction, the deeply personal, soul-baring exercise, the creative public spectacle of my demise. The slow grinding degradation. The self-immolation. I gave up on sending tricky smoke signals through semiautobiography.

Why did I tell that story of her on the plane and me back home? To embroil Robin, to mythologize her, to upset her, break her open. I'd convinced myself that everyone wants to be immortalized in a work of art. I told that story because it confused me. Because it felt good to scratch the itch of that confusion. Because the work of telling it became a consolation. Because when I worked on it, I took hold of dark matter. I felt an ecstatic thrill seeing my work on the page. I wanted to leave my mark. I thought

I could transform it into something else. Because if I didn't somehow address these ideas, I was literally thinking myself out of existence. Which, I guess, was what I'd done, which was why I didn't want to be alive anymore, and why I went to my suitcase to find a belt and hang myself.

TWENTY-FIVE

Someone had thrown my suitcase on the floor and was lying in the nearest bed, staring at me. A woman with bare shoulders lay in my sheets in the dark.

"Hi, funny bunny."

"What are you doing here?"

"Looking for you."

I sat down beside her on the bed to steady the visual. Her eyes were dark. She'd tried and failed to make some kind of knot on top of her head, and part of a ponytail fell across her massive forehead. She looked like a stunned gymnast trying to get up off the floor.

"You're all wet," she said, and leaned into me. Her skin against mine for the second time in one day wiped out the hours in between. "Your face is wet."

"It's raining." It was fated and epic. It had meaning and destiny.

It was too much to take in. We kissed and she touched my face and I leaned back and squeezed alongside her. Maybe I could've laid down on the other bed, but if I did, in this state, we'd be like invalids in some ward.

"You smell like booze."

"I'm so drunk."

She explained that after I'd left her dormitory she'd heard the voices of her returning suitemates. They sat with her for a few minutes, and were nice, then let her sleep, and when she woke up it was dark and she packed up and turned in her conference pass to campus security. But then in the parking lot she couldn't locate her car key, and came here looking for me, and found my door open.

On the night table I noticed a bag of cherries I'd brought from home, a can of club soda, and the bottle of OxyContin, now empty. Between the painkillers and the Valium she'd had enough drugs to level a hippopotamus. They'd also given her an anesthetic to put her in some twilight state of amnesia. Despite my own inebriation, I figured that if she'd driven home with all that in her, four hours in weekend summer highway traffic, she'd be dead by now.

"How is it?" I touched the splint.

"Hot," she said. "This thing holds steady at about a hundred and forty degrees." I remembered the ice melting out there on the grass where I'd dumped it. "I was awake anyway," she said, "thinking about all this." She seemed on the verge of apologizing for what happened in her dorm this afternoon. "I don't want to go home," she said. "I know it's wrong, but it doesn't feel wrong." She reached over to me. "My hands fit your face. I love you here next to me." She touched my cheek.

She was being nice. She put her head on my chest and said she loved listening to my heart. Uncontrollable brain-stem functioning and preorgasmic jizzing scattered into doubt and muddled sensations and further reversals of mood. I shoved my face into her hair, sniffing, wondering how long she'd been lying here, wondering whether we had a future, how we might survive. She loved me. She looked forward to seeing me, but then Mike figured it out and got horny and jumped my girlfriend. One day she hoped to have something better, maybe not with me but then who? I thought of high-ranking church officials begging for her support, scientists and art collectors, meeting her for coffee, kissing her on both sides of the mouth. Museum directors, social entrepreneurs, animal activists, education reformers, emailing, phoning, pleading for money, staring at her breasts. I tried to get ahold of myself.

She said, "I love when you're above me. Did you know you close your eyes? That's when I like to watch you."

Maybe she wasn't so irresistible. Maybe she threw herself at men because she wasn't so high on herself. Maybe the early hardships somehow reinforced an innate insecurity. The crummy childhood, rusty car, and crappy house, set against standout athletics and straight A's, and that psycho who tried to bash her head in, her father's death, the unexamined grief and confusion, the humiliating rituals of male oppression that had to be tolerated, had to be withstood. Maybe she liked to be treated badly. I could handle that. Treating loved ones badly was a talent of mine.

"Oh, I almost forgot," she said. "It's our anniversary. Happy one year of insanity."

We made out for a while. It was total heaven. "I waited for you to come back," she said, "and now you're here."

"This is my bed."

"You're the only thing that matters anymore. Are you real?"

"Yes," I said. "Are you?"

"Yes," she said. "I am real."

I imagined an easy, raucous, searing, sexually explosive bond that would carry us through our days. I imagined our multiple houses, landscaped gardens, marble pastry block, weekends with blended families, visits to the Cheneys, a generous stipend, hush money for Robin, a little gold Rolex for Beanie to suck on.

"A year ago we didn't know what we were getting ourselves into," she said, "but now we do. We know the deal."

"What does that mean?"

"We won't be as lost or sad or lonely. I'll know you're listening to me. And I'll listen to you."

"Okay." I sensed intent, a firm design, a direction.

"We can make each other's lives endurable, and even better, we can be more loving and kind to them. We can do that for each other." She was determined, and seemed to be steering us back on course.

I had to admit that the bulk of our emailing had been tame. In our diligent way, we'd tried to know each other. Contemplating this woman from a distance, commiserating, holding her firmly in my mind, responding humanely, tuning in to that shimmering idea had required faith. Thinking about her was an escape, but the sheer volume of time and energy had turned it into a kind of meditation, at times approaching bliss. Although it was also a recipe for fragmentation and unrequited horniness and misery, an overwrought emotional substitute for love.

"We can trust it without challenging the other, without disrupting our lives. With you on my side, I think I can handle anything."

"Sure." This was more of the same old baloney. My love for her made her strong. Loving me helped her fuck him. I sat up and took off my sneakers and poured out the sand. I could hear it sifting through the cracks of the floorboards, into the apartment below.

I had to figure it out. What the hell, I guess I didn't want to die. The shame of this undertaking became enmeshed with the mechanics of survival. If it was a choice between hanging myself and making a comic about this crap, I might as well give it a whirl. I'd sign up for another year as her emotional waste dump, affording her this sense of camaraderie, so she'd be nicer to him and not think anymore about leaving. We'd learn to live with nothing, we'd give this to each other, it would be our sacrifice.

"I guess I thought I could train him," she said. "I thought I could handle it." She associated his unyielding stupidity with masculine power. "But I need someone, too."

"Tell me everything."

She went on listing complaints, fresh ones I hadn't heard before: hadn't packed his own suitcase in years, couldn't be bothered to carry his plate to the sink, or change a diaper, or change a lightbulb. "I have to put his clubs in the car like I'm his fucking caddy." The Escalade sat outside his office all day, motor running, blocking traffic, emitting greenhouse gases. Took the jet to Miami or Cleveland even though there were thirty-five commercial flights a day.

"Two years ago, he took the fund public without telling me. I'm on the board. He had to forge my signature." I started rubbing her rib cage, to soothe and embolden her. "I'm a trustee. I'm legally responsible." I nodded. She was talking about a $20 billion entity. "Don't get me started on the island he rented for half a mil to go surfing for two days with his regulatory compliance team."

"Holy shit."

"My kids don't even look up when he walks through the door at night. Does that seem odd to you? Seems odd to me. . . ." She went on like that. I don't think she was aware of rationalizing her own behavior. I think she believed his actions were indefensible and beyond retribution. When she lifted her good arm, I remembered the bracelet as it slid and turned slightly. My daughter's pre-K tuition: shiny, subterranean, luminous in the dark.

There was something going on between the three of us, between him and her and me. I couldn't figure out how this thing worked, whether I was being used for their marital enjoyment, or she was being used for his sadistic pleasure, or he was being used for ours. I had a fear that one of us would collide with the other two and end up dead, most likely me. His abuse seemed to satisfy some need in her. Maybe it made her feel different from all those stuck-up assholes at her country club. It gave her a sense of control in an otherwise untethered abundance. Or it made her feel saintly, or it was her miserable Irish suffering, or she dug the whole mentality. I'm abused, I'm an outcast, I'm misunderstood.

"From the start, I knew it was wrong. I had to do something, but I all I could do was lie there. Then kids come. Life is busy. But nothing's changed. The years go by. A couple weeks ago, I set up the thing for our burial plots."

"Oh, bunny." I raised her sleeveless shirt and opened her bra.

"He's right next to me," she said. "I'm stuck with him forever." She sighed, her body sliding against mine. "I asked him point-blank how he'd feel if someone treated his daughters the way he treats me, which is always a good way to end the conversation. He got up and walked out of the room. He doesn't know how to act. He never had a girlfriend. He grew up in a house where no one paid attention to him, and figured it all out on his own, and now everybody wants him and he doesn't need anybody." I put my hand down her shorts. "When I met you, I'd been praying for some way to get through it. I thought I could start all over again. But now it's worse, because I know how good it could be. I'm sad all the time, dreaming of a life without him, and I was sad last night, waiting for you to text me, and I was a mess when you left my room today."

"Me, too."

"Keep doing that." I did. "But while I lay there talking to my roommates, your come was running down my thighs, spilling out, dripping down, and I can't believe I'm saying it, but I was happy to feel that. It was beautiful. I didn't want to go home, but I thought I should, to get away from you. And that's another problem," she said. "It hurts here, under my ribs, all the time."

"Same."

"The only time I can breathe is when you're inside me."

I pulled off my shorts. "You can leave him."

"I can't."

"I'll help you."

"No." She shook her head. "But we can go away, somewhere, for a weekend, just the two of us."

"We already are somewhere."

"Somewhere else," she said. "There's a beach on Minorca I want to show you." I yanked off her shorts. "I love international flights. I love the whole thing, the international terminal, arrivals and departures, everybody making out at the gate!" We were excited, pretending together. I'd been here before, hoping, believing. My hope was completely dead but somehow still strong, marching with zombie power and conviction, trampling my sanity. But then she gave me that chastising, serious, injured-gymnast look.

"Even if I'm alone for the rest of my life, I'll never be as sad and lonely as I am now, married to him."

I guess this kind of talk was therapeutic. She was smiling, although the ponytail had come undone, and in the shadow inside her hair it was a sad smile. Beyond sad. Disturbed. "We don't need him," she said. "I told Lily right in front of him, 'Never let a man treat you the way Daddy treats me.'" That line of thinking seemed to revive her. She turned toward me. "Will you do me a favor? Don't sleep with anyone else after I'm gone, or at least don't bring her here. It's our place now."

"Stop." I was sad too, and that she couldn't tell how sad I was made me sadder.

"Don't be sad," she said. "We can be sad later. I've been sad all summer. I feel alive again."

I felt weak and tired. I had nothing to offer, no tricks, and she knew me too well for any pretending. We were closer now, we'd been through some hell, we were into something less mysterious and not so fun. This would've been the place where something real would start, but there was nothing, no future, no gimmicks. I was afraid of the intense bond we'd formed on this crazy day, afraid that I'd never be able to shake it off, that I'd fallen too far. These were the panties I'd pulled off earlier, nude with scratchy lace. I knew her body now and worked it like it was my own. I sat up and banged my skull on the beam over the bed and grabbed my head, thinking I'd probably just gotten brain damage.

"Something else I need to tell you," she said. "You'll be happy to hear it."

"Okay."

"I'm getting my period." With her shoulders back and boobs out she looked like a bust on a wooden ship. "I know how it freaks you out to think of some little towheaded kid popping out of me. You don't have to worry." But when I thought about it, I wasn't afraid of the possibility, or maybe I liked the idea. "No one will ever know."

"Okay."

"My dalliance," she said, staring into my eyes.

"Your what?"

"We'll take this to our graves."

I let go of her and lay back on the pillow and rested. On closer inspection, the skylight above us was plastic, not glass, and had cracking ice patterns and chips around the flanges. It was not what it appeared to be, and neither were we. This was something between us, a lapse, a misdeed. Light drizzle came down from above us, but if you tried to pull the skylight closed, pieces of rusty stuff rained down on your hair.

I drank some warm club soda. We had nothing else to say. I was ready. I'd been like this at seventeen, like a cow that needs milking. It was nothing at all but the relentless durability of our attraction. It turns out that all you need for kundalini multigasmic monkey sex is two people who know each other just well enough to feel safe but don't share a kitchen. I'd never have her, I'd never lose her. It wasn't real, it didn't matter, would never sour, never fail.

It was more intense than the afternoon session, crammed into less space, both of us more desperate, all of our movement so fluid, sliding my palm down to shield her glaring white hip, caressing the dizzying nexus, moving in with the confident momentum of athletic routine. We cursed softly as we banged against that beam, then toughened up and suffered through the thump of bone on wood. I worried that it would ruin the sex, but nothing could. We stuck our tongues and fingers in each other's ears and mouths and asses, like a single crazed body reconnecting, or like a family of Chihuahuas molesting a turkey leg, and sucked on each other's lips and privates.

"Angel."

"Oh my God, I love you." She fell back, and in the dark I could see her tan lines, her splint, blue and white, her fingers dark, almost purple. Just look at her, laid out on my bed. You can't have it. The guy who can have it anytime he wants it hates her. She planted her feet on the ceiling and made lovely faces as she lay there, staring up at me, taking me in. "This is how I'll remember you," she said sadly, "just let me look," and as she stared at me I realized she was stupid and had no judgment, because I was horrible and dead inside.

"I'm like a cow," I said, and tried to explain.

"What?"

"Moo."

I knew it was sick, knew it was wrong, but had to keep going. Anyway, she wasn't dying of cancer. She had one broken bone and the best drugs in the world and there was never a question of whether we would. I touched her and she turned and hugged a pillow and I kicked off my undies and sank into her, my eyes rolling into my head, my face wedged into the ceiling, forgetting to breathe, having and losing the feeling of flying, soaring, swooning, falling.

"Holy moly," she said. "I prayed for this."

It was the pill I needed to survive, to get me through another year, a scene, a place to park my soul through months of cold and diapers and screaming. The fog of goodness and responsibility needed to be burned off, gotten past, needed endless badness and rebellion.

It didn't feel so much like an abrupt mounting, more like a frenetic angling with these parts pressed into service, and then a distinctly new angle and new sensations, and in between in a herculean feat I crawled down between her legs and she came, kapow, gesundheit. When we began again it was like the B side of an album. I hovered over her, quietly, in control, no movement to it other than the movement itself. She shivered a little, saying, every now and then, "You're killing me," shuddering while I made delicate adjustments, like an artist with his pen, and we fell into a timeless rift of hopeless, helpless, perfect contact. I had no thought in my mind except that I would pay dearly for this or maybe had already paid and earned it. One hand supporting her head, sifting the soft secret hairs of her nape, the other touching her collarbone, measuring the hollow place along it, covering the thin freckled plate of muscle across her sternum, kissing her forehead, kissing her mouth, saying I love you.

In the kitchen I found an old muffin tin and filled it with water to make ice cubes for her, for the morning, and placed it in the freezer. I felt good. It was like driving sixty miles an hour through a car wash and coming out on the other side, shiny and clean. Then I ran the faucet until it got warm and found a washcloth. The windows rattled in the breeze and the Barn creaked, breezes blowing in on all sides, flinging curtains. The rain came harder, slashing the roof.

She lay calm and still while I pressed the warm washcloth to her and cleaned her gently, and for that moment I think we both imagined this as our home. Then she got bored and wondered instead if she could make it to a meeting in the morning, since she couldn't paint and didn't want to waste the day.

"What meeting?"

"A brunch. Really interesting thing. Amazing." She was being asked to fund a project in Afghanistan where farmers were paid to swap poppies for saffron, inspiring foodies while fighting the Taliban with capitalism. It didn't matter what it was, one small part of her overall push to reform our planet, one small ship in her armada.

"Where?"

"Midtown." She meant Manhattan. I asked how. "Chopper," she said, using his word, saying it sarcastically. I smiled to acknowledge her sarcasm, and to allow the absurdity of choppering into Midtown to pass between us. I kept my smile in place, surprised to feel newly devastated and betrayed. The talk of choppering silenced me, forcing me to accept the unrelenting farce of my position. I lifted the washcloth to show her that it was tinged with rust.

"Oh, that's nothing," she said, unmoved by the sight of her own blood. "You just wait." She looked at me thoughtfully. "I'm a bleeder."

I'd grown used to the heady, tainting power of our lovemaking, our biochemical froth and forgivable expressions of joy and despair. But blood carried some unnerving element of permanence I hadn't considered. She didn't seem bothered by having shared it. She thanked me for cleaning her, and I felt dismissed, and tossed the washcloth on the floor. She put her hand over her heart, with my bracelet on her wrist. "I have never in my entire life been treated this well by anyone. Never been this well loved, until now, by you." She studied me with renewed intensity. I felt puzzled over and adored. I'd forgotten the feeling of this scrutiny, of being marveled at by another living being. It had been a long time since anyone had looked at me that way. I remembered that look from my mother.

"You're gifted." Now came the pity.

"It's my blessing."

"But you never get it at home."

"It's also my curse."

"Let's call it a skill."

"A knack."

"If you could package it and sell it, you'd make a fortune."

"Okay."

"There are so many women I know who could use it." She tried to pull me to her, but I resisted, and instead mentioned price points, naming my services and dividing them into grades, Standard, Elite, and Concierge class, for the discerning lovelorn lady. I might've been having fun to combat the choking power of her arrogance, or maybe I meant to engender more pity, or maybe I wanted to remind her of the uselessness of her dough, that financial remuneration devalued our bond.

"Hopefully my new customers will pay a little better."

"Stop it."

"You started it."

"Come here," she said, exhausted.

"You'd dress me like a gigolo and sell me to your friends."

She pulled me to her. "We were both joking," she said.

I lay there, depressed as hell, with my head between her boobs, and tried to put a value on the services I'd provided to her, the sacrifices I'd made, like a common-law spouse, significant contributions to her well-being, which now seemed beyond measure, like that dough of hers, which fit no human scale, or was scaled to all humanity.

She yawned, then started snoring loudly like she was about to suffocate herself. I figured it was the drugs, and couldn't even pretend to sleep until her breathing changed, and crawled out from under her and into the other twin bed, and lay there.

I wanted to get paid. She had enough money for a thousand jerkoffs. A basic level of support, half a million a year, was nothing, a weekend island rental. Azamanian's billions were like a weather phenomenon that forced the natural world into contortions, turned dune scrub into rarefied architecture and putting greens. His crazy blown-out beach house made money sexy or scary but not real. But the proximity to her dough had worn me down, whatever protection I'd had from it. She loved me, but how much? By now Robin would've received an email alert of our zero balance. Or maybe they didn't send them out on weekends. We could've transferred funds from our savings account, but we didn't have a savings account. I'd broken our trust, which I'd only be destroying again through my artwork, by using my indiscretion as a source of inspiration. I couldn't stand it. I had goals and dreams. How long would I have to wait to make them real? For now, though, I needed money from my brother, or half from him and half from Robin's dad, right away, this week, for Kaya's preschool. There were other bills I couldn't let myself think about, but that one had to be paid. I told myself it would be okay. Amy wouldn't let me starve. She'd never let me suffer. Then I remembered that she'd offered some kind of support, up in her closet in Connecticut, while I lay on the floor with my pants down, and I'd told her to shove it.

TWENTY-SIX

Sunday morning we waited in line for coffee, sniffing milk containers, listening as Dennis Fleigel gave Mohammad Khan a cost-benefit analysis of last night's fundraiser. Weather had moved in off the ocean and sat over us like wet gray wool. Roberta stumbled through the fog in dark sunglasses and ducked under a tent flap. Alicia Hernandez Roulet reached past me for milk, trailed by her little goblin, and I bent over to scratch his belly. The blood rushed to my head, and I almost fell down. I felt sick, but also solid, dense, and concentrated, jacked with endorphins from screwing and falling in love. I stroked his fur, girded by this small task, sensing a past-life kinship, and dropped to my knees and spoke to him.

On the planet where we came from, you were free to love and be loved. On that planet, the system didn't beat you into submission. You could lie on your back with your weenie out, and no one stopped you. I read his name tag. Rabies on one side, Piccolo on the other. I felt happy, and a little insane, but I could do whatever I wanted, and whispered in his ear that his real name was Bubbles, and sang him the inchworm song, which was one of Beanie's favorites. The two of them were about the same size and length. I picked him up and cradled him and called him my child, my son. There were black spots on his wet pink tongue. He had his lipstick out. So much love to give.

I understood him, because I'd considered hanging myself just last night—and in that liminal space had received a kind of grace. I didn't want to hurt myself anymore. My self-destructive urges had been replaced by a rush of pity for the seven billion assholes of earth, even Robin, maybe her most of all, out there on the straight and narrow, going it alone. I thought again of my hand in Amy's hair, her mouth before we kissed. Sex, afterglow, possession, elation. I'd write a happy story of transformation, growth, and forgiveness, drawn without inflection or ambivalence. It would be easy to do. The work would go quickly. My pages would look schematic. I'd crank out an entire book in six months, zip zip. My hero would thrive.

Early this morning the Barn had rattled in the wind, blowing curtains. A mist fell through the skylight, dripping onto our blankets. I climbed back into her twin bed, and we listened to the soothing tap upon the roof, and talked the way we had over email, rambling away in gravelly voices about our first summer jobs, the pickup truck I drove delivering auto parts, the neighbor she babysat for, their kitchen AM radio and the songs it played that summer, catechism class, brushing her grandmother's honeyblond wig. I loved lying there. We'd slept naked, and our legs were cool and smooth. Her arm had started to throb but not too badly. I reminded her of a family trip she'd once told me about, it took place thirty years ago, the parents and kids in one tent in some state park on the ocean, how it rained all weekend and her father sang in his Irish tenor and they slept in a puddle and were happy.

She said, "Everyone spends their whole life looking for their daddy," and I said that might be true, and she pulled me tight against her and said, "I don't want to go home."

I saw the clock on the stove, and knew I had to get to class. I wondered if she'd figured out her plans. But she rolled onto her back, breathing funny, and said that she wasn't taking any helicopter in this weather. Then she told me Lily had called from sleepaway camp, and it was not the first time, either, in which she'd pleaded to come home. She'd said she was ashamed of the scars on her head, and her cabinmates were mean, although they'd voted her president of the Squirrel Den. Mike had insisted that Lily go away for camp, even though she was seven and had had emergency brain surgery in March, and had missed a month of school because she could barely walk. She hadn't wanted to go, and had never spent a night away from home in her life without her mother. Mike knew almost nothing about his kid's procedure, hadn't been listening during the few doctor's appointments he'd attended, but felt in his expertise that two weeks among strangers would be good for her, hiking, picking up survival skills, learning to water-ski, and, at the end of two weeks, running a 5K race. This seemed like a winning proposition to confirm her recovery and help her regain her self-confidence. It was sick, twisted, and evil. Amy felt powerless to protect her.

She also worried about the neurological stress tests Lily would be doing as soon as camp ended, to see if they needed to open up her skull again. Then she realized that with the next couple days free, she could drive up to New Hampshire, maybe later today, to surprise Lily, to bust her out and bring her home.

I was afraid to mention my own kids' near-death experiences, afraid she'd unnerve me by attacking Robin or demand some gruesome detail. But when I did, she didn't pry any further. My son had almost choked. My daughter was all cut up.

"You need to concentrate on them," she said sadly. "You should go home."

"No." Anyway, I couldn't. I had to teach my class and get paid. I mentioned the pit behind Curtis's, and that idiot Brett, merging that other life with this one, a necessary and welcome violation, a doubling of my selves. I felt bigger, more enmeshed. I told her how grateful I was that it hadn't been worse, that I didn't have to drive nine hours to a hospital so that I could sit by the bed of my kid, and left it at that.

"But doesn't it seem a little weird?" she said. "First Lily, then my wrist, and now your kids?"

"You think God is watching, making adjustments to our lives so we can experience the right amount of pain?"

"Don't talk to me like that."

I said, "If Lily hadn't played soccer that day, she wouldn't have ended up in the doctor's office." The puking and the fainting had led to tests and finally an MRI, which picked up a rare malformation, a weakness in the branch point of an artery under the brain. The room had quickly filled up with doctors who'd never seen it except in an autopsy. "What do you call that if it's not good luck?"

Amy didn't care what I said. She'd had plenty of good luck in her life, and look where it got her. Then, for no reason, we started frantically kissing and hugging. We did it again, sideways this time, spooning, another first in a series of firsts, just as good as the other ways, better maybe, but with more blood. It seemed the parts of us were smarter than the whole. Or dumber, much dumber. I felt sorry for those parts, worn and red and working away down there when all we wanted was to cry. I was sad, patient, and careful with her, but very connected, impossibly close, and as I got closer I could hear her breathing with me. This was undeniably an activity in which we both excelled. We came at the same moment, kablammo, which of course I'd read about in dirty magazines as a youth, and had imagined but never in my life experienced until that instant. I hadn't even been sure such a thing was possible, though apparently it was, and showed the rare wonder of our compatibility, right down to the nerve endings, a sign of this instinctual trust. It was so good we started laughing, like scientists celebrating a discovery after an explosion blew up the lab, banging our heads on the ceiling, giggling when we did. I was late for breakfast, and jumped up and threw my clothes on and kissed her goodbye, "So long, kid," like it was nothing, and had to run out the door with my shirt unbuttoned and my flip-flops flapping.

I stood in the rain, soaked in that remembering, blowing on my coffee, trying to restart the loop, rewinding and freezing images until the boy who worked in the main office banged a stick against a tent pipe to get everyone's attention.

People knew him now and screamed his name in joyful mockery. Christopher! He wore a festive yellow slicker and black rubber boots. He announced changes in the day's shuttle bus schedule, warning us that the clouds would soon be gone and the sun would return. Amy could hop into her car or chopper away in clear skies. More hooting. We were as a group undaunted by weather, awake and alert, as if this were the real world, the one we were born for, and not that other one of petty, groping, pasty drones who cowered all winter in the dark and cold. Boys and girls from the lacrosse camp ran across the far fields, helmets slung on their sticks. A seagull hovered over the garbage can as I moved to the toaster. I was exhausted, and the pain of my exhaustion forced me to move stiffly; I felt it in the sore muscles in my jaw and head.

"I love Mark," said the girl on the other side of the buffet table.

"Who is, of course, a very good friend of Teddy's," the guy said.

"Teddy was terrific in that play." They were referring, of course, to *Puss in Boots* the musical, put on by the University of Michigan. The girl had bright pink hair and sparkly blue fingernails. The guy wore a clean white T-shirt and a Palestinian scarf. There were lines on either side of the table and conversations going on all around me. Earlier this morning, someone explained, a German television crew had arrived to do a piece on Tom McLaughlin, as part of a series on American writers.

"Dearest friend of my life," said a man with salt-and-pepper hair. A woman handed him a coffee. Something dreaded and illicit passed between them. Down the line a conversation turned to last night's dinner, which had been vegetarian, raw and inedible. People openly complained. Last year's breakfast of bagels and cream cheese had been replaced by cooked grains and bricks of rock-hard Irish soda bread, which we sawed at as if it were a tree limb with a knife that wasn't up to the task. And there'd been a fight about the air-conditioning in the dorm between a woman in a Pucci dress and her roommate, who insisted on sleeping in flannel, while a party had raged outside someone else's door at two A.M. A woman in a pretty turquoise blouse told a skinny guy with tattoos, "It's a new poem, dedicated to my future ex-husband's fiancée. I call it 'Stay the Fuck Away from My Kids, You Whore.'" There was some kind of heated, inordinate bonding that happened among grown-ups, forced out of their decorous privacy into visceral closeness, that had the feeling of an open-air loony bin.

I carried my toast and coffee and a single hard-boiled egg, rolling loosely in a white plastic bowl, past Professor Michnick, seated with Alicia H. R. and my newfound, foot-tall, walleyed tongue-wagging interplanetary soul mate; past Carl, who gave me a listless wave, in the wrinkled yellow linen shirt he'd worn to last night's fundraiser and appeared to have slept in; past a table of black actors, black poets and writers. They tended to congregate at meals, triggering my jealousy, curiosity, and involuntary anxiety. Herschel Davies, the playwright, was a buddy of mine. He taught at SMU. His play about coming of age in Cleveland in the sixties was very good; it had been performed here and later ran on Broadway. He'd nicknamed me "the hamster," in recognition of my scrappy defense in our Ping-Pong matches. Their table was full.

I finally arrived without incident at a nearly empty table. Seated alone there was Angel Solito, which I didn't notice until I'd already put down my plate. He glanced up, frowning, and didn't appear to recognize me, but then did, but didn't look any happier, reaching for his books and papers and pulling them to him as I sat, trying to think of something to say.

"Doing okay?"

"Yup." It was like some idiotic cartoonist conspiracy.

"Ready for class?"

"We're learning how to tell a story." His head drooped, from annoyance or exhaustion, or some attempt to commiserate. I couldn't think of a single thing to say about teaching, even though I'd planned my lecture and class was starting in five minutes. "Can't teach the story," he said. "That's *in* you. That has to come *out*." He had pages of notes and lesson plans, textbooks and anthologies. We agreed on the impossibility of teaching, can't teach talent, all the old clichés. I needed to eat. I took a sip of scalding coffee and started to choke. Winston Doyoyo, the old lion, arose from the table of black people, circled us, and landed at Solito's shoulder, placed a hand on his neck and said something as Solito

nodded politely. Doyoyo ducked stiffly out of the tent. Solito
went back to his notes.

"Theory won't do a fucking thing for you," he said.

"Nope."

"Still, Aristotle knew what a story was." He mentioned Shake-
speare. I needed ketchup. Freytag had mapped it out, but appar-
ently that was just an exhaustive examination of the mechanics
of Greek drama. Then he mentioned the Aristotelian three-act
structure of *Star Wars,* then *Gilgamesh.* "Although technically
that's Eastern."

"Wait, what's Eastern?" I couldn't function in this dialectic.

"Gilgamesh."

"Anyway," I said, "I didn't get a chance to tell you yesterday
how much I like your stuff." His eyes were steady. I figured my
praise was suspect. "I meant to tell you." His teeth went in differ-
ent directions. He needed orthodontia. I asked where he'd been
before this.

"Seattle and Vancouver."

"You're staying in the dorms here on campus?"

He nodded. I asked where. Stewart, the moldy, stinko dorm by
the water. Small hands, narrow yellow wrists, darker skin at the
knuckles, narrow face, shining hair, fine features. I felt everything
about him, all at once. We discussed the smelly carpets, ugly
bunk beds made of logs painted brown. At age four, he was pulled
off a bus and dumped in a government facility in Chiapas. Smug-
glers ditched toddlers at the first sign of trouble. He didn't know
his full name. At age eight, his little legs were still too short to
allow him to hop the train. Other kids fell off and were cut in
half. He'd been born into a brutal world, and had made a journey
like the ocean crossing my orphaned grandfather had made, all
alone, back in 1911—if my grandfather had been forced to swim

the Atlantic. I wished him luck on the book tour in Europe. He stared at me, twisting his brow.

"I know your work," he said, looking away, then straightening his notes, "*Suspicious Package* Number 4 came out while I was in grad school." He looked up. "And Number 5. Almost everyone in my program made comics on the side. Not everyone was as dedicated as I was, but we were all tuned in."

"Uh-huh."

"Of the indie cartoonists who'd broken through, the more successful ones making long, serious comics, no one was more talked about than you."

I thanked him. For a second I thought he'd said something nice. Then I realized he hadn't. Something flashed across his face that I chose to ignore. He didn't say anything else. Had he actually insulted me? Or had he only meant to say that my work provoked strong reactions? I felt a sudden pride of my own, a compact thing with jagged stuff inside it. The jagged stuff started hacking its way out. I picked off some eggshell, putting it in the bowl, ignoring his insult, letting him have his little dig.

"Well," I said. "I hope you enjoy your success. I hope it never ends." He nodded, waiting for more. "I hope it brings attention to the issue of immigration," I said. "Children crossing borders, whatever. It's important." I needed salt.

"It's the story of my life," he said. "And that's what people are expecting from me. But is that what I expect from myself?"

"Is it?" Who gives a crap.

"I'm sick of it."

I banged my toast on the table and stuck it in the coffee.

"I have to tell you," he said. "When that story came out in the *Times*."

"Please, tell me." I didn't know what he was talking about.

It seemed that when the profile on Solito was published, it wrecked his outlier status. He became a name. He spoke from deep inside some bubble of invulnerable obsession, locked in, unashamed. "Don't get me wrong—I'm lucky, I know it. I live in airports. I eat out of vending machines. I smile in public and sign books. And they come up after and hug me and take pictures, and I wonder, How am I supposed to survive this? Like, how do you go back to work when people are hanging on your every word and pleading with you for whatever it is they want? Or they haven't even read the book, just read about it and show up at signings and expect some kind of TED talk, something inspiring. Or they don't care what it's about, they want to debunk it, catch me in a lie, did it really happen this way, is it true, oh my God. Or, Hey, can you come to my fundraiser, for nothing, tomorrow at six? I get grumpy after five minutes, and every night there's this huge line and I have to sit there and listen. 'Great question, let me see if I can answer that.' It was packed in Seattle. I have one more in New York before I fly to Amsterdam. It's getting worse."

A guy went by and said something to him in Spanish. Solito turned, waiting patiently until the man was done. His shoulders slumped as he leaned toward me and said, more quietly, "But it's all so singular, my heartbreaking childhood, my continental trek. Like I had a choice. It's not anything I can duplicate."

People were leaving. It was time to head to class. A guy called out to him as he walked by, then someone else said his name. I held up a hand, like, Hang on, we're talking. "I know what they want," he said. "They want to congratulate me, but that's not what I want. They want to touch it, share in it, get close, but that turns me into something, and I don't want to be that."

"Congratulate you for what?"

He rubbed one eye and then the other. "I haven't figured out what all this attention is about. I have to go somewhere quiet and think about it."

"Good idea," I said. He looked relieved, then worried, then went back to making notes.

I tried to steady myself, eating toast, and felt something saintly come over me, felt myself to be a steadying force for him too, in that parental way, surrendering myself for his sake as I peeled my egg. Every night I ripped out the murky parts of myself and submitted, until I was filled with only light, a nurturing object for my son to hold, for my daughter to close herself into, and lay there pretending to sleep until whichever one was beside me would sleep, and in the process I always passed out too, and woke up hours later, fully alert, afraid to wake them as I crawled out and wandered around the house, wincing at every creak in the floor, wondering what happened to my life.

Solito could look forward to a bright and boundless future, unless he'd already shot his wad, at twenty-eight, in which case he'd be better off blowing his brains out right now or preparing for decades of self-imitation, honing his "talk," hating himself for phoning it in, cursed by early fame, like Fat Elvis dying on his gold-plated toilet. He scribbled away at his lecture, talking some, less guarded, delineating his Aristotelian three-act structure. I happened to be free of all that, of cartooning passion and real ambition, and wanted to feel above him, safe from his artistic pain—but I couldn't, because he had what I wanted, whatever that was: public approval, sycophantic praise, suffering, audience, sympathy.

He'd walked from Guatemala, following mule trails through northern Mexico among candelilla men in rags. They tried to buy him from his trafficker in exchange for drugs, but he never forgot their burnished faces, crucifixes hanging from their throats. The wind in Sonora, roughnecks and cowboys. He'd gone missing in the Arizona desert, hallucinated from dehydration, passed through Tucson like a ghost. He'd lived to tell the story, and found his voice, his own drawing style, and a thorny political issue, a rallying cry, and turned that whole miserable thing into art, so readers could pity him, or at least read the thing once, and slap him on the back and forget.

TWENTY-SEVEN

George, the oldest member of the class, had a portfolio of notes and sketches that went back forty years. He was tall and angular, with a narrow, ravaged face, a quaking voice, white stubble on his chin, and gnarled, trembling hands. He'd grown up on a military base, enlisted in the marines at eighteen, and was assigned to carry a thing that shoulder-launched rockets. There were capable drawings of old French forts, Russian and North Vietnamese artillery, and pages of old letters, photos, and official citations. It was a kind of bliss to inundate myself with the muck of other peoples' lives and to address technical problems with simple, obvious fixes.

"I never killed any women or children, but a guy in my unit did. I saw him throw a grenade in a doorway for fun." He stared at me. His eyes were blue and clear and ageless. Was he trying to absolve himself? Maybe. "My little brother went over after I came back and was killed in action." He touched his eyeglasses. His hand shook. It was clear that the war had undermined his life. Maybe he'd come here to resurrect the brother. I knelt between desks to help him get some solid forms beneath the timid lines of his soldiers. We went back and forth, from his thumbnails to his notes. Someone sat on the floor of the helicopter. Blood dripped. Wind shot through the open cab. We inserted key details, excised others.

Mel, the elementary school art teacher, had a good start on a travelogue to the wilds of Borneo. The town witch doctor drove a convertible. The inn where she'd stayed employed a cook who slept in a tree like a gorilla and covered himself in leaves. She made cartooning seem painless and fun. There were movie-like action breakdowns. She used sophisticated camera angles. She knew her anatomy, she'd had training, and she'd produced two roughed-out pages of a working outline.

"Looking good there."

"Thanks."

Carol's stalky red hair stood up and shined as though it had been waxed. She'd begun a feverish and disturbing scene featuring beer and snow and a carload of teenage boys. The scene took place in 1989. The interior of the car was nicely delineated, well drafted, although the sketches were dark, with spectral light coming out of the dashboard, the boys grimly drinking. I had the feeling something bad was going to happen.

"What's it about?"

She studied the page as though she might shred it. "Me," she said, and shook her head. She had a big, loud, unmodulated voice, and let her voice go as deep and loud as she wanted. "Back there again."

Brandon was dim and lazy, and ready to ink. He thought his gay pride sketches were perfect. He worked entirely in stick figures, like a three-year-old. I knelt beside him and we brainstormed for ways to improve his drawings. Working with dumb people was a depressing waste of time that made a joke of our struggle. Sarah was also stuck. She worked in a bookstore in Cambridge, and had Crohn's disease, and had suffered a flare-up two days ago, so she didn't know how much she could get done on her bookstore confidential/Crohn's confession before Tuesday's open studio. Then she started to cry.

When I finally stood up, I could barely walk. I'd been on my knees for an hour. I went down to the basement, where it was quieter, and sat at a computer. Once they'd put the finishing touches on their comic, they'd come down here to scan it and clean it up before printing. I wrote an instructional guide to the software, carefully explaining how to align their panels on the page, crop and make them level, and fix the white-out and eraser smudges. If you didn't get down to the pixel level, you'd have grays in your whites that reproduced badly and made the final product look amateurish. Behind me, under the staircase, students from another class squeegeed paint across silk screens. Out the window I could hear people blabbing in the courtyard. I hadn't checked my email since I'd left home on Friday. I logged on to the campus system and found a note from Robin from early this morning.

She thanked me for my voicemail. Somehow, everyone had slept more or less through the night. Before bed, she'd changed Kaya's bandages, but it had taken an hour because she'd freaked out and cried hysterically. Robin had had to call our neighbor Elizabeth to come over to persuade Kaya to sit in the bath to soak them off. There were heat warnings, and Robin worried that with all the tape and gauze, the camp nurse would not let Kaya in the pool on Monday, even though a swim was maybe the only thing preventing a kid from bursting into flames. And Beanie had gotten ahold of one of my harmonicas but was afraid to put it to his lips because of what happened with the whistle, so he held it at arm's length and had been screaming at it, more or less, since six A.M. Robin had a pitch meeting first thing Monday morning, with none other than Danny Katavolos, her old pal from the Latin American bureau who she'd complained about for years. Danny was a tiresome, artificial person who gave her lingering full-frontal hugs that she claimed to find revolting. At the Nature Channel, he'd moved up from channel subhead to network boss. His idea of great nature television was twenty-two minutes on the oldest living turtle in North America. She hadn't had time to prepare, because I'd been away, so she didn't have any ideas to pitch him, but in order to deliver eighteen episodes ahead of schedule and make the network a fortune, the show would have to be heavily scripted and produced, nothing educational, no environmental lessons, like a married couple beating the crap out of each other on a herring boat off the coast of Norway. Which, come to think of it, she thought he just might like.

Somehow she hadn't seen the message from our bank, triggered by a negative balance. I'd gotten away with things I couldn't bear to keep inside. I'd been operating like Beanie, testing gravity by dropping crockery off the table. I wanted to be discovered, punished, brutalized, and forgiven. She didn't know enough to accuse me. I opened the attached photo of Kaya's scraped and bruised body and studied it, as well as the equally troubling photo of her splotchy face and still-wet hair, after her bath last night, while she was eating ice cream. In the end, I felt better seeing those photos, more secure, knowing they'd survived.

There were several emails from Adam. The newest one had come in just this morning. I scanned my inbox and scrolled down to the oldest, from late Friday night, and worked my way forward.

There'd been a time, a few years back, when my finances had been in even worse shape, when I'd fretted constantly and stared at the calendar and wondered whether Adam had submitted the invoice for whichever jobs had run, terrified that a drawing had been killed or rescheduled, and he'd patiently calm my fears. But then Jerry the tech weenie had taken over, flush with cash, authorizing contracts for regular contributors, and for the last year and a half a check had gone straight into my account at the end of the month, no matter what I did. I felt appreciated and protected.

I figured Adam was writing with some last changes for the Romney drawing or to talk through the Chinese factory piece. But in the email he didn't mention either, and instead explained that Jerry had hired someone named Dave McNeedle, in a role yet to be named, under himself as publisher but over Laura, the heart and soul of the magazine, who'd been running the place for the past eighteen years. I think the email was supposed to sound reassuring, catty, and cynical, but as it went on, Adam seemed less able to hide his alarm. Dave had worked in venture capital in Silicon Valley and had done some huge deals, and was married to Jerry's little sister, Margaret. Jerry's other attempts to optimize life at the magazine over the last two years—a swanky office redesign, free vegan coconut pudding, empowerment lectures by the likes of tennis legend John Newcombe—had also been worth a chortle or two but had never interfered with operations.

Dave had apparently been introduced at a lunch meeting on Friday, two days ago, and offered his thoughts on the future of digital media, lamenting the magazine's economic prospects, using investor jargon and social network data. Then he began criticizing editing choices from the past few months, including a recent cover story on Bobby Jindal's faith that he found "tough sledding." He criticized other sections of the magazine, and praised publications that had successfully moved into the digital age with lists and videos and hot takes. According to Adam, Dave didn't say anything positive about the deeply reported, long-format journalism that had made the magazine necessary reading for U.S. presidents since Millard Fillmore and instead mentioned how much money the publication was losing every year. This bit of hand-wringing from Adam, more than anything else, struck me as worrisome. Adam said he knew that rumors were flying and people were panicking, but he told me not to take too seriously anything I read. He did concede that there would be changes and closed the note by asking me to call him at home.

On Saturday afternoon he'd written again—while I'd been playing softball, getting whacked on narcotics, and licking Amy's coochie—to say that the Chinese factory story had been killed. "You've probably already heard," he wrote, but the number of print issues would likely be reduced from twelve to maybe eight. Or six. Or maybe none. Although there would be an increase in "Web content." A few of the monthly contracts had been canceled, but not mine, not yet anyway, "And I won't let them cancel yours," he wrote. "That's how important you are to the magazine." I should call him at the office, or on his cell anytime.

His third email had been sent late Saturday night. He explained that Laura had quit, although she'd already been fired, but she didn't know that until she read it later on an industry blog. Apparently, surveillance cameras around the office had been vandalized, and several other people at the magazine had quit or been fired, and maybe those firings had been for the best, but for now the bloodshed was over. There were more assurances, uncharacteristically ungrammatical ones that even on a good day Adam would never be in a position to make. "I'm not going anywhere, I'll die at my desk, and so will you."

A last email had come in around nine this morning. "I've been lucky to work at an institution that remained true to its heritage and principles," he wrote, sounding tired, or like a kidnapping victim being forced to give his own eulogy. He said he didn't know what the future would bring.

I combed the Web for stories about the magazine's implosion and found rants, paeans, and deep outrage from an endless supply of stuck-up former staffers who'd gone on to important careers in journalism and publishing, as well as heartwarming recollections of the good old days. I wondered if I'd get my next check, if it would be my last, and figured I was fortunate to be away from home, where no one would notice my chattering teeth and hollow-eyed, thousand-yard stare. The whole thing felt absurd, unbearably contrived, and way too real.

I'd gotten lazy and cocky, ignored phone calls and emails from other art directors; I'd shunned friends at other magazines, ad agencies, and design houses. I had nothing on the horizon, hadn't attended an industry party or award ceremony or bothered to respond to invitations to join a panel or judge a contest since Kaya's premature arrival. It would take weeks or months of begging, with backbreaking charm and jolly banter, to get the attention of anyone in a position to hire me, and how long after that to scrape together an assignment—at the given rate, no leverage—and 90 or 120 days after that to get paid. We were about to be broke like I hadn't been broke since I'd quit advertising. Any unforeseen expense would blitz my credit card and start a full-scale war at home. I started to hyperventilate, and began to see sparks in the air. I saw myself wearing the wool liner from an old army coat, wheeling a milk crate across a catering hall in a

luggage caddy, setting up an easel to do caricatures at a bar mitz-
vah.

I sat there flipping mindlessly around different news sites,
keeping my brain in neutral, trying to process what had just hap-
pened, maybe hoping to find a funny animal video to distract me,
when a headline caught my eye. For only the second time in its
history, a major book prize had named a cartoonist as a finalist for
its highest award. For a moment, I wondered whether it was me.
But the accompanying photo of Angel Solito, who I'd eaten
breakfast with, cleared up any confusion about why people had
been congratulating him. In the photo he stood in a gray T-shirt,
arms crossed, with a defiant look. I logged off the computer and
pushed back the chair, chuckling to myself, although the sound
began lower, deeper, shivering, rattling. I had to get back to class.

Climbing the stairs two at a time, I felt a wild energy, and
strode into the room, infused with a saintly desperation to en-
lighten and instruct. I knelt beside Vishnu and did the pen-nib
demo he'd requested after our first class, pointing out the parts of
the pen, the barrel of the nib, where the ink was held, demon-
strating to him how to grasp and hold the nib, moving quickly,
showing off, controlling the line, pulling it toward me, turning
my arm, rotating the paper.

"As a general rule of thumb," I said, in a loud, sharp, patroniz-
ing tone, "the pen can only move in so many directions." As I
raised the pen, he gave me a worried look. I thought of driving it
through his eyeball, into his brain. "And now it is time for me to
re-dip." On his desk sat a cup of ink, a murky cup of ink wash, a
stack of empty coffee cups, and a pile of inky blotting tissues
from his hours of failed experimentation. I went on, possibly
screaming, about the viscosity of various inks. There was also a
bag from the bagel place, crumbs in his lap and all over his shirt.

"Now you do it," I said. A strange chill came over me. My vision became blurry, clouded with auras. Maybe this was a dream and we were all already dead.

I went around the room, offering harried technical instruction and hollow, condescending compliments and encouragement, moving on when I felt my aggression spiking. "Nice try." "Staircases are tricky." "That looks wrong. Start over."

TWENTY-EIGHT

On the kitchen table in my apartment I found a note. "My arm is killing me," Amy wrote. "I'm going into town for more drugs." Her handwriting looked like the goofy scrawl of a child, since her good hand was purple and immobilized. "P.S. Where is my car key? I have to go." Good. I wanted her to go, get as far away from here as possible. We'd had our fun, although it was nothing really, and fucking her was killing me. "I'm going to New Hampshire to get Lily, then I'm heading home to deal with Mike." The paper was creased from her effort and her letters had smudged in the struggle to keep pace with her thoughts. "I've had it with his attacks and blame and projections." Maybe she was using her broken hand. I couldn't tell. "I am working on myself. I'm trying to be better. If I dropped dead tomorrow he'd trip over my carcass and not notice, although he is generous to others." Then the note broke up into random upper- and lowercase block print. "He is rude to me on a daily basis." A grapefruit I'd brought from home had been demolished, and she'd left its pits and guts on the kitchen counter.

I went to the bed and sat, holding the note. She'd never confront him. Nothing would come of it. I bowed and smelled the clothes on the bed, her T-shirt, bra, and underpants, taking my time with each, moved and overcome, engaged in the sensory knowledge, holding poignantly to the memories of her parts.

I had some raging, sicko crush on an emotionally stunted zillionaire, and she had a weakness for losers. It was silly and hopeless, and we'd never make it to Minorca. I found my shorts on the floor where I'd tossed them the night before, soaked from the late-night bike ride in the rain, with her key and earrings still in the pockets. I put the key on the kitchen table and placed the earrings in a teacup beside them.

There were some shopping bags from a store in town, and I picked up one and gave it a squeeze. I'd figured she might try to bribe me before she left, as a way to make light of last night's suggestion that I prostitute myself to her wealthy friends. A gift, or cash or a check, a couple thousand, maybe more. And I'd laugh it off, so she'd pretend to shove it in my pants or something, more laughter, but then she'd get serious and plead, but I'd hold firm. No thanks, I'd say, I don't need your pity, and shake my head with disdain. So she'd break down, she'd beg, and I'd cave.

I opened the bag to see what she'd bought me and found a gray polo shirt with a duck stitched on the breast and a three-pack of Fruit of the Loom boxers, price tag still on, $16.95. Rolled up at the bottom, like an afterthought, was a yellow necktie with brown loops on it. I examined it carefully, ashamed and confused. It looked like one I'd worn to my Aunt Doris's wedding in 1979. She'd purchased this stuff at a creaky old store on Main Street that also sold smelly candles and beach toys. I couldn't understand. Cheap, sensible clothing for the budget-minded male. Apparently I meant nothing to her, which I already knew, but now I knew how little nothing actually meant.

She blew $26,000 on her dog's knee surgeries, destroyed a one-of-a-kind custom-made ball gown because she couldn't find the zipper. Though she could also be thrifty and practical. She used old bread bags to carry her lunches, reheated leftovers, tossed in a sprig of rosemary to freshen her pot roast, wore shoes that hurt if they couldn't be returned, hunted down mysterious charges on her credit card bill and hammered the people who'd tried to overcharge her.

She'd dragged herself out of the working class with the strength of a locomotive, and looked back now with something like contempt. We'd turned into a nation of moochers, she'd told me once, and the attitude of entitlement bothered her. She worried—not that all gains went to the top, that Romney promised to overturn *Roe v. Wade,* but that our pride was gone, that the moochers didn't value things, like after-school programs, that were given to them for free. No matter how poor these people were, she'd gone on, it was better to make them pay. Then she'd explain the fee structure at some center she funded.

They lived in a monstrous stone-and-shingle masterpiece and also owned a $20 million duplex overlooking Central Park, and a "crappy" place in London, and a "nice" place in Chamonix. She employed a French-speaking Moroccan chef named Yasmine. I hated her life but thought I should have it. One hundred and twenty million dollars a year was the GDP of the Marshall Islands. If I worked for two thousand years, I'd earn the same as her husband did in one. Their net worth was a concept, like infinity. Easy to say, impossible to imagine.

We were an economic and planetary system at war, victims of a political farce. There'd been moments over the winter when I'd wanted to interrupt our epistolary love affair to unleash a searing rant of impeccable erudition—on the history of unstructured capitalism, twentieth-century U.S. imperialism, American workers forced to compete with Asian slave labor, private for-profit mass incarceration, Donald Rumsfeld, the Koch brothers, Citizens United, and the coming worldwide extinction—but I never got around to it.

I went through her purse and found some used Kleenex, hair ties, gum, a tube of Pantene Overnight Miracle. Eyeglasses, a kid's toy pen that looked like a cucumber. An Air France deck of cards. In her wallet I found $367 in bills, some dimes and quarters, a discount punch card for a pet food and supply store, credit cards, random business cards—"Win Win, matching Wall Street executives with nonprofit causes."

I'd been waiting for summer, for her. I'd wanted someone to save me. I wanted to lick her hand like a dying animal. I felt a horrible sadness twisting my face. From the start I'd been trying to function, to win her, to compete from a position of moral, material, psychic, and sexual subordination, underemployed, underfunded, improperly adorned. Loving someone is already so debilitating. To do it from this lowly place was so much worse. I saw an ordinary middle-aged man, unable to meet his responsibilities, jobless and abandoned, hurtling toward a last phase of doom.

I started to scream. It was the scream of a man who had no sense, who panicked and threw terrifying tantrums, smashed things, and sometimes smacked his own kids. I had vowed a long time ago that I would never become him, and I didn't, tried not to, but I'd become him anyway. Overwhelmed, destructive, destroyed.

I shoved the kitchen table out of the way with surprising ease. The old wooden ladder was heavier than it looked. I dragged it out from behind the filthy plaid sofa and hefted it vertical, vaguely noting the name of the old shipyard burned into one end and the worn wooden dowels that served as steps. I opened it up beneath the cupola's box of bright sunlight and climbed. At the top of the ladder I took in the view in all directions, the glinting water of the blue-black harbor, sailboats running spinnakers, feeling suddenly more alive, seeing colored spots, blinking and panting. Car traffic backed up all the way to the fish market. Across the highway, undulating dunes went out to the point. The dowels hurt as my flip-flops slipped against my sweaty feet. I swallowed back fear, still a little fuzzy on what I meant to do, as a feeling unimaginably corny and sad took hold.

Who hasn't felt this way at least once in his life? Who hasn't thought, at least once, Enough, stop the merry-go-round and let me off? Suicide is a selfish, pathetic, disgusting act. A weak, manipulative, evil thing that leaves behind nothing but the tortured souls of loved ones, twisting in limbo. I've lost everything, I'm a misfit, no one understands me, I want out. What a coward— I wanted a coward's death. I undid my belt and tossed it over the rafter, then cinched it around my throat. Dare me to do it. Dare me to jump! I leaned into the belt to test its strength, felt it tighten, heard the silence of suffocation. I couldn't catch my breath, but even breathing seemed like one more thing to worry about. My own death felt neat and simple. It felt portable, viable, and private. I started to fade, and panicked, and stepped up to undo the belt buckle, thinking I'd maybe taken this joke too far, as a flip-flop caught on the rung. I heard a loud bang and went flying.

OBSCURE CARTOONIST FOUND DEAD BY STINGY PHILANTHROPIST

Richard I. Fischer, 42, of Takoma Park, MD, a failed artist whose small illustrations appeared from time to time in a magazine that no longer exists, died Sunday from injuries related to accidental strangulation. An autopsy confirmed that the deceased had ejaculated several times in recent days, while attending an annual conference here in the Outer Beaches area without his wife, Robin Lister, 38, also of Takoma Park. A part-time television executive generally considered to be thin, loyal, and attractive, Lister had been hoping since June to shoot or stab Fischer in the testicles or chop off his penis. His only book, a graphic novel entitled *I Have Suffered Greatly,* had been out of print for several years, although he'd hoped to revive his career by basing a new semiautobiographical comic upon his recent adulterous experiences. The deceased had been under considerable financial strain and heavy psychological stress and had been looking forward to his annual visit to the Outer Beaches, with its pleasing climate and abundant national seashore. In the evenings he'd enjoyed the sight of many small bonfires behind the motels on the bay, and in the mornings, during his walks among the dunes, along the maze of tall grasses where gay men often came to rendezvous, it had cheered him up to see used, brightly colored condoms, flung into tree branches, dangling in the scrub.

I felt a sharp pain and heard myself groan. I wasn't dead, or even dying. I'd landed on my back on the kitchen table. Through a quick examination, I detected no serious injuries. Underneath my back, I found a broken pair of Amy's eyeglasses.

What the hell. I couldn't even manage to kill myself. The belt lay draped around my neck. The metal prong on the belt buckle had snapped off and was gone. Maybe I'd done it wrong.

Maybe I wasn't supposed to die yet.

I had to stop this, whatever it was, this experiment—stop treating my life as fodder for a story, stop treating the story as a way to take revenge, as a secret code to friends and lovers, as a suicide note. I had to stop, but I couldn't.

As a kid I'd climbed too high and fallen out of trees, experimented with the contents of friends' parents' gun cabinets, knocked out my front teeth on a dark, twisting road in the family Cherokee after figuring out, at fourteen, how to ease off the parking brake and roll down the driveway. Sexual high jinks, psilocybin, thrill seeking, abortions, back taxes, frivolously, flippantly impractical life goals. Marriage and kids had merely distracted me from the task, the need to hurl myself like a madman, to run the experiment until I'd torched the lab and had to sift through the debris for clues. There was shame from having tried, the tantalizing suspicion that I'd tripped on purpose, and the sickening relief at having failed again to die.

Standing, bending over unsteadily, I gathered things from the floor and put them back in her purse. I picked up her phone. It didn't ask for a password. She had Sprint, which apparently worked better on this end of campus.

What could I possibly have been looking for? I knew everything from our ten thousand emails, and in these last two days I'd learned more. She'd shipped her seven-year-old to sleepaway camp against her better judgment, four months after brain surgery, still twenty pounds underweight. Her husband forced himself upon her as she lay there grossed out, wondering whose fault it was. She'd agreed to spend eternity buried next to that fascist.

I began scrolling through her latest messages: an overdue notice from the town library, Harry Potter, fifty cents; a note from a tour operator with an outline of the Rapazzo family's fall cruise off the tip of South America, private transfers, five-star yacht, Magellanic penguins. Lou Ann Haney from her spin class wondered where she'd been all week. Her hair appointment with Gregory was confirmed. A museum board chairwoman apologized for some unintended slight at a social gathering. I saw only bare-bones communications between her and Mike: "home Friday," "no, can't, in mideast till 11th." She hadn't exaggerated; it was like Morse code. There were polite exchanges between his secretary and wife to arrange his tee times and doctor's appointments. A letter from the chapter head of a Franciscan monastery in Boston thanked Amy for a generous contribution, a "considerable, sustaining gift."

I found a spreadsheet from her assistant, Danielle, listing tax-deductible donations from the last two months: a Fukushima relief fund, a hospital in Macedonia, a project to help slow real estate development along sensitive wetlands areas. The donations added up to almost $11 million. It seemed that she couldn't be bothered to uncap her pickle pen for less than seven figures. What about me? I could ask for a loan at least, a measly three thousand bucks.

I'd already googled her a thousand times, found rumors of political front groups that received Mike's help, organizations that wanted to put Romney in the White House, to end all regulatory agencies, dark-money cash machines and fake grassroots charities with patriotic-sounding names. I'd tracked down, then wished I hadn't, publicly disclosed campaign contributions of Michael V. and one Amy D. Rapazzo, backing gubernatorial, House, and Senate candidates, state reps, right-wing candidates from across the country.

One mystery leads to the next, exposes a deeper question, pushes it out into the open. Who was she? How did I end up here?

I'd been given unimpeded access to her domestic perversions, her agonizing fears and deliberations as the umbilical cord went taut across too many miles. She'd shown me that good luck wasn't necessarily good, money couldn't replace the veins in a child's head, that a parent's worst nightmare might still come true. I'd sent heaps of love letters, presided over the realm of her body, an apparently invulnerable place of wet and warm, of cool and sorrow, of subdermal pulses and deep red blood. Gave her eighteen orgasms, loved and cared for her in a way no one ever had, and in return I'd been graced with her attention, a thing of value beyond the mechanism of her wealth. All I'd wanted was someone strange and new, to restore some wonder to the reason we exist. Amy had given me that.

She'd been emailing a Sotheby's agent just this morning, about the house for sale next door to hers, "Pheasant Ridge, a significant Georgian manor on seven acres." Meandering meadows, three-thousand-bottle wine cellar. Asking price: $28 million. She wondered about the highest bidder's escalation clause. But why? Was she planning to outbid him? So she could move across the driveway under the cover of darkness? To split from Mike without the public humiliation? In letters to me she'd floated several scenarios, including his possible relocation to the Frankfurt office or a more permanent move to their digs in New York. She wondered whether their kids would even notice. She'd also discussed blowing out their pool house or adding another floor to their already massive pad, to get him out of her sight. She seemed to think it could be done without telling anyone, not even him.

Or maybe she wanted to buy Pheasant Ridge for me.

TWENTY-NINE

I sat at the kitchen table, staring at her phone, listening to her walk up the stairs. She went to the bed, moving stiffly, picked up the T-shirt she'd worn to sleep, and shook it one-handed. "They wouldn't give me anything," she said. "Except this." A blue sling suspended her arm on a strap around her neck. She turned to me with slanted eyes of Irish sorrow. "I don't remember taking all six pills."

Her hair had a bump on the side and a jagged part. The pain went through her shoulder, she said, up the side of her head. She hunched, not smiling, distracted, looking worn, her face gaunt.

I'd loved her just this morning. I'd loved her as much as I could. I suggested that maybe her pain threshold wasn't as high as she'd thought. She searched my face. It was a wistful, bitter acceptance.

"My doctor called in the refill, but the guy at the pharmacy said it's illegal to prescribe that stuff over the phone. He said if he gets audited he'll lose his license. He said a ten-milligram pill has a street value of twenty dollars." The sarcasm seemed to relieve the pain. "That's a thirteen-dollar net."

She dropped the T-shirt on the bed and came toward the table, blinking wildly, her jaw opening, testing the ache. Her purse lay on its side. Some of her stuff had fallen on the floor again. She lifted one half of her eyeglasses to her face, then dropped it.

"I almost forgot," I said. "Thanks for the shirt. You didn't have to do that."

She looked at me strangely. In return, a forced smile plastered itself under my nose. I tried to change it but couldn't, so I arranged my face to say that these meager offerings were too pitiful to acknowledge beyond a few insincere words. She picked up the shirt and tie and carried them to the couch.

"This stuff is for Mike," she said. She moved in a kind of modified creep, then came back and got the boxers. If she kept moving, she said, she could distract her body from the pain. She began folding her own clothes on the bed, breathing loudly, carefully packing them into her bag, with a throbbing energy that barely hid a suppressed spiritual agony. She held it in, cold and resigned.

She stuffed her sandals down into her bag one-handed, and threw the bag on the kitchen chair. Then she hurled herself onto the bed, rubbing her feet against the old cotton bedspread in a writhing motion as if to soothe herself.

"You missed your meeting in New York."

"It doesn't matter."

"Send them a check." She ignored me, wincing, adjusting her arm. "How much did you give the people you were on the phone with yesterday?"

"None of your beeswax."

"Your assistant needs to enter it into the spreadsheet."

She turned back, a little astonished, squinting at me, then noticed her playing cards on the floor and her phone in my hand.

"Was there anything else you wanted to know?"

"Why are you bidding on Pheasant Ridge?"

"I'm not." She looked away sourly. "Quit looking at my fucking phone."

"But why were you talking to the agent?"

She fell back on the pillow. Her expression gave way to something dark and remote. "Because I was sad."

"Sad?"

"I thought I could donate it to St. Anne's, my church, as a home for adolescent mothers and their babies."

"And that would make you happy?"

"Yes. Or a lab to study the effects of overdevelopment on the local water table. But a real lab, part of the university."

"I don't think it's zoned for that."

"I'm not sure."

"Why are you giving money to those goatfuckers?"

"What?"

"Are you a Republican?"

She let her head fall back. "No." She closed her eyes. "I'm nothing."

"How are you nothing?"

"Although I do believe that in some situations, private enterprise can succeed where big government fails—"

I grabbed my head and yelled. She stopped talking. We waited. Then she asked quietly, "You're talking about my campaign donations?"

"Yes."

"That's Mike's list."

"You're full of shit."

"He wants a united front," she said. "Because it looks better that way."

"You do this stuff and then you blame him."

"No." Her eyes were closed. "It's not mine." She winced in pain and shifted her arm. "Nothing is mine. Not my kids or my work or my own body, or even my own name. If he wants it, it gets taken. If he does something disgusting, I have to live with it. If I do something good, something I support that he likes, education reform or my projects in the Baltic states, he takes it, he makes a call or writes a check and somehow my name gets cut from the press release and no one can tell me how that happened." She looked at me. "The only person I want to help I can't," she said. "You don't need my help, do you?"

I could've told her about our debts and loans, back taxes and whatnot, my endangered job at the magazine. I said no. She smiled. I think she knew. "Do you want the bracelet back?"

"No."

"Because you could return it." She flicked her wrist around so the pearls moved. "It's the nicest thing anyone ever gave me."

"Keep it."

"You know I'd do anything for you."

"I know."

"You're not an environmental cause or a school with two thousand kids. You're just some dude with nice lips."

"Thanks."

"I wanted to help you but I never figured out how."

This was merely one unfortunate thing among many, most of which did work out, on a miraculous scale, all over the world, and in return she received sincere gratitude, plaques and speeches in carpeted ballrooms over white linen with heavy hors d'oeuvres.

"Can you understand that?" I said yes. She could've fixed my life. She'd fix her dog's knees instead. I couldn't bring myself to ask. Borrowing money from the billionaire you've been screwing is tacky, and looks like blackmail, and turns you into a bimbo. A breeze caught the papers on the kitchen table. They fluttered.

"So your plan is for us to go our separate ways," I said, "and when things get desperate we toss it in an email?"

"That was the plan, yeah. Is there a problem with it?" She lay back on the blanket and looked up through the skylight.

"Well, there's the magnitude of the lie, the risk of getting caught, and the way it ruins everything."

She didn't care. She needed me to be a part of it, to shield her from him.

"I can't give up talking to you. I can't go it alone. I think I was dying. You brought me back." The curtains blew softly in and out. "I spent the whole morning chattering to you in my head." She lay with her head back, sighing, her feet rubbing against the bedspread as she shifted her arm to a better position. "When it's quiet, your voice is the one I hear."

Throughout the time I'd known her, there'd always been a sense that the fantasy could not be killed or even weakened, that each of us contained the other and could function independently.

Downtown, the noon whistle blew. Then it was quiet. For a minute, I listened to the cicadas buzzing out in the sunshine. Her chest rose and fell as she lay there.

"Can I ask you something?" she said.

"Uh-huh."

"Do you enjoy the sound of Robin chewing granola?"

"Sure."

"How about watching her stare at herself in the mirror, sucking in her gut, bragging about her paleo diet?"

"Granola's not on the paleo diet," I said.

"I told him, but he doesn't care."

She lay back in a white, rigid state of resignation, self-condemnation, postponing judgment, holding it in. "I'm so tired of being invisible."

There was still some crap from her purse on the floor under the table. The table was made of enameled steel. My neck hurt. There were four places worn into the enamel by a lifetime of meals, so that the metal showed through. We both believed there was a rich erotic life out there that we'd been denied, that strangers knew how to access.

"Does your wife still lie on the floor every night with an ice pack shoved down her sweatpants, saying she tore something in her hip and her foot is broken from her Miu Mius?"

"Yes."

"Saying her foot hurts or she can't find the Advil and thinks she has rheumatoid arthritis or Lyme disease?"

"Yes."

"And it leaves you lonely and missing the person right in front of you?"

"Yes."

She sat up, staring at me. I went to the freezer and dumped the ice from the muffin tin into a dish towel, and brought it over to her.

THIRTY

While putting on her clothes, she called the camp to let them know she was coming, then walked downstairs with her shirt on crooked.

I thought of her, alone, in pain, in the car. I couldn't move, couldn't get out of bed, but it was worse than that. A soft, dull, blanketed weight. There were cracked muddy smears on my thighs, her blood on my naked parts. Out of her, something torn, a wound, our imaginary family. The sight of her disemboweled grapefruit on the counter filled me with horror. I went to the bathroom and sobbed. My circuitry had been jangled. Windowless and dank, wallpaper buckling, the hum of the fluorescent bulb, the black line of mold in the grout, deep black fuzz in the fan vent, vinyl floor tiles that had come loose and been stuck back on crooked, terrible caulking, dirty handprints on the ceiling, water stains and wood rot from leaks in the walls. My sobbing had the obscene quality of a broken, cynical victim fake-laughing, desperate for revenge. Even by my own ridiculous standards, this scene went a little overboard.

I took some time wetting and drying my face, waiting for my personality to return, bawling like a pussy. I was so sick of losing her while also losing to her, by every conceivable measure. Her children would not fall into a junk-filled construction hole. Her marriage was endowed. Their winnings were secured offshore.

I looked around at the warped dresser, the cloudy mirror above it, the gouge in the wall behind it, the ladder, still standing beneath the cupola. I stared hard into these objects, like a little kid waiting for a seed to grow. I threw away the grapefruit and carried the garbage to the dumpster, grabbed my bike, and rode out to the ocean.

As I arrived, cyclists were parking along the highway, locking their bikes to the guardrail, and walking through dense scrub to the dunes. The column moved, more or less single file, leaderless, trudging. Climbing into the sun, we looked out over a Saharan moonscape, our ankles sinking into deep pouring sand. Every step was a different useless thought: I missed my chance. It just might work. I'm such a shit. I need my kids. I love my wife. Then the loop restarted. I'd crossed these dunes before, but they'd changed over the winter and I didn't recognize the path. At the top of the rise the whole mountain fell sharply away. Beneath us, kids had flung themselves, tumbling, down the dune. I marveled at the strange geology. From this distance the ocean looked like nothing, rows of fun, frothy, rolly waves glinting beyond the sea of umbrellas. I had come to perceive the lonely existence of fatherhood and monogamy as submission and defeat, saw my own children as some kind of moral betrayal of artistic purity. How did other people do it? My neighbor Curtis watched Bobby Flay after his family went to bed. In the fall he planted bulbs and raked leaves. I needed more than yard work. And no matter what, I would never stop loving Amy. I would take her to my grave.

At the bottom of the dune were some old preserved wooden buildings, roped off with signage, and a hand-painted taco truck. Hipsters sat on picnic benches in porkpie hats and bikinis, smoking, watching the action on the waves. Surfers and kiteboarders in half-zipped wet suits ran across the parking lot. Little kids in neon shorts flipped their skateboards and fell and assessed their injuries. As I got closer the sea appeared tipped, as if coming from above me, bearing down. The sand was hot. The beach was packed. The wind came up. I stopped and put a hand up as a visor to study it, a roiling cauldron with heaving barrels crashing at bad angles and surfers flying into the air.

An incoming wave sounded like an airplane taking off, followed by a house collapsing. Almost no one was swimming. I had an insane headache, the worst in my life. A hundred yards down the beach, I was still looking for a spot to spread my towel. Heaps of burped-up algae lined the shore. Thick bands of slimy green stuff floated in the water.

Two lifeguards sat high up on a lifeguard chair, in hats that looked Australian, with chin straps cinched up, binoculars raised, noses painted white, in long-sleeved shirts. They flew the yellow flag. A man below them on a towel in the shadow of the chair wore his own wide-brimmed hat and long sleeves. It was Dennis Fleigel, still pink, his face painted white. He looked like the property of a civilization of larger beings, throned above him, imprisoned for later use as a ritual sacrifice. When I got close, he exploded in anguish.

Tom McLaughlin's German TV crew had commandeered Dennis's well-lit, wood-paneled classroom, so Dennis had been shoved into a windowless closet. Carl didn't care who he humiliated. Worse, tonight's featured event, a reading by Dennis from the Coco Chanel bio in progress, had been shifted to a dead zone tomorrow afternoon in the basement of Stinson. "It's not fair," he said. "You know I'm right." He wasn't asking. I didn't feel like being yelled at. He didn't know how to get along. When I couldn't stand it anymore, I moved on.

A piece of what looked like a telephone pole lay among some sunbathers. A red industrial fishing buoy had washed up, like a beach ball, covered in rusty slime. Whatever had happened here last night had left crap all over the place. The destruction felt true to me, a manifestation of bad thoughts. Farther down, Frederick Stugatz seemed to be meditating, elbows on his knees, hair combed, shirtless, muscled, tanned, thin, a flat middle sucked in as though he'd been holding his breath all day. He raised his chin and examined me from behind sunglasses. And even though it was clear that he'd been waiting for someone else, he was friendly.

We sat and watched the water. I'd never seen so many surfers so close to shore, skimming and flying across the waves. I'd never seen kiteboarding. There were aerial acrobatics and fantastic wipeouts. The lifeguards were busy. It was a strong surf with riptide conditions. Now that Amy was gone I felt saner, but I also hoped I'd see someone drown.

We talked about last night's party. Frederick had the latest gossip. He and I were friends to the extent that we'd shared brief, odd, intense experiences over the years, like a flight crew who'd come through bad turbulence with a full load of drunks. Marty Azamanian had poured a bottle of Pellegrino on Bonnie Raitt's boyfriend's head for blowing the punch line to his joke. Later he'd slapped Carl across the face for interrupting him, a light, fun smack Carl hadn't appreciated. At one time or another, we'd seen Marty leaning out an upstairs window of the pool house with his younger son, armed with powerful water-pistol machine guns, scattering the crowd. We took it, because we liked to eat lobster at his beachfront showplace. After the party, Burt had needed fourteen stitches in his head.

I lay back and slept with the thrum of the ocean beneath me, and woke sometime later to a family of cretins who'd spread out their blanket inches away from us. Next to them were two men under a Bolla wine umbrella. They were dark, hairy, and muscular and looked like Mafia killers who'd slap you for kissing their sister, then leave your bullet-riddled body in the town square. I felt the constant slamming of the surf through the ground. I wanted a wave to come up so it blotted out the sun and blasted our bodies to pieces that washed up miles away. Down the coast I noticed three modern white windmills, so huge in the distance they looked like something in a dream.

A whistle blew. A lifeguard pulled hard in the surf, with a yellow rope around his shoulder, as another guard paid out rope from a garbage can.

It was hot but too dangerous to swim, so we left our towels and walked down the beach toward the state park. Farther down, there were pitted areas of wet sand, puddles, logs, garbage, a Fritos bag, a Mylar graduation balloon, a depression full of large, smooth rocks dug into the beach. The crowd thinned. Cigar butt, cigarettes, a big dead bird laid out like an Egyptian mummy. Beyond the cordon of lifeguard protection, the beach was almost empty.

A woman came toward us, in a wifebeater and bikini bottoms with big black sunglasses. It wasn't Amy. A little girl walked along the water, holding a smaller boy's hand. They were nobody I knew.

Frederick looked ahead and said, "How's her arm?" He lifted his chin and pushed his lips together, as though he were patiently adding small numbers, then made an expression of contempt or boredom, as though he'd been forced to sigh and explain that he knew, or everyone knew.

"It hurts."

"I'm sure."

"She's gone. Went home."

"I guess it's no fun to be here with a broken arm."

"I told her to get the hell out." He turned his head. "I'm kidding. I'm being an asshole. She wanted to go."

Our last one had been the longest, the deepest, the most loving, the most kissing, the saddest and most tearful. And when I came inside her I felt healed, and finally began to forgive her.

"You're trying to do the decent thing."

"Not really."

"Do you have plans to see her again?"

"No."

"Maybe it's not over."

"It's over."

"Is it?"

"Yeah."

"I don't think so," he said. "You'll write." He smiled. "Can you imagine, twenty years ago, writing a letter and walking it down to the mailbox five times a day? Calling her at home at midnight and hanging up if he answers? Do you say you love her?"

"No."

"It's not over. You'll see. Winter comes, you get sentimental. So much time goes by you figure it must be love. It gets stronger. Every second, it's right there in the palm of your hand. A few words are all you need to start again. Who will pull the other one in after a period of silence, who will draw the other one out. Who cracks first and begs for attention, who shows greater disregard for their sanity. You have that to look forward to."

"No."

"I can't write a three-word text to Ilana I haven't already sent a thousand times, because nothing ever changes and I've already said it all. I've already heard her same goddamned bullshit complaints. Stick around for that. Stick around for the times when you'd rather be fucking your wife but you do it anyway, when you feel guilty for loving your wife more than the one you're supposed to be so hot for. This is five years I can't get back, when I should've been saving money, planning a family vacation, thinking of something else. I guess it's a trap. I don't regret it. I didn't hurt anybody."

"We couldn't even make it through a year."

"And when you run out of stuff to say, you send photos of yourself as a baby, or tell her things that put your humanity on display—you helped an old lady wheel her groceries out, whatever. She'll respond to that, that works for a while. You talk about your kids and she'll pretend to love them, too. Or someone has some big event, my father died, she had cancer. Just wait. Stuff happens. You'll turn to each other."

"Ilana has cancer?"

"She did."

"She talked to you about it?"

"Every day, for months. You can't put that on someone you live with. It's too heavy. But how much time does it take to read an email and write back 'I love you'? Twenty seconds? Ilana also did that for me. It's nice when someone says it."

Even during years when their time at the conference went badly, compared to previous summers, they'd head home revived by some deranged new thinking. Five summers, with all the excitement leading up to it, all that time afterward to relive it and compare notes. They'd meet in other places too, but the conference was better for pure release, a block of days to rid themselves of awkwardness and flinching at phantasms, without the humiliation of skulking around a hotel lobby. This was, after all, a work trip; they taught the class together. And even while it remained impossible to touch the other in public, they went ahead and assumed we knew. We did.

Four years ago, Ilana moved to L.A. with her husband and son. Got lost in the shuffle at her record label, fought with producers, went through years of limbo hell. Scored movies that never got released, had a mastectomy, called herself "Frankenboob." Her son missed half of eighth grade with mysterious ailments and ended up in a private school for stupid rich kids. Frederick's father died, he lost his teaching job, found a new one at a state school an hour away for less pay.

There were teary messages and missed birthday phone calls, sudden ill-timed fevers of horniness, flurries of nude selfies, hot messages on Christmas Day, smelly hotel rooms in Boston and L.A., windows facing an airshaft, horrible carpets with squares cut out, exposing cement and glue underneath. And afterward, alone, feeling shifty and wrung out from a sleepless night of heedless fucking, he walked alone at dawn in the bracing wind of November on Columbus Avenue beside Thanksgiving Day balloons. Later, when he gave in to melancholy and combed through their early letters, those ancient correspondences, he was unrecognizable to himself, talkative, lyrical, and boisterous, full of steamy excitement and the thrill of the unknown.

Frederick told me everything. They never wrote a musical together. Half of the songs they'd written were unfinished. None were good. They never met each other's kids. Other things had also once seemed inevitable. This year, for the first time since the year of her lumpectomy, they hadn't seen each other once between conferences. Neither one could muster the energy or manage the logistics. And when, two nights ago, on Friday, they'd finally gone off together to discharge their affairs, she'd fallen asleep immediately and he could see in her sleeping that their sex hadn't changed her. It hadn't changed him either, until he saw her lying there, then felt jealous and panicky and couldn't sleep, and in the morning was forced to go through the motions, while her motherly mollifying made him feel like her idiot son. Saturday afternoon had been an improvement, though only from repetition. But last night, after the party, down the beach from the Azamanians, in the rain, beneath some billionaire's heavily anchored volleyball net, they screwed once more, on the sand, and it was perfect and wiped out everything.

"It was nice," he said, nodding his head.

"I bet."

"We've been lucky."

We had turned around where the beach narrowed at the trailer park and had circled back, and were at our towels again. At five, the lifeguards blew their whistles and packed the equipment onto their ATVs and left. The wind had died down, which seemed to calm the water. Frederick's secrets had left me in a weird state. There were gaps between sets of roguish waves. It was a trap, another vow, another job. I ran like a maniac and dove under the rolling surf. It was cold and I stroked spastically. The waves were biggish but not demonic, and I watched them coming and tried to get a sense of an approaching surge. It was all in pieces. I got slammed and half the ocean went up my nose. Farther out was a smooth rolling sea, and I had no problem treading water.

Looking back at the shore I saw her at our towels, perched on one knee but not sitting. Ilana had come to the beach after all. Good for them. He looked up but not directly at her. Soon the sun would begin its shameless, cornball, rhapsodic routine, a perfectly engineered, lurid light show of color, softening slightly at this hour before it turned a golden pinkish yellow, fading the world. Sandpipers dipped their wings and flew past. Fred had been trying to warn me, as a brother, as a friend. Or maybe he'd just been relieving himself of the burden so he could get back to business. Or maybe he wanted me to know how lucky he'd been; how he'd found this arrangement that demanded nothing; that he'd been careful not to blow up his marriage; that Ilana had become an old friend, a comrade, who he joined once a year for these magically efficient sexual interludes.

If she hadn't played, hadn't slipped, if I hadn't rushed it, or wasted half of her pills. If they'd given her drugs this morning she'd still be here, with her arm in an umbrella bag, treading my same water. What a pig I was. What a disaster. We owned that dumb little bed but never got out of it, never saw the ocean, never got the chance to have our own fun. She was different from Robin; that was all that mattered. Her height, her shoulders, her smell meant freedom. Fred slid over, and Ilana sat beside him. Look at them. Please sit. Stay. I would take her back, broken, miserable, and blind to my needs.

Who would cave first? Who would show the least restraint for their sanity, who would crack? Would we keep this up for years as some soul-sucking, double-secret support group?

A wave bore down and pulled me into a trough and I curled up and waited until it passed. I was fifty or a hundred feet from shore. Then another, and another. I got spun inside a washing machine, legs flung supernaturally back and behind, my body bent in half like a doll, eyes peeled open in airless panic. I shot to the surface and caught a wave, riding high, like the driver of a Greyhound bus. It tossed me right up onto the beach a little ways from them, hacking and spitting as I stood, pretending I knew what I was doing.

THIRTY-ONE

Smoke from the outdoor grill blew by as the cooks started dinner. The air was softer here. The grass felt warm underfoot. I went to the tent for something to get the taste of seawater out of my head.

Burt sat at a table in the corner, arms folded across his stomach, beard resting on his chest, gauze wrapped around his head like a soldier from World War I. Carl sat across from him, with Mary, the administrative coordinator, and Chris, the kid who made announcements. When I walked over there, Carl stood up and stepped away from the table. He still wore the yellow linen shirt, wrinkled like a boiled chicken.

"I got a report that you were causing a problem last night at two A.M."

"I was trying to break down the door to Randolph Hall."

"Well, don't let it happen again." He was pretending to be angry at me, but he actually was angry, which made his pretending less convincing. I didn't care. If after fifteen years he hadn't figured out how to run this thing, it was his tough shit. Banging on a dorm door at two A.M. was nothing compared to crumbling buildings, unpaid tuition bills, housing spats, noise violations, student disappearances, stonewalling from the state, or any of the usual travel disasters, teacher flake-outs, broken computer printers, underage drinking, chest pains, lost wallets, dogs trapped in sweltering cars, food complaints, in-class threatening behavior, broken air-conditioning, bruised egos, leaking ceilings, rattling windows, psycho participants pleading for help. His mood was not my fault.

"Didn't you see me wave to you at breakfast?"

"No."

His eyes lit up. They were a luminous green. The top of his face was mottled and shiny, while the lower part was loose and heavy, the color of steak, capillaries dark with iron.

"What's the matter?"

"Nothing," he said. "How are you?" His long gray hair looked slept on.

"Great."

"How's class?"

"Fantastic. Carol Dugan's doing a comic on being gang-raped as a child."

"Jesus Christ."

"And George Frost's brother won the Navy Cross in combat in Vietnam, but they gave it to him after he was dead."

"God."

"There are a few really disturbing ones."

He looked crazed. "How can you stand it?"

"Why are you looking at me that way?"

"Did you really not see me wave to you at breakfast?" He was demented.

"Yes, I thought you were saying hello. I didn't know you needed anything from me."

"I need something."

"What?"

He looked over at the wine table. I guess he needed a drink. I still had a gallon of seawater in my head and hopped up and down on one foot and instead it came pouring out my nose. Carl made his own sour face and waved for me to follow. We went up the porch stairs of the main building to his office, on the second floor. His shelves had books on seabird ecology and marine vertebrates, and novels and poetry by past summer faculty. He had a case of books on a table, signed hardback editions of Tom McLaughlin's West Texas memoir, to be given as gifts to donors. The paintings on Carl's walls were ones students had left behind. His windows looked out over the lawn, onto the scene below, conference attendees coming this way for dinner. I sat on the couch between piles of books, boxes of art supplies, poster tubes, and stacks of sweatshirts donated by the media mogul. He asked me to sign some of my posters, laid out on a table, for swag. I was flattered. He mentioned Solito and the book prize nomination and said it was good press for the conference. "We asked him to give a slide talk tonight."

"You bumped Dennis? That poor fucker." I hated him and started laughing. Carl ignored me and asked if I could introduce Solito. I stopped laughing, because I had no choice. Faculty members were contractually obligated to participate in these things.

Solito had had a similar reaction when Carl approached him. "No thanks, but maybe some other time." Carl's eyes blazed when he repeated those words. He told the kid that the conference had paid $1,200 to have his slide talk advertised on the radio.

Carl handed me a copy of Solito's book. On the inside flap, critics described it as "mesmerizing," "simple and moving," "a tale of suffering," "a story of humor and courage." I opened to the first page and it all came back to me, and was better than I'd remembered: the drawing of his mom, the smoke from her cigarette curling, catching her eye, reflected and dancing on the surface of a single teardrop. I went to the outer office, to Mary's empty desk, to work on my intro, looking for reviews and articles. Carl followed and opened the freezer and took out a bottle of vodka, poured a drink, and sat in a chair by Mary's desk, jingling his ice cubes. "So?" He gave me a leering look. "Having fun this year?" He wanted my dirt. He'd been standing over me when I'd knelt beside her on the softball field. He knew from Burt that I'd been at the clinic, and that it was her dormitory door I'd banged on at two A.M.

"If you want me to do this, go away."

I found material on Solito. One reviewer used the word "voracious." They called him versatile, a tinkerer, comedic, a magpie. They referred to the book as a "meticulously documented autobiographical triumph," "real events in words and pictures," and "a haunting graphic novel." One reviewer wondered what Solito's life would've been like if the United States hadn't destroyed a legitimate Guatemalan government just beginning to enjoy the blessings of democracy, leaving behind death squads, poverty, and decades of civil war. I read the blurbs on the back: "His sensibility is utterly unique, his characters are utterly real." The book was titled *The Crossing: A Picto-Narra-Graphic Allegory.* I pulled quotes and listed Solito's honors, fellowships, and awards.

But as I worked, I worried that audience members who knew me would look on in horror as I groveled in submission to a rising star. I worried that the ones who'd never seen me before would assume I was some sniveling ass licker trying to steal the limelight. I worried that my envy and roiling hostility would muddle my words, or that I'd start cackling madly and drop my introductory notes, grab Solito by the collar, and kick the shit out of him. I worried that any attempt to illuminate his work would reveal my inferiority. But after I printed the introduction out and read it over, I couldn't help but admire him, and felt protective even, proud to be associated with him, and maybe also a little swollen and greasy.

An hour or so later, I was seated at the bottom of a steeply banked chemistry lecture hall, beside Tom, Trudy, Charlene, and Roberta. I had showered and changed, and Solito was late. It was a packed house, with people standing in the back. I glanced over at Carl, who shook his head, grinning furiously. Ten minutes passed. At a quarter after seven he gave me another look, and I got up to announce that the evening would be canceled. The room quieted as I turned to face everyone. At the top of the hall I saw Solito, coming through a side door in dark clothes, holding a folder. I went ahead and read my goddamned intro, standing behind a long, narrow, black-topped science table with goose-necked sink plumbing and gas valves, under a feeble overhead light. I felt myself entering a trancelike state, soothed by the sound of my own voice, yielding as elegantly as I had at breakfast. It was a thoughtful and affectionate introduction. The audience applauded.

Solito walked down the steep staircase and went to the lectern and sipped some water as I took a seat. He turned on the overhead projector so that it flashed a bright blank screen. Hesitant, speaking slowly, in a practiced and self-deprecating tone, he said that it was a pain in the ass to be introduced by someone he admired, in a way that confused me. Some artists made him anxious and insecure, but I had reached out to him or whatever. He started talking about my book: "These days, bumbling antiheroes are commonplace, even quaint, but six years ago . . ." What the hell. He used a few of the same terms I'd used about his work, "powerful," "piercing," "blunt," forcing a comparison between my forgotten comics and his internationally lauded life-and-death struggle across a continent, to make me look like a footnote maybe, a sideshow, while at the same time intentionally mocking my introduction, twisting the flattering and conciliatory things I'd said. I peered around to see if anyone else had noticed. It seemed that no one did. The compliments felt like punches in the stomach. I sat there dazed, not sure if I'd just been ripped apart.

He put a page from his book up on the screen, giving us time to examine it, unhurriedly, then spoke with confidence about decisions he'd made in constructing each section. Then he repeated the process with another page. It took thirty-four minutes. The lights came up, and he answered questions with deep sincerity, as though the Dalai Lama had materialized in his saffron robe. He embodied the geopolitical dilemma, this problem of human migration. I am the border, the scar, the wound, the bridge between worlds. Big deal. Shut up. Blow me. He was calm and amiable. A man crawled around on the floor in front of me in what looked like a bulletproof vest. He held a camera in his hands and had another hanging from the vest. You wouldn't have known that Solito hated the routine or how, as he'd told me at breakfast, these questions were destroying him day by day. He'd admitted in interviews and again here that certain scenes conflated his own experiences with those of a younger cousin who'd made the journey with him, who he'd cut entirely out of the story. He confessed to this audience something I hadn't read in any article: that it was some third relative, and not him or the cousin, who'd been pulled off a bus at age four and placed in detention for months. They had the story, but that wasn't enough. They wanted the story behind the story, they wanted to get the facts out of him, so they could decide for themselves whether his suffering was real.

THIRTY-TWO

I woke up before dawn, gasping, suffocating, flopping around like a dying pigeon. We had no money. We'd lose the house. I felt that iron will, the force, the cult of Robin, the rules I had to live by. Did I even see her anymore, or did I only see things I imagined, the lie of my hate-filled projections, the cartoon of a wife I'd created?

The best times were with them: these beautiful people who called me Daddy and were never afraid, who didn't have a scary father and didn't know I was crazy. At home I was a part of something beyond my understanding, whole evenings spent in a daffy haze of singing, clapping, lifting, swinging, blowing up tiny balloons, my face turning purple, touching and examining every inch of them, like a violinist inspecting his instrument, kissing their sticky, doughnut-smelling feet.

It didn't matter. It was never enough. I needed life beyond them. I wanted more: people, praise, battles, conquests. I wanted to travel beyond myself, to explode out and out and out.

I thought of the monster who'd beat Amy and left her there bleeding. I couldn't fly back in time to protect her. I felt the crust of blood on these sheets and thought chaotically of the eclipsing impenetrable blackness of her obscene fortune, strange tax breaks, Shenzhen factories, unbreathable air, Cardinal Performance Capital grinding out millions under byzantine debt structures. Solito's wounded border, his continent of pain. Our hijacked country, sliding into rising seas. I saw Iris, Robin's mom, seated at dinner, head bowed forward, ignored by us as she waited for death.

I heard birds outside singing their wake-up songs, and felt myself tire of fear, like a rubber ball bouncing slowly to stillness, changing from night to day, from a night mind to a day mind, from fearful and blind to fearless and lucid. I understood why Amy married Rapazzo. She could use his money to reform education and eradicate poverty. Together they'd smash the old world with technocratic muscle and raise up the masses, that wad of scum beneath them. Or maybe that's what she hoped, or maybe that's not why she married him.

I recalled our final moments on Sunday afternoon. We'd been screwing for an hour, she needed to leave, drive to New Hampshire and rescue Lily. Her wrist throbbed, the pain went all the way up into her jaw. She shivered. "Ask me to stay," she said. I'd already imagined that first shitty one-line text she'd send and how that would excite me. She refused to put her clothes on. She loved the Barn and wanted to live here forever. But then, with her broken arm, she pointed out things she'd change, recalling the loft-like space of the ski chalet they'd once rented in Idaho, and some colonial-era money pit a friend of hers had renovated. She'd start with the windows, the kitchen, the plumbing and light fixtures, then scrunched her face and decided to gut the whole place.

A canister of room freshener had been sitting on the night table beside the broken lamp, left there by the cleaning crew, and in a dubious and insulting way, she suggested places around the apartment that needed Febrezing, the kitchen walls splattered with cooking oil, the moldy shower fan and broken front door. The ants in the kitchen, the spiderwebs and grease stains. In thirty seconds, the place had become something to be fumigated or demolished. I went along with it, and suggested Febrezing the couch, my armpits, a few of the moldier conference participants, like Beverly, who used a walker and an old-fashioned cigarette holder and thought she was Norma Desmond. We laughed our heads off. Together we were sharp and quick. Then she pinched her eyes shut and launched herself forward in one motion, bent over, leaning her body against my legs, sobbing. I thought she'd somehow bumped her arm.

"I'm so miserable," she said. It really was that bad, or maybe it was because we'd been laughing, acting silly, free of our frozen resentments. "I've been this way for years." Then she groaned like she'd been punched in the gut and said, "I never wanted this," and I figured she meant all of it, not just him and their heavy contract and those obligations that required such obliterating concentration, but also us, this cheap plastic fantasy that got us through our days.

It was the loneliness of her first pregnancy, nights alone in their overbuilt house in the woods, nursing at all hours, waiting for him to appear. "Staff up," he'd said, refusing to lift a finger when she asked for help. It took a year or two for her to figure it out, to give up, wondering when he'd notice. Sharing the joys and heartbreaks—someone's first tooth, someone's first cartwheel or dance recital—with her nanny or cook or the guy who mowed the lawn. Shoved between meetings and vacations, cringing when he spoke, taking it. His adolescent tries at humor were lame, sexist, sometimes revolting. It was like life in the old days, before cassette tapes, when telephones had bells inside them that rang and rang, and ChapStick came in a metal sleeve, when a man spent his days how he liked, and a woman hoped he'd behave and show up for dinner. "Remember what I told you," she said one night, covered in goose bumps, prickly with hatred, speaking to her daughters, who sat dumbstruck as her husband started to laugh.

THIRTY-THREE

In the rain the bay looked frozen. To the east, three heavy gray military planes from the air base an hour south roared up the coast. I got in line for breakfast. Eva Rotmensch, the dancer turned actress I'd met at softball, was standing so close I could smell her. She wore her same tiny pink corduroy shorts and a purple rain slicker. I smiled and she said nothing as I reached across her for a miserable slice of Irish soda bread. She stepped around me but I couldn't make eye contact. I felt invisible, historical. She had a thin body and breasts so high you could cup them in your hand like a firefly. The young man with the tattoo on his neck and fine golden skin, Ryan, the actor, stepped up behind her, and leaned over her shoulder as, together, they scanned the tent for a place to sit. They were groggy and beautiful, lean and muscled, and had obviously been screwing since the minute softball ended. I hadn't actually seen Ryan in a shirt until now. Of course it had the sleeves cut off and showed his smooth shoulders. It might've been the first shirt he'd ever worn in his life. You could sense in them a kind of psychic unity or harmony that comes when two people form that radiant bond. I stood there, wretchedly buttering my toast, cautious, middle-aged, middle-class. I wanted to apologize to the generations that followed: You don't have to get old. This was my mistake. I stepped past them carefully, eyes on my tofu scramble.

It hurt to wait patiently at the coffee table. I wanted to merge. We had somehow known just when to push, when to grind, and when to be still, locked together. A sadness came over me, then the whiplash of guilt. God, what screwing we'd accomplished. I wanted her in a terrible way, wanted to curl up in a ball and cry for what couldn't be. Rain spilled off the edge of the tent, splattering into mud.

Farther down the breakfast line they were talking about who vomited last night, at what hour, and the funny thing someone named Kaitlyn had said. Sadness gutted me. Chris from the office made announcements in his slicker. I sat at a table of familiar faces and couldn't help thinking they were such awful people. Tom imitated the German accents of the TV crew from Sunday, annoyed by the demands of his fame, working it into a routine that got old. Roberta was feeling youthful, and wanted to try ecstasy, and wondered if there was anything to it. We all agreed that we needed to lose weight. Heather explained that her dad had died of alcoholism. He'd died bad. Only by writing about it did she find some peace. This sounded canned, like a line from a lecture. The rest of them had gone drinking last night, and stayed out late, and looked fragile and bloated.

Ryan and Eva walked by. We had been young once, too. Vicky sat beside me, scowling at her coffee, wondering where I'd disappeared to last night after the slide talk. Winston Doyoyo sat silently on the other side of me, frowning up at his wife, Ingrid, a tall Scandinavian woman who walked back and forth across the tent. At last, she put down a plate of food in front of him and sat, exhaling loudly.

Tabitha confessed that there was no director, no financing or stars attached. She wanted to close the TV deal so she could get paid, and went on humble-bragging, repeating the producer's name, Kevin this, Kevin that, which infuriated Dennis. He wore a starched white linen shirt, the collar sharply pressed. His face looked pink and cold.

Ingrid spoke in a flat, administrative tone, with almost no accent, explaining that the money from these conferences came in handy, that the Nobel Prize Winston had won ten years earlier had gone into the houses of his children and a hotel in Pretoria that had burned to the ground. Winston watched her. She wanted us to understand that there was nothing left, that they lived off his appearance fees. He had an omelette in front of him, with watercress heaped on one side, and sat, incredulous, with something sadistic going on in his face, stronger than interest, more like disgust. Then he turned to me. "How old are you?" he asked.

"Forty-two."

"I'm seventy-eight. Get me a fucking napkin!"

I did, and noticed Frederick and Ilana at a table in the corner, at the far end of the tent, both with freshly wet hair. A few minutes later, we all got up and headed to class.

Up ahead, Vicky made her way across the field, with a cigarette in her mouth and a cup of coffee in each hand. Smoking in the rain seemed especially morbid. There were years when she and I had eaten every meal together, sat beside each other at slide talks, tramped on the beach late at night. Last year, until halfway through the conference, when I met Amy, Vicky and I had been close. There was that feeling of knowing what the other one thought, while Dennis ruined our meal, or in the middle of a particular moment at a reading or a play, like the one about a giant baby, played straight by a grown man in a diaper who needed a shave and was doing, essentially, Reverend Jim from *Taxi*.

I caught up to her and we walked together. As we did, I linked my arm in hers and grabbed her cigarette and took a long drag, and in a German accent I wondered what she thought of Solito's slide talk last night, mispronouncing words with a Hessian flair. "Vut vuz it?" I asked. Was it autobiography if parts of it were conflated? Were conflated parts definitively fiction? What if fiction was mostly made of facts? She didn't care, and misquoted Faulkner, with Kissinger's Bavarian lilt, but said she thought there was something "litigious" in his work, and that his answers had sounded strange.

I'd had feelings for her, while we'd been lying together on the beach on a bedsheet, of a sibling bond, answering questions about Robin and my kids, bumming her cigarettes and listening to stories of her ex boyfriends. Two of them were dead. The first one either choked to death or had a heart attack in a restaurant. She'd kept him alive until the ambulance arrived. The other one got hit by a New York City bus. And although I was subordinate to her, there were similarities in our art, at least with her more cartoony work—a piece about life in a Mexican garbage dump, another about donkey basketball, and one of painted color fields with scribbled questions about porn and eye-popping insults directed at her audience, interspersed with detailed drawings of an assault she'd survived in a subway station.

I saw them crossing the field, heading to the auditorium, walking close. Ilana and Fred were of average height, with the same dark coloring. I jealously studied their movements. There'd always been a laughable attempt to hide it, moving through a crowd, mixing in. There was a clear, quiet, concentrated energy between them, as though together they'd escaped a burning building, and were charged somehow, connected on a profound level. We got to the door of Fine Arts.

"See you later, fräulein."

She dropped the accent and asked again why I'd missed drinks and where I'd been. I said I'd been tired and had gone to bed. I thought that if she didn't look directly at me, I could say it, especially since it was true. But I'd been living with my story for so long, and had muddied the elegiac and ecstatic elements with terror and shame, and hoped that talking about it would give me some relief.

"Do you know her from somewhere else?" She crinkled her face at me. "The one who broke her arm?" She raised a hand above her head to indicate a person of great height. "The glamazon?" She rolled her eyes at me. "That big Wookiee!"

They were curious, but also pissed. They didn't want a happiness to go unsullied. They wanted the story, but if they had the story, they wanted the story behind the story, to punish the ones who had grabbed them and held their attention.

I was late for class but wanted to say one thing and be done with it. I thought she might understand. I didn't need to go on the way Frederick had about tearful Christmas phone calls, but I wanted someone to know. The seriousness of my expression implied that we'd destroyed each other's lives.

"Do you meet on the sly? Do you think of her when you're with your wife? Are you good at lying? Do you feel like a sleaze?" I said yes. "Do you know the husband? Do your families go on vacations together? Does it get easier with practice?" I said no.

THIRTY-FOUR

My classroom smelled lived in, pre-breathed, bodies but not enough air. I could see by the rate of progress that several of the students had pulled overtime since yesterday's class. Someone had spent the night, and lay wrapped in a beach towel at the back of the room, fast asleep. By the powdery bottoms of her feet, I knew it was Mel. I went around quietly with the handout I'd made yesterday, the guide to scanning and software. George had done a drawing of the interior of the bar at the infantry club at Fort Benning, circa 1965. I envied the steady breathing and quiet noises of humans at work. The intensity was palpable, but they were taking too long to draw. From this point they'd be stuck here, breaking for meals, powering through the night, blearily uploading their work, fighting at the scanners, complaining about someone's music, stapling or stitching the binding by hand.

Helen Li was slated to start med school in Boston in the fall, but she still had a few things to say about growing up in Taiwan, where the school day was twelve hours long, with homework until two A.M. If she swore, her mother smacked her with a shoe. The sadists who ran the school hit kids with books, made them line up and squat, then kicked them over like dominoes. At the far end of the room in her spot by the sinks, Rachel sat with her head bent, scribbling, wearing earbuds, lips moving, hearing voices, going hard, talking to herself.

I stood behind the printing press and listened. What I heard instead was Amy's breaths coming faster, those sweet, soft sounds. Then her tired voice, fumbling, reconciled: "Even if I'm alone for the rest of my life, I'll never be as sad and lonely as I am now, married to *him*." I wrote this down on the back of the handout. I had to stop fetishizing my cartooning blockage and look past my crippling envy to see the complexity in her, the potential storylines, huge ones of corrupt elements of power, but also small ones of people living in these fugue states of depressive, combative paranoia. Some cruel, killing part of her had flicked away the truth of my financial woes. Something despicable had risen up in me as I'd witnessed her crumbling façade, by the flagpole, then on the ball field, and in the clinic—an inadvertent meanness.

I wavered, in the middle of my classroom, drowning in this soup of confusion, accosted by fragments. I was seven inches taller than my wife and outweighed her by sixty pounds. My anger had frightened me, so I could imagine how it must've been for her. I felt an animal terror. I attacked out of fear of being less than, or when Robin treated me like the nanny or cook, or when Amy saw me as a gigolo, moments when I'd lost my individual identity. Emotional commitments and lifelong guarantees had turned me into an object of someone else's neuroses. I used Amy to divert my aggression away from Robin. In contrast to Mike, I was a goddamned hero. I humiliated others, swiped at phantoms, and feared for my life. I had to get it all down.

I needed concentrated hours, days of quiet in a nurturing atmosphere, to experiment with tools and materials, shielded from parenting, domestic hostility, taxing freelance work and students, in a place where I could safely lose myself in the process and surprise my eyes with emerging themes, to build out with images that mapped our emotional landscape, to explode out from there with memory and imagination. I made a few thumbnails, then got up and paced around the room.

Rebecca had added a new character to her ambulance scene, a paramedic in charge. He looked like a hockey enforcer, with a lined scowl and a heavy brow, sitting in the ambulance across from the younger Rebecca, counting off as she performed CPR, telling her to stay calm.

"He's dying," the hockey enforcer explains. "You're not dying. You're okay."

"The old man's rib cage crackled like brittle twigs," Rebecca wrote in a narrative box. "I worried his skin would tear."

In the second panel, the old man flatlines. In the third, the other paramedic bags him, forcing oxygen into his lungs. In the fourth, she hits him with paddles, over and over, to bring him back to life. Since yesterday, her pencil sketches had grown in complexity: the faces looked disturbed, the old man radiated illness. It was tight, spare, intense. I wanted her to start inking. She said she thought she might toss it in the garbage. I asked why.

She tapped her pencil against the side of her glasses, wincing. "Because I killed him." I wasn't sure what she meant. "Not on purpose."

"Okay."

"He's not the only one."

"You killed other people?"

"I saved other people." She made a serious face. "I killed mice."

"You what?"

She showed me how she'd done it, in a lab in college: yanked the animal by the ends, snap, pop. You could also gas it or chop off its head. She thought her story demanded an exploration of her role in each of these deaths. I knelt beside her and told her there wasn't enough time.

Carol's comic had structure, like Rebecca's, but almost no dialogue, and just a few captions. She'd knocked in the background of the snowy, beer-drenched drawings I'd seen yesterday. The first three panels were almost identical, as if this scene of boys grimly drinking inside a car in a snowstorm went on, in a loop, forever. In the fourth panel, a girl sat on the front seat, in her underwear, lit by the radio dial, kissing one boy, the hand of another on her breast, and two more in the backseat laughing and talking about her body. Even though I pretty much knew what was coming, reading this scene broke my heart.

The second page showed four nearly identical panels of the cassette deck radio dial. The drawings were dark. The repetition slowed time down, building tension. In each panel, she'd written a caption in a box. In the first one, "You try to hold it in, but eventually the pain will express itself." In the next she wrote, "It's better to face it directly than have it come out through illness or failed relationships." In the third one she wrote, "Recovery takes place." In the last one, "Healing takes place."

Maybe it worked on me because I knew the victim. Maybe it's easier to push this stuff aside when the cartoonist isn't sitting right there. She had one arm laid on the table, pencil smudges on her nose, and ashy graphite all over her hands. She put her hand over the drawing of the girl.

"I wish I had a better story to tell about that day, but I don't." She'd enrolled in my class as part of her recovery. "It hurts to think about, but I'm the one telling the story now. I'm the one who gets to decide." She lived in town and had an appointment with her shrink this afternoon. She took out a red bandanna and blew her nose. At the next desk over, Rebecca glanced up at her, then went back to her own work.

I made some practical suggestions for both of them, and threatened them with tomorrow's deadline, and walked to the far corner and stared at the floor. If someone looked up, I tried to hypnotize them with my mind. Tell the story. The story is in you. It has to come out. I could hear pencils on paper. I remembered standing here last year, and the year before that, trying to will them through.

"Went to a party last night," my new friend, Angel Solito, explained during the coffee break, his shiny black hair pushed into a rooster comb, wearing his hoodie and a checkered ska belt. The rain had forced both classes to congregate by the woodstoves. He'd begun by warmly and politely thanking me for facilitating last night's discussion, then complained that journalists had been hounding him all morning by phone and email. The party had taken place at some donor's swanky beach digs. "I met a man from Tennessee," he said. The man owned the largest private collection of Greek statuary on earth, he explained, and had invited him to come visit.

THIRTY-FIVE

I swept the floor, scrubbed the stains off my sheets, and put the ladder back where I'd found it. Threw away her broken eyeglasses and her playing cards, and cleaned off the table so I could work. Rain splattered onto my mattress. I tried and failed to close the skylight, went back to my notes and sketchbook and started to hyperventilate. Like Rebecca, I'd have to omit key pieces of information, conflate others. These omissions would absolve me of certain sins. Like Carol, I had only one story to tell, didn't want to tell it, but knew I had nothing else to say.

In *The Crossing*, Solito attempts to go north on foot and on buses. Later he clings to the tops of freight trains. In those scenes, there's nothing in front of the train, no horizon, no destination. We don't know where this boy will end up, and that's really the story of children trying to reach the United States from Latin

America. I still had Carl's copy, and noticed the fine brushwork of tree branches that ducked down to knock sleeping children off the train. I reread the scene of him getting robbed and beaten in Jalisco, before crossing the border, a child walking into the Arizona desert with some men who later died of dehydration.

I'd been trying to lower my anxiety level, to make Solito's accomplishments seem accessible, to inspire myself. I wanted to be great, too, wanted prizes and love from strangers. Instead, his stuff superimposed itself over mine. The reviews I'd read last night, the apoplectic praise and hysteria over his talent, youth, and ethnicity all went to work on me. His experiences were historic, monumental.

But until the day people stopped wishing they could cram their spouse into a dumpster, my story was relevant, too. Until we stopped accepting the destructive force of monogamy, until we stopped constructing other selves in secret, I had the edge: my story had yet to be told. And given the intensity of these past days, I held reserves of emotional capability no one could match.

Maybe you had a crush on a co-worker, or came to find some erotic charge in the dimpled smile or soothing voice of a neighbor or friend. You began to tamper with your repressions, the prison of your own making; you craved the slightest attention and the physiological boost that came from easy conversation with some sympathetic, similar-minded soul. Was this nourishing emotional connection a violation of trust? Your life felt rehearsed, performed; your most significant gestures only mimicked real emotion. Routine insincerity had inadvertently hollowed out your entire existence. What passed for candor became an act of nostalgia, loyalty, compulsion. Your drives and urges got sublimated into oblivion, for the good of something better, renovated master bath, shorter commute, authoritative parenting, the load-bearing walls of your house cracking and settling all around you. You became ashamed of senile arguments about how to sauté broccoli, you tuned out bleating babies and bug-eyed children, so that they had to scream to reach you. You peeked through the bars of your cage. Your heart jumped from a five-second exchange with a fair-skinned, ginger-haired stranger in the supermarket's frozen-food aisle. Married life was too strict, isolating, cruel. You could still recognize a certain look in the eyes of a friend when she laughed at your jokes, touching your elbow, sitting beside you at dinner, and said good night with a damp kiss and a flicker of pain, a reflection of your better self, possible lives, better days. Was there someone out there who wanted to enter an immersive illustrated fictional experience on this provocative matter? I shuddered at the thought of the mind-boggling complexities involved. Years of intense labor lay ahead.

I read through my sketchbook and found notes and drawings that fed ideas and strategies. Another world revealed itself to me, with lyrical imperatives. I made a few thumbnails. I imagined a web of unpleasant characters, trafficking in artistic misery, free markets, abstruse financial loopholes. I saw several moves ahead, my hand tracing lines only I could see, hovering somewhere between work and play, between necessity and escape. And yet, even as I worked, I knew it would cost me. Robin would withhold her body forever, or kill me in my sleep. I'd never live it down. Still, the sketches gave me pleasure.

On a clean sheet of paper I drew our little bungalow from the street, wooden porch, burnt lawn, the building planted squarely on the land. In the next panel I drew a tired man, characteristic receding hairline, long birdlike nose, him, me, kneeling in the glare of the television, folding laundry. In the third panel a woman sits on the rug beside him, in leggings and a yoga bra, stretching, her legs in a split. He's watching *South Park,* one where Kenny is dead and the boys build a ladder to heaven to try to get ahold of his winning lottery ticket. In the fourth panel I drew Kenny. In a box beneath Kenny I wrote:

Fuckless weeks, excused by parenting, had turned weirdly okay. Marriage had changed, become solid, had become newly grim as they learned, together, what it was to not be young.

"Let's hope they sleep," the woman says. "Wouldn't that be nice?"

Clean, folded laundry fills the basket. They stand, hugging. She presses her face into his shoulder. He sniffs her hair. "It's late," she says, her way of saying no. He hugs her but keeps his frontal parts back from this deeper embrace, creating a shaft of space between them as he stands impassively.

"What if," she says, "we just keep being nice to each other for a few more days?"

This is what stands for hope, when two people run up against the limitations of aging and married love. Then I roughed out a scene at the wealthy woman's house in Connecticut, the hot couple going from room to room, past the egg-shaped tub, then rolling around on the floor in her closet.

When I looked up, two hours later, it was as if no time had passed. I had eight pages of tight pencils, and four dense pages of notes. I stood and stretched. In a hidden cabinet in the bathroom I discovered a stash of clean sheets and towels, made the bed, gathered dirty dishes from around the apartment.

The teacup sat on the kitchen table. It was cracked, the cracks stained, the handle gone. It had roses painted along the rim. I lifted the cup, and the earrings rattled. I dumped the earrings into my palm and held one up to the light. Easy enough to overlook while packing and leaving. Easy enough to miss if you're crying. Easy enough to understand why the owner might avert her gaze at the sight of a gift given as a reward for tolerating spousal abuse. The stones were bluish white and packed with rainbows. A gift she didn't want, for an act of punishment she hadn't deserved, meant to signify obedience, humiliation, surrender, disgrace.

I should've handed them to her while she was packing her clothes, but in the haze of emotion I'd forgotten, although I could've handed them to her before that, but maybe I didn't want her thinking I was tracking her valuables. In her dorm room she'd asked me to remove them. I'd done nothing wrong. Of course I'd stolen them. Instead of feeling worse, I found mitigating thoughts distracting me. What if she'd left them here on purpose? What if this was how she'd decided to help me? Was she messing with my mind?

I walked through the rain, clutching the earrings as if any jostling might cause their disintegration, and entered the computer room of Crabston Hall, where, in a darkened hush of still bodies clicking mice and keyboards, I began to construct a quick, witty note, to let her know I'd found her baubles. They were bigger than a pencil eraser, smaller than a raspberry. I searched the Web for tips on how to tell the difference between a real and a fake diamond, and estimated their value between $29.95 and $20,000.

I would let her know, then toss them in the mail.

I found myself opening our secret folder, rereading the very last email she'd sent, from the hospital, back in March. I'd forgotten those photos of Lily, in post-op, still sleeping, all tape and tubes. Before that, Amy had complained that her roofer had accidentally backed into her security gate, so now it wouldn't open.

A neighbor from the building in Manhattan where she and Mike owned their duplex said the Russian businessman in the $39 million penthouse had demanded board approval for new security cameras, locks, and doors, because he worried he'd be kidnapped off the roof.

She didn't need these earrings.

Their wealth came from hundreds of millions in commissions sucked out of the Cardinal Capital Fund in untraceable fees, from the invested pensions of state workers, from the salaries of cops and teachers. Mike used those dollars to push reforms that turned dollars into votes, to disrupt a functioning democracy, to seize power for his own enrichment. He managed the savings of workers while maiming their rights through his philanthropy.

Most people figure out how to get by, save some and waste the rest, while the thought of dominating humanity might pass by in a daydream. I personally had no longing for supremacy. I'd never thought about it growing up. My dad tried to make some dough but didn't have the stomach for it. My mom saw her job as a way to give a little back.

She'd spent her life in a red brick elementary school two towns over from ours in the New York suburbs, teaching music to ten-, eleven-, and twelve-year-olds. My parents now lived almost entirely off her pension. In her retirement, she taught piano and swam at the Y. For the last forty-seven years, she'd been cooking my dad's meals. If, God forbid, she died before him, she'd need to remember to throw a chicken in the oven first, so he wouldn't starve. I loved her with a confused and heated passion. Once or twice, early in her brief career, I think she sang on Broadway. As a kid, I'd go over to her elementary school to see the shows she staged. I quit going as soon as I got my driver's license. A bouquet of flowers at the final bow, my mother walking out of the dark, reaching up to take them, then walking back into the dark. In the weeks before the show she'd play those old records, *Oklahoma!*, *Annie Get Your Gun, The Pajama Game, Oliver!*, on a wooden phonograph in our living room. I knew those shows by heart, knew where each of those records skipped, and sang the songs accordingly.

She led a fairly dull existence. Her youthful dreams fell away by necessity. Most people don't have it in them to change the world, don't harbor some secret fantasy so deeply buried and believed in that it gets confused with what's real.

Jerry accidentally destroyed the magazine. Marty ruined Hollywood, cable news, and FM radio. The Tennessee toad hoarded the treasures of all antiquity. Amy remembered the neediest, but she also owned a private jet and a live-in gardener, and caved to the whimsy of her redneck fascist owner.

To all the world, she was the lucky one. But I knew the truth, and kept it a secret, this thing that she herself could not keep secret, couldn't contain. She'd saddled me with it, infected me, inserted this sadness into me so that I went around burdened with it, tied to her. Now I'd be required to carry these valuables down the street to the post office, to mail them back to her, certified mail, heavily insured. Who would repay me? She could've made a real difference in my life, could've changed it forever with a flick of her pen. But instead, she left me here to rot.

I added up everything I'd ever given her: Christmas sweater, accidental bracelet, blouse, necklace, in addition to the dinner I'd bought her here last summer, bouillabaisse, braised vegetables, plus the gas I'd used driving up and down the East Coast so I could detour to Connecticut to hump her in her closet. It came to four grand, or nearly 7 percent of last year's income. Whereas 7 percent of her husband's income was $8 million. If the stuff she'd sent me—sweater, scarf, Italian leather gloves—added up to $800, then she'd spent less, much less, proportionally speaking. I was a fucking lot more generous.

I watched a video on the History channel with the volume down on the pitfalls of selling stolen goods to pawnshops. They interviewed criminals on what to say, how to act. I'd end up in jail or worse. I took notes.

THIRTY-SIX

Vast marshes of cattails looked beleaguered in the rain. At the end of town I hit the highway with a hysterical sense of self-justification, guilt level holding steady, howling inner voices mostly suppressed. Looking back in my rearview mirror, I lost sight of town, and broke the spell of the conference.

Thirty minutes later, I exited the highway and entered a quiet, stiff, old-fashioned, intolerant picture-postcard seacoast village, with a monument to dead soldiers of World War I, strolling tourists, and geese floating in the pond. I missed the weirdness of my temporary home, the dildo stores and street buskers, the drag queens scaring children.

The jewelry store was located inside the lobby of an old hotel. A woman seated under a bright light in the corner raised her head. A man in a suit came out of an office. Above us I noted closed-circuit cameras. It felt as though someone had taken the blunt end of a broomstick and banged it into my guts. We, my family, had decided to liquidate some heirlooms, I said. You gave them something airtight and unassailable and kept it short and sweet. He led me into his office and clasped his hands over a thick white pad covered in gem diagrams. He began listing his bona fides—licensed, certified—then talked about precision and magnification. "You can trust me," he said, "because I trust myself." I didn't know what I'd been hoping for, but this was not going to work. I explained that we kept everything in a safe-deposit box in Rhode Island but I could come back as soon as my Aunt Bunny gave her consent. He nodded, ignoring me, then pointed to Mrs. Nelson, sitting behind the case, who happened to be even more highly certified than him, he said. "But we can't advertise her certification without an AGS-approved lab."

It got worse. Historically, the trade in gemstones has been somewhat secretive, he explained, resistant to any kind of auditing or regulation. New developments had raised the reputation of the industry, helped standardize appraisal methods. This guy was some kind of fucking moralizing gemologist.

"What percentage of jewelers are licensed?"

"Oh, most."

On the shelf behind him were family photos, including one of him in a burgundy fez. He said something about an old lady who came by with a six-carat diamond. "I've been here for thirty-one years," he said. "I've been named personally in people's wills." He'd done thousands of transactions. We made an appointment for next week, and I stood and thanked him, feigning relief at having found an honorable soul, and gave him my name, Dennis Fleigel. I assumed I'd be arrested as I stepped out of the hotel, handcuffed, maybe stabbed, waiting hungrily for the blade to part my flesh.

I'd made a list of places to try within a hundred miles, and drove to the next one on it. The woman behind the counter needed proof of my ID, and sent me to the copier place two doors down. I got back in the car. Other places were too crowded or had gone out of business or had a bad vibe. One guy mostly worked with cuckoo clocks, beneath strips of peeling wallpaper.

Twenty miles down the highway I reached a fusty resort town on the state line, the last place on the list. A single storefront window displayed fine jewelry. I had to be buzzed in. I didn't give a shit anymore what happened.

"What if I have something to sell?"

He wore an orange golf shirt and held a newspaper, folded in thirds.

"What if I found it?"

He looked bored. "Am I the lost and found?"

"But how does this work?"

"I'm not a broker." He wore a big silver chain. "Typically, I want to get paid." He motioned with his hand. I gave him one of the earrings. He examined it with the loupe. "Does it have papers?"

I didn't know what he was talking about. "Just tell me what it's worth."

"A piece like this," he said, but didn't finish. He handed it back to me. "Take it to New York. You won't do better. But take it somewhere else, and if he offers more, then you know I'm fucking you. If you can do better with him, do it, but you won't. That's why I say, go somewhere else." There were cards on the counter. This store had two other locations, in Palm Beach and Rotterdam.

"What if it's insured?"

"Not my concern. If you have insurance and you get rid of the piece, cancel the policy because you don't own it anymore."

I asked if there was a way to identify it, repeating what the first guy said about laser whatever.

"Oh, what a pain in the ass."

"But if it's on there?"

"You take it off." I asked how. He looked irritated. "You polish it."

The cops would find me. Insurance investigators. A cuckolded billionaire with every kind of connection would take my life and pulp it, hire a ninja, God knows what, sink me into debt that would bury my grandchildren.

"They got these things now measure every angle, every facet. It's bullshit. One cut and the weight changes, it's a different stone. Look, they got this stuff helps people sleep better at night. Good for them." He picked up the loupe again, annoyed. "You got the other one?"

I couldn't move. He thought I was being coy. He closed his hand.

"It's funny because you can hold it in your fist, but it's worth a lot of money." He smiled. He'd been foggy when I'd walked in but had fully woken up. "I have to look at it under the light and weigh it." He turned and motioned for me to follow him into the back. I figured I'd be shot in the head when I stepped through the doorway.

"Someone walking in off the street with a piece like this? It's rare." He flipped on a bright light and talked about the stone while he looked at it under a microscope, describing the thing in technical terms, jotting down notes. Behind him was a flat steel door painted beige that I continued to stare at for the next ten minutes, trembling like a fish. I shook the way Amy had, last summer, on the beach. I felt most alive when I was doing something rotten.

"What's this?" he said. I froze. "A stone taken out of the ground. Hey look, if we left these things buried, nobody would know. The world could go to hell tomorrow and this stuff ain't gonna help.

But the labor involved in digging them out, plus they're rare, and people like 'em. D color, flawless, three carat and above, you're talking about an investment, easily transportable, and they hold their value. A few of them is a house on the beach."

I took the other one out of my pocket and slid it across the desk for him to weigh and examine. Security cameras, bank records. Of course I'd get caught, because getting caught had been my goal, that's what I'd been hoping for, real punishment, real pain. I called myself every disgusting name I could think of. Then I was happy because I could say no, walk out. I hadn't gone through with it yet. Then I was happy, thinking I still might.

He stuck his glasses on his head and gave me the grading info, the offer per carat, then multiplied it by the weight of the two diamonds. The number had no shape. I tried to find its contours, its boundaries. The upper limit of my earlier estimate had been off by $221,000.

Who would play softball with something like that in their ears?

I hated money. And I hated people who had money, it was disgusting, it made them do weird stuff. I'd rather suffer. I knew how to suffer.

"In a case like this, what I'll do, I have a few ideas of who I'll call. And to be honest, I have to throw some percentage on top and hope I don't queer the deal. I want you to know I'm paying the most, but I want him to think he's paying the least. Although, look, these days, anyone is happy with a sale."

He picked up the phone and asked whether I wanted a bank wire or a check. His face went slack as someone answered, and he opened the steel door. "It's me," he said. "Put Murray on the phone." He pulled the door closed behind him.

Dear God in heaven, I wanted a sump pump. In a heavy storm I could take a thousand wet-vac buckets out of my leaking basement, up the back stairs, and dump them in the yard. Sometimes the wet-vac accidentally sucked up pieces of the crumbling floor. Sometimes when it rained, weird stuff from the kitchen sink, like Cheerios and macaroni, floated up out of the basement drain.

The earrings sat in a velvet-lined dish on his desk.

I also had some lingering dental issues. The crown cost $1,600. Or maybe the root canal cost $1,600 and the crown was more. I'd been chewing crookedly on that side for a year. And the retaining wall in my backyard had fallen down and spilled into the alley in chunks. I'd gotten two ominous warnings from the city and a $4,000 estimate from a structural engineer.

I wanted to knock out the pre-K tuition, call an oil-burner repair man, open a retirement account, start a college fund. The murmuring through the door, not the content so much as the cadence, somehow mediated the experience. There was still a layer of protection between reality and me. They were discussing the potential sale of some hot rocks. This guy was either crooked, stupid, or crazy, or maybe he knew the trade well enough to handle a high-grade diamond with no documentation.

I also needed life insurance, a new dishwasher, and those screens that keep leaves out of your gutters. All I'd ever wanted was to save her from him, but I had been kidding myself. They belonged together.

There were too many stories of stupid, vicious, dangerous, cruel, or disgusting things he'd done to her, and to his kids, things she'd encouraged or enabled. Here are your secrets. I don't want them anymore. I'm giving them back to you, in a story I'll write and donate to mankind. Better yet, I'll write to Rapazzo, tell him I've been banging his wife, send a few naked pictures of her and threaten to splatter them and every horrible thing she'd ever said about him all over the Web unless he promised to be nice to her. I'll write to the SEC, I'll do something. I stood, grabbed the earrings, and walked down the street in the rain to my car.

THIRTY-SEVEN

College fund, new front yard, a year of unmolested time to work on comics. Driving back to campus, I would forget the number, then remember it again. A few seconds would pass, then it would come back, along with everything I could do with it. I would play with the number, subtract all or part of our credit card debt, another five figures laid out in horrifying installments to the IRS, other unpleasant amounts to the bank and my mother-in-law and whoever had signed the note on my car.

I wasn't sure whether to be afraid. On the highway, drivers in cars going the opposite way looked worried, too. The world was the same for them. They feared rain, they feared life. I tried Robin. She didn't pick up. I called Adam. He was afraid, couldn't sleep, had planned to do the principled thing and quit, but hadn't quit yet because he had three kids and no one else had offered him a

job. We wondered if there would be more cuts, but the damage
was done. Everybody good had left. Eventually we discussed my
next assignments. We agreed that the future looked terrible, and
then I hung up and didn't worry about his sorry ass anymore.

I made a list in my head of a dozen former colleagues in adver-
tising. I would send them chatty notes. I'd give my former pub-
lisher a call. "Hey, asshole, thanks for giving up on me," I'd say.
"I'm back from the dead." I'd send him new pages in a month or
two. I needed to register on a job board for teachers in fine arts,
graphic design, illustration, and cartooning. I needed to write a
letter of interest and dust off my CV.

I called my parents. My dad had been answering the phone
since he'd retired, but I still wasn't used to it. Of course I only
ever called to talk to her, but she was out. He liked to start in the
middle of a sentence, as if I had just watched an instant replay of
his morning and had called to hear the follow-up on the latest
rash between his toes or a dead bat in the attic. Maybe if I'd taken
the money and could give my parents $75,000 I would've felt dif-
ferent, but I felt the same, suffocated by adult burdens, amazed
and enraged after almost two decades of this feeling that no one
had warned me about how hard it would be. He'd spent his
morning raking heaps of algae out of his friend's scuzzy pond, to
use as fertilizer in his garden. His elbow hurt, but he'd saved a
couple hundred bucks. He offered an update on his macular de-
generation, and how much that bastard charged for eyedrops,
and the sixty-eight-dollar co-pay. Then he waxed poetic about the
benefits to his intestines of unsweetened cranberry juice with a
teaspoon of lecithin granules. He talked to me now the way he'd
always talked to her, offering a kind of inventory that I tried to
discourage.

Bioflavonoids, grapefruit, wheatgrass, ginger.

I think that at least half the world grows up with a parent who's scary and a little nuts, and he'd been mine, and I forgave him a long time ago, but I didn't want to hear about his granules, I didn't want to be his friend through this next phase of degeneration, and I sure as hell didn't want to be his wife.

"I love you, Dad."

"Give those kids a kiss from us," he said. "Tell 'em we're nuts about 'em." When he let me go, I felt worse. We were a defective bloodline, destined, blighted; my fears had been confirmed.

I kept drifting back to the beautiful discovery in the teacup and the conditions under which the earrings had been lost. I was meant to take by other means what ordinary life had withheld. But I couldn't do it. A quiet descended, a simple and damning quiet of living within my means. I'd ended up right where I belonged, and it was looking to be a bad rest of my life. Amy was the one who'd earned those things. She'd lived through brutality. She had paid.

Fog had come in and covered the town, and I parked on campus and walked down Main Street. A fine, warm rain blew sideways, right into my open mouth, the bay at high tide, waves washing into the street, big puddles everywhere, people taking cover on the steps of town hall. I went into the post office and stuck her earrings in a box. The line snaked around the lobby. It didn't seem to be moving. The woman in front of me wore a waitress apron and tapped her phone. A wet, smelly dog with sandy feet who didn't seem to belong to anyone trotted into the lobby and shook himself, prompting obscenities. I called to him, and held open the back door, and on second thought followed him out. He cut between the post office and a motel on a soggy path to the beach. He watched me, ready to play fetch. I ripped the earrings out of the box and threw them into the bay.

A little farther down Main Street, someone had laid rubber floor mats in the doorway of the hardware store. People pushed in and out. Two little boys bought stickers for their skateboards, and a girl behind the counter patiently unrolled their wet money, three dollars, flattening the bills.

I went into stores, touching all the things I couldn't afford, waving at clerks, requesting information. I sat in furniture, smelled genuine leather. A small boy walked past me carrying a turtle. He held it gently by the edges of its shell, beaming, delighted.

The money was like a noxious cloud. It wouldn't let me breathe. I keep thinking of what I should've done with it. I went back to Stoler's Jewelry. They greeted me warmly. We were old friends. I sheepishly placed three wire bracelets on the counter, thin pieces of junk for sixty-five dollars, for Robin, paid, and walked out to the beach again and stared at the bay, yanked off my shirt and ran out there in my sneakers, thrashing around in the dark green water, grabbing handfuls of hard sandy bottom, then quit, grieving, and slapped myself dry. I went into a children's store and calmed down, and bought a rubber alligator for Beanie and a pack of hair bows for Kaya. My soaking-wet sneakers made clown farts.

Back on campus, I stood in the lobby of the main building, listening to Carl, a puddle forming at my feet. The whole conference was still buzzing from last night's slide talk, he said, most of what comes along is just filler, great work is rare, but blah blah. It was clear that he'd hired Solito without having seen even a page of his work, saw it for the first time yesterday. In six years, Carl had never asked me to give a slide talk on my own work at this fucking conference, although my first year here I'd given a lecture on the history of comics, starting with the cave paintings of

Lascaux, the Codex Mendoza, and Commodore Perry's arrival in Japan with *Punch* cartoons; eleven people had shown up. When he noticed that I had nothing to add, he pulled an envelope from a wad of them in his binder.

"In case I don't see you tomorrow," he said. It was my check, $2,750. After all these years, he'd given me a raise.

THIRTY-EIGHT

I sat on the porch at the back of the main building in a wicker love seat, looking out at the flagpole in the rain. Kaya picked up, sounding normal, a credit to the supernatural healing powers of a four-year-old kid. I didn't interrupt as she let go a partly understandable solid wall of words. Something about Sammy, a cross-eyed three-year-old from camp, and Rigby, a boy who never smiled and chased her around with a territorial scowl, and Molly, who told her there were "witches in our country."

"There are no witches, honey."

"If you see a witch, you gotta chop off da head."

"Did Molly tell you that?"

"Yah. Do you know dat spiderwebs can trap your hands?"

"Did Molly tell you that, too?"

In the background I heard the mason jar of macaroni being

opened, the lid rattling on the counter, the sound of pasta hitting the glass measuring cup, the whoosh as it spilled into the pot. I could feel in Robin's silence her exhaustion, disorientation, and rage. I did my best to set Kaya straight on the occult. I could feel the kitchen's silent appraisal of me, of my acts of liberation, my remorse and rationalization, and of my failed experiments with the plutocracy.

I could almost see the newspapers piled on a dining room chair, the cat lying on Robin's dirty gym stuff, old mail on the kitchen table, barf rags, nursing bras, filthy socks, running sneakers, Tupperware from old lunches, swim goggles, shredded sweetener packets, tubes of sunblock. I could hear Beanie in the bouncer we clipped to the kitchen doorway, spronging up and down on a steel spring as he stared ahead like a little zombie as, somewhere in the distance, a recording sang to him from Winnie-the-Pooh.

I wondered about her meeting with Katavolos, who had followed her to the Nature Channel and now ran the network. She took the phone from Kaya. When she finally spoke, she sounded less broken than I'd feared, surely benefitting from my absence, the simplified power dynamic, the relief of assaults upon her soul from my critical glances. "Please tell your daughter not to go in Mommy's bed tonight."

I heard a small protest in the distance, "But my baby was crying," though she meant Polly, her doll. Robin didn't say anything. Kaya asked, "When will Polly grow up?"

"She won't grow up. She's made of plastic."

"Well, she might be made of person or she might be made of plastic or she might be made of bones."

"Well," Robin said, "she'll be fine either way." Then she let out a sigh and I waited. If she'd gone on to say that the feds had been looking for me in connection with a class B felony for trafficking in stolen property, or for oral and sexual mishandling of a Mrs.

A. D. Rapazzo of Crumberry, Connecticut, or that a gang of hired killers had slit the tires of her car, dismembered the cat, and burned down our porch, or that she'd somehow gotten wind of my shenanigans, delivered in an envelope by a private investigator, I wouldn't have been surprised. I would've been ready. The events of these past days had stomped all the juices out of my adrenals, but I could still feel the terror, the consequences of my choices, the potential horror of real loss, the jewel of my life, lost.

Then she would explain the malfunctioning psyche of an emotional cripple like me, defended against vulnerability, predisposed to fantasy, pain avoidance, and cynicism. Forty years earlier, as I'd been lying there in my diaper, some bored lady had flirted with me, told me I was irresistible, and I had the valence for it, and believed I was a Casanova. The more recent bored housewife who'd picked me out of the crowd at art camp had merely prolonged the delusion, blocking genuine intimacy and the intolerable awareness of death. Then Robin would inform me that the locks had been changed, that her dad's attorney had filed a restraining order and I'd never see my children again, that as individuals we were nothing but together we'd made these miraculous beings, that I'd be broke for the rest of my days supporting them, as they drifted farther away and those bonds dissolved and turned toxic and became the unworkable torment of my life.

"We need floss."

"Okay."

"And toilet paper."

"Yokey-dokey." I said I'd get some on the way home.

She carried the phone to the table and put it on speaker while they ate.

"The meeting went fine."

Sounds of chewing. Beanie gabbled away in the language of his people.

"There's no job, but they offered me an episode of a show on what used to be the Crime Channel, which is now called something else and is part of the War Channel, which is now called the American Century Channel. We do crime reenactments, things like historical reenactments of train robberies from the Wild West. Next week I have to fly out to New Mexico to blow up a train."

"Who offered you an episode?"

"What?"

"Who did you meet with?"

She didn't sound evasive or annoyed—just detached, free of obligation to me, to my structural assaults.

"Was there a couch in his office?" She didn't answer. "Did you let him feel your boobs?" She laughed. "Did he put his hands in your pants?"

She laughed again and said she hadn't been wearing pants. "But he wanted to know why I'd leave Connie's production company for this. I think he thinks I'm following him around." It was a big, throaty, confident laugh, a sound of relief that reminded me that for the last couple years I'd been living with a depressed person, that it had infected us both, that together we'd grown into people who, upon waking, did not look out the window to examine the day's weather. Then she told me about some old men who ran the company, who she'd bumped into in the halls, who'd grabbed and hugged her and asked where she'd been all these years. The channel those guys started in the mid-eighties had been a place for beautiful nature documentaries, flora and fauna, with a stress on cinematography, shows about world history and anthropology. For years now, the channel had been in a race to the bottom.

Then she gloated about her lunch meeting with Karen Crickstein, and all the old friends she'd heard about, former staff EPs and VPs who'd screwed up, aged out, or got fired, or who'd put out their own shingle and were hanging on, hoping for the big comeback.

I listened to them eat. Everything would go back to the way it was, only worse, because I'd given up. No more tricks, no gimmicks, no narcotics or lubricants, no funky aftertaste. No fake hysteria or narcissism, no more armoring self-hatred. Just dinner, stories, singing, bedtime, followed by calling, begging, weeping, and throwing up, until at some point, it was quiet. Just a feely guy, full of zinger insights and stunning sensitivity, preparing with humility for true interpenetration by and with his life person. How do you do it? How do you span the nothingness? Through love, through music, through art, through the sharing of food, fucking, and experiences. Inside my chest I imagined a lump of unpolished quartz, pink and cold, with veins of lighter pink in a cloud of white. The cloud, the aftermath of an explosion, had fine debris floating inside it, still to the visible eye but with some radiant nuclear dust, moving out, exploding.

"Oh, by the way, the washing machine broke. Stuff's all wet at the end."

"You have to run the spin cycle a second time."

"I did."

"And did it work?"

"Yes."

She didn't ask whether I'd seen the low balance in our checking account, didn't say a word about it, didn't wonder whether I'd lost my mind, and when it was clear that she wouldn't, I asked her. She said quietly that she'd ordered four pairs of boots and was planning to return three. The account had been wildly overdrawn, but I was so heartened by this news of her spending that I decided to announce my raise, and assured her that I would deposit the check ASAP, but she wasn't listening or didn't care.

"Don't poke your brother with a fork."

"I just wanna toch."

"Cut it out, sweetie."

"He likes it, Momma!"

Beanie screamed. Robin threatened Kaya with the loss of weekend television. He sat in a chair clipped to the side of the table, and clocked his sister warily. When it seemed that Kaya had lost interest in poking him, he went back to his applesauce.

"I'm finished."

"Eat your avocado."

"What's dessert?" Robin told Kaya to bring the cookies.

Then she told me about her night. Beanie up at ten, then up at one for an hour. When he went back down, she worried that he'd wake up again, and that if she couldn't fall back to sleep she'd be too tired and would blow her meeting. "Then I'm lying there worrying, trapped in this room, stuck in this bed, trapped like a convict, waiting for a peep from him, and every creak and bird noise and car out there sounds like it's pretty much happening in my ear, my heart starts pounding and I wonder if I should get up and work, but I know I'll hate my work and be infected by this insecurity about everything—then Kaya's standing by my head, shoving a plastic doll in my face, and I'm so happy to see her I want to cry."

I waited for her to direct the blame.

"Does that happen to you?"

"Yes," I said. "Every night."

"How do you stand it?"

What if it wasn't my fault?

"How do you get anything done?"

"I don't."

"And my face is covered in rosacea, on my chin, under my

nose, behind my ears. I have stuff on it that makes it hard to move my skin, and when I do it cracks and burns."

What if I was forgivable? What if this was just a phase? What if, in a few months, things improved? What if, underneath it all, she wanted what I wanted? What if, in the meantime, our needs for intimacy were mostly being met by our children? What if we'd been temporarily blown off course and still had a bright future ahead of us, with some acceptable level of insistent sadness woven into the fabric of time?

After the meeting she went to Iris's house and talked to the caregivers about hygiene, then sat beside her mother for two hours. "I told her about my meeting. She was really proud. 'You're so smart, so beautiful.' I think that was the best part of my day. I told her about the new show. 'My beautiful, beautiful—'" Robin was quiet for a second. "'Hey, what's your name again?'" She sighed. I tried to picture it. "I guess that was the worst part of my day." I told her I was sorry.

I'd done a lot of horrible things that couldn't be undone, and planned to write about those things, and was already sorry for that too, for how I was made, sorry for the way I am, that I wanted more, sorry for how badly at that very moment I missed being in bed, in the Barn, listening to the rain, buried deep inside Amy, breathing when she breathed. What did it mean? It meant new life. The first time I felt it, I thought I'd live forever. But I wouldn't. I was just a body whizzing through time.

"Dementia," Robin said, "is connected to estrogen. My dementia will start when menopause starts. But I'm not sure if it's from not having enough estrogen or from having too much. I can't remember, which is actually a sign of dementia."

"You don't have dementia."

"Promise to kill me when I get like that."

I promised, although I knew that what she really wanted was for me to be nice to her, to be kind and patient with everyone, and maybe in a few months our goddamned baby would sleep through the night.

But I wanted more. I wanted Robin to ask how I'd slept, whether I'd gone to the beach, was I having fun. I wanted some time to show her again who I was, for an hour or two on Sunday mornings, to lie in bed with nowhere to go, feeling cool sheets on my legs, talking about what we'd make for breakfast, listening to the sounds out the window of cars and birds. I wanted hugs and petting and inside jokes, us against the world. I wanted daily eroticism, dishy sex talk, innuendo, full-frontal hugs with her boobs mashed against me as she pinned me against the dishwasher, short bursts of stolen kisses while our shrimps played a room away, a warm body welded to mine, merging for a few seconds before we went our separate ways. I wanted her to put on a show, every night, wanted to feel as though she, or someone, would die from desire; I wanted her to want my body and call me beautiful. I wanted her to say "pussy" every once in a while, "my pussy," whisper it in my ear, that sort of thing, use the different words for penis now and then, "cock," "prick."

What if I could ask for it in exchange for loving her, and for dragging her hair out of the shower drain, and carrying the fucking AC units up and down the basement steps, hauling the five-gallon water jugs, garbage and groceries, making sure to pay her parking tickets, dandling our babies every night, cooking light and tasty meals, scraping old rice off the floor under Beanie's chair, folding and neatly placing her lacy undergarments back in her drawer of frilly things?

"Are you flying out to New Mexico alone?"

She didn't answer. I was jealous. Although I was no more jealous than I would've been imagining Amy bending over to take it from Mike. Because I'd been away and had touched someone new, Robin had become strange to me all over again; her situation felt new and precarious, and tinged with excitement.

I recalled a night seven or eight years earlier, before we moved to D.C., seated in the corner of our kitchen in Lauraville, with our view of the cemetery. Danny and his wife, Elaine, had come to dinner. They had a new baby in the Snap-N-Go and Elaine was already pregnant again, which tormented us because we were in the middle of disgusting fertility stuff and our being able to have a kid was not looking good.

They'd brought us ice cream and candles. There was a competitive energy between Robin and him, and all these shared experiences. I sat across from Elaine, shoveling food into my face, feeling pitiful. Danny sat across from Robin, staring at her as they talked about wherever they were heading next, or Alejandro the Chilean fixer, or the night they spent on the side of the road in the Darién Gap, one of the times he'd acted like Johnny War Zone and almost got them killed. She looked like Audrey Hepburn in the candlelight. Then they started speaking in Spanish, and I hated to interrupt them to ask for the grated cheese.

She looked at him, with her hollow cheeks and smooth, olive skin and hazel eyes. It all sat at the end of her nose. I must've felt proud watching Danny court my wife. It must've felt good all her life to get that kind of braying attention from guys.

But instead of answering me about her flight to Albuquerque, she got nervous and started babbling: "The average amount of television the typical viewer watches of crime-reenactment shows is a hundred and twenty minutes a sitting, four times a week, eight hours of this one stupid show. The average amount of television a person watches who watches that much crime reenactment is four to six hours a day. That's six to midnight, with no break for dinner. Can you believe it? It's disgusting."

Maybe they never touched each other. Maybe she liked being flirted with or just needed to go back to work. She used to complain that he spoke Spanish like an old lady, and after two days on the road he smelled like a moldy sneaker, and almost got them macheted to death in a market in Port-au-Prince, wandering around like an idiot.

Or maybe she'd loved him for ten years. Maybe they cooked up reasons to go to places so they could live their other life. Maybe she was frustrated from having been denied his bodily pleasures and took it out on me, or him, or herself. Maybe it wasn't just survivor guilt that had pushed her into war zones all over Latin America. Maybe it was because of guilt from two-timing me that she needed drugs to sleep. Maybe the years without him had made her heartsick. Maybe we were both better off when she was more in love. This was probably all in my head.

Robin ran through some of the pitches they'd come up with for her crime-reenactment show. The episodes were all the same: someone is in danger and doesn't know it, and someone evil is coming to destroy them. "Artistically speaking, my attitude is 'Here you go, dumb pigs, eat some slop.'" She laughed.

Were we safe? Was someone coming to destroy us? She had loads of work to do. The sooner I got home, the better. "Anyway, I'll do the best I can, and embrace the fact that it's about ratings, and hope that people will want to watch. And that's a good feeling."

"Sure."

"Isn't it?"

"Yes. It's good enough."

the last thing they say to each other

THIRTY-NINE

The rain had stopped. As I crossed the quad, I tried to imagine them at that moment. After dinner, Beanie liked to sit on the rug in the living room with a piece of cheese in each hand, making coyote sounds. Kaya liked to scatter dollhouse furniture across the rug, little grandfather clocks, tiny cakes and clothing, and naked Barbies in a pile. She liked to place the Barbie with a flower sticker on her face beside the Ken doll, on a too-small canopy bed with their feet hanging off the end. At their feet she'd arrange some dollhouse people, a mismatched girl and boy, into a family of four, pretending to sleep. She liked to stage these family scenes, and didn't want to take them apart at the end of the night.

She'd leave these things around the house: a stuffed Dalmatian wearing one of Beanie's swim diapers, resting on the couch; a brown-skinned plastic baby, in sunglasses, flat on a kitchen chair on a dish towel, stripped to its panties. A feeling streamed toward me from a monkey in a tutu, with a teacup and saucer, cowering under Robin's desk or crammed into a toy high chair beside a green knitted frog in dolls' pajamas, propped against the bookcase like Tiny Tim. I thought she staged these props for a reason, to remind us of what we were really here for: to protect smaller, helpless bug-eyed creatures.

While she played, one of us cleared the table and the other gave Beanie a bath. Then came pajamas and a reading from *Curious George*. The tinted darkness, cream-colored walls of our bedroom, humidifier's huff, noise-canceling machine's whoosh, Thomas the Tank Engine's face smiling sweetly from the nightlight. I'd take in Beanie's smell of crackers and fruit, the lingering fragrance of his bath, place him in the crib and lean my head against the rails, singing softly. With terrific strength he'd stand and grab my shirt and cling. I'd lay him back down and cover him with his gacky as he closed his eyes. I'd lie on the floor for a brief eternity, out of his line of sight, serenading from the rug beside the crib with "Mary Had a Little Lamb," then crawl on my hands and knees, turning the knob like a safecracker, tiptoeing into the hall.

Some nights it was like splitting an atom. Panicking, bargaining, surrender, or the telltale burping that signaled vomiting at will. Other nights loneliness overtook me and I hauled him into bed. Some nights it went okay.

FORTY

Burt stood in front of me in the supper line, twisting his beard, reading the chalkboard. Fresh seasonal fruit cocktail, Jell-O for dessert, and chicken française, with the "française" crossed out. A light yellow stain oozed through the bandage on his head. There were announcements too: Lions Club bingo, poetry reading at seven, "Bump and Grind" beach party on the cove at nine, and a drum circle at midnight, clothing optional.

I looked around but didn't see anyone I knew, so I sat with Linda, who wore a visor from a casino in Atlantic City, and Shari, who was bipolar and on lithium and unable to utter a sentence without diagramming her mother's destructive narcissism, and Ginny, a nature poet from the Pacific Northwest. The conversation turned to Solito. Because I'd introduced him the night before, they gave me the chance to weigh in. When I didn't, they took turns. A great artist gave everyone in his proximity a sense of what's possible, he lit the path, gave you hope, and so on.

I was still full of hate, but I had the sense that a fever had passed. I'd gone through it. My wife and kids were getting ready for bed. Amy was somewhere north of here. Our final moment hadn't exactly crackled with resolution. I ate another barbecued chicken leg. They discussed the polishing of memories, the skeleton of facts a writer illuminates through feeling. I would do what he did, make something out of nothing. This experience of turmoil and ecstasy deserved my attention and respect.

I had one last night to get through, and one more day with my students. I wanted to eat and head back to the Barn to look over my lecture notes so I'd have something to offer in the morning, although I was in no particular hurry. I was afraid to be alone and knew that when I went back to the Barn it would be worse: it would be quiet, it would be all Amy, everywhere. The kitchen cutting board, the curtains—each object would trigger some thought, image, words. The steel bar of the bed frame that she'd wrapped her hand around. We fit, locked together like puzzle pieces. She pulled me in and gave me life from the deep spring inside her. My own genetic material had lived inside her. And what if it still did? A creamy burst, a microscopic explosion would bind us. Then I remembered the party at the Azamanians', the big, slimy oysters I'd eaten while they were still alive. Did they swim inside me? And the lobsters, boiled alive but served cold, and the bay, warm and solid, strange plankton glowing in the sand at night, and the ocean everywhere around us; cold and roiling and teeming, it flung living and half-dead things upon the shores. I wondered when I would stop thinking about her. I could rub my own face with my own two hands, and those hands would be her hands, and she would hold me in her arms and I would go crazy. I started to go crazy anyway, wondering what was real.

Where was she? Had she made it to New Hampshire in one piece, only to find her daughter writhing on the grass, bleeding from her brain? Or were she and Lily already safe at home? Had Mike returned early, in an expansive mood? Had the sight of his injured wife inspired his compassion? Or had he sensed in her some troubling, independent spirit that would incite his need to dominate and destroy?

Would I be haunted by her ghost, be woken in the night, would I check my phone, lie there in cool sheets and think of her until it all came rushing back? We'd agreed to leave each other alone, to write only if necessary. This was a natural stopping point. Would I cave first? Would she write something beautiful? "I know what I'd do if you were here in my bed." Would she tell a rambling story about the photo lab she worked at after high school, during that strange year after the attack, when the keepsake images of strangers gave her something to look forward to?

Would it ever end? Would I spend years sadistically refashioning events, squeezing life's nervous contradictions into scene and action, would I write to her from time to time, asking for help with the details of her life, answering her questions about my children or my own attempts at happiness? Would this go on until the secret history and madness lost its power, the familiar click in my heart replaced by a cooling, a nostalgia, and a sense of camaraderie?

Cigarette smoke blew by. The clouds broke and sunlight poured through. The sudden beauty reassured us. We agreed that if it weren't bad for us, we'd smoke five packs a day, take Ambien every night, ride motorcycles, and stop eating kale. It was one of those kooky, freewheeling conversations grown-ups have in an idyllic place when they're trying to shake off the sorrow that it's ending and they know they're running out of time. Then Shari stood and went back for seconds, and Ginny went off to find a homework assignment for her final class.

On the second floor of the main building, I made copies of work to show my students: a few pages of Crumb, from an underground comic he did in the sixties—acid-tinged, id crazy—where this feminist chick beats up some cops, who tear off her dress, so she runs naked through the supermarket, knocking down all these repressed old hags. And Art Spiegelman, who used adorable mice to bring genocide to life, and proved to the world that comics could be literature. The main office was empty and dark. Fish swam on Mary's glowing screensaver. And newer work, Phoebe Gloeckner's obsessive rage tour of her abusive childhood and years of promiscuity. And Alison Bechdel's lovingly wrought family drama, her dad in the closet, her own coming out, in fine black lines and gray-green ink wash. These were pages I'd burned into my brain and tried to steal, went crazy over and knocked my head against but just couldn't beat, cartoonists who made me want to be one, until I came up with my own thing, before I quit.

For a while, in my twenties and thirties, I told stories that hit close to home, that were crucial to my existence, of love and sarcasm and maddening envy, daily mortification, sexual pity and raging insecurity, stylized fictionalization of stuff taken from my life. I stole the moral and ethical problems of friends and relations and gave them to imaginary beings, then worked like hell to turn line drawings into walking, talking flesh and blood.

I checked the page numbers, skimming to make sure I'd copied the right ones. I found myself rereading scenes I'd read a hundred times before. It seemed to me then that I'd missed the point of everything, and had ended up on the wrong side of the divide. It wasn't up to me to judge cartoonists. The only thing that mattered was finding stuff I loved. I didn't hate comics. I hated the need to make them. I loved comics. I hated the lifetime of pain and struggle it took to create a thing that anyone could read in an hour.

Downstairs, a kind of cocktail party spilled off the porch. The after-dinner crowd clustered at the drinks table and slumped on wicker couches. Along the front of the main building, conference-goers headed off on bikes to watch the sunset. The sky had cleared. The bay glowed a strange, prehistoric silver.

On the porch, a girl with freckles and a ponytail pushed by me, followed by a man with a flat nose like a boxer's, holding a pen in one hand and a book in the other, for Tom McLaughlin to sign. Tom smiled back brightly but didn't budge, holding his wine. He was worn out. The guy blanched. Dennis stood beside Tom, ignored by him, with a red nose.

I went over to a side table and poured half a bottle of wine into a cup, eavesdropping on a man with a bulging forehead and a woman in espadrilles offering her chicken recipe with leeks and mustard. A witty former student of mine, Ruth Gutenberg, Googlebaum, took my chin in her hand and, with a cocktail napkin, wiped some barbecue sauce off my face.

"My dearest darling," she said. "My sneezy, dirty, grumpy little elf." I had to grab her wrist. I hadn't seen Ruth yet this summer. "Did you miss me terribly?" she asked. She looked different, thinner and older, with shorter hair. She called everyone "darling" and "crumpet." "Nothing will ever come between us again." She was still joking around but I remembered how, a few years earlier, nothing had: lying under an open window, in a moment of pure stillness, all our nerves on edge. We did everything in that dormitory bunk bed except sing "I Got You Babe," and slept like babies, and had breakfast in town the next morning. I gave her a hug, banging her on the back like a long-lost brother.

She introduced me to Nancy, mute, agreeable, soft, and sensitive, and Russell, sturdy and angry, hadn't gotten as much done as he'd hoped, planned to write a hundred pages in August. Somehow, we turned to the subject of Solito. Russell wondered how the cartoonist was able to recall scenes and conversations verbatim from infancy on up. "He used real names," Russell said. "Does that mean everything actually happened?" We talked about screen memory, emotional honesty, and other stuff.

We were joined by a tall woman wearing lipstick and a guy in gold-rimmed glasses. As Solito's star had risen, several articles had appeared, exploring the story behind the story, with photos of Angel and other family members pulled from social media, along with evidence of blurry paperwork from his detention in Oaxaca at age six. He'd changed some details about key characters, had altered the chronology of major events, and he had admitted that freely. He'd used real people as a means, boiled them down, strained and stripped out whole through lines and tossed them away, kept other parts, shifted blame, moved ugly things up into the foreground or back, depending on what he needed.

I didn't want to hear what they thought. I already had my own response. Solito had been given the opportunity to actualize his dreams, and then he'd handed those dreams over to literary critics, professional cranks whose only means of support was to shred the work of others, and beyond that to the wider world of opinion generated by every asshole with a keyboard. I didn't want them to tear him apart.

"There's a difficulty in any sort of autobiographical writing," the guy with glasses said. "It's a stew of self-analysis, reporting, biography, imagination, and also some heat, a core of wanting, of strong emotions, who knows."

"That's why my book is labeled a novel," Russell said.

"Dearest, it doesn't matter what you call it," Ruth said. "Telling stories about other people is immoral. A ten-year-old knows that."

The poetry reading ended, and bodies flooded through the doors of the main building. By the traumatized looks on their faces, you could tell how it had gone. They dragged themselves into the fresh air, gasping foggily, not looking back, drawn and pale, shoulders fallen, bellies out, stepping toward a table with a melted wheel of Brie, moving gingerly to protect the psychic wound.

"Are you part of the conference?" I asked Nancy. She nodded. "Are you enjoying everything so far?"

She wore a pale orange dress that left her half-naked in back, stitched with little green flowers whose leaves were embroidered with tiny holes through which you could see her bra and tanned pulsing skin. Around one wrist was a plastic bracelet from the Pretty Pretty Princess game. I asked her who made it and she showed me a picture of a girl in a shiny pink leotard with her face pressed against her mother's larger head. I took out my phone, and we showed each other photos and gave their names and ages.

But then the poet emerged, in a wool suit coat and tie, looking flustered, with a conference handler dutifully stationed at his side, loudly offering him some wine, as members of his audience falsely congratulated him. It became impossible to ignore the metallic vibration of his foul effects, we wanted to get as far away from this scene as possible, and followed Ruth off the porch, along a dirt path, up the hill, to a party in the windmill. Above us in the dark sky, its massive fan blades had been trimmed in white lights. Powerful spotlights lit up its exterior. A small tent had been set up outside with a jazz trio, sponsored by a vodka brand.

Following Ruth, we ducked through the doorway of the oddly shaped building, like something a hobbit might live in, and entered a room lined with a heavy stone foundation. I read the plaque. The guts of the windmill—the mill, et cetera—had been removed. Built in 1811, the structure had been dragged to the campus in 1860 on horse-drawn skids, when the campus had been the estate of a gunpowder merchant. I recognized several trustees coming down the steep staircase, and other funders of the conference leaning back on the banister, stepping slowly, carefully, smiling and red-faced, as though they'd been locked inside a sauna. When our cohort mounted the stairs to go up, I went out to the vodka tent.

I'd worked hard these past days, done foolish things, run around with my blood pumping. It had been a kind of terrific nightmare, a product of a feverish delirium. It had been useful, but there was no point in pretending. I'd become what I would've been anyway. I'd tried to disrupt the smooth conveyance of myself into middle age, obedience, whatever, to destroy my own likely future by posing as a bumbling incompetent, forcing myself through outlandish behavior, while cagily implying some authorial control.

Nancy walked slowly around the outside of the windmill. She gazed upward, angling her body in the spotlight so that I could look at her, backlit in her dress, while she studied the building. Then she took a seat and told me how it had been made, using pegs, braces, and trusses. We sat on teak chaises that had been arranged beneath the tent. The town she lived in, near Boston, was full of old mills and tanneries. She worked as a designer at her husband's architecture firm. Historic preservation was about consistency. There were rigid guidelines. I could feel then that she had nowhere to go. The band played "Tangerine."

We lay there, in a breeze as soft as butterfly wings, as the wind lifted the hem above her knees and the fabric fluttered over her body. I felt the light from her body enter my brain. She wore leather sandals on tanned feet, her toenails painted pink. Their firm was busy, doing well, had just finished a retail build-out of the train station so that it reeked with economic vitality. The thing to do here was probe more deeply, with a light touch and genuine concern, to file away details and assemble them later, to reflect them back to her in a flattering way. She talked about some old coffered ceiling and her daughter's ballet schedule and son's hoop camp. I pretended something interesting was happening out on the bay, and in fact there was, the tide flowing out, the beach wide and flat with bonfires all the way to the cliffs.

"My husband does very well," she explained. "He's a wonderful father." She had a small face framed by thick brown hair. "But he doesn't talk about his feelings—not to me, anyway. It's a problem."

"Oh."

"He loves to ride his bicycle." Her eyes went to my face, around my face, for whatever she was looking for, and I felt the pressure building. I had no more space inside me, no more room in my face or in my heart. I already loved as many people as I could.

"You have no right to complain, you have a good life, but he freezes you out, and it's a sham, and you're stuck."

"You know what it is?"

"What?"

"Lack of privacy."

"Sure."

"Everything is communal. Nothing is yours."

"Exactly."

"We're together all day, and with our kids at night. Nothing goes unseen. Nothing goes unmeasured, unmentioned. Nothing is secret. Nothing is hidden."

"That's true."

"Quantity versus quality."

"But we like it," I said, "because it takes out the guesswork."

"That's marriage, measuring everything, like a speed trap. Your speed is communal property. Your kids belong to the community. Your tendencies will be noted." She had one hand tucked under her armpit and the fingers of her other hand pressed to her lips, as though she'd forgotten and then remembered some terrible news. I felt her body's energy, felt it flashing and beaming. She said, "I shouldn't take it for granted."

"I'm trying to stay positive and think of the nice parts."

"I find I'm often faking it."

"Sure."

"Is that sure like 'whatever,' or sure like 'me too'?"

"I know what you mean."

"I pretend to care about whether to save leftover chicken. I pretend to like hip-hop with disgusting lyrics when we're alone in the car."

"I pretend to snore so my kid will fall asleep, but then I really do fall asleep."

"Maybe you don't know what I mean."

"I probably do."

"You have it easy. Some people do."

I just kept looking. Something stood up in me. It had a mean grin, and a chip on its shoulder from a cynical, isolated, cutthroat victimhood. Looking at her body, at her face, was like pulling up to the curb with my U-Haul. Then I'd say, "Do you want to see the eighteenth-century barn I'm staying in?"

I couldn't do it. She talked about her husband a little more. I pretended not to listen. She got up.

I saw that ugly little walleyed dog, Piccolo, coming up the paved path to the windmill. He scampered around the tent, licked my shoe, and pissed under a side table before following Alicia through the door of the windmill. He gave me a last goggle-eyed look. I couldn't bring myself to flirt with him, either.

The theater performance let out, and the crowd came across the lawn. Winston walked slowly, heavily, with Ingrid behind him, and Charlene, Roberta, and Nada Klein. A clot of faculty assembled. I went over there. Carl came out of the building, his long gray hair plastered to his neck, with Barney Angerman leaning on his arm, and said it was too crowded in the windmill, the stairs were too steep, and asked if I would walk Barney home. I introduced myself, and bent down as Barney's other arm hooked around mine. I wasn't sure if he'd been given any say in the matter. He was entirely deaf and looked up at me and smiled. We prepared to descend, and carefully took the first step down the paved path to the lawn.

He stared ahead, his hair glowing white, in a kind of pompadour, his stride short and uneven, his eyes steady. His shirt had stains all over it. His ears looked like something that had grown in the black dirt at the base of a hobbit's tree, his nose resting against his upper lip. As we descended, I didn't say a word for fear of distracting him. We navigated a dark wooden staircase, and he paused to catch his breath, pulling hard on my elbow, and when we started up again I tripped, almost yanking us both down the stairs, and he let out a creepy, warbled laugh.

We exited the campus gate and crossed Main Street. He was staying in a salt stained cottage on the bay. We went around back, where some men and women were sitting in the dark, drinking and talking.

Barney pushed past me on his own power and lowered himself into a patio chair. A candle burned in a jar. Someone handed him a cup of wine and he took a sip, letting out a sigh, and someone else politely asked me to sit except there weren't any chairs. The average age here seemed to be nearing the triple digits. They talked about places they'd rented or owned around town over the years, and who owned them now, a house that caught fire one

Fourth of July, and recalled their first trip out here decades earlier in a white '73 Eldorado convertible. It felt good to be young among them. There was a raft lying on the patio and I lay down on it. I could pretend I was nothing, or anything, depending.

Barney explained how, one summer forty years ago, on an empty floor of some factory in Manhattan, two men whose names he couldn't remember invented disco. "We thought it was paradise." He took a long drink. "Dancing until dawn, barely able to stand, stoned on ethyl chloride." It ended when he fell in love with a guy named James and moved out here, to a one-story shack on Route 7 while he wrote *The Dancer*, his best-known play.

I lay there on the raft, looking at the stars. I thought about outer space and how we're in it, wondering what it is and where it ends, because it has to end, and what's over the roof of space, who made it, and what if I stood on my roof back home, would I be able to see stars? I missed the night sky, a heaven above me in which things occurred. This was my world, my universe, it had been given to me, and I lay there, amazed, and tears streamed out, quietly, like rain down a window.

Air flew weightlessly across the sea, against the crisp blackness, in the beauty of this night. The stars were so big. Beneath them bits of fog puffed by, and the bigger stars winked behind the veil, and then it was clear again, and the heavens were so huge, and the Milky Way so bright, a path of spilled breadcrumbs, an explosion of particles frozen in the sky. We're particles of the same particles, we eat each other, we are stardust. I was so small, and raw from the blowing wind, and I started to feel good, and wondered how I could ever feel bad again.

The bay was wide and dark. I could see TV sets glowing inside motel rooms and an airliner overhead. I heard the shushing of the bay, the sea slapping pebbles, rattling stones, and saw, bathed in

the ugly orange glow from a streetlight, a condo where a student
had hosted a cocktail party years earlier. *Shoosh. Woosh.*

I woke up on the raft on the tiny brick patio at sunrise, six A.M.
The steel cable of a catamaran whanged against the metal mast
in a steady breeze as it sat in the yard next door. A loud horn, the
final boarding call, blared across the harbor from the ferry termi-
nal.

A yoga class floated out in the glassy bay on paddleboards in
downward-facing dog. The deck of a restaurant two doors down
was swarmed by seagulls, pinned to updrafts, shrieking and
squawking and landing on the rail, waddling and pecking and
pooping on the planks. The bay was tea-colored, and beyond the
jetty the white sea foam stood out crisply. I took off everything
and swam. Still air, so quiet, birds, high soft clouds, a bright hard
sun, cold, clear bay water. I floated over a hard sandy bottom in
what felt as buoyant as Jell-O with glowing green blobs of algae
that moved softly against my hand. I made my way by breast-
stroke down the curved harbor, past morning kayakers, rowboat-
ers, anchored sailboats and sculls.

Walking through town in the clear morning light, wet and
partly clothed, I saw a woman wearing a dog in a backpack. A shirt-
less boy set down his boom box, unfolded his sheet of cardboard,
and danced. People threw money at his feet. A French-speaking
family stopped to eye some kitchen gadgets in a storefront win-

dow. A huge, brownish, immature eagle with patchy white flecks perched on a telephone pole on the bay side above a wine store, scaring seagulls. I sat and had coffee and some toast. We were twenty miles out in the ocean, on a skinny piece of sand, bathed in light. Along the upper stories of a brightly painted bed-and-breakfast, blossoming vines mounted columns, spilling off the roof deck, drinking in the light.

We came for the light, the nearness to nature, the solitude, the convergence of elements. It hummed. It grabbed you and pulled you in every direction. It drove you back to something in your memory, made you want to try to repeat it. It made you crazy. It gave you hope or sex or courage. I passed the Crabby Sailor and two barefoot boys with sand on their calves. In front of the hardware store, a woman removed a long chain that wove through gas grills, patio furniture, and surfboards. There was a farmers' market on the town green, with bright white stalls. A sign advertised a spaghetti dinner at the firehouse. A brand-new coffee shop had opened, with tables shaded by umbrellas out front. Every summer new places tried where old ones had failed, and the traffic got worse and drunks got arrested, and swimmers drowned on the rough side of the point. Broadway stars and summer rep took over the old theater until the end of August. A drag queen named Tasty Burlington sold out her two-week run. Then came Carnival, then Bear Week, then Labor Day, and then it was over.

There's no such thing as a reliable narrator. There's more reliable and less reliable, but any light that passes through that lens is shaped, bent, divided. You willingly create distortions and those distortions are misleading, designed to stir up, revise, reverse, undo, shift, shape, sing. A story is an interrogation, an act of aggression, a flirtation. It's slippery, squirrelly, and rascally. The conference had helped me return to meaningful work, but I'd lost faith that the project would gird me. Instead, a darker feeling filled me with longing. I imagined myself years into the future, and felt the inevitable letdown of having produced anything at all, of putting myself into it and giving it away.

People lined up to get on the ferry, dressed for someplace else. Men, women, and children shuffled off the boat, carrying luggage, blinded by the sun. I walked home with my shirt in a ball. I still had an hour before class. The siren blared across the bay. In the Barn I stood under hot water in the shower stall, then fell onto the soft, worn flowered bedspread with its rusty stains, all clean, wrapped myself in it, and slept.

ACKNOWLEDGMENTS

I'm grateful to the organizations whose encouragement and support made this project possible: the Whiting and Guggenheim foundations, Johns Hopkins University, and Stony Brook Southampton.

The work done by individuals on my behalf, offering inspiration, edits, and new ways of seeing, touched every page of this work. Thanks to Jessica Blau, Rebecca Curtis, Nicholas Dawidoff, Dana Flor, Eric Puchner, Paul Tough, and Andy Ward.

Thanks also to Chelsea Cardinale, Sarah Chalfant, Tom Chalkley, Max Culhane, Alix Clyburn, Todd Dimston, Michael Kessler, Brian Klam, Dave Kornhaber, Alice McDermott, Liz Mozden, Robert Reeves, Nathan Schreiber, Jillian Tamaki, Stephen Von Oehsen, and Conor Willumsen.

A Q&A BETWEEN MATTHEW KLAM AND
CURTIS SITTENFELD

Curtis Sittenfeld: Your story collection, *Sam the Cat,* came out in 2000, and your super-fans, of which I am just one, have been eagerly awaiting another book from you ever since. I know you worked on a few other novels. What made *Who Is Rich?* the one you finished, the one that worked?

Matthew Klam: From 2002 to 2008, I had other ideas for books, and got about a hundred pages in several times. My track record indicates some kind paralysis in those years, but I did write a book's worth of long-form journalism in *Harper's Magazine, The New York Times Magazine, Esquire,* and *GQ,* among others. But in my heart I really didn't know what to care about, or maybe I did and spent years after my first book pretending I didn't know. I'm envious of fiction writers with a strong, steady output, and writers who can work on more than one story at once. I'm sure it's hell for them too, but from the sidelines I feel nothing but awe.

I started *Who Is Rich?* in 2010. It took six years to complete. I remember thinking, a few months after I started, that I hoped the story would end at short-story length, under forty pages. Then, at seventy-five pages, I began writing a flashback, and it was almost thirty pages long. When I finished the flashback, I knew it was on the wrong scale for anything but a novel, and yet it seemed to strengthen the momentum of the story, rather than weaken it. That was an indication that I should go on.

As I worked on this story and came to understand that it would essentially be a conversation about marriage and parenting, carried on between two people who were married to other people, I found my groove. That they would insist on remaining dedicated to the institution of marriage—while violating all sorts of norms of decency—also seemed tantalizing, perverse, irresistible.

CS: Do you have advice for writers on how to find their groove?

MK: Maybe take the spirit of this if nothing else: Follow your nose. Go to your obsessions, don't be afraid to be interested in the things that fascinate you, and don't be disdainful of them. I have a big nose, but that doesn't make it any easier to follow. It took a while for my worries as a father, husband, teacher, artist, animal lover, and so on to emerge. It also took a while to admit to a sort of "second self" that doesn't always match up perfectly with who I present to the world. We function in this world using a beautifully articulated persona, the one we engage with co-workers, neighbors, and friends, and when we model behavior for kids—but there's more to us than the people we become in order to get along. It took time to admit to all of this, and that I was entangled in it and would be better off trying to write my way out.

CS: You write really well about sex, in all its weirdness and glory. Do American sexual mores feel different to you now than they did when your story collection came out?

MK: I think we're as conflicted as we've ever been. Our bodies and appetites and impulses freak us out and disrupt our images of ourselves. I don't think that's changed in seventeen years. I hear people over forty talking about "hookup culture," as evidence of our degradation, but I look at the stories of the multitude of nineteen-year-olds I've taught over the years and it's the same as it was for me in 1983, the longing for connection. Hearts get broken, and people regret things they said and did and wonder what went wrong and whether they'll ever find love.

CS: Everything that happens in your fiction is plausible and realistic, and also often cringe inducing and hilarious. I know from my own experience that readers often conflate "plausible" and "autobiographical." Do you care if people assume your fiction is true or semi-true?

MK: Some people assume everything in my fiction is true, and that the narrator is me, and in this new book I tried to have fun with that assumption, addressing the issue directly. A narrator is nothing but a set of demands, a way to get from A to Z. But of course everything in the book *is* true, because I'm writing about what I know. But what I know includes the totality of my experience, thoughts, actions I've regretted or fantasized about, dreams I've had, stories I've been told that stuck with me, the treasure chest of literature I've read. The book has always been linked in my mind to the second half of *The Sun Also Rises,* the seven days in Pamplona, where people do things they wouldn't normally do and totally unravel. And *The Age of Innocence,* the heartsick crush Newland Archer has on Ellen Olenska that never ends. But for anyone who thinks it's me: making a character is a huge pain in the ass. Imagine, for instance, composing an email to someone with some complicated nugget of information: a complaint to your child's principal that the math teacher has been psychologically abusive, your child has witnessed it but not been the victim, or something. You're trying to assemble with language several complicated concerns. You don't want to get the teacher fired. You don't want to blow it off either. Creating a character is hard like that. You need to know their motives, their style of speaking and history and beliefs. It's not paint-by-numbers. So even when I've been influenced by a real person to create a certain character, even if I'm the person I'm basing a character on, that influence is mostly a security blanket for me, and it doesn't answer the essential questions, which are, What happens next? How do I show it? What do they say and do? How does that fit with the rest?

CS: Relatedly, do you show people you're close to, like your wife or your parents, your work before publication? Do you give them veto power?

MK: I don't show my work to anyone outside the editing process, and I try to avoid offending friends and loved ones. That's also a concern I wrote into the narrator's anxieties about making art, as a way for me to address it directly. I'm married to a psychoanalyst, and she has a pretty clear understanding of human nature. Psychologically minded people know that our unconscious drives are part of our essence and spirit and are ever-present, and that we get into trouble when we try to deny that aspect. Engaging in a fantasy is, a psychoanalyst might say, a healthy sublimation—like writing.

CS: What do you look for in fiction as a reader?

MK: In my work and in the work of others, I'm looking for an expansive sense of humor, not just in the storytelling, but in the act of writing and putting oneself on display, a kind of reckless self-examination and visceral honesty that exposes shame and human frailty, and elicits a cosmic gale of laughter.

MATTHEW KLAM is the author of the acclaimed short story collection *Sam the Cat*. He is a recipient of a Guggenheim Fellowship, a PEN/Robert W. Bingham Prize, a Whiting Award, and a National Endowment for the Arts grant. His writing has been featured in publications including *The New Yorker*, *Harper's*, *GQ*, *The New York Times Magazine*, *The O. Henry Prize Stories*, *The Best American Nonrequired Reading*, and *The Ecco Anthology of Contemporary American Short Fiction*.

matthewklam.com
Twitter: @MatthewKlam